SCOURGE OF GODS

Book 2

Lair of the Serpent

-by-

Thomas A Farmer

ISBN-13: 978-0-9987679-3-2

ISBN-10: 0-9987679-3-X

Published by: Black Knight Books, 2019

For the Authors in Abstract Crew, Mike and Whitney.

You make sure this stuff stays fun.

Chapter 1

Victoria awoke, screaming, flailing for the dagger still strapped to her naked calf even in sleep. Dreams, her own mixed with those of the dead lives that came before her, warred with reality. She had no idea how long she slept, her memory stopped the moment her head touched the impossibly soft pillow, but she now lay on the floor between the bed and the wall, drenched in sweat.

She brandished the dagger, threatening everything and nothing until her heart calmed and her eyes fully focused. Slowly, she came to her feet. The white sheets on the bed where she first fell asleep had been stained an ugly mix of gray, brown, and black. A swatch of browning red discolored the carpet under her where she tore the stitches in her side as she slept.

Still holding the dagger, but now with the relaxed grip learned from experience rather than the white-knuckled panic of moments before, Victoria paced around the room. Everything seemed the same as it had when she went to sleep. Her black mastigas-fabric suit still lay crumpled on the floor where she discarded it. One dagger sat on the small table next to the bed. Her baton was hidden in the seemingly random folds of her fallen clothing.

When Pallasophia brought her to the room, Victoria had been too tired to truly examine it beyond a cursory inspection for threats. Once it fully sank in that she was no longer in danger, it seemed the fatigue of her time in the damnable labyrinth of Aphelion's depths caught up to her. All she could think about upon leaving Doctor Iro's office was sleep.

Now, she looked around the room, marveling at the soft pastel colors of everything. It was all so unlike anything she experienced before, that simply walking around the room gave Victoria a strange and almost dreamlike sense of calm.

Then, she found the mirror sitting atop an otherwise innocuous dresser and the horror returned. Doctor Iro's office had mirrors, but Victoria never really looked *at* them. She had seen herself reflected in water and metal, and she thought there was nothing that glass could tell her that those materials could not.

As it turned out, she was wrong.

Those imperfect reflections hid many of the scars and bruises from fighting the mastigas. Now, her broad shoulders and bronze skin showed the marks of dozens of wounds. The wound in her shoulder, thanks to the quick heal, was already closed, but the skin itself was a twisted mass of pink and red, flesh torn apart by the sophont's bullet.

Likewise, the wound the elite gave her continued to ooze where two of Doctor Iro's expertly-done stitches tore out as she thrashed in her sleep. She touched that wound, remembering the cold chill of the elite's sword as it effortlessly sliced through her flesh, stopping just short of fatal damage. The scar was clean, straight, almost like it had been drawn on.

Other scars were fainter, from less-serious injuries. Little marks here and there covered her skin where her defense had not been perfect, even with multiple lifetimes worth of practice. She barely noticed those. At best, they were potential memory triggers, but most of the time those myriad cuts and wounds were just another part of her skin.

Victoria moved on to the next thing that interested her: a set of curtains on the wall next to the bed. She reached out and took hold of the strong, but still impossibly soft, material. It slid with a series of rings on a bar overhead, softly rattling as it went.

When she looked out the window, her heart stopped. It was *open* out there. There was no ceiling on the other side of the window and, for a terrible moment, Victoria forgot that she was inside at all and the infinite sky seemed to draw her in, reeling and enfolding her forever.

Her hand reached out instinctively to catch her and impacted the cool glass of the window. That brought her back to reality and she was finally able to get her breathing under control. Some time passed while she stared out at the stars overhead, simply processing exactly what it was she was seeing. The longer she looked, the less afraid and the more fascinated she felt.

The landscape beyond the facility glittered with crystal clarity. Things outside her window curved away sharply. Barren, gray rock backlit by a pair of burning stars just above the horizon stretched as far as she could see.

A billion billion stars glittered in a velvety black canopy overhead, driving every other thought from her mind. With the window between her and it, the vast open space was at once appealing and terrifying.

She saw her face again reflected in the window, gray eyes peering back from the starscape. Almost automatically, she looked over at the actual mirror, and it finally sank in that, no matter what else she did, Victoria *had* to clean off the grime of the labyrinth. Her stomach then took that moment to rumble, reminding her that she had very little to eat down there, even after meeting Pallasophia's team.

As she enumerated a mental list of things she needed to do, Victoria realized she was still holding one of her stolen mastigas knives. The feeling of the grip in her hand was so familiar that it failed to consciously register. She looked at it for a moment, trying to wrap her mind around the idea that, at least in this place, she had no need for the weapon.

Very slowly, she placed the knife on the dresser and stepped away. Her fingers itched to hold something, anything that she could use as a weapon. Victoria knew she was not defenseless—she had killed many mastigas with her bare hands, after all—but the sensation never went away.

That went on for a full minute as she examined the rest of her room. It only had three doors, so exploration was a simple matter. One led to an empty closet and another to the hallway beyond. On the way back from that door, her hand instinctively closed into a fist as she dropped into a fighting crouch in response to the click of the door lock.

She took that moment to retrieve her baton from inside the folds of her clothing on the floor. The heavy, arm-length metal rod looked much the same as it did her first day alive. Even when she took it from the mastigas giant, it was scuffed and showed the telltale signs of use.

Victoria tried not to think about how many human skulls it might have caved in before coming into her possession. Yet, in taking it from the mastigas giant, she turned it from a tool used to destroy human life into one that preserved it. In that thought, though she had no idea where it had come from, she felt a strange sort of comfort. She slipped the loop tied to the grip around her wrist and continued her inspection of the room.

Her stomach rumbled again, and now her bowels protested as well, forcing Victoria to add yet another thing to the top of her list. Before she ate, she had to attend to the other end of things. Finding the toilet, fortunately, was easy enough. She only had one more door to check, after all.

She stepped off of the carpet and onto cold tile. The abrupt shift sent a shiver up her spine, but it was no worse than stepping off of tattered carpet and onto bare stone on the levels below. Unlike the facility's stone flooring, the tile quickly warmed under her feet, and she supposed even this might be comfortable.

Functional plumbing had been nonexistent in any useful capacity in the labyrinth. By and large, the mastigas had either destroyed it, or it poured nothing but polluted water. Faucets were more or less universal, and the few she came across in the depths of the facility made obvious the purpose of the sink and the bathtub.

The toilet, of all things, puzzled her. In the labyrinth, such things had been simpler. When it became necessary, the only thing available to her was a quiet corner where, like her sleeping and eating spaces, she hoped nothing would try to kill her. Other than the elite's refuse pile, she never found evidence that the mastigas had a place for such things either.

Now, the idea of wasting so much water to do something simple felt strange, and she wondered if she was making the right assumptions. She glanced at the shower; that would be the simpler option and would result in less water loss, but it had a mesh grate over the drain. It clearly was not the right choice.

A few more minutes passed while Victoria poked and prodded at various things around the room. She had no idea what most of the chemicals and various bottled liquids were. Some of them smelled sweet and pleasant, while others reeked of antiseptic.

Vivid memories of choking on her own blood after another mouth and throat had been torn apart by similar-smelling liquids told her enough about what she could and could not drink. They seemed to follow a pattern: safe things up high, dangerous ones below.

In all the time Victoria had been alive, she had never bathed once. Assuming, she reminded herself with a wry quirk of her lips, she excluded the time the mastigas tried to drown her. The Technocrats smelled different than she did; their sweat was different, covered by floral and spiced scents. The doctor, on the other hand, smelled clean, like Victoria herself on her first day.

Obviously bathing had neither been a priority, nor really even an option, while running and fighting beneath the arena. Her mastigas clothing and armor kept most of the blood off of her skin after the first day, but some of it still remained here and there in places like the crevices

5

under her fingernails. Her skin was covered in the residual dryness of old sweat.

For the moment however, she had a *definite* list of things her body was telling her to do. First, was to finish her business in the bathroom. Poking at everything made it clear that her original assumption was correct; the object the assumed to be the toilet was in fact exactly that. Operating it was simple enough. It had two large buttons on top that even someone who had never seen one before could figure out.

Victoria stopped in front of the sink, laying her baton next to the basin whose hand-washing purpose seemed obvious enough. An internal urge, a natural-seeming one rather than the artificial memories given to her, told her to at least wash her hands. Cleanliness was a survival skill. That was the logical reason for the sink being there, after all.

Experimenting a few minutes before told her how to operate the sink, and that one knob produced cold water while the other produced hot. By mixing the two, she found a temperature that was comfortable. She had grown used to the frigid water of the labyrinth, but that by no means meant she wanted to continue using water that cold.

The very idea of warm water sent a wave of pleasure over her skin. To think that something so mundane, so basically necessary to life could itself be a comfort was strange, to say the least.

The water that sluiced over her hands went from clear to a dark brown in moments. The dirt, sweat, and blood had all accumulated so steadily over the previous nine days that she was never really aware of exactly how dirty she was getting. The water continued running brown, though the color lightened after a moment, when she picked up the waxy bar next to the faucet. Being so close to the sink meant they were probably used together, and so she ran it across her hands. The white foam it produced turned brown and then black under the constant stream of warm water, and so she continued massaging her hands until the warm water ran clear again.

Victoria set the soap back down and shut off the faucet, and marveled at the difference between her hands and her arms. Her skin was skill the same burnished bronze color, but the smears of blood and dirt were gone along with the salt that crusted her skin from endless hours of sweating.

A single look at the shower was all it took to convince her that whatever the Technocrat customs for cleanliness were, she herself wanted to clean up before doing anything else. Her hands and wrists now felt profoundly different than the rest of her skin. The shower looked straightforward enough with controls like the faucet and a clear door to, she presumed, keep water off of the floor.

She stepped into the shower and gasped as icy water shot from the sprayer above her head. She reflexively jerked the red-colored hot water knob and in moments the water went from ice to warm to burning hot. On her bare skin, the heat was not terrible, but it burned at her exposed wounds. A few more moments of adjusting and she finally found a comfortable temperature between those two extremes.

All thoughts left her mind after a few moments standing under the spray of hot water. The heat and pressure seemed to hit every one of her sore and tight muscles and joints, massaging them with a relaxing ecstasy she would not have imagined possible ten minutes before.

She had no idea how long she spent in the shower. The hot water quickly filled the little glass-walled shower with steam that warmed her from inside like the water warmed her skin. Most of that time, she simply stood there letting the water warm her up and loosen her pervasive tension. She had no basis for knowing how common this was, or if Pallasophia as "Project Director" was privy to luxuries unknown to the common people, but it was certainly something she could grow used to.

Finally, the growls in her stomach intensified to a point that she was paying more attention to them than to the pleasant warmth of the water. The hunger pangs might have been far milder than anything she would have considered urgent in the labyrinth, but Victoria had no reason to put them off with a fully stocked kitchen nearby. She reached for the soap and finished washing.

Satisfied, or at least too hungry to stay in any longer, she shut the water off and stepped out of the shower. Hanging on a bar nearby was a long rectangle of fuzzy cloth. It looked absorbent, and so she reached for it, assuming its purpose was related to the shower it hung
next to.

Clean and dry, she hung the towel back on its bar the way she found it. Her baton sat on the sink, a glowering black oil spot against the otherwise clean countertop. When she picked it up, her hand came away greasy and dirty. She had handled it so many times before without even realizing how dirty it was because she was that dirty as well.

So she set to work washing it, too. It was too long to fit under the faucet, but she was able to clean it in the shower while staying dry by reaching through the door and scrubbing it until the metal shined a dull silver rather than the blotchy gray it had been before. Even then, she continued scrubbing using the soaps meant for her skin until the water stopped running ugly and gray.

She repeated the process with her daggers, though washing their sheathes left them soggy and wet. The wet fabric rubbed unpleasantly against her calves, so she left them in the bathroom to dry. The strip of fabric around her baton was easy enough to squeeze dry, and she tied it to her arm, affixing it just above her elbow. Safe or not, having something close at hand put her nerves at ease.

She looked in the mirror again, amazed at the face that looked back at her. The overall color of her skin had not changed, but it was warmer now, cleaner. The grease and dirt were gone and even her wounds had been washed clear of the caked blood that built up between her visit with Doctor Iro and the shower.

Satisfied, she turned and left the room. The hallway outside was the same temperature, a pleasantly cool medium between the chill of the labyrinth and the heat of the arena. A soft breeze, one that had not been present in her room, caressed her skin.

The carpet under her feet was a pleasant, if unusual, shade of light blue. The walls, at least in the hallway, were a shade of off-white that made the space feel wider than it was. The high ceiling overhead, however, was black and studded with silver speckles that reminded Victoria of the stars outside.

The hallway held six doors, including the one to her room. A quick inspection revealed that the two smaller ones went to closets and the other three normal sized doors were locked. Her room was the second from the end on one side. A path worn into the blue carpet, little more than a slightly darker trail, led to the door at the very end of the hall. Victoria suspected that was Pallasophia's room.

A short distance away, a staircase led to a large open area. It was decorated in a wide variety of colors, none of which seemed to clash against one another in her eyes. Seating, primarily a series of soft-looking couches, was arranged in a semi-circle in the center of the room. Here and there other chairs and even a pair of small tables were scattered around. Five doors dotted the walls along with a staircase going up to another part of the upper floor.

Victoria took her time exploring. Pallasophia told her where everything was, but now she looked at it with an eye for utility. Always the back of her mind held the thought of how she could use the various spaces and objects around her in a fight. One table had a stone top—heavy, but excellent cover. The other was lighter, made of glass, and would be useful as a distraction or even a source of sharp shards. The couches were heavy, and were as comfortable as their overstuffed appearance made them look, but they were soft and would make bad cover.

Up the other staircase was a work room. A large desk sat in the center flanked by chairs. Two smaller desks stood against the walls, which themselves were crammed full of shelves. It had a used, well-worn feeling about it. Much more than the common area downstairs, the workroom felt to her like a place where people spent a lot of time.

The biggest desk was covered in control surfaces. Victoria had a vague knowledge of what they were. Gesturing at them, which brought up various top level menus and password-input forms, confirmed her assumption. The two smaller desks were covered with ceramic tiles. The largest piece occupied one entire desk and contained the written, and still mostly unreadable, lines she had found in the elite's chambers. The other desk had been piled high with the tiles that contained the elite's personal records of the battles it fought. Those scenes again triggered painful memories of death and dismemberment, and so she left them well alone and returned to the main floor.

The doors in the main room each led different places. The largest went outside, which was a largely meaningless term, because "outside" was simply another corridor. However, the suite seemed to have been designed to feel like a home, and so it had a front door. She left it closed and investigated the other areas. Another door led downstairs, which she had been told held little beyond computer mainframes and climate machinery.

A third door led to a bathroom and the fourth nearby to a closet. The fifth led to the kitchen. It had a smell of grease and food about it as well as spices and char. Off of the kitchen was the dining room, an area almost as large as the main room and dominated by a long table with six chairs. Paintings and sculptures decorated the walls.

She returned to the kitchen and encountered another problem. In the labyrinth, she had made a fire by relying on the implanted memories of one of the previous ninety-nine subjects that told her how to make heat with friction. She had no idea how to work any of the gadgets in the kitchen, nor any real idea what most of them were. Nothing was labeled by function, only brand, and "*roufichtra*" did not exactly tell her what it did.

That meant it was back to experimenting. Victoria pressed buttons and dials and knobs, trying to figure out what everything did. A half an hour later, she had a general idea. One wall held three boxes with hot, dry interiors. Another box hummed when she tapped on the buttons, but nothing seemed to happen. She passed by a glass plate set into one of the counters several times, hitting buttons each time, without understanding it.

Finally, she came back to that large glass plate, finding one part of it hot and glowing red. Heat meant cooking and cooking meant food. Her stomach growled again as she shifted the goal of her search to food itself. She felt it a safe assumption that anything she found would be better than what passed for food in the labyrinth.

A very large box-shaped machine stood against one wall. The inside was cold, and the bottom section was frozen with a crust of ice on the inside. She found meat and vegetables inside, and more of the same in the frozen section. She removed several things that looked appetizing and set them on the counter behind her.

She found pots and pans near the stove, and located the pantry a minute later. She never stopped to consider how she, eleven days old, could read the labels and things around her in the first place, simply taking it as a given much like sight or hearing. Wherever the ability came from, the labels on the food were easy enough to read, unlike those on the appliances. Thus far, her limited culinary experience was not helpful. She knew that she needed heat to cook, but knew nothing about spices, seasoning, or anything that went into actually preparing a meal other than heating it until any residual disease was dead.

Victoria decided to improvise. She placed one of the larger skillets on the hot eye of the stove and let it heat. Experience had not taught her much, but it had taught her that searing something on a hot surface often made it better. While it heated, she chopped up several pounds of vegetables and meat. With no idea how much food actually went into a meal, she used as much as would fit into the heavy metal skillet.

She mixed a few spices, once she found them, into the food by smell and let it cook. Meat was done when it was a different color all the way through. Someone else's memory told her that, though she wondered how much that had to do with real food and how much was simply burning away the filth of the labyrinth. Still, she preferred to be safe rather than dead—perhaps she could get Pallasophia to teach her properly later—and let her meal cook until the slices of meat were done.

The smells of meat and vegetables quickly filled the air. The pan started to smoke and a fan kicked on overhead. Victoria started to remove the food from the skillet, but the meat was not yet done.

Perhaps it was supposed to do that, she thought and stirred the dish with a large spoon. Doing so dislodging several chunks of blackened food and a puff of smoke that quick dissipated. The food sizzled louder as uncooked pieces hit the hot metal.

That made yet another new thing learned in the last few hours, she thought to herself. As the food continued to cook, she stirred it every so often. Finally, she deemed the meat ready to eat and turned off the stove. A cabinet behind her held plates and bowls. Another beside it had been filled with glasses and mugs.

She remembered that the chilled cabinet held several bottles of liquid and went back to it to get something to drink. None of it was water and nearly everything was a different color. She opened and sniffed various things. A few of the bottles had obvious warning labels on them listing them as poisonous or only for cleaning, which made the decision rather easy. She settled on a red drink that fizzed when opened and smelled vaguely sweet and earthy as the same time and poured it into a glass.

She gathered her food and drink and, after a quick look indicated nowhere to set them in the kitchen, she went to the dining room. The food steamed, so she let it sit for a minute while it cooled.

Something bothered her about the entire process. She examined the decorations in the room idly while mulling things over in her mind.

The dining room was fairly large, but obviously single-purpose. There was enough room to move easily around all sides of the long table, but little else. A few cabinets sat against one of the walls. One was filled with lightweight, delicate-looking glassware and another full of dusty bottles in a variety of shapes and sizes. She smelled one, noting the acrid tinge and alcoholic vapor it gave off, and put it back.

She paced around as her food cooled, inspecting the busts and paintings along the walls. The paintings, two per wall on opposite walls, each showed a different landscape. Those places were strange, open, and the wide skies filled her with uneasy fascination the same way the stars outside her bedroom window had.

A series of nine busts, four men and five women, on pedestals dominated the fourth wall. They all looked severe, yet wise, as though the sculptor was trying to capture wisdom and power in the same facial expression. She made her way down the row of statues, examining each of them to see if they stirred any memories, either her own or those memories given to her. She felt no recognition from the first eight, but the ninth was clearly a stylized and rather imperious cast of First Lord Tritogenes, easy enough to recognize from the picture Pallasophia showed her. The face on the statue lacked the lines around his mouth and eyes that the real man possessed.

It hit her.

Looking at the bust of the man who had, in a very real way, designed and built her, Victoria suddenly realized where her feelings of discomfort came from. The statue in front of her was a perfected version of a real man. Age and wear and fatigue and tiredness had all been erased by the sculptor's hands. That left a piece of art that showed the subject as it should be in an ideal world, not as it was in reality.

She thought back to, of all things, the bathroom upstairs. Surely, human children took time to understand the rules of cleanliness, how and when to wash and why. Perhaps they learned quickly, perhaps the process took a long time, but of one thing she was certain. No human

13

being learned those rules in half an hour. Perhaps animals had an instinct to keep themselves clean, perhaps even the mastigas knew even that much about civility.

Yet, here she was, eleven days old, and everything she looked at, she understood as an adult human being. A human being with, perhaps, the veneer of civilization stripped away, but an adult nonetheless. True, she did not know how Technocrat society worked and it had taken time to understand how and why the things in the suite worked, but she came at them not as a child learning about the world, but as an adult with a few unfortunate gaps in her understanding.

Victoria turned away from the bust and gazed at the still-steaming plate of meats and vegetables waiting for her at one end of the table. The process of cooking had taken trial and error, yes, but surely real human children destroyed more food than they prepared when they were learning to cook. Despite that, she had produced a fully cooked—if amateurish—meal on her very first attempt.

She turned back to the bust of Tritogenes, aiming her questioning thoughts at it and using that stone image to polish the questions she would ask the real First Lord when she saw him in person.

She knew, had known, how to do things as though she had been comfortable with many of them already. Even the things new to her had been easy enough to learn or figure out. Just how much of her mind, she asked the statue, was someone else's creation?

Her stomach growled. Whatever the answers to her questions, she was still human. She had to be.

***

After eating, she returned to her room with another glass of the sweet, red drink. A small table with what the voice in her head identified as a computer sat in the middle of the room, and Victoria pushed it against the window. She set her glass on it and picked up the tablet, examining it for a moment before her eye fell on her pile of clothing.

She frowned. The black mastigas-fabric suit she made for herself sat in the floor, stinking and filthy. Having washed herself and gotten away from it for even a short time, Victoria was now acutely aware of *exactly* how dirty that pile of clothing was and had no desire to put it back on. She dragged it into the bathroom and left it there for the time being.

Returning to the table, she again picked up the tablet. It had no apparent controls and, while the voice identified *what* it was, it gave her precisely zero indication how it should be used. The only clue she had was watching some of Pallasophia's soldiers using similar devices. Most of them bore holographic menus awakened by a tap, or taps, on the tablet's surface.

So, she did.

The tablet came to life, vibrating softly as if to convey a tactile message that it was now functional. Victoria eased into the chair, examining the menus. Most of them seemed focused on mundane things, news and other events from Limani. Victoria knew that as Tritogenes's planet, and pieced together the identities of the other planets from Pallasophia's mentions of the Hexarchs in passing.

As she navigated what she new to be basic knowledge, Victoria found herself torn between boredom and fascination. Boredom because, if she was honest with herself, most of this information was the sort of thing she found hard to care about. It was too mundane, the type of knowledge people who grew up in that world would take for granted. In fact, she resented that she had to learn it at all, especially when intimate knowledge of how to field strip and repair several different military weapons had been provided.

"Why that," she growled with a voice still not used to speaking aloud, "and not, say, the identity of the Hexarch of Pteryga, or the results of the last System Olympics?"

After several minutes of browsing, an icon blinked to life in the upper right corner of the holographic screen. She tapped it and the words

"NEW MESSAGE" appeared. The sender was listed as "Second Lord Philip of Limani."

She tapped on the notification and the news and other information sank to the background. The image of a young, handsome man filled the display from his shoulders up. Long hair fell into a sleek braid that disappeared below the video pickup, and stark overhead shadows made discerning the color of his eyes almost impossible, but Victoria thought she saw a hint of bright blue, or perhaps green.

"Good day," the recording began. "My name is Philip. I'm a personal friend of First Lord Tritogenes. He didn't tell me your name, but he did tell me you were victorious and had reached safety. Other than the staff of your facility, and Tritogenes himself, I suspect I'm the only one who knows your location, let alone your existence in the first place."

The recording laughed, a bright, clear sound. "No, I know what you're asking yourself. Tritogenes did not ask me to contact you. In fact, I doubt he knows I've done so at all. I'm also not going to bore you by telling you the same thing you've no doubt been told over and over by now. You're very important, Titan, but that status isn't the reason why I'm contacting you.

"My first reason was, as I said, simply to express my happiness at hearing of your safety. Tritogenes and I spoke at length about," the recording paused and he frowned. A moment later, he continued, "about the Project. I am glad it's over."

Victoria scoffed, but said nothing. Interacting with a recording was pointless.

Philip continued speaking a moment later, as though he anticipated the need for her to react at that moment. If he was as charismatic in person as his smile indicated, Victoria had no doubt that he could read people, and predict their reactions, with ease.

"My second, and primary, reason for contacting you is that now that you're safe, I fear your skills may be needed sooner than anticipated. A

16

few days ago, Tritogenes asked me to investigate a group he called the Ouroboros Society."

That name, and the way Philip delivered it with a marked frown, sent a shiver down Victoria's spine. It transferred itself to the pit of her stomach where it sank into a cold chasm as Philip continued speaking.

"I could find no information on them. Titan, you must understand how impossible that is. My profession is to uncover information, especially information that could be of use, or danger, to Tritogenes.

"That I have been unable to do so is, at best, a matter to be concerned about. My contact details are included in this message. Please, if you hear anything about this group, forward the information to me. Rest assured I will do the same for you.

"Selene's Grace be upon you, Titan."

The recording ended and Victoria's news feed returned to the front of her holo-display, but she had no time to think about it as a roaring shudder ran through the facility at that exact moment.

She threw herself out of her chair, tucked into a roll, and brought the baton up in a guard as natural as breathing. Nothing happened, not even dust from the ceiling, and Victoria prowled the room until she returned to the window to see a shuttle flying away from the facility. The identity of the craft was provided by the same guiding voice in her brain that named most things so far.

Pallasophia's suite, which she referred to as a "modest residence," occupied three of the facility's upper floors. The only things above it were the landing area for personal shuttles and the first security checkpoint for the facility itself. Together, they formed the only parts of the facility to protrude above the surface.

Above her head, the ceiling creaked and Victoria jumped again. When nothing kicked in her door or tore through the wall, she forced herself to lower the baton and breathe normally again. Possessing a reflex that told her to kill anything that might threaten her only made her jumpy when nothing was a threat.

17

With a sigh, Victoria sank into her chair again. Perhaps, given enough time, she could learn how to interact with her fellow human beings as more than a weapon wary of its new surroundings.

Chapter 2

Exactly on schedule, First Lord Eurybia's liner slid into orbit around Prosgeiosi, the Technocrat capital planet. On her authority as a Hexarch, she pushed through the normally-lengthy process of finding a parking orbit and gaining clearance for her lander. Within an hour of her order to find a suitable parking orbit for the ship, she and her guests were on their way to the surface.

Given the certainty that Eurybia had bugged the cabin, neither Tritogenes nor Enyalios wanted to discuss anything about the Project ahead of the Council meeting. The most either of them said on the subject was a comment from Enyalios about how he considered it a shame that Project Titan, for all its success, had so highlighted the divisions within the Council.

At the time, Tritogenes scoffed. He knew the older Hexarch was right, but he was not about to admit it aloud.

Fortunately, the lander had more than enough seats for the three Hexarchs to sit comfortably. Their staff, including Second Lord Daniel, Enyalios's Titan, waited in a larger lander that would be making its way down through the queue the normal way. After being relegated to the same suite for the trip because Eurybia's liner only had one spare room, even Tritogenes and Enyalios were tired of one another's presence and sat in silence an amicable distance apart.

Eurybia sat on the opposite side of the cabin, though not as far removed as Tritogenes would have expected. Her body language, and the one-sided holo, said that whatever she was reading was something neither of them were welcome to see. Likewise, Enyalios was engrossed in a novel, probably some sort of romance if Tritogenes had to guess, and so he simply watched through the window as the land sped past beneath them.

He did not object that no one wanted to engage in conversation. For his part, Tritogenes simply had too much on his mind. If he was being honest, he felt a great deal of apprehension about meeting Victoria. She also would not arrive for several days, assuming she and Pallasophia had even left Aphelion, which he doubted.

It was just as well as far as Tritogenes was concerned. The first planet settled by the Technocrats nearly twelve-hundred years before, Prosgeiosi was a spectacle unto itself. In the time between that historic event and Landing Year 1181, the population of Prosgeiosi had swelled, reached some four-hundred million. More people called that planet home than any other settled planet in the system. The night side, just visible as a crescent at the edge of the planetary disk, glittered with uncountable tiny speckles of light.

The orbitals above them were alight with ships—engine flares studded space like a thousand manmade stars. Closer ships blinked with running lights that carried farther than the sight of the ship itself, reducing them to a sea of red and green sparks moving at a pace rendered glacial by distance.

The lander descended slowly through the clouds. Like nearly every vehicle used by the Hexarchs, the little ship was equipped with heat shields which would have allowed it to drop to the ground quickly, but they were in no rush. Eurybia had, Tritogenes suspected, pushed her way through the orbital procedures because she could, not because they were in any danger of being late.

Descending through the atmosphere at a speed which would not heat up the hull very much took almost as much time as the original orbital insertion had. Tritogenes supposed that, had their ship been forced to go through the normal procedures that Prosgeiosi's millions of other guests went through, the atmospheric descent would have felt rather swift. As it was, time seemed to crawl until he could see the lights of the capital blinking at him, brilliant even in the daytime.

Odyssey, the capital city of the Technocray, gleamed like a pearl below them. In terms of sheer size, it was one of the smallest cities on any of the seven inhabited planets, but it was here that the Hexarchs held Council, and here that the most important business and socioeconomic work was carried out.

Space was at a premium for Odyssey's inhabitants. Those born in the city often found the wide, open homes and buildings of the other planets in the binary to be too large, agoraphobic even. For what Tritogenes had paid to renovate his palace's bedroom suite, he would have been lucky to mortgage a condominium half that size inside the walls of Odyssey. Yet the people for whom opportunity presented a way to acquire one of those expensive dwellings rarely turned down the chance.

The city, like the entire capital planet, was ruled directly by the Council of Hexarchs. The other six planets were governed by a single Hexarch and decisions that only affected that planet or that Hexarch's holdings—something that in practice rarely happened—were unquestionable by the other five. By contrast, any decision involving life on Prosgeiosi had to be agreed upon by the entire Council. It was often a time consuming process, but the day-to-day of the city could carry on easily enough while the First Lords and their direct subordinates conducted business in the rarefied air of the Council chamber.

Despite the cramped accommodations and the sheer expense of living in Odyssey, it persisted exactly as it had for some thousand years.

Other cities grew and spread, sprawling at times hundreds of kilometers across fields, plains, and mountains. Odyssey never did. Smaller cities sprang up around it, but those cities were never actually part of Odyssey, no matter how large or how closely they crept to the capital's opalescent walls. If those other cities were comfortable homesteads, Odyssey was a hive, buzzing with activity every second of every day.

Odyssey remained the same, always.

That ancient city also had something those other, more expansive, cities would never have. Odyssey had a history that stretched back far beyond its role as a capital city. It never expanded because it never could expand, not and still be the same thing it had always been. For more than nine millennia, the thing known as Odyssey had been a massive ship crawling its way through the stars at a tiny fraction of the speed of light. Launched from Earth at what Technocrat history called the end of the Golden Age, it cruised through space looking for a new home for its millions of inhabitants. Civilizations had risen and fallen aboard the Odyssey. Technocrats were only the latest of them, but it was they who had made the decision to find a place for their ship to land, and so they had found Prosgeiosi, and for nearly twelve hundred years had called it and its sister planets home.

The sight of the city of Odyssey was nothing new for any of the First Lords in the slowly-descending lander. For Tritogenes even less so, because he had grown up on Prosgeiosi. It was only after being elevated to First Lord and assuming the responsibilities that First Lord Ophion left in the wake of his death, among which included the governorship of the planet Limani, that Tritogenes relocated.

Familiarity, however, had never quite rid him of the sense of awe he felt whenever he saw the massive edifice. A desire to get "in there" had driven him most of his life. Once he achieved the rank of Second Lord, and thus was allowed to participate in Council sessions, he rarely missed one. Until his final elevation, however, and to his continued frustration up until that point, he was never able to secure a position lucrative enough to afford a suite in Odyssey proper.

Now, as a Hexarch, he owned a "suite" in Odyssey only marginally smaller than the area Second Lord Pallasophia carved out for herself atop Aphelion. Usually, such suites were rented out to a Hexarch's most loyal Second Lords, the ones who oversaw the vast commercial and technological empires that served as power base and source of income both.

He could, if he needed to use it, force her out temporarily or bring his things in for as long as he needed. He could also, now that he had the wealth to do so, simply purchase another suite for his use. He never did that either, rental accommodations were enough for whatever short-term purpose brought him back to Odyssey.

Gaining an apartment inside the dome might have been his driving force through his youth, but once Tritogenes actually achieved that goal, he found Odyssey's cramped interior to be exactly that—cramped. So he allowed Pallasophia full-time use of the suite instead.

Tritogenes held controlling shares in dozens of industries and businesses, most thanks to his "inheritance" from First Lord Ophion. He also, though he had to be continually reminded of the fact by the corporation itself when they needed something, owned one of the larger media conglomerates in the binary. He certainly had the wealth to spare, but he preferred to spend it other ways. Reinvesting in his companies in the form of benefits and wage increases quickly shot many of them to the top of their respective industries.

More to the point, if he was going to invest in Prosgeiosi's local economy, there were other ways he could do it. Banquets, parties, theater—those things brought him joy in ways that no Odyssean suite ever could.

All those thoughts swirled through his brain as the ship approached Odyssey. The top levels of the dome that had once been the habitable section of the massive ship were studded with landing pads and bridges.

Some modification had been necessary to turn *Odyssey* the ship into Odyssey the city, but they had been as minimal as possible.

The lander's pilot went through a complex security procedure, one that not even First Lord Eurybia was prepared to forego, that granted them access to the special landing area at the very top of the old ship's dome. A few other landers sat there—other Hexarchs who had already arrived.

A brief flash of unease passed through his body, especially legs and stomach, as the lander shut off its artificial gravity. Thanks to the inertial dampeners, none of the little craft's passengers felt a thing as it moved through space, accelerating, twisting, and turning at speeds far in excess of anything that an unprotected human body could handle. Even so, every transition from artificial to real gravity induced in him a brief moment of nausea. The fields were never quite aligned perfectly and the instantaneous shift in balance was something few got used to. The sensation passed in the space of a heartbeat and they all stood, more or less simultaneously, to exit the lander.

"By the by, First Lord Tritogenes," Eurybia said. She stood, watching, as a Fourth Lord appeared from the front of the ship and opened the hatch. She waved away the next offer of assistance, navigating the three steps to the ground slowly but with better balance than Tritogenes had seen her exhibit in several years.

"Yes?" he inquired, following her down the short steps.

Behind them, Enyalios waited a moment at the top of the steps. Tritogenes thought he was simply avoiding making conversation with Eurybia, but then he glanced back and saw his friend watching the horizon, where a lander slightly larger than theirs, but still painted with Eurybia's ensigns, descended past the upper levels of Odyssey's dome.

"I meant to ask earlier," she said. "When will your Titan be joining us?"

Tritogenes froze for half a heartbeat. His hesitation that lasted a few seconds longer than he would have liked, covering the moment by summoning his holo and flipped through the information there in order to check his calendar. "Soon, First Lord. She should be undergoing her final medical evaluation today or tomorrow."

She nodded, allowing a slight smile. "Excellent. I would hate for the last few years to have been wasted."

"The years have been many things. Wasted is not among them," Tritogenes said, perhaps more tersely than he intended.

"It looks as though Second Lord Daniel made it through the traffic queue in short order," Eurybia observed, nodding her head in the direction the other lander had gone.

Enyalios descended the stairs, allowing the platform to withdraw into the lander. "Yes. Almost as fast as we did," he replied. Tritogenes thought he detected an unspoken continuation in Enyalios's subtle frown: "and he did so without rushing Orbital Control."

"Oh, and Tritogenes? Do join me for dinner tonight." Eurybia said, phrasing the imperative as politely as she could. "I will be meeting First Lord Aegesander and his Titan."

Tritogenes, to his surprise, seriously considered her offer. Despite his lingering dislike of the woman, and the rudeness with which she treated Enyalios's staff before they left Katarraktes, Tritogenes was starting to remember some of the reasons he actually liked her. For all her rough edges, Eurybia remained charismatic and quite easy to talk to.

Plus, he admitted with a smile that ghosted across his lips, he really wanted to meet Helena, and he could put up with Aegesander for an evening in trade for that opportunity.

And so, after a moment, his smiled turned genuine and he nodded. "I would love to, thank you. Forward the details to me when you get them worked out."

A single gesture from Eurybia brought up her personal holo, then dismissed it. Tritogenes chuckled, amused. Apparently she already had the information pulled up and ready to send, confident that he would agree join them.

He glanced over his shoulder. "Enyalios?"

The other Hexarch shook his head. "No, but thank you. I promised Daniel I would give him a tour of the city this evening."

He nodded. "Of course."

Eurybia turned to leave again, stopped, and smiled over her shoulder. "Thank you, Tritogenes. We'll see you tonight."

As she walked away, Enyalios finally came to stand beside Tritogenes. He spoke, controlling his voice so that it would not carry. "You know she still hates you, right?"

Tritogenes shrugged. "I know Aegesander does, and some of that's bound to rub off."

Enyalios laughed. "You know, Tritogenes, I'll always be impressed by your inability to hold a grudge."

He laughed in return. "If that's my only flaw, my friend, I'd say I'm doing rather well."

"It's not your only flaw, no." Enyalios laughed again, then slapped Tritogenes on the shoulder. "Come. We have an hour or so before Daniel makes it through the checkpoints. Would you care for a drink?"

"If I say no, you'll be bored, and then I'll feel responsible for whatever mischief you get yourself into."

Enyalios laughed a loud, tension-draining laugh. "My dear friend, we are Hexarchs! We do not get into 'mischief.'"

Tritogenes echoed the laugh, and they began the short walk to the door that would lead them inside Odyssey's walls. The next minutes passed in silence broken only by their footsteps and the unobtrusive whispered conversations of their staff and security.

Finally, at the door, Enyalios spoke again. "I overheard her talking to Aegesander this morning. Apparently he's come to Prosgeiosi already, as has Hyperion."

Tritogenes shrugged. "That's no surprise."

Enyalios's eyebrows rose in a conspiratorial grin. "This is, and Eurybia seemed as taken aback by it as I'm sure you'll be. Apparently Hyperion and Aegesander are meeting for d—"

"Meeting *one another*? Are you crashing serious?" Tritogenes demanded, louder than he meant. Their staff pointedly did not hear.

Enyalios nodded. "I couldn't tap into the call—Eurybia's security is damned good, I'll give her that—but I was able to listen in on her half of the conversation. Apparently, Aegesander finally reached out, using the Project as an olive branch."

Tritogenes hummed. "I honestly don't know what to make of that."

Enyalios, for his part, laughed. "Me either, but I can tell you one thing."

"What's that?"

"The Titan reveal is going to be one *hell* of a celebration if those two are talking to one another again."

***

First Lord Eurybia returned to her suite to find the soldiers who should have been guarding her door conspicuously absent. There were no signs of a struggle, at least nothing obvious with a few seconds worth of examination. No blood or even disturbed decorations in the hallway gave anything away; they were simply gone.

Eurybia grit her teeth for the barest moment as she surveyed the scene. She could get the names of those two guards from her security coordinator and, once they were found, she would see to it that their careers were ruined at best. True, this was Odyssey, and the odds of anything untoward happening to her, or to anyone for that matter, here on the upper levels was nearly zero, but "nearly zero," and "actually zero" were not the same thing. More importantly, she had been paying them quite well.

Before reaching for the door, she retrieved a pistol from within her robe. Unlike several of her fellow Hexarchs—in fact, this was one of the few things she had in common with Tritogenes—Eurybia had no formal combat training. Still, a quick trigger finger and short distances did a great deal to equalize things between herself and any potential attacker.

With the pistol leveled in one hand, she reached for the door lock. As soon as she touched it, she realized something was off. The pad under her hand was not the proper lock for her door, but rather a veneer placed overtop.

She jerked back, raising the gun as she did so.

Nothing attacked or otherwise threatened her directly, but the pad disguised at her door lock blinked once, softly, and projected a hologram in front of the door.

In lurid orange, the image appeared. It was still, little more than a stylized logo rather than a photograph or holovideo. Suspended in the orange light was a circular glyph, a serpent eating its own tail, trapped in an endless cycle of death and rebirth.

Just inside the circular serpent, a ring of text grew in brightness until it too was legible. To her surprise, it was written in Lexeis Archaeo, and it took her a moment to remember her school lessons from decades before.

"Evil becomes good in the minds of those whom the gods would destroy."

The words themselves were nothing new. Everyone who stayed awake through basic literature in school read them in one language or another. Seeing them projected onto her door alongside an ouroboros, however, was something else entirely.

With an annoyed snarl, as close to anger as she would allow herself to get in a public area, Eurybia swatted the fake door lock off of the wall. It fell to the floor and the holo on her door vanished. She picked it up and stuffed the device into a pocket, not wanting a random passerby to stumble upon it.

With that annoyance out of the way, she pressed her hand to the actual lock on her door. It blinked green and a small slit opened in the wall above it. She leaned her face in close to that spot, letting the retinal scanner do its job as well. Once the system was convinced she was who she was supposed to be, the door itself unlocked and slid aside.

Eurybia stepped through, and immediately jumped backward.

On the floor, laid out neatly side-by-side and still showing no signs of struggle, were the two soldiers she hired to guard her door.

The door slid shut behind her, and now that she was in private, Eurybia cursed. "Gods between. Now this is a problem."

***

Tritogenes read over the tablet, carefully concealing his surprise and even anger. If it was that obvious to Eurybia, she knew Aegesander, in the next seat over, could easily pick Tritogenes's feelings apart. That Aegesander did not immediately pounce upon his reaction was proof enough to Eurybia that Tritogenes had nothing to do with the stunt in her suite. She would not have suspected him, logically, but it paid to cover every potential avenue before moving forward.

After a minute, Tritogenes typed out a quick message on the tablet before sliding it across the table. It came to a stop in front of Eurybia's plate. She read it and waved the message away. Once their conversation was done, the security program Helena wrote would wipe the tablet's memory irrevocably.

"Why are we not doing something about this?" it read.

"It's being handled quietly," she typed, then slid the tablet to Aegesander.

He returned it to her with an added line of text that simply read, "whoever they are, they want us to acknowledge them. We'll not give them that."

She nodded and slid it back to Tritogenes. His fingers danced in the air for a moment before he returned it to her. "Who else knows?"

"Just us," she typed out, then added, "keep it that way."

Aegesander again intercepted the tablet. It sat so that Eurybia could read it as he typed. "When your Titan arrives, tell her. Otherwise, we will speak with the others as they arrive in person."

29

Tritogenes nodded as he scanned the tablet, then passed it back to Eurybia. With that handled, she tapped the code that would activate Helena's program. In moments, all record of that short, text-based conversation was gone. In fact, any record in the tablet's memory that it had been used at all was gone. As far as the little device itself was concerned, the software inside was brand new.

***

While that secret conversation was going on, a more normal one was happening verbally.

"Good evening Tritogenes," Aegesander said, nodding respectfully. He indicated the two cybernetically-enhanced people sitting next to him with a flourish. "I'd like to introduce Second Lord Helena and Second Lord Panatakis, Titans of Dasos and Kokkinos, respectively."

Tritogenes introduced himself to the two Titans while Eurybia finished typing out the first message, detailing everything from the hallway and the relevant parts from inside the suite. She told Aegesander before coming to the restaurant, speaking with him privately under guise of needing to discuss "sensitive economic policies."

In a way, Eurybia supposed having Tritogenes here was a boon. The whole thing had been very theatrical, so dinner would either implicate him or allow him to use his extensive theatrical training to help piece apart exactly why her still unknown harassers did things in the manner they did.

She slid the tablet across the table now for the first time, saying, "have a look at this, Tritogenes. Tell me which you prefer." She laughed. "Aegesander would rather I build the statue, but I think they're *so* played out these days."

This had been rehearsed, or at least discussed beforehand, and Aegesander picked it up without pause as Tritogenes read her account. "There's tradition in statues, Eurybia."

"I have to agree with Aegesander," Panatakis added. His contribution had not been planned, but it helped their cover. "Especially ones properly made and positioned. When the sunlight hits them, it's like a symphony of shadows."

Tritogenes put the tablet down on the table and typed on its surface.

"I believe I must agree with First Lord Eurybia," Helena said. "I find the relaxing atmosphere of a garden to be many times more preferable to a mere statue. In fact..."

Eurybia raised an eyebrow as Tritogenes slid the tablet to her. "Go on, Helena."

"Apologies, First Lord. I was wary of being too precise."

She laughed. "Don't feel bad, Helena. Opinions..."

"Especially about art!" Tritogenes interrupted.

"Are best when they're detailed."

Helena nodded. "I will remember that. As I was saying, a statue may change slightly as it weathers, or it may be moved or painted, but it is otherwise static. A garden is ever-changing. Flowers bloom and wither, leaves grow and die, and new plants come up in places where before there were only weeds and dirt."

Helena smiled, and for a moment Eurybia could understand exactly why Aegesander was afraid of her. There was something entirely too intelligent and calculating behind those glittering, sky-blue eyes.

Helena's gaze was different from Panatakis's. His cybernetic synesthesia ensured he never actually looked directly at anyone. He was always looking off to the side, around the room, or at some interesting noise. That was odd, but she got used to it. After all, she knew people without cybernetic senses with similar movement patterns.

In contrast, Helena stared, as she was doing now. Eurybia never knew her before the implants, but Aegesander told her that such behavior was new, probably a result of the high level information-processing software she possessed. Whatever the cause, Helena's eyes always seemed to bore holes in whoever she was looking at.

After a moment, Helena added, "if we're voting, I vote for garden."

Eurybia nodded, sliding the tablet to Aegesander. Fortunately the conversation they were having was productive, because she *had* allocated funds for some sort of monument in honor of Project Titan to be erected in her palace on Kokkinos. She was leaning toward a garden herself, but Aegesander's arguments in favor of statuary were compelling enough to warrant using that very real discussion as cover for their secret, text-based conversation.

Aegesander nodded and passed the tablet to Tritogenes. "Think of it, though. A statue of each of you, memorialized in stone quarried from your home planet."

"I admit," Tritogenes said, eyes flicking between Aegesander and the tablet. "I admit that I appreciate the poetry of your idea, but think of it this way. Kokkinos is largely desert. A garden would symbolized their resilience and ability to thrive."

Rather than reply, Eurybia caught the tablet with one hand as he slid it across and with the other gestured at Tritogenes as though to say, "see? He understands!"

"You could put the statues on Dasos, First Lord," Panatakis quipped.

Aegesander hummed. "I suppose I could. That would seem to settle that, then. Eurybia will have her garden and I my statues. That does leave one question, Tritogenes."

"Hmm?"

Aegesander's eyes darkened, the lids and brows lowering slightly. Mere millimeters marked the change, but his gaze suddenly took on an intensity it had not held before. If not for the smile on his lips, she might have called it predatory. "If I am to use stone from each planet, as you yourself said was a good and poetic idea, I find a hole in my information. Where, my friend, was your Titan born?"

Tritogenes waited a moment before replying. In that instant, his face was under such careful control that Eurybia doubted even Aegesander could read him.

Helena's lips quirked into what might have been a smile, then she too put on a passive mask.

"She was born on one of the rim colonies."

Aegesander's face lit up, a reaction Eurybia knew to be done entirely for Tritogenes's benefit. "Ah! How very exciting. She must have been very young when the mastigas attacked. I assume she was raised in your care?"

Again, that curious pause. This one was more nuanced, but the primary emotion Eurybia read from it was anguish.

"You might say that, yes."

Aegesander nodded once as a knowing smile crept across his face. He shifted in place as though he was about to pat Tritogenes on the shoulder before realizing the table was too big.

She knew exactly what he was doing. Aegesander had done the same trick to Tritogenes—and to her—more than once in the past. Tritogenes knew Aegesander did not care for him, and yet here he was, taken in by his charisma. More to the point, Eurybia wondered what his purpose was. Tritogenes would reveal all of that information fairly soon, either at the Council meeting or no later than the parade.

So, she asked herself, why now?

By this point, the tablet with their secret conversation had come back into her possession, and she wiped it. They continued passing it back and forth, now typing random messages about this or that. That way, the tablet still contained an extensive conversation history, but now it was about nothing more important than—Eurybia glanced down as it came back into her possession—recent popular music concerts.

"I'd very much like to meet her, Tritogenes, sir," Helena said. Her face had opened, showing more expression than Eurybia ever remembered seeing there. In her peripheral vision, she saw Aegesander shift nervously.

Tritogenes smiled. "I suspect you two would have a lot in common, Helena."

She canted her head to one side slightly as a questioning expression crossed her face. "Why is that?"

Tritogenes hesitated, obvious even across the table. "You're both unique. From what Aegesander's told me, you've given a lot to the Project."

Helena touched her implants with a gesture so automatic that Eurybia wondered if she was even aware she did it and said nothing for a moment.

She turned slightly, aiming a questioning glance at Aegesander.

"I've told him nothing," he mouthed.

Movement out of the corner of her eye caught Eurybia's attention, but it turned out to be nothing more than an errant smile and laugh from Panatakis in response to some comment Helena whispered into his ear.

Helena smiled bright and turned it on Tritogenes. Eurybia shuddered, again certain that there was something fake there. Hexarchs often put on a false face with one another, but it rarely felt so mechanical as when she did it.

"Haven't we all?" Helena asked.

***

<He seems nervous,> Panatakis quipped across their mental link.

On the other "side" of their ethereal conversation, Helena's mind bubbled amusement. Somewhere in his mind, Panatakis was aware of an odd feeling of affection growing. She never let such emotions appear in the physical world. He wondered if something happened with her implants to harm her ability to express herself any way but mentally, but that particular conversation had never come up. Instead, he was content with the way things were.

<First Lord Aegesander has reacted disfavorably when events are not in his control two-hundred eighty-se...> she paused, then, <many times.>

<What's your take on all this?>

<My take? Ah, you mean my opinion.>

<Yes.>

<Aegesander,> she replied, then stopped. It was rare for her thoughts to come to such a complete halt like that. Usually, they might wander off into mathematic noise or abstraction, but he only once heard her speechless in their brief acquaintance. Finally, she "spoke" again. <He is afraid.>

<Of the people who went after Eurybia?>

She passed along the mental sensation of a brief nod of the head, but it was feeble, hesitant. <I believe so.>

<And you. Something's bothering you about this.>

Again, she hesitated. <Did you see Tritogenes check his personal tablet earlier?>

He shook his head, both physically and mentally. The sensation transferred easily enough between them. <No.>

Helena's mental presence faded away for a moment, then returned. With it came the distinct feeling that she was carrying something. The same sort of second-hand feeling that was associated with watching someone carry a heavy weight, the sympathetic tightening of the core muscles, hung around his mind now.

With a brief mental grunt of exertion, Helena reached out and gave the file to Panatakis. It took him a moment to get to the important part, past all of the packaged security layers, but in the center of the mental bundle was a short text conversation.

He automatically read it "aloud," mentally voicing it exactly as he would while reading in private. If Helena minded, or even noticed, she said nothing.

<First Lord Tritogenes, forgive the intrusion. This message is from Helena. I am using my implants to record this message. Please do not react, and treat this conversation as more private than the one you are passing between you.>

<How can I help you, Titan Helena?>

<You seemed ill at ease upon reading First Lord Eurybia's account.>

<It's a problem when someone gets to a Hexarch like that.>

<I believe there is more to it than that. Forgive me, First Lord, but I believe you know more than you are letting on.>

<Before leaving Katarraktes, I received a warning about the Ouroboros Society. That warning included a note that very little was actually known about the group.>

<And you suspect it was the same group.>

<It's not a symbol someone would choose lightly.>

<I see. Please pass any information you gather to me, First Lord. If this is truly a danger to the Hexarchs, I would see it dealt with swiftly. And, if I may, please introduce me to your Titan soon. Again, if this is a danger to the six of you, I would like to have as many resources available as possible.>

<When she comes to Prosgeiosi, I will make sure you two meet.>

<Thank you, First Lord. I will trouble you no further. Thank you for your discretion. You are a skilled actor.>

<Thank you. I think.>

Panatakis mulled over the conversation for several moments. Finally, he said, <you really think these people are a threat?>

<I think they want us to treat them like a threat, and until I have more information at my disposal, that is exactly how I will treat them.>

Panatakis hummed in his mind, then conjured an imaginary chessboard inside their shared mental realm. <Can I interest you in a game while we eat?>

Privately, where it was only visible to someone who could see her mind, Helena smiled. <I would like that, yes.>

Chapter 3

Second Lord Pallasophia entered the spacious suite to find it quiet. The scent of food still lingered on the air, but the main floor had fallen silent. She opened the door to the dining room slowly, but found no one there. The kitchen was likewise empty, though a plate, glass, and skillet sat in the drying rack. She inspected them and found them much cleaner than expected; all traces of whatever food Victoria must have prepared and eaten were gone.

Pallasophia found it impressive enough that Victoria managed to prepare a meal for herself. The fact that she cleaned up afterward was doubly impressive. She checked the pantry and refrigerator, found the missing vegetables and meat, and made a note on her tablet to order extra food for the duration of Victoria's stay. Judging by the amount of missing food and lack of leftovers, her strength and stamina came at a high metabolic cost.

For the first few minutes, she was surprised enough by the simple fact that Victoria had figured out the kitchen, cooked, and cleaned without any outside instruction that Pallasophia failed to be surprised at how short her absence had been. She had been gone less than six hours, and expected Victoria to still still asleep.

Pallasophia half expected to find her in the office. She kept most of her files there and would not have been surprised to find Victoria pouring through her notes on Project Titan. Victoria seemed to understand everything else well enough. Pallasophia supposed she would simply take it in stride if Tritogenes's "perfect soldier" understood genetic engineering.

She stifled a laugh. Of course, there was a chance Victoria understood genetic engineering just as well as she did, Pallasophia thought. When Tritogenes compiled the original list of skills he thought their experimental soldiers would need, she had not double-checked the list for "extraneous" things. It had been enough, she thought at the time, to include obvious subjects like cleanliness. There had been no need to review the information at that point. Even if there had been, she likely would have had an underling do it while she focused on synthesizing combat data. For all she knew, Victoria came out of that shell in the facility with an innate understanding of differential calculus and orbital mechanics.

Her office also contained one of the more expensive perks of her position. The fact that they were here, rather than her actual house on Limani spoke to just how much time she spent here, buried inside a tiny piece of rock a billion miles from home. Against one wall, flanking the window that looked out onto the rocky terrain of the asteroid and the endless starfield above it, were a pair of wooden bookcases. Each was filled with row after row of real books. Most of them had leather covers, though a few were wooden or some variety of plastic, but they were all physical copies of single volumes. In the space they occupied, she could have housed a rack of data drives large enough to hold the accumulated knowledge of the entire Titan Project, but instead they contained, in print form, so little data that a dozen scanned copies of everything on those shelves could fit on a palmdrive and still have room to spare.

Some of those books had been bought with her own money long before taking the job as Director for Tritogenes's branch of Project Titan.

The first one she ever purchased, a two-century old copy of a book from Old Earth called *The Lord of the Rings*, had cost half a year's salary as a Fifth Lord. Others had been purchased here and there over the years since, culminating in a gift of a five-volume set titled *Odyssey: Ten Thousand Years Among the Stars* from Tritogenes himself on the first year anniversary of Project Titan's existence.

Taken all together, the book collection represented an investment of well over a million credits. The sight was familiar enough, but the knowledge of the value of the two humble-seeming pieces of furniture still surprised her. Knowing that it was hers, value aside, never failed to sent a little rush through her nerves.

She spared a moment to look over the tiles Photeos's team removed from the elite's bedchamber. The drawings of its kills were fascinating in their way, but represented little more than basic iconography. They showed a modicum of intelligence, but what truly fascinated her was the block of written text. Pallasophia looked it over again, and again felt a cold pit in her stomach as she processed the words written there. The elite's handwriting was crude—its hands were not delicate instruments suited to calligraphy—but the ideas expressed there were clear enough.

She smiled. Working on Project Titan had its perks, she thought. Long hours—endless hours, if she was truthful about it—and an overall disappointing and disheartening series of trials made the job more difficult than anything else she had done in her decade and a half as a Second Lord. Tritogenes had given her a large budget and very little restrictions provided she did not detract from the Project itself. Much of her personal stipend had gone into the suite and the small library, leaving more than enough to upgrade the facility's food budget and keep everyone fed with the best cuisine she could import through the dozens of layers of security.

Thinking of food reminded her of the primary reason she came back to the suite and Pallasophia adjusted the bag she held over her shoulder and went back down the stairs to the main floor. She crossed it, went to the other staircase, and made her way to the small wing that held the bedrooms.

Pallasophia turned, going away from her room and towards Victoria's. She hesitated for a moment. The suite's sensors could have told her whether Victoria was awake or not, but somehow after monitoring her entire life, no matter how long that actually had been, turning the sensors on seemed wrong. She knocked on the door and waited.

"Come in," Victoria replied after a few moments. She sounded awake, which was good.

Pallasophia did so, opening, stepping through, and then shutting the door before looking around the room. It was just as simple as hers had been five years ago. She struggled to remember her room looking so plain and found the memory obscured by knickknacks she collected over half a decade of work.

The large bed sat in the middle of the wall, flanked by night tables, with space on either side. Victoria's knives sat on one of the tables, while the other seemed untouched. The sheets were rumpled, but Victoria seemed to have made an attempt at making the bed at some point. Her scavenged mastigas clothing and armor were nowhere to be seen, but a small puddle of water just inside the open bathroom door indicated that Victoria had probably made an effort to wash them.

Victoria sat, naked, at the small table under the window. A large tablet sat on the table in front of her. The holo had been set to single-direction, and all Pallasophia could see was a blank, green rectangle sporting Aphelion facility's logo in a darker shade in the center. Next to the table sat a half-full glass of something red.

Eyes the color of steel, a striking contrast with the bronze face that framed them, regarded Pallasophia with curiosity. She swiped across the holo display to dismiss it, watching Pallasophia as she crossed the small room. When Pallasophia crossed the midpoint of the room, Victoria rose to her feet in a single, fluid motion, still with the same curious expression on her face.

Pallsophia supposed she had no idea what the proper Technocrat greetings would be. Such things had been omitted from her "training."

She looked Victoria up and down. She had seen Victoria's face and body during their time in the Labyrinth, but there was something clearly different between the dirt- and blood-smeared human weapon from then and the woman who stood before her now. Doctor Iro's report indicated excellent health and muscle tone. Pallasophia could confirm the second, at least, herself. Victoria's muscles rippled with every movement, long and lean under her skin. The rest of her, Pallasophia thought, seemed to be in excellent condition as well. The sheen of sweat on her skin, despite the cool of the room, could easily be explained by the long towel laid out on the floor like a traditional exercise mat.

"By the Ten Thousand," Pallasophia muttered, staring. Most of the scars crisscrossing her body had been concealed by grime, but now they stood out in stark detail. At least a half-dozen newer slashes and cuts shone red against her skin. A large part of her stomach and lower ribs stood out even darker, showing the sickly purples and greens colors of an old bruise. The scar from the elite's sword was so clean as to be art, but the wound in her shoulder where she had been shot was still a mess.

She was also keenly aware of Victoria's eyes on her. Her gaze swept across her, her robe, and the bag dangling over her shoulder. Most of Victoria's attention seemed fixed on her clothing, likely already starting to put the pieces together after seeing two Second Lords in their Blue.

"I was wondering when you would be back," Victoria said, apparently oblivious of her condition. Her eyes were now fixed on Pallasophia's face, almost uncomfortable in their intensity.

"I had several errands to run. I confess, I expected you to still be asleep," she replied, wondering even as she spoke why the words came out with such stiff formality.

Victoria shrugged her broad shoulders. "I slept enough, ate as well."

"I noticed."

"I tried to clean everything up afterward. It... didn't seem right to leave everything dirty."

Pallasophia smiled. "You did well, trust me. Many who grow up around the luxuries of civilization fail when it comes to cleaning up after themselves."

Victoria crossed her arms over her breasts. "I suppose, however, you didn't just come here to compliment my ability to feed myself."

Pallasophia laughed, both at the absurdity of the situation and at Victoria's comment. "No," she replied. "I brought you a gift."

"A gift?"

Pallasophia took the bag off of her shoulder and held it in front of her. She had been somewhat distracted by Victoria's appearance and her initial errand slipped her mind. When Victoria did not take the bundle herself, Pallasophia withdrew a mass of black fabric and let the now-empty garment bag fall to the ground. That let her unfold the black cloth with both hands. When she was finished, she held the plain black robe by the shoulders. It was significantly longer than her own and she struggled to keep the hem off of the floor.

She held it out for Victoria to see, then draped it over her arm. She spoke stiffly, formally, aware of the tension in the air. "This is for you. You are not officially a Technocrat citizen, but you do need clothing. Black is the color of someone without a formal rank. It is typically reserved for those with religious objections to the social order, but not always."

Victoria frowned. "So I'll be an outcast."

"Perhaps at first, but..."

She shrugged. "That's fine. I haven't decided yet if I *want* to be a Technocrat."

Pallasophia hesitated. This was not going as planned. "I understand."

"It's blank," Victoria observed, glancing at the myriad of symbols and patterns embroidered in gold and silver thread on Pallasophia's blue robe.

The Second Lord nodded. "It's traditional for each person to design the symbols for their robes. You'll find, though, that it's not completely blank. An intricate design takes time to produce, but in the time I had, I was able to design a small pattern for you."

She held out the black fabric for Victoria to take and waited a moment while she inspected her new garment.

After a few moments, she said, "here, on the collar," and held it up. A thin tracery of silver thread wrapped around the neckline of the robe. "What does it mean?"

"It's a mathematical representation of what Tritogenes said to me when you killed the elite. 'She has done the impossible.'"

Victoria ran a finger across the comparatively unobtrusive design. Pallasophia watched her face as emotions swam across it, never settling for long on any one thing.

"Other symbols," Pallasophia added, "will be up to you as time goes on."

Victoria smiled. "Thank you, Second Lord." Her gratitude seemed genuine. Pallasophia had been afraid that Victoria would reject the robe.

"Unless we're out somewhere among other Technocrats, you can simply call me Pallasophia if you like."

Victoria nodded. "Pallasophia it is."

"Now," the Second Lord said, holding out a hand and stepping closer to Victoria, "if you will permit me to show you how, let us get you dressed."

Victoria tensed for a moment at the sudden proximity, but relaxed and handed over her robe a moment later. "And then?"

"And then," Pallasophia said, "how about tea?"

"Tea?" Victoria asked, raising an eyebrow.

Pallasophia laughed. "There are many luxuries in life you do not yet know about. Let's let tea be the first one."

Now it was Victoria's turn to laugh. "No, I think the shower was the first one. Tea can be second."

***

Victoria sat on the couch in front of the room's artificial fireplace, one arm draped over the end. Her legs were crossed at the ankles, leaving her in a position that would, if it became necessary, let her spring up and off the soft cushions in one fluid movement. Despite that, she felt strangely relaxed. The black robe helped, she supposed. It was something other than the black mastigas fabric she had been wearing, and between that change and her shower, she felt rather different. The knowledge that she was safe, that nothing would leap from a shadowed corner and try to kill her, was starting to sink in as well.

Of course, much of her physical sense of relaxation came from the combination of the soft couch her and the feeling of the lush carpet under her bare feet. Pallasophia brought several pairs of shoes to wear, but none of them had yet suited her as well as going barefoot. Pallasophia re-entered the room carrying a large iron kettle in one hand and in the other a silver tray with two cups and various other odds and ends. She set the steaming kettle on the table in front of them and the tray beside it.

"It will take me a while to get used to this robe," Victoria mused. Watching Pallasophia move effortlessly in her shroud of blue made it obvious how much she still had to learn. She needed help to put on the deceptively complicated thing, to say nothing of trying to walk in it.

"It's customary for Technocrats to wear their robes in public," Pallasophia replied. She took a seat at the far end of the couch.

"Why?"

She thought for a moment, then simply shrugged. "Unless you need to wear something else, like the uniforms we wore when my team came to rescue you, these," she shifted and held up a fold of her robe, "are simply how you dress."

"Does comfort come into it at all?"

Pallasophia laughed. "Some. At home, things are less strict. If you know the other person well, then it can be a symbol of trust to go without."

Victoria raised an eyebrow. "And now?"

"Now," Pallasophia shrugged. "Wearing your robe now will help you get used to it, to the trappings of civilization. Once the fabric wears some, it will be comfortable enough."

"I fail to see how. Skin tight clothing, or less, is more comfortable for moving around. I suppose for sitting or standing and looking important, these work well enough. I feel less capable of violence in this than I did out of it. "

Despite the seriousness of the comment, Pallasophia laughed softly. "It's a symbol. The robes stand for our accomplishments. To shed that is to present a much more vulnerable side of yourself than most people want to expose."

Pallasophia waved a hand through the air, opening a holographic menu. The text and icons floated above her arm, tethered to her movements. "The tea will take a minute to finish steeping. While it does, there is something you need to see."

Victoria felt a wave of unease radiating out from the other end of the couch. That put her on her guard. "What is it?"

"I promised you answers," she replied, deliberately not looking at Victoria. "This will clear some things up, I hope."

Victoria watched her as she maneuvered through a series of menus. The feeling of unease never left, and she could see Pallasophia's neck muscles, some of the only skin visible around the robe, tensing as she worked.

The holoprojector came to life and the lights in the room dimmed. An an empty room hovered above the mantle. A long table sat under a holographic window. Through that window, the room beyond was bright, but the angle of the video prevented them from seeing anything beyond.

The timestamp in the lower right corner of the screen told them that the video had been taken four years before. Dates were straightforward enough to follow after the broad look she took into Technocrat history. "LY 1176," claimed the stamp.

A lone purple-robed figure sat at the table with his back to the camera. His hair was pulled back into a tight ponytail. He sat with his shoulders hunched, both elbows pressed into the top of the table as he hammered furiously away at the holographic keyboard in front of him. Even with his face out of view, Victoria recognized Tritogenes by the designs on his robe.

He shifted in position, drawing his shoulders up straighter. With his back to the camera, his voice came out muffled and with strange rises and falls in volume as the camera caught or missed various words.

"There's a problem. Trial Number Eighteen," he said. "Failed. Subject was unable to overcome even a single mastigas in combat, even after being given a weapon and two days of training."

Victoria wondered why she did not remember this alleged training. She had skills that she certainly might have gained from being taught to fight rather than trial and error as the "trial subjects" ran out, but her mind could recall nothing from a period before Aphelion Facility became Aphelion the labyrinth.

Tritogenes was still talking in the recording. "...lasted longer than Subjects Seventeen or Eighteen, though. Number Nineteen exhibited a remarkable ability to analyze his enemy's tactics. Unfortunately, his physical failings, much like those of Sixteen and Eighteen, proved to be the fatal flaw. Twenty is down there right now, and..."

Victoria felt increasing unease at hearing Tritogenes talking about the Project, herself included, as merely "trials" and "test subjects." To hear him say those things in such a dispassionate tone sent shivers down her spine. His posture said tension, frustration, but the tone in his voice

46

sounded less like regret for lives lost and more like the tone a scientist might take when a certain chemical reaction came out differently than expected.

On top of that, she knew she was "Number One-Hundred." What she was watching was the early stages of the Project, long before her life began. Some eighty dead lay between her and the time in the video. It was not a comforting thought.

"I must find a way to increase the test subjects' endurance," the First Lord continued. "All the skill in the binary will not save them when they tire before the mastigas are dead. We must press on and..."

The door flew open. It sat outside the camera's pickup, but the sound of it being flung open and slamming against the wall of the workroom were clear enough. Previously, the only light had been from the window, and the sudden shaft of light cast by the door in the dim room was startling.

"First Lord Tritogenes," a female voice from off camera called. The voice panted, out of breath. Victoria detected, of all things, fear in the voice. "First Lord..."

Tritogenes growled. "What?" he snarled, then straightened his shoulders and turned. His face was a mask of civility as he addressed the off-screen voice. "Yes, Third Lord? I trust you have something of importance to tell me? Something that could not wait?"

"My apologies, First Lord," the voice replied. She was getting her breathing under control, but the tremors of fear still rattled her words. "But the project heads on the lower levels said to find you immediately and tell you that the worst we prepared for has happened."

Tritogenes shot to his feet with such force that he sent his chair skidding backwards. He turned on his heels and faced the unseen door. For a brief moment, his eyes were wide with an unreadable, roiling mix of emotions. That was over in a flash, and the tension in his face drained, flowing down his shoulders and into his hands which he clenched into white-knuckled fists at his sides. His face, however, calmed and resumed its mask.

"Explain," he ordered.

"The project heads said to bring you, First Lord. I can tell you on the way, but they stressed that we must go now!"

Victoria heard denial in his voice. "Are there no plans in place? Can they not handle their own tasks while I see to mine here?"

"Yes, First Lord, but the project heads said that you are needed immediately." The voice was practically pleading now.

"Why did they not comm me direc—"

"Sir," the voice interrupted. Anger flashed across Tritogenes's face, but it, too, was quickly suppressed. "First Lord, forgive my interruption, but the project heads were insistent. they have tried everything in the official policy you set down and all options have failed. They did not want this being overheard, but gave me permission to say it should you, in Second Lord Kyros's words, 'insist on being bullheaded.'"

Tritogenes's eyes narrowed.

"Second Lord Kyros said that it was officially a Code Black, Omega Grade."

Tritogenes's eyes snapped all the way open. His face went from shock to anger to confusion to fear and fluctuated between them all for several moments as the muscle in his jaw clenched and slacked. Despite everything he could do, Tritogenes proved unable, at least for several seconds, to contain the sea of emotions under his skin. His face reddened.

"Go!" he snapped. "Return to Kyros and tell him I am on my way. Tell him to maintain quarantine as long as possible. Run as fast as you can. The devil chases you! Go!"

The sound of running feet was the only thing that answered Tritogenes's hastily snapped orders. He turned back to the table and leaned against it, pressing his knuckles into the tabletop for several seconds as he simply breathed. His heaving shoulders eventually slowed and he stood up straight. He sighed, then, in a flash, snatched up his tablet from the table and flung it directly into the camera pickup.

The holo went black.

It immediately segued into another scene. The time in the corner showed that the events they were now watching happened twenty minutes before the scene they just watched. Victoria realized she had clenched her fists in her lap and forced them to relax. Even recorded, Tritogenes seemed to have a way of infecting everyone in the room with his emotions, and right then the tension had been terribly palpable.

The new scene was a room Victoria recognized from the labyrinth. This time around it looked very different. Where she remembered a dark room with only one functioning light, smashed furniture and broken equipment, and a bare concrete floor, the room in the recording was clean and bright. People, mostly in the greens and yellows of Third and Fourth Lords, milled around it, moving from workstation to workstation with methodical precision. They all seemed to be talking, their voices rising in a murmur that the video failed to isolate into anything useful.

The tone shift from the previous scene was jarring. Tritogenes had been tense, even before the news of the disaster reached him, and here these people were working as though it were any normal job.

A green light on one console flickered and burned red. The room fell silent.

"Number Twenty has been killed," the yellow-robed Technocrat sitting nearest to the light announced.

Another, this one in a green robe, commented that, "preliminary reports indicate she killed the first mastigas she encountered..."

Despite everything Pallasophia had told her about Technocrat reservation and their usual social taboos against showing extreme emotion, the room erupted in a few moments of unrestrained cheering and applause. When it calmed, the technocrat who had last spoken continued.

"Subject Twenty, according to telemetry, came across the sophont ahead of schedule. We had no reason to suspect the sophont had moved away from its assigned area. Second Lord Matthias, please dispatch a security team to sector seventeen, level nine and detain the sophont. First Lord Tritogenes will want a full report and suggestions for better containment before subject Twenty-One is ready to decant."

"Yes, Third Lord," a voice replied from offscreen.

The screen blinked and jumped ahead five minutes. The workers had moved around the room and a definite air of tension had settled, but otherwise nothing changed. That persisted for exactly seven seconds before someone announced, "the security team just went dark."

"Sensors?"

"Negative human contacts."

"Mastigas?"

"Sensors show them converging on level nine."

A blue-robed Second Lord shoved another worker aside and leaned toward one of the consoles. She tapped a series of buttons. "Executive comm override. Second Lord Matthias, do you..."

"...behind you!" a voice screamed, distorted by the little speaker on the console. "Positive contact! Three gigas and seven fonias on our nine."

Gunfire erupted across the comm line.

"Second Lord Matthias!"

More gunfire, accompanied by incoherent yelling.

"Second Lord Matthias!"

"Second Lord Kyros? We are being overrun. Repeat, we have a Code Black. Recommend reinforcements."

"Reinforcements are en route. Can you hold your position?"

"For how long?"

On the holo, Second Lord Kyros hesitated. She straightened and looked around the room. One by one, the other Technocrats made eye

50

contact with her and then looked away. Victoria watched as she chewed on her lower lip, unable or unwilling to reply.

"Kyros? I need an ETA!"

"ETA Unknown. Hold position, Second Lord. Go with the suns," she said and tapped a switch on the console before any reply could come through the comms.

"Second Lord?" one of the other Technocrats said. He spoke quietly. "There are no reinforcements, are there?"

"Reinforcements are already on their way. I tripped the alarm as soon as they left, just in case. But they're going to be half an hour out."

One of the Technocrats made a small x-shape in front of his chest with the first two fingers of each hand. A few other others made similar gestures, though most remained still and seated.

"We have work to do," Kyros said. "Anything we can do, do it. Power up every system in the facility with a draw, tap into every sensor and scanner you can get code into, and..."

The comm clicked on again.

"Hello," came the voice. It rasped with an inhuman quality. Victoria knew that voice before anyone in the video identified it. She watched in horror as every motion in the room froze in an instant as the realization of what was speaking to them spread.

"You!" Kyros pointed to one of the Technocrats. She stood. "You placed in the games last year, yes? As a runner?"

The other Technocrat nodded.

"Go! Tell First Lord Tritogenes. Get him down here! I need personal authorization to seal the facility."

"Second Lord, I..."

"Go, blue screen it!" Second Lord Kyros snapped. Her curse rippled through the room, stirring the others from their stupor and into a flurry of activity. "If Tritogenes insists on being bullheaded, then tell him it's a Code Black, Omega Grade. He'll know what that means. Just get him the hell down here!"

Kyros prodded her way through a series of touch-screen menus before bringing up what she apparently sought. The screen was hidden from the camera, but the look of her face seemed to turn somewhat toward satisfaction for a moment. She pressed her hand against the screen and waited a moment.

"Level twelve sealed," an electronic voice announced.

One of the Technocrats stood up. There was a gun in his hand. "You would seal us in?"

Kyros turned halfway around and addressed him. If she saw the gun, her posture never changed and nothing on her face indicated she cared. Most of her attention was still on the screen beside her as she moved things around on the touch interface. "I would seal the rest of the facility off from the mastigas first. We know they are not yet above us, but were I to seal the level below only to have them appear in our midst," she turned back to her console and with utmost formality said, "if we can stop them, I will unseal the doors. If not, it is well that I seal them now."

The worker who had protested held the gun a moment longer before his shoulders slumped. Defeat hung there, and he turned back to his own console and leaned over it, going back to work.

Kyros pressed her palm into her screen again. In a quiet voice, Pallasophia explained that she could seal the levels but all she had the authority to do was drop the security doors and lock them. Without the First Lord's personal approval, granted by his palm print, she could not activate the protocols that would drop the armored hatches and weld them shut, truly sealing the facility.

"Tritogenes could have left the doors locked and sent in more troops, but he chose not to do so," she added.

"Why not?" Victoria hissed.

"He would not tell me," she confessed. "You, in fact all eighty who would follow number Twenty, were still down there. Perhaps he was afraid you would be killed even before you were born in he tried to take the facility by force."

52

"But he kept the Project running!"

Pallasophia nodded. Her voice was quiet, dark. "There were eighty of you. We hoped that one of you would survive and free yourself."

Victoria scoffed. "Was I everything you wanted in your Project?" she asked, voice dripping with scorn.

"More. Now watch, there is one more thing you have to see."

"I think I know what happened now."

Pallasophia shook her head. "There is more you ought to know. This is about the mastigas themselves, and may help explain what we saw in the elite's room."

"Alright."

The screen changed again. Along with the date and time, the camera was also labeled, "level seven, sector four." It was now ten minutes before Tritogenes would get the news of the disaster.

Two mastigas gigas and four of the knife-armed fonias wandered down a well-lit hallway. They ambled with no real apparent goal other than "the other end of the hallway." The six mastigas hissed and growled at one another.

The hunched posture of the fonias made them look bestial, not like the assassins in darkness they had been when she met them. The gigas were another matter. They stood much higher than she did, nearly as large as the elite itself, and they were broad across the shoulders with arms that reached to their knees. Where the fonias crawled and crept, the gigas lumbered.

Suddenly, the six mastigas snapped to some measure of attention. Their path down the hall straightened. Three of the fonias took point in front of their group while the fourth dropped to the rear and started looking over its shoulder constantly. The two gigas synchronized their pace, thundering down the hallway in unison.

Another mastigas stepped into the video feed. It was smaller than the others. Taller than the fonias and thinner than the gigas, it nevertheless stood just barely taller than a human. Its long, spindly legs moved with an insectoid grace. It walked with its arms folded behind its back, like a sergeant addressing his troops. Two smaller arms nestled in tight against its chest. Its head was the most unnerving thing about its appearance. The skull was too large for its frame, held up by a thick neck out of place against the thin limbs.

Victoria recognized it on sight. She killed it herself. The spindly-limbed thing owned the voice that taunted Victoria all through the labyrinth, before she found it and tore it apart. It was also identical, as far as she could tell, to the one that confronted her and Pallasophia's soldiers in the pod room.

On the screen, the sophont addressed the other mastigas with a combination of words and arm gestures. "Come," it said in its wet-rocks voice. "Come, fonias, knives in the dark. Come, gigas, mover of mountains. Above us waits the elite of our kind, and above that waits a thousand humans!"

The two gigas, in perfect sync, bellowed.

Chapter 4

All around the feast hall, people were enjoying their first round of drinks. The clamor of conversation was quieter than it could have been, and definitely quieter than it would be later, once things really got started. For the moment, the buzz still qualified as "background noise," and it was easy enough to talk over without anyone having to raise their voice very much.

For a "feast hall," the facility was rather small. Instead of using one of the so-called grand ballrooms inside Odyssey itself, this little facility sat on the riverbank of one of Eantio's canals. The windows facing Tritogenes's chair gave a view of the far bank of the canal and the still-bustling shops there.

Their dinner was no secret, and the doors had been open to the public right up until the house manager booked the very last seat. At Hyperion's insistence, the seats had been free to anyone with enough gumption to walk through the door. As a result, the room held a dizzying array of colored robes.

He laughed to himself as the last people through the door stood in bewilderment as they realized exactly what sort of event they just walked into. Two women, either second or third lords by their blue-green robes, stood hand-in-hand and seemed to be staring directly at Tritogenes from across the hall. Hyperion did not advertise exactly who was putting on this particular celebration, nor why, only that it was free to the first hundred people to walk through the door.

He nudged his fellow Hexarch with the back of his hand and pointed to the couple as the house manager directed them to their seats. "Somehow I doubt they expected to meet half the Council this evening."

Hyperion laughed. Eyes of purest blue shone out of his wizened, amused face. Six rubies twinkled in his beard, the only decoration of his that stayed the same no matter what else he wore. "Exactly why I wanted to use this place, my friend. Odyssey is so full of its own business, but even this close to the dome, these people have very little interest in the politicking that we do up there."

From the seat next to Hyperion, Enyalios snorted a laugh. "Politics." He held up an empty mug. "I'll toast to anything but that."

As if on cue, a Fourth Lord finally came to their table with a large clay pitcher. He refilled their mugs one by one. Tritogenes instantly recognized the drink being poured and allowed himself to laugh in amusement. He never, personally, cared much for the watered-down wine-and-honey Hyperion always served, but neither did he expressly dislike it.

But, he thought, raising his now-full glass in a toast, he would never turn down a free drink, certainly not from someone like Hyperion.

With a wry grin, Tritogenes said, "to surprising our people."

Hyperion and Enyalios clanked their mugs against his and they all took long drinks of the subtly sweet wine. Around the hall, very few of the guests took notice of their impromptu toast.

Again, Tritogenes laughed, though he declined to explain why, no matter how inquisitive Hyperion's glance became. Far be it from him, Tritogenes thought, to remind his erstwhile mentor exactly how little their current setup surprised him. Hyperion, thought Tritogenes, always wanted to either be in the exact center of the spotlight or nowhere near it.

Instead, he disguised his amusement as interest in his mug. On the surface, the clay vessel was fairly simple, but an up-close look proved exactly how wrong that impression was. The tan clay had been shaped into a tapered cylinder, larger at the base. Into that clay had been carved a landscape scene from Hyperion's home planet of Pteryga. The one Tritogenes had been given showed mountains, themselves stained a darker brown, with rivers flowing down to a blue wash at the base of the mug. Jewels the color of straw had been set into that base.

The marks from the potter's hands were obvious, he thought, and that was where the value came from. Anyone of reasonable means could have outfitted the dining hall with machine-made mugs that looked, from a distance, even better than these did. Hyperion, however, had filled the hall with hundreds of handmade dishes.

Once their guests realized who threw this particular event, Tritogenes thought with another amused snort, the quality of their tableware would put the spotlight firmly back on Hyperion.

Tritogenes set the water and wine mixture back on the table, now less a good third of its contents from moments before. He turned slightly, taking the moment to examine a glimmer at Hyperion's wrist. Small silver plates, etched with words of poetry from Earth, adorned his cuffs. The poems were short, just a few lines of text on each wrist, but Tritogenes still remembered what each one said.

That Hyperion chose to wear that particular piece of jewelry that evening was a good sign as far as Tritogenes was concerned.

Hyperion, still drinking, caught his interested glance, and his sapphire eyes glittered with amusement, but neither Hexarch said anything. That gift had been years and years ago, back when Tritogenes was a Second Lord.

On the far side, Korakti and Daniel, the Titans of Pteryga and Katarraktes respectively, had paused on the way back from their joint trip to the kitchen. While Tritogenes watched, Korakti seemed to be challenging a random guest to a drinking contest. They were out of earshot, but a moment later both she and the still-unnamed guest raised their mugs and proceeded to attempt to down them in a single gulp.

Suddenly feeling out of place having stopped drinking, Tritogenes picked his back up and took another long drink. Putting it down, he said, "I must admit. You have always known how to throw a lavish feast."

Hyperion's eyes flicked up and he smiled, amused. "Ninety years of practice indulging the appetites of Prosgeiosi's elite gives one a certain ability in that regard."

Korakti dropped heavily into the seat next to him. Tritogenes noticed with amusement that she was much like her Hexarch in that regard. He had not seen her cross the room, but now that she wanted to be noticed, suddenly her entrance was the center of attention for their table.

Adding to her entrance, Korakti heavily set several full mugs of beer down on the table. Tritogenes did a double take at the sight of the mugs—it was definitely beer in them, and a dark one at that. Where she got them, in a hall full of Hyperion's honey wine, he he no idea and was not about to ask. She pushed mugs in front of everyone except Daniel—he carried his own to the table.

"My most esteemed Hexarch has a reputation to uphold, you understand."

"Korakti, my Titan, did you convince the kitchen staff to open the cellar again?" Hyperion's voice was, on the surface stern and full of discipline, but Tritogenes had been around him long enough to hear the amusement in it. He suspected Korakti did as well, because she simply smiled, laughed, and said nothing.

Tritogenes laughed, directing his comment at Korakti. "One he's cultivated for many decades."

"How many of these did you attend as my pupil, Tritogenes, hmm?" Hyperion smiled again, and added, "before Ophion, rest his thoughts, took you from me?"

The young Hexarch laughed again. "It feels like you threw one a week, some years."

"I most likely did," he agreed. "Open to the public, too. Like this one."

Tritogenes nodded. That last remark had a bit of a taint of sadness to it. He thought he detected some anger, but it was gone in a moment. Sadness, regret even, replaced it.

Before he could reply, First Lord Enyalios, sitting to Tritogenes's right, spoke up. "Speaking of, Tritogenes, don't you have a message to deliver?"

Tritogenes glanced at him out of the corner of his eye, moving his head just enough to bring the other Hexarch into view. He regarded him for a moment with annoyance, then shook his head with an amused sigh. "I was hoping to leave unpleasantness until after dinner."

"Unpleasantness?" Hyperion echoed. He raised the beer Korakti placed in front of him. "If there's to be bad news, we need more drink."

As one, the five of them lifted their mugs and drank heavily. Tritogenes amended his previous assessment. He would have preferred more of the honey wine to this heavily spiced, thick beer, but as Enyalios often said, the best drink was the one someone else brought.

Hyperion dropped his mug back to the table and wiped foam from his thick beard. "So, I assume your 'unpleasantness' has to do with the esteemed Hexarch of Kokkinos?"

Tritogenes swallowed, taking that moment to collect his thoughts. He was not surprised that Hyperion was able to put two and two together and get the proper answer. "Word has already reached you of her visit to Katarraktes, I see."

"And of your meeting with them last night."

Tritogenes frowned, more at himself than anything. Aegesander had been, for all that he said very little during dinner, rather pleasant and neither he nor Eurybia mentioned Hyperion once.

Hyperion was his friend, his mentor, but he did not particularly like being put in the middle of his feud with Aegesander.

"I was more interested in meeting their Titans, if I'm telling the truth."

Hyperion raised an eyebrow. "And?"

"I'll tell you more later," he replied, flashing a quick hand sign that he and Hyperion had not used in decades, one that indicated he wanted privacy for that conversation. "But the short version is that I found both of them to be rather fascinating. When Victoria makes her way here, I suspect she will be fast friends with them both."

Korakti dropped her mug to the table. It rattled with an empty thud. "I want to fight her!" She laughed raucously. "With your permission, First Lords."

Hyperion chuckled. "Is there anyone you don't want to fight, my Titan?"

She jerked a thumb at Daniel in his seat next to her. He sipped almost reverently from his mug, but watched the others over the top.

"Me?" he asked, surprised.

"Without your armor, it wouldn't exactly be a fair fight," she replied, giving his bicep a quick squeeze. "And with? Gods between, even I'm not that strong!"

After the laughter died down, Tritogenes asked, "so Eurybia's visit isn't news to you?"

Hyperion grinned. "Many things are done around our system by people who think I do not know about their activities. More to the point, Tritogenes, her visit was no secret. I spoke at length with First Lord Aegesander that day and he informed me of her intent to stop at Kataraktes."

Tritogenes concealed his shock behind a demure raised eyebrow. "Did he?"

Hyperion nodded. "From the other side of a holo, the Lord of Dasos is almost amenable at times."

"You two were friends once," Tritogenes ventured. Historically, he and Aegesander had worked quite close together, but that was before Tritogenes had been born. In his lifetime, the two of them—and Aegesander's close ally and confidant First Lord Eurybia—had very little to do with one another. As the years went on, they seemed to have less and less contact, and what contact they did share was bitter, angry.

Hyperion never told Tritogenes what brought about the shift. For the barest of moments, less than a heartbeat, Hyperion's expression made it seem like he wanted to share that information. Instead, he chose that moment to take another long drink of his beer. His sapphire eyes continued to watch Tritogenes; even as he drank, they seemed to study him.

Finally, he set the mug down and folded both hands on the table. "What *did* our dear comrade Eurybia have to say?"

Tritogenes stifled a look of annoyance. Hyperion, it seemed, was going to ignore the question once again. With a sidelong glance at First Lord Enyalios, he said, "Eurybia came to visit First Lord Enyalios on her way back from her mines in the belt. She very generously offered the use of her personal liner to transport us here."

Hyperion nodded. "Aegesander said as much, but Eurybia can be pleasant enough company at times. Why bring it up now?"

He paused, wondering if it was even worth bringing up. After a moment's consideration, he assumed that, if it was important enough to mention at all, it was best to get it out of the way before dinner proper started. A moment longer, and Tritogenes inhaled deeply before beginning. "She asked me if I would, ah, check on you, First Lord."

Hyperion raised one eyebrow, but his face remained otherwise still. "Check on me?"

"She claimed to be worried about your health."

Tritogenes was sure no one outside their table saw the gesture, but Hyperion spared a half-second's glance at the mug of honey wine abandoned in favor of Korakti's beer. His immediate suspicion, and the insult behind it, would have been clear enough to anyone who saw it.

Hyperion replied, "I am in excellent health."

Korakti, after several drinks of short succession starting to show only the slightest hint of intoxication, interrupted with a bark of laughter. "Did Eurybia not see my prize fight? The Boss Man here almost kicked my ass!"

Hyperion smiled, a fleeting gesture. To the rest of the table, he said, "Korakti was tired at that point."

"Tired, nothing. Look, Hyperion nearly had me. Look it up, watch the holo. Best damn fight of my career!"

Again, the table broke out in a round of laughter, dispelling the tension that built up over the previous few minutes.

Hyperion took another drink, emptying the mug of beer Korakti brought him. "So, Tritogenes, why do *you* think Eurybia asked after me?"

"She said because it had been so long since you met with them, and with Project Titan being so stressful, she and First Lord Aegesander were concerned for your well being."

He scoffed again, this time with open derision. Quietly, so that only Tritogenes, and perhaps Korakti on his other side, could hear, he muttered, "Aegesander has not cared for my well being in twenty years, Tritogenes."

"If I may, with the Project Ending..." he started, then hushed. Hyperion had already blown off this particular line of questioning once before, but if Tritogenes took another tack with it, he supposed he might have better luck.

"We have been on equal footing for twenty years, my friend. Whatever you were about to ask, go ahead."

Tritogenes hesitated, but only for a moment. He took a deep breath. In all their years, he had hinted at it, but never came right out and said anything directly. It was time to change that. "What happened between you and Aegesander twenty years ago?"

Hyperion's face darkened. Tritogenes could tell the frustration was not directed at him, but he had not seen the elderly First Lord that angry more than a handful of times. The dark cloud passed as quickly as it came, replaced with Hyperion's usual control over his emotions, and he said simply, "I lied, my friend. You may ask about anything but that. There are things you are better off not knowing."

Tritogenes started to argue. "But..."

Hyperion closed his eyes and shook his head. The movement was firm, decisive. He would accept no argument on the subject. "No, Tritogenes. This is for your own safety. Do not pursue this."

Tritogenes sat in silence for a moment, then nodded slowly. Whatever it was was secret enough that the "usual" espionage game the Hexarchs all played with one another had not uncovered it, which meant that Hyperion—and Aegesander—had gone to great lengths to keep it hidden.

The older Hexarch continued, "in any case, I will thank First Lord Eurybia for her concern," a pause, a frown, "at the next Council meeting. I will thank Aegesander when I see him next."

"When you?" Tritogenes asked."You're going to meet with Aegesander?"

Hyperion nodded, once.

"So then why the secrecy?"

"Just because the Lord of Dasos and I are attempting to mend our relationship for the future, it does not mean our past issues are any less problematic."

Hyperion stopped, then turned to face Tritogenes, locking eyes with him for a brief, if intense, moment. Under that piercing stare, Tritogenes was reminded exactly how he felt as a Second Lord working for Hyperion, feeling like the man was a force of nature instead of a mere human. To his surprise, however, Hyperion simply said one, quiet word.

"Please."

Tritogenes swallowed the uncomfortable feeling in his gut, conscious that the others at the table were watching and listening to their conversation. "Of course, First Lord."

Hyperion smiled. "Yes. Until then, let us speak of more pleasant subjects. What skills does your Titan possess, my friend?"

Tritogenes explained as much as he could about Victoria. The more he spoke, the more he realized he really did not know much about his own Titan. Pallasophia had taken care of that end of things so successfully that he had not kept abreast of her updates like he should. When she killed the elite, he left to share his success with First Lord Enyalios before she had even been extracted safely from the facility.

He couched his explanations in as much vagueness as he could, relying on things he did know. He stressed her mental flexibility and "extensive" training. She was, he argued, well suited to the unknown environment aboard the mastigas ship.

"Whatever's there, I promise you Victoria will be able to handle it," he concluded.

"Victoria," Hyperion mused. "I never really thought about it before, but that's an odd name."

"She picked it herself." As soon as the words were out of his mouth, Tritogenes realized he now had to come up with a reason why she might have named herself rather than simply doing what every other Technocrat in the binary would have done and gone by their given name. After a moment's indecision, he added, "after she passed the final trial, she declared that it would be her name from then on."

It was, he reflected, only a small stretching of the truth.

"What was this final trial?" Hyperion asked. He had turned in his seat to look more fully at Tritogenes. Over his shoulder, Korakti leaned forward in her seat, eager to hear the story as well.

Tritogenes explained the trials he had set up for his branch of the Project. He explained them as they should have gone, starting with easy fights and slowly building, as the subject grew more skills, into the puzzle door and the showdown with the elite.

He did not mention how things had gone terribly, disastrously wrong.

"And she killed a mastigas elite with her bare hands?" Korakti asked. Excitement showed plain on her face.

"Of course not," Tritogenes replied. "That would be ridiculous."

Korakti's excitement faded somewhat.

Tritogenes grinned, and added, "she used a knife."

Pteryga's Titan's excitement was back. "By herself though?"

Tritogenes nodded. "Yes."

"Well! Now I definitely want to fight her. When did you say she should be arriving, First Lord?"

"Soon," he replied. "Before the Council session, anyway. Tell me, Second Lord, what do you bring to the Project? I watched your exhibition matches, but beyond that, your Hexarch has been rather recalcitrant in that matter."

She glanced a question at First Lord Hyperion, one whose meaning was lost on Tritogenes, and the older Hexarch nodded.

"I can use any and every weapon we have, First Lord. Close or long range, anything from personal arms to the main gun of a warship. I trained with the best soldiers First Lord Hyperion could find for at least eight hours a day, every day, for the last four and a half years."

Tritogenes nodded, stroking his chin. That was a gesture he had not performed in some time which was, he thought for an amused moment, a testament to Hyperion's infectious charisma. The long-bearded Hexarch did it frequently enough that Tritogenes thought he looked unusual without a hand on his white beard. Now, after a only a few hours around his old mentor, he picked the habit right back up.

"Impressive."

Before he could say anything else, Hyperion added, "what she is not telling you, my esteemed fellow Hexarch, is that Second Lord Korakti was Pteryga's champion wrestler and open-form fighter for seven years? Eight years?"

He had directed the question to his left with a slight turn of his head, and she replied, "I held the wrestling title for six years, First Lord, and the open-form title for nine."

"I was close," Hyperion replied, amused.

"Indeed, First Lord."

He turned back to Tritogenes. "And she was the champion marksman for all of Pteryga for three years in a row."

"It sounds like she was an impressive woman to start with."

Hyperion nodded. "And she has only become more so. I do not brag when I say I have no concerns about her ability to fight mastigas."

She slapped Second Lord Daniel on the back. "I have to admit, when I saw pictures of the Aegis, the suit First Lord Enyalios made, I was more than a little jealous."

"It comes with its own share of annoyances," the Second Lord replied. Louder, he said, "not that they haven't gotten better with recent upgrades."

Korakti laughed. She turned to Daniel as the two of them excitedly started comparing various weapons systems they had trained with over the half-decade of the Project. Tritogenes started to eavesdrop when a comment from Hyperion broke his reverie.

"You never mentioned your Titan's rank, First Lord." He emphasized Tritogenes's own rank as a contrast.

His mind raced. At ten years old, all Technocrat citizens were automatically granted the rank of Sixth Lord. That rank numbered in the millions across the binary, the largest out of all of them. Nearly everyone rose at least one social rank by the age of twenty, and it was not uncommon to see Fourth Lords in their early twenties.

Tritogenes was sixty-five years old. Having held the title for a little over two decades, he was also the youngest Hexarch on the Council— even First Lord Rivka, who had only been a Hexarch for five years, was twenty-years his senior in age. Only Hyperion himself had been younger when he assumed the rank ninety-five years before—a mere thirty-five years old.

For an adult not to have a rank at all was almost unheard of. Other than children, the only ones without rank were criminals and...

"She had religious reasons," he supplied.

Hyperion's eyebrows rose slightly at that. "She's not a metastellist is she?"

"No, she has," his momentary pause, as he again thought of what to say, was long enough for Hyperion to notice, he felt, but not quite long enough for the other Hexarch to interrupt. He continued, "too close a relationship with technology to be a metastellist. I have, in fact, never asked her religion directly."

"As long as it doesn't interfere with the Project."

Tritogenes grinned, unable to resist poking a little bit of fun at his friend and mentor. "If she was going to sabotage the Project because her gods wanted her to re-launch the Odyssey, I don't think she would have gone along with it in the first place."

Not that she had a choice, he added silently and ruefully.

Hyperion's blue eyes twinkled with amusement. "Of course," he said, then with what Tritogenes might have called a wistful tone coming from anyone else, he added, "you know, I should be glad Ophion won your loyalty in the end."

Unlike his relationship with Aegesander, Hyperion's friendship with Ophion never faltered until the latter's death. Still, Hyperion had always expressed a friendly sort of resentment toward his former fellow Hexarch for "stealing away his prized Second Lord."

After a moment, when he realized Hyperion was not about to say anything else, Tritogenes simply asked, "why is that?"

"Had you remained in my employ, you would still be there. Ophion's passing allowed you to assume his seat and, while I may miss him greatly, it has been an honor working beside you these twenty years."

67

Hyperion's face took on a strange, thoughtful expression as he went on. "Without you, no one would have proposed Project Titan and we would not now be ready to fight the mastigas on our terms for once."

"Surely one of the others..."

Hyperion interrupted, a rare thing. He was firm. "No. None of the others would have done it. You saw what happened with First Lord Diomedes."

"We weren't sure how to proceed against the mastigas, especially not after we lost so badly early on," Tritogenes protested.

"Thirty years ago when the mastigas," Hyperion paused, then, "when they arrived. Where were you?"

"I was a Second Lord," he replied, unsure where Hyperion was going with his question. He had been there, after all. "In your employ. As I recall, I was in the dressing room after the final run of *I Kori Kai O Trovadorous Ippotis*. Why?"

Hyperion's eyes had taken on a faraway look, almost like he was reliving the events in question. "I was in the Council chamber when the news broke. A huge ship had been detected in the outer reaches of our system. We were," he paused, "curious. And worried. When the mastigas destroyed the scout ships, we knew they did not, as the saying goes, come in peace.

"But we did nothing, Tritogenes. Nothing. Because of our inaction, our lack of foresight, our," another pause, and his voice hardened, "foolishness, people died. And we did nothing to stop it.

"This is our chance to right the wrongs of the past and atone for our sins."

***

Tritogenes watched as Korakti and Daniel interlocked arms and each downed an entire cordial glass full of dessert liqueur. The empty glasses joined several others on the table in front of them. Daniel had a pronounced wobble to his movements, even seated, but Korakti hardly seemed to be affected by the copious amount of drink she consumed over the course of the night's festivities.

Enyalios called their night-long drinking contest a "team building activity" in the same breath that he used to threaten Daniel with an early start the next morning. Hyperion promised similar, but neither Titan seemed to have slacked in their enthusiasm. If anything, the threats from their Hexarchs seemed to spur them on.

As the feast started winding down, the three Hexarchs made their way around the hall, talking to the various attendees for a few minutes. This particular district of the city was home to mostly locals, people born on Prosgeiosi. Tritogenes always enjoyed meeting them for many reasons, not least of which because he was from Prosgeiosi himself. People born on the capital planet, where each of the six Hexarchs held nominally equal sway, tended to have a much more cosmopolitan view of things, which he enjoyed.

He laughed and patted his most recent "new friend," a wealthy painter who lived just a few streets away from Hyperion's banquet hall, on the shoulder. Halfway to the next table, he caught a sudden shift in Enyalios's posture out of the corner of his eye. His fellow Hexarch had been deep in conversation with a table of people who all sat like soldiers, an assumption backed up by Enyalios's enthusiastic pantomime of marksmanship.

In the middle of what looked like an engaging story, Enyalios stopped and stood straight. He gestured to the table he had been entertaining and stepped away. Tritogenes then noticed that the rest of the banquet hall seemed to have fallen silent as well.

Instinctively, he looked to their table. Korakti patted Daniel vigorously on the shoulder, gesturing to the door.

Hyperion could fend for himself, Tritogenes thought, turning to the door. There, stepping in from the late evening dusk stood a man in a glittering purple robe whose embroidery and stiff drape made it appear like it was decorated with actual gold and silver rather than thread.

Aegesander's makeup had been applied to accentuate his deep eyes with broad strokes of black and brown.

At Aegesander's side stood a disarmingly petite woman swathed in a deep blue robe whose hem brushed the floor with a gentle caress. Helena's implants had been highlighted with a subtle reddish purple on the skin around them.

Nothing terribly fancy, Tritogenes thought, but crashed unexpected.

Now, his eyes swept across the room to find Hyperion. The senior Hexarch had, like Enyalios and the Titans, stiffened at Aegesander's approach. Despite Hyperion's attestation that he and Aegesander were starting to repair their once-strong friendship, he did not seem at all happy to see the other Hexarch here.

Helena glided across the room to the other Titans. Tritogenes balked at the cliché description in his mind, but that was the best way he could think of to describe the effortless way Aegesander's Titan moved. He barely saw her shoulder shift and the hem of her robe, so long that most people would have trouble not tripping over it, merely rippled slightly as her feet brushed against it.

Without adjusting her pace or faltering, Helena turned her head to regard him for a moment with her piercing blue eyes. Her gaze bore an eerie resemble to Hyperion's, especially in that Tritogenes felt very exposed by the intelligence he saw there, but there the similarities ended. Had he not been looking directly at her face, Tritogenes would have missed the subtle nod of her head before she turned her eyes forward again.

In its pocket inside his robe, his tablet chimed to indicate a new message. He summoned a small one-sided holo as Helena introduced herself to Korakti and Daniel.

"No new information," the message read. It had no listed sender, but that part was not hard to determine. He tried not to think about the fact that she had not sent the message through any of the normal messaging programs. Rather, her note appeared as a system dialog from his tablet itself. The positive was that the note was untraceable that way. The negative was that it meant Helena hacked through several layers of security in moments.

A brief chill washed over him as Tritogenes pocketed the tablet. He sympathized with Aegesander's feelings, he realized. Helena's ability to utilize her implants was frankly frightening.

For the moment, though, he had potentially more pressing matters to worry about. Hyperion and Aegesander were already engaged in conversation by the time he made his way across the room. The banquet hall had an open space in the center ostensibly for dancing which meant the nearest tables were just out of hearing distance as conversation resumed around the room.

It was there that Hyperion intercepted Aegesander, and there Tritogenes met both of them in time to hear Hyperion say, "...a surprise, First Lord."

Aegesander smiled, disarming and fake all in the same moment. "My invitation must have gotten lost."

"There were no invitations, First Lord," Tritogenes said, interjecting himself into the conversation. "Hyperion and I were talking earlier and we decided to open this hall for the evening."

Aegesander extended his hand to Tritogenes, who took it. They clasped wrists and shook once. The greeting was unnecessary, but it immediately dispelled any burgeoning feelings of annoyance at Aegesander's sudden arrival. His eyes twinkled mischievously, and Aegesander said, "so it was your idea, my friend."

Tritogenes laughed. "It was, yes. I wanted to use one of my halls over in Parikia, but Hyperion insisted we do this here instead. Between the two of us," he leaned in closer, pretending Hyperion was not standing a meter away. He continued, "I think he just wanted to show off."

Aegesander smiled. "Of course. He does have that streak in him, doesn't he?"

Tritogenes gestured to Helena where she had joined Korakti and Daniel at their table. Korakti, in the few moments Tritogenes had his back turned had managed to produce another round of beer, including one for Helena.

"I see Second Lord Helena has wasted no time introducing herself."

Aegesander nodded. "She spent most of the Project working alone and, now that we're here on Prosgeiosi, has been as social as possible recently." He glanced at Hyperion as though suddenly remembering the other Hexarch was there. "Much like your Korakti, I would imagine."

"Korakti always went for the spotlight, even before the Project," Hyperion replied. "But let us not waste time, Aegesander. What brings you here, now, at the end of the night's festivities?"

Aegesander put on a hurt face that was quite obviously fake as he turned to face Hyperion directly. The gesture would have fooled no one, yet Hyperion replied with a genuine expression of apology. No words passed between them, but after a few minutes, the tension seemed to lessen somewhat.

Aegesander shrugged. "I came because I heard my good friends were throwing a party tonight. I apologize for not showing up earlier; it was all I could do to get away from Odyssey when I did."

"No ulterior motives?"

This time, Aegesander genuinely looked hurt. Tritogenes knew the expression was at least a little manufactured given Aegesander's usual iron control over his emotions, but it felt as though Aegesander were showing them a falsely-poor attempt to control a real reaction rather than a truly false reaction. "Must I have some other reason? Helena wanted to meet your Titan, Hyperion."

"I would have been happy to entertain her, Aegesander. All you needed do was let me know she wanted to meet Korakti and I could have included Helena in this banquet."

Aegesander frowned. "But not me." It was not a question.

"You're a Hexarch, Aegesander. You're not forbidden from any location on this planet outside of the home of a private citizen."

"Which this is not."

"It is not."

"Then, why, my friend," Aegesander began.

Despite his calm and collected tone, Tritogenes saw the frustration bubbling beneath Aegesander's surface. Worse, he saw the same thing in Hyperion. Had they been in private, he would have let this escalate where ever it went, to argument or even to fist fight. Hyperion and Aegesander both made it clear to Tritogenes that whatever the cause of their feud, it was none of his concern.

But they were in a public venue, and the last thing they, as "The Council," needed was for two Hexarchs to start a fight in front of a hundred-plus people.

"First Lords," he began.

"Stay out of this, Tritogenes," Hyperion hissed.

Aegesander ignored him completely.

Nonetheless, Tritogenes repeated himself. He placed his hands firmly on their shoulders, tightening his grip perhaps more than was needed to get his point across. His voice was firmer the second time. "*First Lords*," he said. "Should be not be celebrating right now? Project Titan was a success! Surely whatever problems existed in the past have remained there."

Neither Hexarch interrupted him, and so he signaled a nearby Third Lord who, he hoped, was on the banquet hall's staff. She brought over a trio of cordials a moment later, sweet liqueur served in tiny onyx goblets.

Tritogenes raised his cup. "To the future."

Hyperion followed a moment later. "To the Titans."

Finally Aegesander raised his. "To our health."

"The feast is winding down," Hyperion said. "If you wish to stay, Aegesander, you may."

73

"How very generous, Hyperion, to allow me the dregs of your celebration, but I'm afraid I must be on my way. I came to introduce Helena to her comrades, not to rehash past arguments."

He waited just long enough for Hyperion to raise his voice to be overheard and say, "go with the suns, First Lord," before turning and leaving the hall.

Once Aegesander was out of earshot, Tritogenes stepped closer to Hyperion. "What..."

Hyperion cut him off with a rare burst of annoyance. "Not now, please. A foul mood has settled on my mind just like it's settled on this room."

Tritogenes frowned. "You're going to tell me what's going on between the two of you."

"No."

"As a Hexarch..."

"As my *friend*, Tritogenes, you'll stay out of this. I will hear no more about it. The Lord of Dasos and I will make amends or we will not."

Tritogenes sighed, scanning the room. Hyperion was right. The general mood had soured considerably. "I feel like this is partly my fault. I should not have pushed the issue. Let me make it up to you, old friend."

Hyperion smiled as the dark cloud that settled on his face seemed to part. "I know that expression, Tritogenes. You have something in mind, don't you?"

He grinned. "Always. Let's just hope I remember it all, hmm?"

Tritogenes cleared his throat. Without any introduction, he began to sing. In moments, conversation around the room stopped as his rich, operatic baritone rang out. Even the air itself felt heavier as he sang, as though the notes themselves warmed and weighed it down.

"*I set my eyes on eternity. To rise above, must we burn as we always have? For the dawn, for the stars, for the salvation of humanity, if someone must burn, let it be me! O gods, stand between these flames and my people...*"

74

The aria lasted a full eleven minutes and, as it turned out, Tritogenes remembered every word despite the thirty-something years since he performed it last. When he finished, the banquet's attendees applauded for two full minutes and, to his delight, the overall mood had improved considerably.

"Well done," Hyperion said, embracing Tritogenes as he stepped away from the center of the room. "For a moment there, I was back in the box seats on opening night, sharing drinks with Diomedes, Meriones, Ophion, and even Eurybia and Aegesander. Thank you, my friend."

Korakti appeared at his side a moment later, pushing a mug of beer into his hands. "Well done!" she said, beaming with the smile of minor intoxication. "Opera isn't my thing, but if the Boss says you did it right, then who am I to argue?"

Tritogenes laughed, took a drink, and laughed again. "It felt good to get to perform again, even for just a few minutes."

"Good, good! Because we've got a bit of a problem over here."

"What's wrong?"

Korakti laughed. "There's still beer left! Come on, First Lord. Help us finish!"

Tritogenes eyed Hyperion for a moment, then shrugged. "She's *your* Titan."

Chapter 5

The liner felt empty with only the two of them and the little ship's crew aboard. They left early in the morning from Aphelion, delaying only long enough to pick up gear personally fabricated for Victoria by Second Lord Glaukos in the armory. The suit had been designed to mimic the look of her old clothing, clothing that now hung alongside her helmet, the elite's helmet, and its swords as more of a trophy than a functional garment.

They could have taken a smaller ship, one that would not have felt quite so empty, but Tritogenes had taken the only high-speed shuttle stationed at Aphelion for his trip to Katarraktes. The liner, larger and with more powerful engines, was the fastest long-distance ship currently stationed there.

Victoria had watched the little asteroid fall away from their ship through the windows of her cabin. The ship's inertial dampener—a term she only knew because she asked the pilot and then had had to look up much of the technical jargon on her own—all but eliminated any sense of motion or acceleration. Outside the window, the asteroid shrank from something large enough that her mind registered it as "the ground" to a small rock falling away as though she had dropped a pebble out the window.

The facility itself was even less impressive. From the outside, Aphelion facility was a featureless gray rectangle protruding a few stories above the equally dull, gray rock. Aside from the shuttle landing area atop the little tower, it was as featureless, and undetectable, as possible.

By contrast, the liner, at least on the inside, was anything but featureless. Victoria supposed that since it belonged to Tritogenes, rather than Pallasophia, it reflected his personal taste in decor more than hers. Red carpet edged with gold ran along the hallways on the passenger level, colors whose warm brightness was emphasized by the dark brown paneling on the walls. Lights shone from brass candelabras on the walls rather than overhead as they had in the suite.

Her room, one of six staterooms, was less extravagant, but not by far. The four-poster bed she slept on was just as comfortable as hers had been in the suite, but the room had been decorated with small odds and ends. A real, physical book printed on paper had waited for her on the nightstand. One wall held the window. The door to the hallway, flanked by lights, occupied the next wall, and the third was filled by her dresser, mirror, and the door to the bathroom. The fourth was dominated by a painting of a green and gray mountain range ringed with fog.

Victoria finished drying off after her post-workout shower and hung the towel back on its rack. Crossing the room, she checked the embroidery machine in the corner. It had been working slowly and steadily on her robe since some time the previous evening when she, with Second Lord Pallasophia's help, submitted her first design.

The small light atop the machine glowed a steady blue color. Prior to her shower, it had been red. She removed her robe from the complex system of arms and wheels inside the machine and held it up.

A series of glyphs shone across the front. The first was an entwined pair of spectral lines, one visual and one thermal, that displayed the physical conditions inside the arena. The second was a map of the molecular structure of the sand underfoot. It had been further enhanced with small details spiraling off in fractal patterns that, if she looked close enough, represented the ordeals she had gone through to get to the arena in the first place.

The final glyph was not as mathematically detailed as the others. The first two had been designed with Technocrat assistance. This third one came directly from a sketch she made herself and stylized for the machine. A three eyed skull, impaled with a blade passing through the uppermost eye and out the base adorned the left side of her chest, just above her breast.

Satisfied with the outcome, she donned the complex garment. They were less than a day out from Prosgeiosi now, and she had spent most of the time so far in her robe, learning not only how to move in it but how to simply wear it.

Victoria adjusted the robe in her room's large mirror until she was happy with it. The designs fell exactly as they should, which pleased her. Part of her determination had been to simply get something on her robe beyond the little sonic graph across her collar. Even the lower-ranking staff had robes that were full of designs showcasing their achievements. Until she settled on the three images that now adorned her black robe, a sense that the featureless black fabric did not fit in kept her from wearing it for long.

Even now, she preferred her combat uniform or nothing at all.

She picked up the book from the dresser and carried it over to one of the chairs in the spacious room's reading area. The fact that she could read at all still surprised her, but she supposed it was yet another skill Tritogenes deemed necessary for her to have and so had installed it in her brain before she had been "born."

Still, the book, a story of a world whose minds were trapped in a computer simulation, was interesting enough. She had only gotten a few pages further than her previous bookmark when the door chime sounded.

The automated system announced that Second Lord Pallasophia was at her door, not that it could be anyone else. She had asked the ship's staff for privacy and they agreed to her wish with an eagerness she found off-putting.

"It's unlocked," Victoria called.

The door opened a moment later, admitted the blue-robed Second Lord. She smiled. "I was about to warn you, again, about leaving the door unlocked, but I suppose you don't have much to worry about from anyone who would break in."

Amused, Victoria smiled in return. "I suppose not."

Pallasophia gestured to Victoria's robe. "You finished it."

She nodded. "A few minutes ago, yes."

"It looks nice."

"Thank you," she said. Victoria was about to turn back to her book when the note of tension in the Second Lord's voice roused her interest and her concern at the same time. She placed the bookmark, closed the book, and asked if everything was alright.

Pallasophia took a moment to reply. When she did, she made an effort to drop the formal tones and tenses she had been using. "We're getting close to Prosgeiosi. I've never much liked the capital planet, to be honest. There's such an air of judgment there that I wonder how anyone gets anything done."

"It can't be that bad."

"It probably isn't," she admitted, "but that doesn't mean that's not how it feels."

"Sit," Victoria said, gesturing with her book to the empty chair across the reading nook from where she sat. "I'm sure you didn't come see me just to vent your frustrations about visiting Odyssey."

She did so, arranging the folds of her robe to prevent their creasing as she sat. A moment passed as she relaxed and settled into the seat and she said, "I came to see if you would like to have lunch with me. You've barely come out of your cabin since we left Aphelion."

Victoria watched her for a moment, wondering if it was concern she heard in the other woman's voice or simple curiosity. Finally, she settled on a mix of both, though concern seemed to be the dominant emotion in her voice.

"I don't see why not."

Pallasophia smiled. "Excellent." She waved a hand over her wrist, entering a short command into the holographic interface there.

Victoria stood, indicated the door with one hand, and followed Pallasophia out into the hallway. The door slid shut on its silent track behind them and she said, "you're worried about my mental state."

Pallasophia turned and arched an eyebrow at her. Victoria's statement had intentionally not been a question, and she watched as the Second Lord processed it. They spent considerable time together since leaving Aphelion, almost all of which had been in Victoria's cabin, asking the Second Lord an endless string of questions about the Technocracy and its people.

"Honestly?" she asked. "Yes."

Victoria nodded. "I assumed as much."

"You sent the staff away, haven't left your room more than twice, and, most importantly, you're traveling aboard First Lord Tritogenes's most luxurious transport mere days after scrounging for your very life amid the ruins that he, personally, locked you in."

Victoria snorted, amused by the superficial absurdity of that statement.

"I would understand if you were having trouble."

Victoria nodded. "Thank you for the concern, really. I've spent most of my life, such that it is, alone. Even the small crowd of staff that run this ship is larger than any I've ever been around. At least," she added with a smile, "any that's not been trying to kill me."

"Prosgeiosi is going to be an even bigger change of pace, you understand."

"I understand," she emphasized the verb, "but that doesn't mean..." They passed a green-robed Technocrat. Victoria had not seen her before and she wondered what section of the ship she worked in. As the woman passed them, Victoria almost automatically switched tones. She finished with, "that I would be comfortable amid such a sizable crowd, especially given that I, and my five pseudo-brethren, am likely to be the center of their attention."

Pallasophia nodded, waiting for the Third Lord to pass and round the corner behind them before replying. When she spoke, she was still using informal tenses. "I can understand that. Selene knows I'm not fond of the crowds there."

Victoria relaxed again. "Is that why you took the job at Aphelion?"

"Part of it. I also believed in the Project. That's why I wasn't willing to give up even when," she trailed off, struggling between meeting Victoria's eyes and avoiding them.

"Even after the Incident, when everything went to hell."

"Yes."

Victoria folded her arms across her chest. Her robe had been cut for movement, with narrow arms, and the voluminous fabric did very little to hide the musculature there. "You're tense again."

"Yes."

Victoria sighed. "If you expect me to trust you, Pallasophia, you need to trust me."

"I do."

"You don't. You're tense. I can see it in your eyes. You're talking to me like..." she trailed off as a yellow-robed Fourth Lord passed them. When he realized the the blue-robed Second and the mysterious black-robed Champion had fallen silent because of him, he hurried his pace. When he was out of sight, Victoria continued speaking. "Like I'm a caged animal and you're afraid if you say the wrong thing, I'll kill you."

Pallasophia stared at her for a moment, then flushed and made a show of looking down at the crimson-and-gold carpet under their feet. "Come," she said, gesturing down the hall.

Victoria followed, mulling over her thoughts silently.

Pallasophia did not speak until the door to her private cabin closed behind them. "I apologize."

Victoria stopped. That was not what she expected to hear. "For?"

Her voice was stiff and formal. "Treating you that way. I should not have done so."

Victoria folded her arms over her chest, emphasizing her height and making space between them. "What else would you have done? How else could you have approached the situation?"

"I should have made myself more comfortable around you and..."

Victoria interrupted. "I'm what you made me. Your caution makes sense."

"You're more than that."

"Am I?"

"What do you mean?"

Victoria realized she was pacing only after starting. She stopped. "When we sparred yesterday, did you win?"

"No. What does that have to do with anything?"

Victoria's tone came out tight, accusatory. "You won tournaments for martial arts in college, you said."

Pallasophia wavered between defensive and confused. "Yes. I fail to see what they have to do with this, though."

"I've never trained."

"That just makes your skill more impressive, not less."

Victoria shook her head violently. She was silent for a moment, clenching and unclenching her jaw as she tried to put her thoughts into words. Finally, she said, "those trophies and awards you showed me? You earned them. Your rank, you earned that as well, right? It wasn't given to you?"

"No," she replied, hesitant.

The black-robed woman pressed on, ignoring anything Pallasophia was about to say. "I didn't earn those skills. I just," she groped for words for a moment. "Have them."

"Most people would be happy to wake up with a hundred lifetimes of skill."

Victoria snarled, even though Pallasophia's regret-filled expression made it clear the other woman realized she said the wrong thing. "Those people would have been give a choice! I was not!"

Pallasophia struggled for words for a long moment. Half-formed sounds came and went as a dozen thoughts all seemed to vie for dominance. Victoria simply stood and fumed, watching the Second Lord struggle.

Pallasophia said, "you survived in the facility when no one else did."

"That's my point," Victoria countered. "I *survived*. I didn't elect to go down there and fight that monster. I didn't spend my life training for the opportunity to excel and to showcase my skill in that arena. I woke up. That's all."

"You excelled, though. To the Technocrat people, you're an inspiration, a champion."

Victoria thought she sounded like she was pleading with her, but the impact of her words was lost amid her frustration and anger. She growled, then snapped out, "I excelled because of how I was made!"

Silence fell in the cabin as realization dawned across Pallasophia's face. "That's it, isn't it?"

Victoria glared. A part of her brain realized that Pallasophia seemed to be starting to understand and the glare softened into merely an intense stare. That lasted for several moments before she said, "you fought for everything you have. Me? I was given all of this, a lot of it before I was even born. I was given the genetics and the skills were," she searched for the word she wanted, "installed in my brain before I ever woke up."

She stopped talking for a moment, watching how Pallasophia's emotions played out like a book across her normally reserved face. Victoria's voice was softer, quieter, but only a little less angry as she continued. "Imagine that you were just a number. That everything you accomplished was because of the number you drew. Not because of who you were, but because you hit the right spot on a checklist. Imagine waking up to violence and murderous things you don't even have a name for, naked and unarmed, and that being the first real memory in your brain. And the voices of a hundred dead are shouting at you in the place where your instincts and reflexes should be!"

Victoria stopped, breathed, and blinked as unexpected wetness rolled from her eyes down her cheeks. Instead of acknowledge her tears, she continued staring straight into Pallasophia's eyes, watching for her reactions instead.

Something that was not regret, something much more intense, passed across The Second Lord's face before she repeated her earlier sentiment. "I'm sorry."

Victoria took in a deep breath, letting it out through her teeth. She wondered if control of her emotions was as simple as control of her actions. She could strike hard or soft, fast or slow. So what, she asked herself, was the difference between that and emotion?

Carefully, she forced her anger aside as something tugged at her. She felt the urge to empathize rather than condemn building in the back of her brain. Intellectually, she knew that too had to be another "gift" of the Project, but as the feeling grew, her anger ebbed.

She reached out a hand, slowly, and placed it on Pallasophia's shoulder. Resentment still burned in the back of her mind, but yelling at the one person so far who had attempted to understand her would not help matters any. "Apology accepted."

Pallasophia nodded, once. The wariness in her face remained, but it had diminished. The muscle in her shoulder under Victoria's hand, however, remained tensed. "Thank you. You're wrong, though."

Victoria pulled her hand back and stepped away. "How?"

"You're more than you think. You're not some homunculus built only to fight. You're more than we expected."

Victoria raised an eyebrow. "What were you expecting?"

"A killer," she replied, spreading her hands in a gesture of helpless honesty. "You're," she grasped, almost physically, for the words, and failed to find the right ones. "Human."

Victoria crossed to the cabin's window. She indicated the starfield beyond with an expansive wave of her hand. "I love this. It's beautiful. Did you expect that?"

"No," Pallasophia admitted.

"And this," Victoria added. She called up a series of pictures on the holographic display floating above her wrist. "I spent the morning looking at pictures from your seven planets. They're all beautiful in their own way, each different from the others. I want to visit each one and simply stand beneath their skies. That's not something a killer would want, is it?"

"I don't know," Pallasophia replied, following her to the large window. Together they looked out at the starfield for several long, quiet minutes. Pallasophia finally turned away from the window and raised one arm. With the other she pointed to a line of code that ran vertically under her left arm from her hips to her armpit. It was embroidered in glittering gold thread, sixteen rows of small type. "Do you know what this is?"

Victoria looked at it, but coding was one of the few skills she had not found to be installed in her brain. She shook her head.

"This is the block of code that laid the foundations for the process to transfer memories and skills from one generation to the next. I came up with this code after we lost the first two of your ancestors."

Victoria looked from the sparkling text to Pallasophia's brown eyes and back several times. The words and symbols made no sense to her, but if the Second Lord was telling the truth, then that small block of text, small enough to turn into ornamentation for her Technocrat robe, was the reason she was who she was.

She had no idea how to feel about that. Emotions swirled around her brain, refusing to coalesce into any single thing she could make sense of. Her brain wanted to settle on wonder while her heart tried to be angry and her guts sank into cold uncertainty.

Could she, the things that made her *her*, really be summed up in such a small piece of text?

Victoria decided that it could not be that simple. There was more to being alive than one's memories and skills. Even if many of those memories and skills were not, truly, her own. Perhaps, in that case, the distinction was even more important. If she was the sum of her skills and memories, then she really was "Number One-Hundred," and nothing more.

If, on the other hand, she was really her own person, then there had to be more. That code, those words and symbols, helped shape who and what she was, but they were not the author of her mind.

Tritogenes and Pallasophia, great as their contributions to her life had been, were not the ultimate cause of her mind and thoughts. She was herself, built upon the foundation they set down for her, certainly, but she was not solely their creation.

"Victoria?"

"I was thinking," she said, and pointed to the code running under Pallasophia's arm, "about that. Without it, I might have been someone else. Someone else might not have survived the labyrinth."

"No," Pallasophia said quietly. "Only you could have done that."

***

Despite the ship itself belonging to a Hexarch, Pallasophia apparently lacked the authority to override the landing queue. She told Victoria, in between arguments with Orbital Control, that she— probably—would not abuse the power if she had it.

After the third time they had to re-confirm something with the seemingly uninterested Fourth Lord on duty, even Victoria's patience was starting to wear thin. Victoria told herself that, were she the Hexarch, she would also not abuse that power. The longer things dragged on, the less sure she was of that.

Pallasophia finally lost what was left of her patience and demanded to know what was taking so long. After being put on hold again, she explained to Victoria that, usually, even on high traffic days the landing queue was no more than an hour. Four hours was unacceptable.

The yellow-robed woman appeared on the screen again. She seemed no more interested in their problem than she had been before, but Victoria did notice a slight hint of apology in her expression and tone.

"We've got more incoming than usual, and we're working to reroute landing traffic through the outbound lanes, but you must understand that is neither a slow nor an easy process, Second Lord."

"What's the issue?" Victoria asked. She stood away from the lander's video pickup, where her curious black robe would not draw questions just yet. Her voice carried well enough, though.

The traffic control officer almost seemed to perk up for a moment. "If I had to guess, it's the Titans. A lot of people are coming from off-planet to watch the parade."

"Parade?"

The Fourth Lord nodded. "It's supposed to be larger than any the Hexarchs have thrown in years. First Lords Hyperion and Aegesander appeared on the news this morning to talk about it."

Victoria muttered, hopefully too quiet for the system to pick up. "Why was I not informed of this?"

Pallasophia, still in the center of the video pickup, frowned. She turned and mouthed, "I was going to tell you after we landed," but said nothing aloud.

"I have you a position in the queue, Second Lord," the traffic controller announced. Any trace of excitement or animation in her face was gone now that they were back to talking about work instead of any celebrations.

Pallasophia nodded. "Thank you, Fourth Lord."

She returned the nod just enough to be polite. "Of course. Good day."

The transmission cut before Pallasophia could say anything else. Under her breath, just loud enough for Victoria to hear, she said, "bureaucrats."

"She didn't want to be there any more than we want to be here," Victoria offered.

Pallasophia sighed. "I know that, but it doesn't make it any less frustrating on our end. When they got the liner parked in geosynch in twenty minutes, I had high hopes that we'd be able to land within an hour of hitting orbit."

"Understandable."

Pallasophia chuckled. "Why aren't you upset about having to wait?"

Victoria shrugged. Unbidden, memories from her previous lives flashed across her mind. Death and pain caused by not taking those extra few minutes to prepare. She might have shuddered at the sudden influx of sensation—such things were coming less often these days—but she was not sure. Either way, it passed in a moment. "I learned very early on that rushing things was dangerous. It annoyed me, yes, but I saw nothing to gain from pushing the issue."

Pallasophia eyed her with a curious expression Victoria could not identify. It was some part confusion and another respect, but something else lurked there, behind those surface emotions, that Victoria could not place.

As the shuttle descended, Pallasophia pointed out various landmarks. Mountain ranges and oceans became mountains and lakes as they drew closer to the surface. From there, even they fell away as the shuttle approached the great plain upon which Odyssey itself sat, flanked on all sides by lesser cities.

Victoria had to admit that the sight of the Technocrat capital was impressive. From the outside, Aphelion had been underwhelming, bland. By comparison the dome that encompassed the capital city itself gleamed like a pearl under the twin suns. Her mind struggled to take in the vastness of it all, instead imagining the sprawling chaos below them as a particularly detailed model.

Nothing could be that big, that open, she thought.

That thought came again as the shuttle settled onto its landing legs and the hatch opened. Light, brighter even than the lights of the arena spilled through the open door. With it came a warm breeze and the sounds and smells of Odyssey. Intermingled with the smells of the shuttle, herself and Pallasophia, the remnants of lunch, and the mechanical smell of the little ship's components, it was hard to tell exactly what was what.

Sound came next, rumbling loud enough to cover up the subtle hum of the shuttle's engines and the other noises she had grown used to on the trip down. The low roar of airborne traffic circulating around the outside of the dome or going to the abutting cities ran together into background sounds. Another shuttle took off nearby. Its engines were not necessarily loud, but they stood out against the white noise all around her just the same.

Pallasophia stepped through the hatch and down the steps first, motioning for Victoria to follow.

Victoria placed one hand on the side of the ship's hatch and stepped into it. Not through it, but now she stood under the arch of the door itself. One foot rested where the door had been and the other, slowly, she set down on the top step of the landing stair.

The first thing that hit was the light itself. She preferred things dim, like they had been in the facility. Even Pallasophia's default settings were brighter than Victoria preferred. The unfiltered light of the twin suns overhead stung her eyes like knives in her skin. Reflexively, she screwed her eyes tightly shut and shaded her face with a hand, cutting the unacceptable glare.

While she waited, she took deep breaths. The sharp scent of ion thrusters from the shuttles around her mixed with grease and oil. Under those smells she thought she could just barely detect something sweet that a voice in her mind identified as belonging to the blooms of thousands of flowers and trees.

Finally, her eyes started to hurt less, and she forced them open a sliver. For a moment, Victoria stood there, blinking against the glare as her eyes slowly adjusted to a sky brighter than anything she had ever seen.

Then she looked up.

Open sky stretched above her, and her heart started racing. It thundered in her ears as she craned her neck upward to take in the vast, infinite stretch of blue. Her breath caught in her lungs as reality sank in: nothing lay above her air and space, infinite emptiness reaching through the atmosphere until it faded into icy wisps, and thence blackness and stars.

Victoria focused on the task ahead of her. If she could overcome bloodthirsty, green eyed monsters, she reasoned that stepping out of the shuttle would not be that hard. Pallasophia waited for her at the foot of the stairs, a curious, concerned expression on her face.

She took a deep breath, focusing on the scent of the flowers blowing in the breeze. The open sky and burning light from the suns meant they grew like they never could on Aphelion. If the sky produced something like that, Victoria tried to convince herself that it was not all bad.

If anything, she reasoned, keeping her eyes on the ground made things easier. It kept the adrenaline rushing through her system to a minimum as she took her first step down the stairs themselves.

The second step was easier, and the third easier still. By the bottom of the stairs, the vast open space above her head barely registered on her mind. Being lower down than the tops of the shuttles and short towers around her helped somewhat. She could tell herself that they represented the ceiling, that the stretch of blue between them was simply an artfully painted fresco overhead.

She still wanted to get inside.

Pallasophia extended a hand to her as Victoria reached the bottom step. She took it out of politeness, but was steady enough on her feet without help.

"Where do we go now?" Victoria asked.

"Customs," Pallasophia replied. She laughed, then, "just like everyone else."

Keeping her eyes on Pallasophia meant Victoria was not looking at the sky and its terrible openness. She smiled. "Do they make the Hexarchs wait in line?"

"Here?" Pallasophia asked, smiling herself now. "Everyone waits in line."

Victoria nodded. "Good. Then let's get inside and get it over with."

***

Inside proved to be much more pleasant than outside. For one, it was so much less bright that, for the first few moments, Victoria again felt blind. Once her eyes adjusted a second time, she found the light level to be much more comfortable. The ceiling overhead also helped her mental state significantly.

She commented on the former, the light level, to Pallasophia, but did not mention the latter issue at all.

Victoria took mental notes on everything they passed on their way to the customs station. Very little stood out on its own merits. The walls were a pastel green, lit by a soft glow of lights overhead. On the surface, it looked very much like any anonymous corridor from Aphelion.

On the trip to Prosgeiosi, she read up on the history of the city, how *Odyssey* the ship became Odyssey the city. Here, inside the walls, the Technocrats made a conscious effort to preserve as much of the former ship's structure as possible. Knowing that she stood in the presence of history sent a chill down her spine.

That thought kicked off another one, and Victoria laughed quietly. The paint, she reasoned, was not ten millennia old. Was it?

The check-in desk was located in the middle of a small room, past a half empty waiting area. The few Technocrats there, mostly those of lower ranks, stared as she passed. What they were staring at, she could not say for sure. She towered over Pallasophia, which could have caught their attention. Most likely, she thought, it was the black robe, the embroidered elite skull over her left breast, or a combination of both. None of them said anything to her as Pallasophia led her past those waiting.

"Do these people know who I am?" she asked in hushed tones.

"They know who I am, and so they suspect."

A Third Lord sat on the far side of an ornate desk. She looked up when the door opened, and the bored look on her face vanished. What replaced it was a swirl of emotion, interest, confusion, and excitement all vying to be dominant.

Despite the excitement on her face, her tones were of utmost formality. "With respect, Second Lord, since the pair of you simply came in without being called, I assume that your unranked companion is the guest of one of the Hexarchs?"

Pallasophia nodded. "Victoria should be on First Lord Tritogenes's list."

The Third Lord looked down, scanning the contents of a one-sided holoscreen behind the counter. Either the list was short or her name was near the top of it because the Third Lord's eyes doubled in size after a moment.

She rose and sketched a quick bow. "I did not know you would be arriving today, Titan. Orbital Control did not pass along your identity. I apologize for any inconvenience you might have gone through. Please, proceed."

While Victoria was processing the sudden shift in the receptionist's attitude, Pallasophia cleared her throat. "This is her first time in Odyssey."

"I see," the Third Lord said. She turned to Victoria. "I greatly apologize, Titan, but there are procedures and rules that must be followed, even for a guest such as yourself."

"Worry not," Victoria said, doing her best to affect the formal tones and tenses she had heard Pallasophia and other Technocrats using. She felt silly using the stiff tones and overly formal speech. "I am in no true hurry to reach my destination."

"Thank you, Titan."

The receptionist then walked her through a multi-step registration process. Victoria's finger and palm prints were scanned and saved, along with her retinal print. All of them, she learned, could be used to access various areas inside the city. Finger or thumb prints would get her into all public areas, palm prints were required for personal areas, and her retinal print was the only thing that would allow her access to the Hexarchs' area.

"If I may, Titan," the receptionist said, rising again. "Could I beg your indulgence for a moment and shake your hand?"

Victoria stared at her for a moment before recognition of what she asked sunk in. Pallasophia told her that Project Titan itself had not been secret like Aphelion itself was. Some of the Titans, even, had been public figures during the Project. Either way, the population of the binary had been waiting and hoping for half a decade that the Project would be successful.

Looking at the expectancy in her eyes, Victoria supposed she could not blame this Third Lord for her attitude. Pallasophia had been right about one thing, though; if everyone was going to react like this, Victoria would be spending a lot of time either alone or in the company of the other Titans. A few excited faces was fine, but an unending throng of thousands would, at best, impede her ability to prepare for her mission.

Still, Pallasophia had also instilled in her an appreciation of how public image could affect things. Tritogenes, after all, owned the Technocrats' largest media corporation. Putting on a good show for the population was at least as important as actually defeating the mastigas. As long as it did not become more important than her mission, she could indulge things some.

After that consideration, Victoria nodded once and held out her hand, assuming she might as well act as the social senior and take initiative. The receptionist followed, grasping Victoria's arm by the wrist as awe spread across her face. Victoria's fingers tightened slowly, testing the strength of the other woman's grip. The Third Lord's hand tightened on her wrist, stopping far short of Victoria's own maximum grip strength.

Victoria placed her other hand atop the Third Lord's hand as the Technocrat did likewise, completing the little ritual in its most formal iteration. After a moment, they broke contact and the receptionist stepped away.

"Thank you, Titan. May the Grace of Lady Selene watch over you."

Victoria nodded. "And you as well." Once they were out in the hall and alone, she said to Pallasophia, "I wasn't expecting that sort of reaction this soon."

"I warned you."

Victoria laughed, more amused at the Second Lord's reaction than anything. "You did, but I wasn't expecting it to be that intense."

Pallasophia smiled. "Neither was I, honestly, but we'd best get used to it."

Victoria raised an eyebrow. "We?"

She nodded. "I plan on staying close by until you and the others leave. You need someone to show you how things work here in the 'great city of Odyssey.'" She punctuated the last part of her statement with a sarcastic wave of her hand at their surroundings.

"Plus," she continued, "the only easily available room is the spare bedroom in my suite. I hope you don't mind."

Victoria shook her head. "I don't, no. It will be nice to have..." She paused, unsure of exactly what the Second Lord was. Finally, she settled on, "a friend. Especially if working with the other Titans if going to be as intense as I expect."

Chapter 6

The binary star system that was home to the Technocrat civilization was vast, far larger than the Sol System that birthed the human race. The same twin suns that produced the massive habitable zone with its seven Earth-like planets extended their joint reach far into space, and the system's Kuiper belt lay far from anything bearing human life.

Somewhere, the exact location known only to the people who worked there, Aphelion Facility slowly circled the twin suns, hidden by the vastness of space itself. On the opposite side of the vast stretch of rock-studded Nothing, the mastigas ship lurked. As they rampaged through the outer limits of the system, more and more colonies and bases were abandoned until none were left.

Long before the mastigas attacked Kipos and Tritogenes proposed Project Titan, one of then-newly-elevated First Lord Enyalios's first acts was to design and construct a trio of enormous warships he called mobile fortresses to keep watch on the mastigas ship—the battleship, he was careful to call it—in case it attacked again.

Asphodel, the first of the ships to be completed, engaged the mastigas battleship directly. The battle lasted sixty-three days, finally culminating in the warship's destruction after being invaded by hundreds of mastigas on foot.

The next two, the *Elysium* and the *Tartarus*, took up much more defensive roles, serving as an early warning system for the battleship's seemingly random course corrections around the system perimeter.

That setup lasted for fifteen years and, by even the most cynical estimates, saved hundreds of thousands of lives. Unfortunately for the twelve thousand souls aboard the *Elysium*, that ship's effectiveness came to an end shortly before the beginning of Project Titan, when the mastigas battleship suddenly changed heading and assaulted Kipos. In its wake, its nuclear missiles destroyed the *Elysium* so thoroughly that neither debris nor bodies remained to recover.

After that, First Lord Aegesander commissioned five more ships, smaller than Enyalios's grand mobile fortresses but still some of the most powerful warships ever deployed by the Technocrats, and assigned them to support the last surviving mobile fortress, the *Tartarus*. Being assigned to one of those ships was either considered a severe punishment or a great opportunity, depending on the outlook of the person in question.

For Third Lords Mihalis and Aella, it was the latter right up until the moment the ship's general quarters alarm violently roused them from sleep.

Mihalis quite literally rolled out of bed, operating on reflex that was several steps ahead of his still-awakening brain. He was on his feet and getting dressed inside of ten seconds after the first warning klaxon shattered his sleep.

He kept his duty uniform next to the bed and had already struggled into the gunmetal gray pants by the time Aella rousted herself from her own bed on the other side of the cabin.

With no end of groggy profanities and protests, Aella slid to the edge of her bed and planted her feet on the floor. She went no further for the moment. Unlike her cabinmate, Aella was in no hurry to get dressed.

Instead, while Mihalis buttoned the shirt that went under his uniform jacket, she picked up her holo computer and checked the reasoning behind the alarm.

"They'll tell us what's going on when we get to our stations," Mihalis said.

Aella shrugged. One shoulder hitched slightly where a yellow-green bruise still lingered after an ill-fated bit of showmanship the week before. "You're not wrong, but I'd like to know what I'm walking into. It'd be nice to know if we should panic or just hustle a bit."

"Doesn't change our orders."

Another shrug, followed by a stiff roll of her shoulders. Mihalis wished she would get dressed if she was going to continue sitting there, at least. It was annoying not being able to look down until she did. He also knew that she knew about that particular hangup, and suspected that her typical unwillingness to get dressed until the last minute was more to needle her cabinmate than any dislike of clothing on her part.

"It might, and," she paused. "What's this? They've done it!"

Something in her tone sent his pulse racing. "Done what?"

"Hold on," she said, and swiped across the holo screen twice. The first gesture silenced the room's alarm, though they could still hear it plainly through the thin interior walls. The second opened another holo window, floating above hers and oriented to be read from Mihalis's side.

"TITANS ARRIVE ON PROSGEIOSI," it read in block text. Below that headline, a smaller line continued the story. "As of this morning, the six men and women who took part in 'Project Titan,' First Lord Tritogenes's initiative aimed at combating the mastigas, have all arrived in Odyssey."

Before either of them could read on, Aella's holo blanked and the room's alarm resumed. She frowned. "Damn it, can't the emergency wait a few more seconds? I was reading that."

This time, the alarm was accompanied by spoken instructions. The siren wailed twice, then, "all hands to battle stations," another two bone-jarring alarms, and finally, "this is not a drill."

The alarm repeated itself with the same pattern as Mihalis finished buttoning his uniform jacket.

He laughed. "I think Second Lord Tryphosa would look at you a little weird if you showed up to the guns naked."

Aella hummed a question, then looked down as though she had forgotten that particularly important piece of morning prep. "Give me a second."

Mihalis turned away as she slid the rest of the way out of bed. He half expected her to throw something at the back of his head, but he supposed that even Third Lord Aella knew when to start taking things seriously. Instead, he heard a dramatic rustle and pop of fabric followed by a satisfied grunt.

Mihalis turned around in time to see her buckle a duty belt around her waist and blouse the folds of her robe overtop. He never did understand how she managed to put on the complicated robe so quickly, but the gray-green garment was well within dress regulations of the Technocrat navy, and so he let it be.

"Where do you think it's going?" she asked.

They locked eyes for a moment. He did not have to ask what "it" was. Being stationed aboard the *Phlegethon* left very few answers to that question, and if the answer did not either begin or end with "the mastigas," then it was so far above his pay grade that the only option he had left was to nod along with the captain and go where he was told.

"Not through us," he replied, deadly serious.

Aella was twenty years older than Mihalis, who had lied about his age on his application to the military academy. While still quite young, the forty-four year old Third Lord had a much different perspective on the mastigas than he did. They tried to discuss it one night, what the system had been like before "they"—he could practically feel the venom she put into that single word—arrived, but Mihalis never lived in that world. To him, the mastigas were the monsters who attacked his home, Kipos, not some invaders from beyond the stars.

An expression of sadness, delicate as it passed over her features, confronted him for a moment. It vanished, replaced with a smile and a firm slap on the shoulder. "Yeah."

She said nothing else before turning toward the cabin door and tapping the switch next to it.

The door slid open, revealing chaos beyond. If Mihalis thought the alarm in the cabin was loud, the siren out in the corridor was deafening. Most of the people out there were running the same direction, to the left from the perspective of their cabin door, but a few headed the opposite direction.

Aella turned right while Mihalis turned left. He stopped, pivoted in place, and yelled above the din, "hey!"

She stopped and turned, raising a questioning eyebrow. With her head, she gestured to the flow of people around them. She mouthed, "I've got no time."

Mihalis supposed she might have actually said something aloud, but it was lost as the siren overhead blared again.

"BATTLE STATIONS," it demanded. "THIS IS NOT A DRILL."

He made a quick gesture at chest level, an x with the index and middle fingers of both hands. The benediction, nearly a silent prayer in and of itself, required no words.

She smiled. Aella did not share his faith, but the gesture never went unappreciated for what it was. She pushed through the crowd so they could speak for a second or two, then repeated his gesture back to him. "Ten Thousand keep you, Mihalis," she said, then grinned, "now let's go stop that battleship."

He nodded, turned away, and joined the greater of the two streams of personnel. He smelled fear around him as he came into close proximity with everyone else. Aella, he was sure, never even knew what fear felt like, but now that he was once again around the press of the crew, the subtle odor of fear-sweat was unmistakable.

He looked around him. Some of his fellow crewmates kept their eyes on the floor or looked anywhere but directly at another human being. Others looked around, eyes darting from person to person, desperate to find a moment of kinship as their adrenal glands did everything in their power to chemically convince them they were all about to die.

Mihalis, for his part, did his best to project an air of self-assurance that he most certainly did not feel. The people around him needed to feel like someone was on top of things, and for the moment, Mihalis decided that person would be him, at least until they all reached their various stations aboard the ship.

It was what his father would have done, he told himself.

The *Phlegethon* was a big ship, and even though he, and those around him, maintained a near-jogging pace, it required nearly five minutes to reach his destination. During that time, the alarm quieted, but did not cease. Men and women of various ranks joined and departed the arterial flow of people all heading in the same direction.

In Mihalis's case, he was headed to the bridge, and the concentration of Third and Second Lords increased the closer he to the bow of the ship he came.

The entrance to the *Phlegethon*'s bridge was a short staircase, up which only he and one other person climbed. Until that moment, he had been so focused on his own thoughts that Mihalis had not noticed that Second Lord Vasia catching up to him.

As though waiting to greet him until he got his head out of the proverbial clouds, she nodded in his direction. "Morning."

He laughed. "Is it?"

A shrug, then Vasia laughed. "In the literal sense that it's after midnight? Sure."

"If you're here, then who..." he asked, but as the two of them hit the top step, the question answered itself.

An old man stood at the navigation plot. An ornate cane with a brass head that was almost certainly a violation of regulations leaned against the table-sized holo projector. Mihalis breathed a sigh of relief at the sight. Vasia could operate the plot's controls well enough, but the last thing he wanted to deal with was fighting with the projector itself.

It seemed, some days, that every time it fell to Third Lord Mihalis to activate the navigation plot that the damnable thing found some new and inventive way to break on him.

"Welcome to the cauldron," Second Lord Anaxagoras said. His voice was the very antithesis of his stooped frame. Every time Mihalis saw him, he expected the senior navigator to have a rasping, harsh voice. Instead, Anaxagoras spoke with a vibrant baritone that would not have sounded out of place coming from a news program.

'The cauldron,' was his nickname for the navigation plot, and Mihalis always felt it was a much more appropriate name. Ordinarily, the *Phlegethon* sat at the center of the plot. Its four siblings stretched out in every direction, with the *Tartarus* in the center. Together, they created a shell with the mastigas battleship at the focus.

This time, as Mihalis and Vasia took up their positions around the table-sized holo, the mastigas ship had been placed at the center. Stretching three kilometers in length, nearly three times the size of the *Tartarus* itself, the ship's silhouette was dominated by an imposing pyramid at the stern.

It was also pointed directly at the *Cocytus,* which hung a mere thousand kilometers to the *Phlegethon*'s starboard side.

"Do we know if it's targeting the *Cocytus*?" Vasia asked.

Anaxagoras shook his head. "All I know is that Hyacinthia and Athanas have been shoulder-to-shoulder for fifteen minutes now."

Mihalis looked over, watching the ship's weapons control and communications officers confer in voices too quiet to carry over the still blaring alarm.

"Silence the alarm," Second Lord Cepheus, the ship's captain, ordered.

"Aye."

The warning lights continued their slow strobe, but the grating klaxon finally fell silent, making it much easier to think and, perhaps more important, converse.

"Lochias Athanas," the captain continued, "what do we see out there?"

"The mastigas ship has increased engine output thirty percent. I believe they've powered up sensors and weapon systems, sir."

"You believe?"

He nodded nervously. "Yes, sir. Even with First Lord Enyalios's upgrades, we can barely see past the first few centimeters of their hull."

"Lochias Valentina?"

Where Athanas's nervousness showed in a slight jitter, hers manifested in a crisp precision. She even saluted out of automatic reflex when the Captain spoke to her. "Sir, the *Cocytus* is reporting an active sensor ping, but nothing else."

"Lochias Anaxagoras, is the ship headed for anything in-system?"

"Negative, Lochagos," the old man replied.

While they spoke, Mihalis manipulated the holo. If it broke, he was out of luck, but while it was working correctly, he had no trouble with it. The field of view expanded until the plot displayed the entire system. They, and the mastigas battleship, shrank into invisibility, but a quick command added the necessary info tags to keep track of their own position.

"Vasia, add the mastigas's ship's vector," he said, polite and quiet.

She nodded. A moment later, a red arrow appeared in what looked like the middle of nowhere. It stretched slowly to what was agreed upon as being "East" relative to the twin suns. A quick reference check told him that nothing important lay over there, but a thought continued to nag at the back of Mihalis's mind.

He lead the plot through a slow projection of the ship's possible course if their blockade was not present to stop them. The mastigas battleship was not fast, especially by the standards of modern Technocrat warships, and Mihalis had to push the simulation nine months into the future before any useful information appeared.

Granted, that was enough time for the ship to change course a thousand more times, but Mihalis had studied this ship his entire life. Long before being assigned to the *Phlegethon*, he learned one important fact about the battleship's behavior: it was not prone to dramatic course corrections. Rather, nearly every time it moved, it changed heading less than ten degrees. That information let him narrow things down considerably.

Mihalis looked up from the plot finally to see Anaxagoras and Vasia's eyes fixed on it as well. Slowly, Anaxagoras's gaze rose to meet Mihalis's eyes.

"Lochagos," Anaxagoras said slowly. "It seems I was wrong. There's a sixty percent chance that the mastigas vessel is headed for Dasos."

The bridge fell silent for a moment, broken only by a single word spoken by the captain. "Understood."

Third Lord Valentina broke the silence next. "Sir, the *Cocytus* is reporting active targeting, and..."

Before she could finish, Third Lord Athanas interrupted. "The mastigas battleship has launched missiles. Repeat, positive missile launch confirmed."

Vasia violently swiped through the plot, resetting it to the default view with the *Phlegethon* in the center. The mastigas ship had indeed moved, and the plot showed its engine output had risen another five percent, but it was still far outside any previously demonstrated maximum weapon range.

"Lochias Hyacinthia!" the captain barked. "Are we within range to support the *Cocytus*?"

"Barely, sir."

"Navigation!" he next ordered, not bothering to differentiate between the three of them, "give me a least time course to bring our point defenses to bear."

"Aye," Mihalis replied. He reached out and sketched a line on the holo plot, one which Anaxagoras refined by running it through an algorithm to maximize efficiency. While he did that, Vasia projected a sphere around the *Phlegethon* to show optimal weapon range.

Satisfied, Anaxagoras, the senior of the three, passed it along to Third Lord Leander, the ship's helmsman. Another copy automatically went to Hyacinthia at the weapons console.

"Blue-screen it!" Valentina cursed. Her hands flew through her own holo, adding commands and information streamed directly from the *Cocytus*. One of the results, the most important at that moment, was that the mastigas missiles appeared on the nav plot.

Not only were the missiles launched from outside the battleship's previously displayed maximum range, but they seemed to be moving at least twenty percent faster.

"By the Ten Thousand," Mihalis whispered. Vasia shot him an angry glare at the outburst, but otherwise said nothing.

Then it happened to her, and Vasia cursed. "Gods between! We won't get there in time."

On the plot, the three of them watched the terrible sight unfold with silent, clinical detachment.

The icons representing the swarm of mastigas missiles streaked toward the *Cocytus* with aching slowness. Across the vast distances, even missile fire took several minutes to reach its target. Ordinarily, that was enough time to prep the ship's point defenses, but if the *Cocytus*'s crew had been as surprised as they were by the attack's extreme range, it was possible that their point defense was not completely engaged yet.

No one spoke in the eleven minutes the missiles took to reach their target. No further orders were needed. Lochagos Cepheus already gave the order to intercept if possible. The only other order he could give would be to abandon the *Cocytus* altogether, and Mihalis knew that order would never pass his lips.

The first wave of missile detonated twenty kilometers short of the *Cocytus*, victims of its point defenses, but as time stretched on, the explosions crept closer and closer.

On the plot, something else moved. Mihalis swiped at it, momentarily re-centering the plot. "Sir!" he snapped. "The *Lethe* is moving toward to attack."

"Confirm Dekaneas," the captain growled in reply. "Moving to attack, not to support the *Cocytus*?"

The angry way in which he nearly spat the word "attack" made Mihalis's blood run cold and he double checked the plot. "Aye, sir. The *Lethe* is moving toward the mastigas ship."

"Confirmed, sir." Third Lord Athanas announced from the sensor console. "*Lethe* has targeted the mastigas ship."

"Fuck!"

"Orders, sir?"

"Get Lochagos Takis on the comm. Now!"

Mihalis bent back over the nav plot. He passed on his report, the mechanical voice of his military duty told him. It was now their issue, and he had his own to worry about. In the few moments that he spoke to the captain, either Vasia or Anaxagoras had re-centered the plot.

His eyes focused just in time to see seventeen missiles strike the *Cocytus* at nearly the same instant. In a single, horrifying moment, the warship that had been home to over four thousand people was reduced first to flaming wreckage and them to a ball of radioactive gasses and metals.

Missiles continued pounding the rapidly cooling bubble that used to be the *Cocytus* for several minutes, even as the *Lethe* launched its own volley and the mastigas battleship turned its spine-chilling attention toward that ship.

Mihalis was aware, in some dim corner of his mind, that the captain was shouting orders. None of them were aimed at the navigators, and so none of the words made it through the numb shell around his conscious thoughts.

That lasted until the captain finally gave them an order. "Plot a course for the mastigas battleship."

"Sir?" he asked, snapped immediately out of his reverie.

"Orders from the Strategos. *Tartarus* says the green-eyes are going to pick us all off at this rate. Either we flee and hope we get outside of whatever damn firing envelope that ship actually has, and we let it slip away long enough to attack Dasos, or we see just what we can do if we all work together."

"Understood, sir," Anaxagoras replied. His voice retained the rich baritone it always had, but Mihalis heard the same emptiness he felt echoed in his supervisor's words.

The three of them laid in a pair of courses, giving the captain options without wasting his time talking about them. One option gave them a fifteen minute intercept with the *Lethe*, and the other a twelve minute shot at the mastigas themselves.

Lochagos Captain Cepheus manipulated his own control holo and the intercept course for the *Lethe* vanished. Mihalis's stomach sank, but he understood. Unlike the *Cocytus*, the *Lethe* was on the opposite side of their formation. Their fifteen minute intercept would put them arriving some four minutes after the mastigas missiles.

Mihalis swallowed hard. They were abandoning the *Lethe*.

The next ten minutes sped by in a blur. The mastigas missiles reached the *Lethe* exactly on time, penetrating its point defenses even easier than they had those of the *Cocytus*. More missiles got through more quickly than they had before. In an instant, the *Lethe* vanished from the plot.

He was too numb to feel anything but a distant, cold ache as the other ship's icon vanished. So soon after losing the *Cocytus*, Mihalis found it impossible for his heart to ache any worse.

And, then, even that proved to be a lie as the announcement rang out over the bridge. "The mastigas ship has targeted the *Phlegethon*."

***

"The *Tartarus* has moved to engage the mastigas battleship."

Even on the highly-sanitized and icon-heavy tactical displays in the *Phlegethon*'s magazine, the situation did not look good. Two ships were already gone, and a third, the *Phlegethon* itself, was under fire. The mastigas had shown a terrifying advantage in weapon range, one that even now they were struggling to negate.

Watching the holo projected above her console, Third Lord Aella reflected on the redundancy of that announcement. The *Tartarus* was the second-largest icon on the screen. Anyone doing their due diligence and paying attention to the tactical situation outside the ship would have seen it.

And yet, she thought, some things were needed because they generated the spark of an idea.

"Lochias!" she shouted, pitching her voice to be heard across the magazine and through the mechanical noises around them.

Second Lord Tryphosa's head rose above her console. "Yes, Dekaneas?"

"We're still out of range of the mastigas ship," she said, another redundant announcement, especially given the alarms blaring from the point-defense consoles. "I checked with the computer. It'll add twenty-point-oh-two seconds to our firing time, but I think we can get the range we need."

"Explain, Dekaneas. Now. Time isn't something we have a lot of."

"Lochias, if we remove the warheads from the missiles..."

Second Lord Tryphosa interrupted with a shout of, "unacceptable!" Then, she added, "if we remove the warheads, we'll barely damage that ship."

"Would it not be better to do minimal damage than no damage, Lochias? If anything, we could help saturate their fire control so the *Tartarus* will have a better time of it."

"If I may, Lochias," a voice from the point defense console offered. Aella recognized the voice, but he was normally on a different shift and she never bothered learning his name. "There is a certain viability of kinetic weaponry in this situation. A precision strike could..."

Tryphosa nodded once, firmly. "Fine. Dekaneas Aella, see to the modifications and be quick about it."

"Aye, Lochias."

She went to work, doing her best to tune out the alarms and announcements that blared around her. The point defense crew's conversation grew louder and louder as the incoming mastigas fire steadily pierced their defenses.

Finally, a joyous shout rose from that end of the room, something important-seeming enough to roust her from her station. Less than three minutes had passed, but the announcement of, "we've entered the *Tartarus*'s defensive envelope!" filled her with something that might have been hope in a less harrowing situation.

Finally, she cleared the display on her console, announcing, "it's done, Lochias."

Tryphosa nodded. "Good. All stations, target the mastigas ship's weapons first. Fire when ready."

During training, Third Lord Aella had qualified, barely, on the pistol and rifle courses. Those were skills she never needed after taking a post aboard a starship, and she was sure her skill now was even less than it was then. Still, there was something satisfying about pulling a trigger that could never be replicated by the cold indifference of a console.

As her hand touched the holographic firing control, Second Lord Aella very much wished her weapons had a trigger instead.

When she turned her attention back to the tactical display, the emotionless icons told her the *Tartarus* had already opened fire. The *Styx* and *Acheron* had increased their engine output to maximum in order to bring their own weapons to bear as soon as possible, but even if they had the same idea she did, it would be several minutes before they could fire.

The mastigas ship, as it had shown several times already, had no such troubles with range. As she watched another cluster of missiles streak her way, Aella wondered exactly how long the mastigas had possessed this kind of range advantage.

Had these missiles always been so effective, and the mastigas simply never used them at maximum rage before? Or, her thoughts continued, were the mastigas smarter than everyone gave them credit for, and had been working to improve their own technology out here in the silence of the rim?

In that moment, she was not sure which was more terrifying.

As she watched the missiles heading for the *Phlegethon*, however, she did not feel fear. Either the missiles would reach them or they would not, and point defense was not her job. It was, in a sense, a strangely liberating thought to realize that her safety and ultimately her life, did not rest in her own hands.

"Three missiles got through!"

She turned her attention away from the tactical plot even as the ship shuddered under the impact of the first mastigas warhead. Her own console indicated that their modified kinetic missiles were finally ready to fire again. With some measure of satisfaction, she noted that the mastigas ship still sat outside the range of their regular, unmodified weaponry.

Third Lord Aella had direct fire control over one quarter of the *Phlegethon*'s offensive capability. Her fingers danced through her holo display, targeting what appeared to be the mastigas ship's own launchers.

Her targeting icons appeared in blue, with those of the other gunnery officers appearing in red, yellow, and green. A moment's hushed conversation passed between the four of them, little more than half-formed words and gestures, and several of the targeting indicators shifted around the ship.

Satisfied, she again tapped the control to open fire.

Several minutes passed, during which the *Tartarus* opened fire for the first time. The *Styx*, now operating in the mobile fortress's shadow just like the *Phlegethon*, came in to range as well, dumping an entire load of unmodified nuclear warheads into space.

"We're being ordered to cover the *Acheron*," Second Lord Tryphosa announced. Her voice was cool, level, betraying none of the tension that pervaded the room.

"The mastigas ship has opened fire."

"Is the *Acheron* within our defensive range?"

"No, Lochias. I'm sorry."

Tryphosa swore, but said nothing else. The ship could only move so quickly, and nothing she did or said could speed it up.

She looked again at the tactical plot. The *Tartarus* was still moving toward the mastigas ship. Missiles were starting to get through their combined defenses, but only in ones and twos. Even mastigas warheads could not do very much damage alone like that. Still, the mobile fortress crept closer, trying to interpose itself physically between the enemy battleship and the *Acheron*, and use the proximity to overwhelm the mastigas fire control systems.

Suicide, said a cold voice in Aella's mind.

Mastigas missiles streaked ahead of the *Tartarus*, this most recent volley all but ignoring them. Instead, the battleship focused on the *Acheron*, still just outside the joint defensive envelope that protected the *Phlegethon* and the *Styx*.

She found herself unable to close her eyes as the green icon representing the *Acheron* yellowed, then turned orange, red, and finally the deep bloody crimson of critical damage. It hung there like that for a full minute, defiant, surviving somehow.

Her heart swelled as a cloud of escape pods shrouded the *Acheron*'s icon, then sank into a very cold, very deep pit as another volley of missiles obliterated the wreckage of the warship and punched city-sized holes in the cloud of escape pods.

"It's targeting the..."

Aella thought the Lochias was about to say, "*Tartarus*," but she stopped mid-sentence as an alarm blared for half a second before plunging the magazine into darkness. The ship bucked and shuddered once, accompanied by a feeling of being thrown sideways that not even the artificial gravity could dampen.

"What the hell..." one of the point defense controllers asked.

"Gods between," someone whispered. It might even have been Aella herself, but she was not sure.

The calm voice of Second Lord Tryphosa cut through the cloud of terror that fell across the pitch black room. "The ship's sensors are down, and whatever knocked them out has done a number on the rest of our systems."

"How long..."

That question answered itself as the room's lights came back on with an audible humming noise. In near unison, holo consoles around the room flickered back to life as well. What she saw there made her heart sink.

On the tactical display, the *Tartarus* was gone.

From the point defense console, someone yelled an announcement. "Incoming! Seven seconds!"

Overhead, the intercom blared to life as a dozen different alarms rang out, then the first explosion ran through the bones of the warship. The deck under Aella's feet shuddered, vibrating like a speaker turned up too loud.

Instinctively, she turned back to her console and triggered another volley of missiles. The mastigas battleship was very close now, and she wished she had a live feed from outside or even a window. It would have been nice to see something more engaging than the tactical plot, she thought.

The ship shuddered again and overhead something popped and crashed. Cold wind whistled through the magazine. She ignored it, already trying to queue up the next volley.

Aella's heart skipped a beat, a phrase she always thought was metaphor until it happened, and she shouted. "We got through!"

She pivoted in place, eager to inform Second Lord Tryphosa of her success, and stopped. The crashing sound she heard was a piece of debris that pierced the magazine underneath Tryphosa's chair, mangling it beyond recognition.

Overhead, the ship's intercom came to life again. She thought it might have been the captain giving orders, but it was hard to hear above the rattling explosions and screams of the crew around her.

When one of the missiles breached the magazine itself a moment later, it became very hard to hear anything at all.

Chapter 7

Pallasophia's first words upon re-entering the suite were, "are you alright?"

Victoria looked up from the book she had been reading, another paper-bound volume signifying the Second Lord's wealth, although this one turned out to be rather more interesting than some of the others.

Pallasophia carried a large canvas bag on one shoulder, which she carried to the kitchen of their shared suite. Victoria did not have to ask what was in the bag, even after such a short time, she already knew certain things like that about the Second Lord. For instance, that bag was what Pallasophia carried when she went shopping for produce in the open-air markets just outside of Odyssey's walls.

Those things could have been delivered to the suite. In fact, in the message queue Victoria read that morning, looking over Pallasophia's shoulder, it seemed like there was no end of lower-ranking Technocrats sending out blanket applications for personal valet jobs.

"It gives me something to do," she had said in response to Victoria's question that morning. "More important, it gives me something *mundane* to do."

Reacting to the question of the moment, however, Victoria simply raised her eyebrows in mute question. When Pallasophia shook her head, smiling a vague enigmatic smile, and went into the kitchen, Victoria finally called after her. "I feel fine. Why?"

"You haven't left the suite since we got here a day and a half ago."

Despite being the only one in the room for the moment, Victoria self-consciously eyed the book she had been reading, then closed it and placed it on the little table next to her chair. Her black robe rustled as she shifted in her seat, tucking her feet underneath her body.

"I've seen busy."

"There's more to do here than read through my library and exercise."

Victoria frowned. She did not particularly want to admit that the primary reasons she refused to leave the suite was their very location. Odyssey was full of people and, while the ceilings overhead might have been more comforting than the open air of the upper levels or of the cities that sprawled at its feet, Victoria did not exactly feel comfortable in those kinds of crowds.

Instead, she said, "I haven't needed to."

"I'm sure the other Titans want to meet you."

Despite the friendly tone in Pallasophia's voice, Victoria was starting to feel a little defensive. She crossed her arms, turning her annoyed frown at the empty room. "I've been exchanging messages with them."

"In person," Pallasophia argued.

"The banquet is only a few days away. I will meet them all then."

Pallasophia came back into the room, but stopped just inside of the door leading to the kitchen. "Tritogenes wants to meet you."

Now, she frowned, angry. Of course he wanted to meet her, she thought. Tritogenes wanted to see the face of the person he locked in a mastigas-infested hell for a hundred generations. The list of things she wanted to say to him was very long indeed, and very few of them were pleasant.

Yet, and her anger seemed to find a new target in the mastigas, leaving Tritogenes alone, she found it very hard to actually be angry at the Hexarch. He was only doing what was best for his people, she reasoned. The thought would not leave, and so she accepted it and turned her mind away.

She shook her head physically, clearing her thoughts. In the few moments she had been lost in her own mind, Pallasophia crossed the room and sat herself down in the chair opposite the one Victoria claimed as her personal reading perch. She spared a glance at the stack of books beside the chair as a mix of amusement and happiness crossed her face.

"You know," Pallasophia said, "I never got around to reading half of those. The ones I would always reread went with me to Aphelion."

Victoria picked up her current volume and placed it on the low table between the two chairs. The title read *Valor and Glory*. "What about this one?"

Pallasophia shrugged. The robe she selected that morning before leaving the suite was decorated with glimmering braid on the shoulders that sparkled and shone even in the dim light—Victoria finally won *that* argument—of the suite. "I haven't, no."

"It's actually good, even though the author can't decide on a genre." At Pallasophia's questioning glance, she continued her explanation. "It starts out as a crime story, but a quarter of the way into it, the main character has seduced both of her fellow team leaders and their enemy."

Victoria shrugged. "It's gotten bogged down in the background of some of the minor characters, but it's been a fun read."

She picked up a book from the top of the stack on the right side of her chair, brandishing the cover. "This one? Don't bother."

Pallasophia laughed quietly and an amused smile settled on her face. "*The Third Hand* is a classic."

Victoria scoffed as she set it back down on her "already read" stack. "It's pretentious."

"But you finished it."

She laughed, loud and boisterous. "I had to know if it stayed pretentious all the way to the end."

"Does it?"

She nodded.

Pallasophia's grin widened. "Good. I hated that book. I've kept that copy around because Tritogenes gave it to me. He said it was a gift from Hyperion, so it's got some sentimental value. Between the two of us though?" Her smile turned conspiratorial. "I don't think Tritogenes liked it very much, either."

"For once," Victoria said, "I can't blame him."

"Why don't we go shopping for something new to read after dinner?"

Victoria froze. Pallasophia's expectant expression told her she stumbled into the Second Lord's trap exactly as she meant her to. Now, going by the previous conversation, Victoria had no reason to object to leaving the suite.

She fought with herself for a moment, trying to decide whether she was going to balk with no explanation or actually talk to the one person she considered a friend.

Victoria unfolded her legs, thought about standing, but instead simply pushed herself back into the chair so that she could sit up straighter for the moment. "Do you remember the woman working at the customs desk?"

Pallasophia nodded. "She was excited to meet you, Victoria. Everyone is."

Her blood chilled a little at that, and she swallowed hard, hoping Pallasophia did not notice. The concern on her face told Victoria that she had, indeed, noticed. "That's the problem."

Pallasophia said nothing. Instead, she leaned back in her chair, projected an aura of casualness, and folded her hands loosely in her lap.

The silence ticked by for several seconds before Victoria continued. "I can accept," she paused long enough to touch the embroidered mastigas elite skull on her robe, "this. I can accept that I'm here to be part

117

of the assault force that's going to deal with the mastigas once and for all. The news keeps reminding me of that, even if all they have to show of my face is a holo from the customs office."

"But?" Pallasophia's voice was quiet, but it cut through the air like a knife.

Victoria sagged back against the chair, then draped one leg over the side. "I don't want every encounter to be like that."

"It sounds strange," Pallasophia began, paused, then continued. "But if you start meeting people now, those reactions will become less frequent. You're the fifth Titan to arrive here, Lelantos is still on Kipos with First Lord Rivka, and already the other four are a fairly normal sight around here."

Pallasophia paused again, taking a deep breath. Victoria almost interrupted, but the other woman's posture said she was not yet done.

"Do people still stop them? Of course they do, especially Helena. Daniel could blend into a crowd if he wanted to. Barely anyone recognizes him outside of the Aegis. But even Helena, with her implants, goes about her business just fine."

"What do you propose? I get it all out of the way now?"

Pallasophia nodded, smiling. "That's exactly what I suggest. Odyssey is a nice place, for all the things I hate about it."

"Like the crowds."

The Second Lord laughed. "Yes, like the crowds. "Why don't we actually go shopping after dinner? Not just books but for your room, too?"

"Why?"

"Because," Pallasophia replied. "Once you start working with the other Titans, it's going to be hard to find time to relax. I want you to enjoy yourself, even if it's just for a few days."

Victoria looked across the expansive combination living and dining room to her own door. Like Pallasophia's door, it stood open during the day. There was no reason to close it off while she was out in the main room reading or eating.

Her bedroom had a few decorations, overflow from Pallasophia's own ever-growing collection of kitsch. More than that, her meager possessions accompanied them on the trip from Aphelion, but there was little decorative value in any of them except the elite's sword which hung like a trophy on the wall above her bed.

Other than those things, her room was bare of anything that might even generously be referred to as "personality."

She turned her attention back to Pallasophia, whose expression might have softened a little, but remained open and expectant.

Victoria sighed. "Alright. Fine. Two conditions, though."

"Alright."

Victoria held up a hand, enumerating things on her fingers even as she said them aloud. "First, no gifts. If we buy something, it's because I want it."

"You're going to have a harder time there than you think."

Victoria frowned. "Why?"

"Remember that customs agent you mentioned? The excited one?"

"What about her?"

"She was a Third Lord. Most of them are fairly well off, able to treat themselves or their loved ones to nice gifts when the occasion merits it. Second Lords like myself, to say nothing of the Hexarchs, often have significantly more disposable income."

Instead of anger or frustration, the overriding emotion she felt in that moment was exasperation. "I don't have much of a choice, do I?"

"You can have anything you don't like shipped to Limani or even Aphelion," Pallasophia said, spreading her hands apologetically. "Beyond that? Refusing a gift is a pretty big insult."

She sighed. "Alright. One condition, then."

"Name it."

Victoria rose from her seat, marveling at the way her robe had already softened after a mere two days of wear. Either that or she was finally getting used to the heavy thing. "I'm making dinner. I'm still not convinced cooking isn't some sort of magic."

She smiled, but it faded after a moment. "Plus, I'd like to develop a skill that's my own, not something programmed into my brain."

Pallasophia smiled and rose herself. "I'll help."

"You're helping," Victoria said sternly, "not doing it for me."

Pallasophia laughed. "Of course." A moment later, she asked, "I'm going to make a request, then."

Victoria nodded, already heading for the kitchen.

"If it's alright with you, I'm going to invite Tritogenes to dinner." As Victoria bristled, Pallasophia continued quickly, "not to go shopping afterward. Just to eat with us, and to meet you."

For the moment, she was glad her back was to Pallasophia, because she knew the expression that crossed her features could not have been pleasant. Victoria felt her eyes narrow and her lips firm into a very displeased line.

By the time Pallasophia caught up with her, however, she had regained control over her emotions and expression, and she greeted the Second Lord with a smile. "I look forward to it."

***

The smell of food emanated from Second Lord Pallasophia's suite as Tritogenes stood outside the door. The subtext beneath her message had been clear enough, and Tritogenes found himself a touch more nervous than he would have expected in any other situation.

Victoria was going to have questions, and probably more, for him when he went inside. That much was obvious even without Pallasophia's partially cryptic warning. They never met face to face at Aphelion, and for that alone, had their positions been reversed, he would have harbored more than a little resentment. With luck, things would work out differently, but until they actually met in person, he had no way to know.

He laughed to himself, nervous and glad that no one else was in this particular hallway of the Hexarch's area. He had to look a foolish sight, dressed and made up as though he were going to a public restaurant and not to a private residence.

He had questions for her as well, and certainly had things to say, but he would let her say her piece first. He owed her that much.

For a moment, his hand paused on the way to the door. Tritogenes did not consider himself a paranoid sort, but the idea that Pallasophia left the suite after contacting him crossed his mind. He had a vivid image of stepping into a dark room, bleak and broken like the pits of Aphelion, and coming face to face with Victoria's black mask.

Tritogenes shuddered. If he was going to die in a pool of his own blood, he at least wanted to do it beneath the suns.

After another moment to rally himself, he pressed the door chime and announced himself. Despite his rank, he could not enter another Technocrat's private residence without permission. He might have owned the suite, legally, but it was hers in practice. The door slid open a moment later, admitting him into the, thankfully brightly lit, suite.

Pallasophia and Victoria both awaited him inside the suite. Sizzling noises rode a wave of spices drifting outward from from the open kitchen doorway.

The door closed behind him, and Tritogenes suddenly had another flash of his thoughts from moments before. "Trapped in here with her," was the thought that raced through his mind, no matter how much be tried to banish it.

The atmosphere in the room changed as both women made note of his arrival. The moment he stepped through the door, Pallasophia's face had been alight with emotion. She smiled and her laughter mixed with Victoria's, resulting in a sound with more happiness in it than Tritogenes had heard from her since she became Project Director at Aphelion.

That happy feeling did not cut off immediately at his arrival, rather it hit a strong decrescendo and then immediately got replaced by a chilly

121

tension. Pallasophia's face quietly blanked, assuming the cool politeness high-ranking Technocrats were expected to show one another in public. It was the sudden tension in Victoria's shoulders that really told him how his arrival changed the room. She sat up straight, pulling her shoulders back and engaging the muscles there, ready to spring or pounce in any direction.

Pallasophia rose from her seat respectfully, then motioned toward Victoria. She stood up as well, and her head and shoulders continued to rise far higher than Tritogenes expected. He had seen pictures and video and had even watched her defeat the mastigas elite as it happened, but none of those things prepared him for the woman in the black robe.

Victoria turned smoothly on her heels like a dancer. Her shroud of black fabric blossomed around her feet, but nothing else seemed to move. In a moment, even that settled. The grace in her actions was eerie.

She frowned at him as a war of emotions both positive and negative boiled at the edges of her eyes and mouth. For a long moment, neither of them seemed to know what to say, so Tritogenes used those few seconds to finally *see* the person his near-failure created.

After her stature, her eyes were the first thing he noticed. The gaze boring holes through Tritogenes's spine were the color of winter's clouds, cold and piercing. He had no doubt she recognized him.

Her bronze-skinned face with its high cheekbones and square jaw had a hard cast to it, like she had been sculpted out of the very sort of metal she resembled. The shock of dark hair on her head, growing only since she emerged from her pod in the lower levels of the facility, remained too short to brush or do any of the sorts of ornate things most Technocrats fancied. As short as it was, it gave her a decidedly military appearance.

Several faint scars crossed her face, with more appearing the longer he looked. The one that stood out the most, however, emerged from the collar of her robe and climbed to just above her chin on the left side of her face. It looked newer, and worse, than the others, standing out as a jagged pinkish-white line.

In person, she was more beautiful than he dared hope.

Finally, he spoke first. Tritogenes kept his voice carefully neutral, betraying none of the emotion he felt. He said her name, "Victoria." Anything else, for the moment, felt like too much, a conversation moving too quickly.

Victoria replied slowly, pronouncing every word as though she was inspecting each syllable. "First Lord Tritogenes. We meet at last."

Her voice came out as a deep, rich alto. It fit her imposing frame, he thought. What it did not do, however, was ease any of his tension. If she wanted to harm him, there was very little Tritogenes could do. Even if the door behind him opened the moment he stepped near it, he knew he could not escape. He watched her fight. Should she so desire, Victoria could be on him in a moment, and Tritogenes would die before he got halfway out of the room.

Pallasophia shifted on her feet slightly, almost starting to come forward and then thinking better of it. Instead, she turned and went for the kitchen to deal with whatever heavily-spiced meal awaited them. On the way there, she said, "Victoria cooked for us, First Lord."

That moment broke the tension. The storm of emotions still warred on Victoria's face, but Tritogenes no longer felt visceral danger radiating from her. Again, he spoke first. "I am sure you have questions and things you want to say. I will listen."

Silence fell again as Victoria continued to stare at him. Finally, she spoke again, giving voice to his thoughts. "I could kill you and walk out of here. I would disappear, probably on one of your rivals' planets. You know that, right?"

Tritogenes felt his face drain of color. While it had been the exact sort of opening statement he expected, to hear it aloud, and to hear it spoken so calmly, brought about a new wave of terror. The confirmation of his deepest fears, not his own death but that she would simply walk away from the Project, came almost as a physical shock.

He swallowed hard. "I am aware, yes. I created you to be the perfect soldier and I have no illusions about your skills."

Victoria growled. "You killed ninety-nine others first."

"The Project did not go as planned."

"I know. I've seen the footage of the Incident. I also know that you could have sent troops into the facility at any time, and chose not to."

"You are not incorrect, yet to abort the Project would have been to court failure."

Victoria's voice was ice. "Ninety-nine dead *is* a failure."

He hesitated for just a moment, gathering his thoughts, before replying. In one of her messages, Pallasophia indicated that Victoria had an uncanny ability to pick lies and half-truths out of a conversation. Victoria expected honesty from him and to give her anything else would be to risk the cold fury of her anger getting worse.

He nodded. Let her hate him for the truth, then. "I would sacrifice them all again if it resulted in your birth."

Her voice lowered to something guttural, more articulate than a growl but only just. "And if I died, you would have just stored my memories, my life, and downloaded them into the hundred-and-first in line to die."

"We are all born to die, and if ninety-nine must be sacrificed to save the human race, then I would pay that butcher's bill ten times over." He knew his voice was taut with tension that he desperately wished was not so glaringly obvious, but at that moment could do nothing about it.

"Do you not understand how heartless that sounds?" Victoria snapped.

"I understand all too well." He vividly remembered the pain in his soul of the first few failed trials. They threatened to become rote as time went on, and that was the thing he regretted most of all. He said, "I am proud of the results, proud of you, but I am not proud of my methods. I can only pray that perhaps one day you will forgive me."

Victoria silently strode across the room, stopping within arm's reach of Tritogenes, and regarded him with a curious expression of detached interest. To have her, still angry, standing so close to him made the Hexarch nervous but Victoria no longer radiated the sense of danger she had before.

She towered over him, a fact of which she had to be aware, and Tritogenes craned his neck upward with well-hidden annoyance to meet her icy gaze. His instincts, most of them coming from his role at Hexarch, screamed at him to move away or push her away or to simply say something to reassert dominance over the conversation, but he stayed silent. This was her time to speak.

"Pallasophia and I have already discussed this," she began. "There is nothing I can say to you that will undo the past. I know how much you regret what you did. I spoke at length with Doctor Iro about it, but that doesn't make it right."

"I am sorry, Victoria."

She nodded once, and Tritogenes had to fight down a flash of anger as he read the expression on her face as *pity*, of all things.

"I know," she continued. "I accept that. You're right, though. Perhaps I'll forgive you." She paused, narrowed her eyes. "One day."

He looked away, unable to meet her eyes until she spoke again.

"I have something for you, First Lord."

He raised his head. In her hands was a sheathed mastigas dagger. She gripped it by the middle of the sheath, holding it out to him. He stared at it, wide-eyed, wondering exactly what it was she expected him to think or do.

The dagger could be a peace offering of sorts, or it could be the threat he expected since opening the door. He looked from it to her face and back, trying to decide which it was. Finally, he accepted it, waiting for Victoria to explain herself.

"Unsheathe it," she commanded. Her voice sounded like Pallasophia's did when she was issuing orders to her subordinates. Tritogenes fought the reflex to recoil away from being given orders—he was a Hexarch, after all—and obeyed. The blade was dirty, marred with brown stains.

"That's my blood on that blade," she said, gesturing with her chin. "Keep it as a reminder of what I did for you."

Tritogenes nodded slowly, feeling a strange rush of emotions as pride and anxiety rushed through his system. He returned the dagger to its sheath and pocketed it.

"May I sit?" he asked after a moment.

Victoria stepped back two paces and gestured to the reading area. Tritogenes went where he was instructed, sparing a glance toward the kitchen in the hope that Pallasophia would appear and defuse the tension again. When she did not, Tritogenes supposed he was grateful; he must have looked silly being ordered around as he was.

Victoria sat on the far side, directly opposite Tritogenes. Pallasophia, finally, came and sat between them. That diffused some of the tension, but not all, not by a long shot. "Ten minutes," she said. "The rice is nearly done."

Victoria nodded in acknowledgment, but her eyes were still fixed on Tritogenes. "How was Katarraktes?"

At first, he did not reply. That question coming from a fellow Hexarch could have had a thousand different insinuations depending on tone, context, and who it was asking. From Victoria, he picked up none of the subterfuge that would have ordinarily accompanied an inquiry like that. Sitting next to Pallasophia, she seemed to relax again and her expression told him her question had been genuine curiosity.

That, he reflected momentarily, was not something he was used to dealing with. For the first time in years, this was a question he could simply *answer*.

"It was nice," he said finally. "The weather at Enalios's palace is pleasant this time of year. Apparently my visit came a few days after a thunderstorm swept through the mountains, and the waterfalls roared with the first snowmelt of spring. In fact..."

Without realizing it, Tritogenes spent the next hour going over everything he did there, from the initial meeting with Enyalios about the Project to Eurybia's arrival and the nightly festivals.

Exactly on time, Pallasophia brought food in, setting the table while he spoke, pausing only long enough to relocate from the soft reading chair to the dinner table. Tritogenes kept expecting Victoria to interrupt or to express her displeasure with things, but she never did. In fact, she sat and simply listened to his story.

Trigogenes finished by explaining what happened to Eurybia, and what little they knew about Ouroboros.

Now, Victoria spoke up. "I was contacted at Aphelion by a friend of yours, Tritogenes. Second Lord Philip? He told me much the same thing about them."

Tritogenes laughed. "I'm not surprised Philip reached out to you. He's got a good mind for things like that."

"I had a hard time understanding how serious it might possibly be until you said what happened to Eurybia. Compared to what I faced at Aphelion, it didn't seem like a secret society could be all that dangerous."

"Compared to the mastigas," Pallasophia added, "there's not much you could really consider 'dangerous.'"

Tritogenes nodded. For the moment, he grew serious again. "Even so, I want to deal with Ouroboros before you leave for the mastigas ship, Victoria. You six are going to need as much support as we can give you, and we can't afford to keep half the fleet at home worrying about Ouroboros."

Victoria raised an eyebrow. "They're that bad?"

He shook his head, words vying to get out of his mouth, and stumbled. "I, we... Gods curse it. I don't know. They got to Eurybia; we have *no* idea what else they can do."

Victoria nodded. Her reply came out as though she were discussing nothing more important than the weather. "Then we take them out."

The conversation drifted again as Victoria talked about some of the things that happened to her in the labyrinth. After several minutes, when Pallasophia again left the room to bring a promised course of dessert, she turned to Tritogenes again, inquisitive and angry.

"First Lord," she began, then stopped herself. "Tritogenes. How much of me is me?"

"I'm not sure I understand."

"I was born with memories, skills, all from the previous generations. How much of my mind is my own?"

He avoided her eyes for a moment. The answer to that question was a more complicated issue than he wanted to get into just after dinner. It bled into debates he and Pallasophia had that lasted all day and all night during the early days of the Project. "You are shaped by your memories, even those that happened to someone else, but you are *not* those people."

"Is that why I can't stay angry with you?"

Tritogenes cursed silently. That, too, was a question he did not want to answer. "The memories..." He stopped himself. That was the wrong path to take. "The skills and information we gave you included certain things. Preferences, goals. Pallasophia told me about your drive to protect her soldiers. That was one of them."

"And my feelings toward you?"

Very, very slowly, he nodded. With every millimeter of movement, he hoped Pallasophia would reenter the room and give him an excuse not to answer, but of course she did no such thing. He knew from experience that she could hear their conversation from the kitchen, and she would not come back until it was finished.

"Yes," he said. "That was part of it."

Victoria sat there, unmoving in her chair. Fury blazed in her eyes and tension stood out in her neck and hands. That lasted several seconds before it passed, either fading or pushed away by force of will.

She nodded. "That's logical."

Pallasophia took that moment to return to the room carrying a tray with three handmade clay bowls filled with ice cream.

Tritogenes waited until the three of them finished dessert in silence and returned to the soft reading chairs to ask his next question.

"Victoria, the fact that you were born at Aphelion, created as an adult..."

She narrowed her eyes into a glare for a moment, but it passed as soon as she spoke. "In your lab."

"Yes. That presents us with a legal problem."

She gestured to her black robe. "I'm not a Technocrat citizen, I know."

"I believe I've got a solution."

Victoria folded her arms in her lap and gestured for him to continue.

"Have you ever heard of a Spatharios?"

He watched as Victoria's eyes wandered like they did when she was thinking. During dinner she told him about the voices in her head, memories of the dead she called them, and he wondered for a moment if she could actually consult them consciously. Finally, she shook her head and replied that she had not heard of them.

"It's an old tradition," he said, "from the time when Odyssey the city was still *Odyssey* the ship. The Spatharii were the personal guards of the Hexarchs around the time we first came to Prosgeiosi and for several generations afterward. Once we learned to stop killing one another, the practice fell out of commonplace use.

"Considering Project Titan's function, and with the threat posed by the mastigas to consider, I feel the position might be revived."

"And you want me to be your Spatharios?"

129

Tritogenes nodded. "It would eliminate many of the issues around your not legally being a Technocrat. The Spatharii were outside the formal structure, sworn specifically to a single First Lord."

Victoria fell silent for several minutes. Tritogenes did his best not to speculate about what might or might not be going through her mind while she considered his offer. He could think of many more reasons for her to say no than he could for her to say yes, most of them logically rooted in resentment over her ordeal at Aphelion. And yet...

"I accept your offer."

Relief flooded through his nerves and he felt his shoulders slump slightly. A great weight had been taken from his back and, at least for a moment, his conscience felt just a little lighter for it.

He smiled. "Thank you, Victoria." He paused for a suitably dramatic moment. "Spatharios Victoria."

She rose again and crossed to where he was seated. This time, instead of terror, her presence exuded an inexplicable magnetism. He wondered if it was an inborn part of her, or if she learned from Pallasophia. Before he consciously decided to move, Tritogenes realized he was standing as well.

Victoria waited a moment, then extended a hand. Tritogenes stared at it for a moment, taken aback by yet another unexpected gesture. Hexarchs, or the social senior, always initiated little rituals like that. Yet here she was, almost certainly knowing that fact, and offering her hand to him instead.

He clasped his Titan's wrist, shaking firmly once as pride swelled in his breast. That feeling lasted exactly four seconds before his earpiece beeped an alert tone. From the sudden look of concern on Pallasophia's face, she got one too. That meant one of two things, either something happened at Limani or Aphelion, or some new piece of information directly relating to the mastigas just hit the high-priority channels.

As the data fed into his earpiece, Tritogenes tried to relay it, but found himself struck numb by the sudden, terrible news. He knew his mouth was open, but no sound came out and he was unable to close it again.

Thankfully, Pallasophia spoke up. In a clinical, detached tone, she summarized the important pieces. "The *Tartarus* has been destroyed and the mastigas ship is moving. We have nine months."

Chapter 8

The city of Molyvos was actually the remnant of two smaller towns that merged together when their steady, mutual sprawl finally blurred their borders too much. Even though those two towns had been gone in all but name for over two hundreds years, remnants still appeared here and there. Architectural styles meshed in strange and unexpected ways as what had once been fingers of the towns wove around one another. Streets on the old peripheries now went nowhere or wound back on themselves in multicolored loops.

Nowhere was that strange meshing of style more obvious than the aptly named Wisteria Road. To First Lord Rivka's left, the buildings of what had once been Galiantra rose in muted earth tones painted over with vibrant murals. To her right, the remnants of Psilolofos looked like even now they were trying to emulate the seaside cafes of a place like Katarrraktes.

Yet, as she looked overhead and breathed in the heady smell of the pale purple flowers that grew there, those differences were what made Molyvos what it was. Aside from this particular road, the two towns came together in bits and pieces, and in parts the distinction was so subtle that one had to uncover centuries-old documents to know to which of the two towns a particular building once belonged.

The vines and their flowers were one of her favorite parts about Molyvos as well. Other cities, like Tavros, clear cut the existing forests to make way for what they undoubtedly considered their modern city skyline. Others replanted trees or maintained small parks here and there to give some semblance of nature, but not here.

She took another deep breath. Molyvos was different. The thing that Galiantra and Psilolofos had in common was a shared love of nature, which perhaps explained why they merged into the sprawling city of Molyvos rather than maintaining their borders as the other cities in Odyssey's shadow had done.

As the cities grew, they simply built around the trees and things that were already there. Certainly, some had been cut down and measures taken to prevent their regrowth through basements or roadways, but as the city of Molyvos spread, the urban planners took every pain to preserve the arboreal landscape.

It had its drawbacks. Molyvos was hardly the cleanest place around. Leaves, fallen flower blooms, and the detritus of animal life were scattered here and there, lost in crevasses just deep enough that only the most thorough of cleanings would reach.

Wind rustled the wisteria overhead. The suns in the sky agreed with the clock on Rivka's holo. It was just after noon, but the purple flowers overhead grew so densely that it might have been early evening for all the light that reached the ground.

She looked over at Lelantos as they walked together down the center of the road. People parted to let them pass in deference of her rank, but only just far enough to let them through. Vacating the street would have been an affront, a sign that she was not welcome among the people living there. Instead, she was afforded just enough space so that no one could be accused of interfering with a Hexarch's business.

133

Rivka smiled to herself. Places like this made her security staff nervous. Hundreds, if not thousands at this point, of people came within arm's reach of her. Any one of them could have a weapon or something else equally dangerous.

She knew they were out there somewhere, probably placed here and there along the road and in other places through the city just in case she deviated from the day's plans. They blended in so perfectly with the regular citizenry of Molyvos that even Rivka could not pick them out of the crowd.

No, she thought with amusement, her staff would have to deal with it. Armed cordons and cleared streets were the stuff of tyrants and leaders who did not have the will and hearts of the people on their side. She also knew how naive that idea was by itself, which was why Rivka still maintained her security force.

Here and there, she also spotted faces she recognized. Even with her memory, she blanked on a great many names. Most of them were just people she had seen in passing or possibly interacted with once or twice in years past. They obviously recognized her, however, and so Rivka would nod or smile politely, sometimes even stopping for a few moments to make context-free small talk depending on what felt the most appropriate at the moment.

Halfway to their destination, Rivka finally saw a face in the crowd that she definitively could say she recognized. The other woman was a long-time associate of hers, and to see her here, now, on Prosgeiosi was either a huge coincidence or it meant someone, somewhere had an important piece of information for her.

The other woman presented as a Second Lord today, wearing a robe whose aquamarine designs blended into the press of people who all considered themselves vaguely important or at least on vaguely important business that day. Her eyes and Rivka's scanned past one another without a moment of contact or external recognition passing between them.

That meant she was here on business, and now Rivka's adrenaline finally dumped. As the other woman disappeared into the crowd, Rivka started scanning faces, looking for more people in the sea of eyes that she might have done business with in the past.

Lelantos, half a step closer to her than he was a moment before, cleared his throat. In a very quiet voice with the clipped rhythms of a minor chronodrug trip, he asked, "is everything alright?"

Rivka nodded, forcing everything back into its proper place again. Thoughts, pulse, adrenaline—all of it had to be tightly controlled. Her breathing never got very fast, at least not enough to alert her security team, she hoped. The last thing she needed, especially right in that exact moment, was armed guards infiltrating the crowd and making a scene.

Extraction, they would say. *Compromised assets,* she would argue.

"It's nothing," she replied.

Lelantos raised an eyebrow, but said nothing. Early on in their working relationship, he would have pried into an answer like that, but now he knew that Rivka would talk if she wanted to.

Privately, she was glad about that. Much like an invasion by her security forces, the last thing she wanted to discuss was why her adrenal glands were suddenly doing their best to convince her that every single person in the crowd around them was going to try to kill her in the next few moments.

She took another deep breath, calming herself and heading off the shakes and other unpleasant and uncontrollable side effects of such moments.

"I thought I saw someone I recognized," she said. Unless her old friend appeared again, that was all that particular conversation needed.

Lelantos laughed. "An ex of yours?"

"An ex? No, why would you think that?"

He laughed again. "Your heart rate spiked through the roof."

She eyed him for a suspicious moment. The feelings from a moment ago had only been assuaged, not completely dealt with. Even from

Lelantos, the apparent non sequitur was nearly enough to restart the raging storm of adrenaline in her veins.

Then Rivka saw the smile on his thin, pale face and Second Lord Lelantos's uncanny ability to calm her nerves finally took effect.

"You were counting my pulse on my neck weren't you?"

His grin widened for a moment, hanging there as his chronodrug-altered reflexes kept the expression on his face just a hair too long to appear completely natural.

Now it was Rivka's turn to laugh. "I should have known."

Several more minutes passed and the crowd thickened. This part of Wisteria Road was home to several cafes which sported large outdoor patios. The flowers overhead and the shade they provided allowed the restaurants here to seat people well away from the building's actual facade without it *feeling* like the customers were far away.

Because of the restaurants, more people tended to visit this part of the city, often coming up one of the side streets before making their way down the wisteria-covered path. That increase in numbers combined with the gradual narrowing of the street meant that the comfortable bubble around herself and Lelantos shrank considerably.

Rivka was fortunate, she supposed, that of all the things that did bother her, crowds were not one of them. In fact, from her days as Lady Whipcord, working as an information broker for Kipos's black market, being surrounded by a such a press of people was actually a comfort. Even in her Hexarch's purple, she felt like she could blend into the crowd for a few minutes and move along unnoticed.

Truthfully, she knew she could. People often only saw what they expected to see, and with everyone milling around like they were, the vast majority of the people she passed would never remember sharing a street with the Hexarch of Kipos.

In the midst of that press, her earpiece came to life. The conversation suddenly flooding across her attention was not directed at her per se, but passed between members of her security team. Ordinarily, a Hexarch

136

would have been oblivious to chatter from their security team, but Rivka personally programmed the protocols that her people used. Among others, one of the features she included was that any high-priority transmissions were automatically sent to her as as they were flagged.

"...probable threat at the Thalassakoi. Orders, Lochagos?"

"Take teams two and three and sweep the area."

"Understood."

Rivka, barely relaxed from seeing her old contact again, snapped to attention. At her side, Lelantos did as well. He was not patched into the security network and so, despite the hand closing on the grip of his pistol, he turned a questioning look her direction.

"What's going on?" he spoke with even more precision than before. The newest chronodrug dispenser was triggered by a muscle twitch in his neck and required no external interaction at all. If he was not on the maximum dose before, Rivka knew he was now.

"I don't know," she said, careful to turn her face toward him as she spoke. "A security alert just came through. More to the point..."

Rivka froze as that same familiar face reappeared from the crowd. "By the Ten Thousand!" she exclaimed, playing the part of an excited countryside fan. Rivka noted, however, that she was talking to her Titan, not to her. In a heavily accented character voice, she continued, "you're Lelantos, aren't you?"

Slowly he nodded. His eyes darted in every direction, the only muscular concession to the chronodrug he allowed at the moment. From the outside, to someone unfamiliar with the drug, he must have looked quite insane in that moment.

After a second, he replied in rushed, clipped syllables. "I am. Yes. Who are you?"

"Second Lord Josephine," she replied, still all smiles and excitement.

Meanwhile, Rivka was doing everything she could to keep her heart under control. It thundered in her chest, turning her sight into tunnel vision as her adrenaline tried to pull her every direction at once.

Thankful, for once, for the billowing sleeves on the robe she chose that morning, she balled her hands into white-knuckled fists where they could not be seen.

"Josephine" continued after a moment, sunshine and bubbles. "I'm from Kipos! I've been following the Project since it started. I had no idea you would be here today!"

Rivka's throat tightened. That was a lie. It had to be. There was no way a coincidence this big could happen, especially without her knowing about it. That she was on Prosgeiosi was no secret, but nothing on the black market channels she checked that morning mentioned anything special about her arrival. For this to happen right as two thirds of her security team were called away was, again, not a coincidence.

She swallowed hard. Something was *wrong*. Rivka started to reach out for Josephine, but arrested the movement before it was more than a twitch in her direction.

Trust, she told herself. She repeated that concept several more times.

Josephine, for her part, was still gushing over Lelantos. "Would it be too forward if I asked to take a holo with you?"

He shook his head. "It would not. I would be happy to do so. It's for you that we will be fighting, after all."

Josephine stepped between Rivka and Lelantos, wrapping one arm around his slender waist. The other manipulated the holographic controls connected to her camera.

Lelantos smiled, the camera clicked with an audible sound, and he frowned. That frown turned into a scowl a second later.

He had no time to warn Rivka what was about to happen. Instead, it simply *happened*.

First, Josephine collapsed downward, then sideways, coiling like a spring. She slammed into Rivka with her shoulder hard enough to knock the air out of the Hexarch's lungs. Josephine's arms were around her a moment later, wrapped tight.

They hit the ground together.

Second, Lelantos sank into a fighting stance. One hand floated in front of his body to ward off any attacking blows while the other drew his pistol. The part of Rivka's brain not completely subsumed by Josephine's sudden attack told her that Lelantos was pointing *away* from her. His drug-sharpened attention was aimed elsewhere, which meant he knew what Josephine was about to do.

A bullet thudded into the ground several meters from where Rivka had been standing. Had she still been there, it likely would have penetrated, and obliterated, her skull on its dirtward journey.

Josephine and Rivka rolled on the ground together as Lelantos let off a shot from his pistol. She knew he was aiming high, over the heads of the people around them. He would not have shot otherwise. Their attacker was far away, probably using a rifle.

The crowd screamed and parted, running. Most of them made for the shops and cafes nearby, but in that panic-stricken moment, no one knew which way to go.

Those thoughts flitted through her mind in an instant as her reflexes fought against Josephine. The other woman held her too securely to let Rivka do anything, however, and for the moment the Hexarch was at her mercy. Josephine wrapped even tighter as they flipped on the ground.

Lelantos fired again. He stood still, tall, inviting return fire to be directed at him rather than the innocent and terrified people around them.

Josephine came up on top of their bundle of limbs, sheltering Rivka from the feet of the people around them. A hole opened in the crowd as people finally realized who exactly was on the ground. Josephine took that moment to twist and heave, flipping Rivka first on top of her then away.

"Run!" she screamed. "Devils chase you, Rivka, run!"

A puff of dirt exploded between them, and Rivka got to her feet. She spared a look backward just long enough to see a spray of red blow upward from Josephine's chest. Her torso bucked, the ground underneath her already staining itself black.

Lelantos, face set in a hard mask, fired again.

Rivka called his name, or thought she did. The sound she told her mouth to make should have been his name, but it got caught somewhere between her brain and her lips.

Whatever sound she made, Lelantos turned his attention to his Hexarch finally. He lunged for her, roughly grabbing her hand and leading her on an unerring path through the crowd and into a nearby cafe.

People voiced their concern and fear inside the cafe, but for the moment, Rivka was too numb to do anything but meet their eyes and nod acknowledgment. She should have said platitudes, perhaps she did; she was not sure.

Lelantos continued leading her literally by the hand through the cafe and out the back. It emptied out into a courtyard with what would have been a beautiful cherry tree if she was capable of appreciating beauty in that moment.

The courtyard, open to the sky, was nearly devoid of people. Still, Lelantos continued wordlessly. He led her through the courtyard and to a nondescript door where he knocked three times.

Finally, Rivka's brain caught up with what they were doing and where they were. She recognized this courtyard and the door.

"Bergamot," replied Lelantos in answer to a question from the other side of the door. It opened a crack and he shouldered through. "Privacy!"

The room's previous two occupants stood up and left the room immediately, paying them no more attention than absolutely necessary to avoid a physical collision.

Lelantos and Rivka fell into a pair of the room's overstuffed chairs. Her world struggled to right itself as she tried to get her breath under control. Her voice squeaked in her throat when she tried to speak, but the urge to say something remained.

She tried to speak again, and again, and again, and again. Each time her throat closed up on her, and now her eyes started watering as adrenaline tore her nerves apart from the inside.

"Breathe," Lelantos said. His voice was firm, but it echoed in her head from somewhere far away. Still, it carried a tone of authority, and so she listened and obeyed.

Rivka inhaled. She exhaled. She inhaled and wiped her eyes. She exhaled and her chest shuddered.

"Breathe," Lelantos repeated.

That process took several minutes to complete, but when she could finally breathe with her entire chest again, Rivka sank back into the chair.

"They killed her, Lelantos. They killed Calliope." She felt tears welling in her eyes, real ones of grief and pain this time. "Why? Who are they? Who the *fuck* are they, Lelantos?"

"I don't know," he said. He spoke quietly, trying not to further agitate his Hexarch. "What I do know comes from a message she was able to pass along."

Rivka brightened, but that feeling of elation was quickly swept away by the flood of rage building in her chest. "A message? How? What did it say?"

"It flashed across her holo, too fast for a normal human eye to read or even see."

Rivka's eyes went wide. "She knew about the chronodrug."

Lelantos nodded. "That worries me as well. Such things were supposed to be secret until the banquet."

A nervous chuckle escaped her lips. "Calliope was always good at her job."

"That's her name? Not Josephine?"

"No, Josephine was just a code name. She probably thought she could get away before..." Rivka waved at the door they came through. "Before that *shit* happened. Calliope was her real name. I'm probably one of a half dozen who know that. Knew that. Damn it."

He took a deep breath. "Her message was fifteen words long and carefully crafted. She knew exactly how much time I would need to read it."

She put aside for the moment the troubling notion that someone outside of her closest staff knew about Lelantos's chronodrug. Her blood felt like it was back under her control again, working properly. Her heart still beat hard and fast, but it too was quickly coming back under control. "What did the message say?"

"Security compromised. Threat here. K.M. Bridge. Two for Rivka. Last meeting. Suspected. Ouroboros is coming."

Rivka took a deep breath and folded her hands on front of her, interlacing her fingers in a series of complex patterns that always helped her still her mind.

"They weren't out to kill civilians," she said.

Lelantos nodded. "Agreed. They had plenty of targets to choose from."

Rivka's stomach turned at that phrasing, but she said nothing. It was accurate enough, and they would have time for niceties when they were no longer trying to analyze the actions of someone who tried to kill her.

"And Calliope," Rivka paused. "You said in her message that she was suspected? By them?"

"It would be logical."

Rivka nodded. "She had to be playing double agent for these people and she," her breath hitched in her throat, "*died* getting me that warning."

"She died," Lelantos echoed, then, "saving your life. Without her interruption, those snipers would have killed you on the spot."

"And my security," she said, then repeated with more emphasis and anger, "my security was compromised! Do they know we're here?"

Lelantos shook his head. "No. I only came here because I happened to remember this place and read this morning's password over your shoulder."

Rivka laughed, dark and haunted. "You're sneaky, Lelantos."

"Yes. And today it saved your life."

"Thank you, my friend. Now what do we..."

Rivka never had a chance to finish her question, because a thunderous roar reverberated through the room. Deep and primal, she felt it in her bones more than heard it as an actual noise. If the room had been any less clean, dust would have fallen from the ceiling, but as it was, several things tumbled from previously safe shelves and hit the floor.

Rivka and Lelantos ran to the door. Having been in the closer chair, she made it there first. Rivka flung open the door, finally with enough presence of mind to draw the pistol hidden in her Hexarch's robes. When Lelantos joined her a moment later, he carried a rifle liberated from the somewhere in the hideout.

Sirens wailed, cutting through the air with their shrill cries. Worse, in the distance, black smoke billowed for the sky.

"Crashed Gods," Lelantos whispered.

"No," Rivka said. "I don't think they're here right now."

***

First Lord Aegesander carefully replaced the teacup on its saucer, staring momentarily at what remained in the bottom of the hand-painted vessel. Reading tea leaves, much like any superstition, cropped up now and then across the binary. No one of any credit believed such things were possible, but in that moment, Aegesander vehemently wished he could glean some sort in insight from the bits of plant matter in the bottom of his drink.

He took a deep breath, banishing those thoughts from his mind. He was a Hexarch, and they all made difficult decisions over the course of their careers. Now, standing on the verge of sending the Titans to deal with the mastigas problem once and for all, Aegesander felt like he was finally about to make the most important decision of his life.

Rather, he felt like he had already made that decision, and now all that remained was to see it through to the end.

He looked across the little table as the wind kicked up for a moment, bringing a whiff of sweet air from the wisteria growing overhead. It also momentarily disheveled Helena's hair. After the raid—because, he asked himself, what else was he supposed to call it?—on Eurybia's suite, Helena dyed her hair a glossy, sable black. Why she did that, she refused to say.

For the moment, Helena's hair covered most of her implants, reminding Aegesander of the young woman who first signed up for Project Titan. For the moment, a look of concern passed across her face. He had not seen such an expression coming from her in some time and, despite his confidence in her skills, Aegesander found himself wondering what exactly troubled her.

While they did not sit in the literal shadow of Molyvos's stadium, that was a factor of the time of day and orientation of the suns rather than distance. In the evening, this entire block was covered with dappled shadows, fractured light passing through marble arches. For the moment, however, the suns pointed the other direction, illuminating the great frescoes that covered the stadium's outer walls.

Aegesander inhaled deeply of the sweet, wisteria-laden air. He liked those frescoes; they had been gifts from Diomedes, granted before his untimely death five years prior and only recently completed.

He looked over the crowd. It was the usual sort of reasonably wealthy people who often crowded Wisteria Road. Second and Third Lords made up the majority of the crowd, but it was a fairly nice day and even lower-ranking Technocrats milled about around them. Aegesander even noticed a number of families, some with adolescent Sixth Lords and others with children too young to have a rank at all.

One of those families passed by and the child, a tiny thing in a gray robe-like garment, caught sight of something and made a break away from its parents. Boy or girl—he could not tell and for all practical purposes it did not matter—the child ran through a sudden break in the crowd toward the very patio where he and Helena sat.

It stopped a few meters away, close enough that it would have made his security team nervous had it been an adult or even an older child.

144

However, instead of doing anything remotely threatening or even disturbing, it simply stood there, eyes wide with wonder.

Aegesander smiled and gave a little wave of his hand, eliciting a cry of delight from the child. Up close, it could not have been more than two years old, probably even less, and Aegesander wondered if it even knew how to talk yet.

In a moment, he had an answer to that as the child's delight turned into a barely intelligible mangle that was probably his rank and name. When the parents arrived, two disheveled-looking female third lords, the child excitedly pointed toward Aegesander's table and said in a clear voice, "Hexarch!"

"We're very sorry, First Lord. She got away from us," one of the mothers explained.

Aegesander waved a hand in dismissal. "Don't worry about it. We were all children once. Go enjoy your day."

The second mother made a deep bow from her waist. "Thank you, First Lord. Come on, Amalthea. Would you like some fruit?"

"Apple!" the toddler exclaimed excitedly, chasing after her mothers.

"You seem ill at ease," Helena observed.

Aegesander's attention shifted immediately back to her. Helena had watched the exchange with the child with an interested detachment. In the few moments that his attention had been elsewhere, she tucked her hair behind her ears, revealing more of the gleaming silver implants that wrapped around her skull.

Aegesander laughed. "I was just about to say the same thing. Does your exposition match against Lelantos trouble you?"

Helena shook her head, then shrugged slightly. Both gestures were small, precise. "I admit to some apprehension, but I believe our skills will be fairly matched. If you will permit me, First Lord, I detect some other thing bothering you today."

"It's the mastigas," he confessed. There was no point in lying to Helena, no matter how much he wanted to. He learned that very early on.

The most he could do was keep things hidden from her, which was hard enough in itself that, that list contained a very few things that were all deeply personal.

She nodded. "The ship is moving. Astronomers on Dasos predict it will take nine months to arrive."

Aegesander frowned. "That's not how I hoped things would go."

"We should engage them in the outer reaches of the binary."

"I agree."

"The farther from inhabited worlds, the better."

"I agree," he said, aware he was repeating himself. None of it was anything he had not said himself, and he wondered where Helena was going with it.

Her face pinched into a tight frown as the muscles moved awkwardly around the bits of metal wrapped around her cheekbones and eyebrows. "We have yet to even meet as a team. No scenario I have examined gives us much chance of success without that crucial element."

He stiffened. "We have nine months."

Helena raised a hand slightly, cutting off anything else he was going to say with that simple gesture. It infuriated Aegesander that she had gained that much power over him, but she so rarely exercised it. "We have nine months until they reach Dasos, assuming that is where their course takes them. We must engage them before that happens."

He felt his face flush, darkening not with embarrassment, not that he would admit to, but with anger. "We cannot let what happened to Kipos happen to Dasos."

"We won't."

Her iron-clad resolve was infectious, but something still nagged at him. "How can you be so sure, Helena? You know as well as I do how important it is to plan things out thoroughly. This attack by the mastigas on our advance screen has thrown all of that into chaos."

"You are concerned."

He felt his face flush again for a moment, but wrapped a tight hold on his emotions. In private, he might have given vent to them, but not here in public like this. "I am," he paused, "concerned, yes. Have we done enough? Have *I* done enough?"

"The only way to insure we succeed, or at least to maximize such odds, is for the six of us to train together. I will speak to the astronomers and we will come up with a window, the latest possible date we can leave this planet and engage the mastigas ship safely."

Aegesander nodded. He had already begun such talks, but it could not hurt for Helena to do so as well. If anything, he thought, a second opinion was rarely a problem. "That's a good idea. You'll make a good team leader."

She fixed him with an intense stare. She smiled, but the expression was limited only to her lips. Her eyes remained impassive, impossible even for him to read. "Thank you, First Lord. Your faith in me will not go unrewarded."

He made himself smile in return. "Of course. Now, let's worry about more short-term issues, shall we?"

"Such as?"

"Such as," he echoed, then made a dramatic show of checking the time on his holo. "Where in the dark are Rivka and Lelantos?"

"Accessing the local networks, I can tell that Rivka is..."

He waved a dismissive hand. "Don't go that far. It takes some of the fun out of things. If I know why she's late, then I can't ask her about it when she arrives." Aegesander waited a moment, then laughed. "In the old days, Ophion and I wou—"

Helena shot upright in her chair. "A sniper is targeting Rivka."

Aegesander blanked. Targeting a Hexarch with a violent attack in public, in a crowded public place no less, was so unthinkable that for several long seconds his brain refused to even process that such a thing was possible. He even asked the question that, even in the moment, sounded silly. "Targeting? How?"

147

The first gunshot went off and the crowd screamed, a collective human wail of terror and anguish. The dull roar of foot traffic crescendoed into a sound so loud that the follow-up gunshots barely registered as noises at all.

Helena rose, drawing a small pistol that had been concealed in the folds of her robe. Even Aegesander had not known it was there, and he wondered if his security team knew. She held it aloft, barrel pointed at the sky, as she scanned the crowd.

"The shots were several blocks away. I can't see any of the shooters."

"Shooters," Aegesander echoed, emphasizing the plural. Now he was on his feet, pistol in hand as well. Unlike Helena, he leveled it, sweeping the crowd and ready to unleash deadly retribution on whoever dared to attack a Hexarch in broad daylight.

"First Lord, we must go." Helena said. Her voice was flat, completely devoid of intonation. Muscles twitched on her neck and the hand that did not hold the pistol slowly contracted and relaxed its fingers. In spite of all that, her voice rang out clear and with iron control.

He took a step toward the stadium, and Helena's hand closed around the collar of his robe. Rather than pull or push him along one of the expected directions of forward, backward, left, and right, Helena shifted and sank. As she pivoted, she dropped her pistol to the ground, the clatter lost amid the sounds of the crowd. With her second hand now free, she darted in closer and threw Aegesander roughly to the stone floor of the patio.

Helena landed next to him, rolled, and pulled one of the heavy metal tables over them both. She covered her ears and pressed her eyes into her knees, curling tight.

Aegesander opened his mouth to speak, but anything he might have said was lost as a cacophonous roar washed over them. The blast pushed the air from his lungs and Aegesander sat there, sheltering under a cafe table and gasping for air for several seconds as the sound of crashing stone replaced the sound of human voices.

The smell of fire and soot replaced the sweet sent of Wisteria on the wind as burning metal and stone filled the air.

His ears rang, but he at least had been able to cover his eyes. Through the smoke and haze of falling debris, he saw a pillar of black smoke rising from what had been the southwestern face of the stadium.

What replaced it was little more than a standing crater, a rapidly crumbling monument to destruction. For the moment, the rest of the stadium stood, but as more and more fell away from the blast site, Aegesander could not be sure how long that would remain true.

"Call," he started to order, but Helena cut him off.

Helena rose, covered in soot and with her hair and robes in uncharacteristic disarray. If she minded, it did not show on her face. "I was just in contact with Rivka. She and Lelantos are alive and moving to safety. Come, we must get back to Odyssey."

He coughed and spat a gob of phlegm tainted with brown dust. "Contact Eurybia. Have her meet me in four hours in my suite. Then once you have confirmation from her, contact the others. Schedule an emergency meeting for six hours from now."

Helena's eyes already looked distant, glazed with the same strange expression she got when accessing a computer network via her implants. Her voice was equally quiet and distant. "As you say, First Lord."

Chapter 9

The carpet in their shared suite did very little to dampen impacts. That thought crossed Victoria's mind once again as Pallasophia dropped her heavily onto the floor. Plentiful quick heal remedied any injuries and even the more severe bumps and bruises, but the experience, in the moment, was not exactly pleasant.

They used different rules for different matches. This one disallowed strikes, but allowed chokes. In fact, that was one of the only effective victory conditions aside from signaling surrender by tapping out.

Because of that, Pallasophia followed Victoria to the floor, moving quickly with the practiced grace of a planetary champion. Her head was exposed, but Victoria was not allowed to strike at that obvious weak point.

In matches where strikes *were* allowed, Pallasophia approached differently, guarding her head and face. Victoria found the Second Lord's adaptability damnably difficult to work around.

Pallasophia quickly moved from position to position, securing Victoria's right arm at the elbow before turning to place her entire body weight across Victoria's ribs. Whether intentional or by accident,

Victoria's own elbow ended up digging into her solar plexus, making breathing a difficult affair.

Victoria had plenty of time to perfect her ability to fight while dodging mastigas knives in the depths of Aphelion. She considered herself quite skilled at it, in fact, and the piles of dead mastigas lay in support of that assertion.

In fact, when they relaxed the rules, Victoria won nearly every match. Pallasophia proved to be, one-on-one, a very difficult opponent to overcome. As they placed more and more rules on their sparring matches, however, Victoria found herself winning less and less.

She bucked her hips, throwing Pallasophia aside. That, at least, was no different. Victoria outweighed her by a substantial margin—not that it mattered very much against the latter's skill—which made simple pins like the one Pallasophia was attempting much more difficult.

Fighting was one thing, she reasoned, but this was something entirely different. This was sport, a combative sport to be sure and one that shared many skills with actual combat, but it was still a sport.

More importantly, it was a sport Pallasophia was very, *very* good at.

Now, Victoria grunted with effort as she tried to keep Pallasophia's arms away from her throat. No matter how tightly she tucked her chin, the Second Lord routinely found the exact angle she needed to slip her arms into position and cut off Victoria's air supply.

Determined not to let that happen again, Victoria fought and pushed against Pallasophia's grip. One arm snaked around behind her head, pulling it up and off the floor, but that alone was not enough to choke. When Pallasophia went to place her other arm against Victoria's throat, the Titan relaxed for just a fraction of a second.

Pallasophia lurched forward, pushing against resistance that was no longer there, and Victoria seized her arm with both hands. One gripped her wrist and the other her elbow. Her position was not exactly the strongest, but between her strength and the leverage now at her disposal,

Victoria twisted Pallasophia's arm behind her back, eliciting a sharp cry of pain and surprise as her shoulder was torqued suddenly backwards.

Still, she did not give up. Pallasophia pivoted away, uncurling her arm out of the painful position Victoria put it in.

Victoria rose without releasing the other woman's arm, moved forward for a pin of her own, but Pallasophia seized her free hand by the wrist. She dropped backwards, planting her foot in Victoria's stomach in the same movement. Pallasophia hit the floor and Victoria went sailing through the air over her.

She crashed onto her back, air driven from her lungs, but she was not about to let something as trivial as the ability to breathe, or see without the world tilting sideways, get in her way.

Victoria rose, arms outstretched, but before she could react, Pallasophia was inside her guard. She wrapped both arms around Victoria's left shoulder, dropped to her knees, and cranked hard.

The Titan of Limani went down on one knee and Pallasophia fell on top of her, intensifying the shoulder lock. Now, Victoria found the size discrepancy between the two of them to be a disadvantage. She struggled for a moment, but Pallasophia planted her knee in the middle of Victoria's back, adding that pressure to the pain in her shoulder.

She kicked, just to make sure, and Pallasophia leaned into the shoulder lock even harder.

Several more seconds passed before Victoria finally admitted the obvious to herself and tapped twice on the carpet with her free hand.

Pallasophia immediately released all pressure and stood. Victoria rolled onto her back in time to see the Second Lord extend a hand to help her to her feet. She took it, coming to her feet in a fluid motion.

"You won. You make the drinks," Victoria said. The words came out in the midst of deep, panting breaths. Now that the match was over, the exertion caught up to her, and her lungs screamed for every molecule of oxygen she could provide.

Similarly winded, Pallasophia simply stood in the middle of the room for a moment, chest and stomach heaving with her body's hunger for oxygen. She waved acknowledgment of Victoria's request, then with the same hand wiped the sweat from her forehead.

Victoria picked up the pair of small towels from the back of a nearby chair. There was not enough room for a sparring area, even a small one, and enough furniture to make the place livable, and so for the moment everything had been pushed against the wall. After they cooled down, everything had to be put back where it was supposed to be, otherwise they would be climbing over the back of the couch to get to the tables.

She handed one of the towels to Pallasophia, who used it to wipe away the rest of the sweat from her face, arms, and legs. The skintight wrestling suits were a matte gray—or they had been before getting soaked with sweat—and left the skin below the elbows and knees and above the collarbone bare. The fabric kept tight compression on the body's large muscles and joints, ultimately making post-match recovery a much less painful affair.

They also, Victoria thought as her eyes drifted downward watching Pallasophia leave the room, provided ample support.

"I lasted longer that time," Victoria said, calling to the next room.

"You did," Pallasophia agreed. "Do you want to go another round?"

"Now?"

From the kitchen, she laughed. "No, definitely not now, but in general. Today, I mean."

"No, I think I'm good. I want to try and figure out how you got out of that hold before we go again. Why?"

"I'm trying to decide if I just want to mix up something with electrolytes and salts in it, or if I want to mix an actual drink while I'm in here."

That decision, at least, required no thought on Victoria's part. "The latter."

"Good, we agree."

"I'm going to throw this in the cleaner if we're done for the day," Victoria said, already peeling the fabric down off her shoulders and arms.

"Don't start it until I put mine in."

"I won't."

The cleaner sat in the wall separating her bedroom from Pallasophia's, and Victoria opened the cabinet-like door and tossed her singlet inside. She briefly considered putting something else on, but she still did not feel entirely comfortable in her robe, and her black combat suit was exactly that, designed for combat. Comfort had not been a priority in its design.

The couch at least, still faced more or less the right direction. After dragging one of the low tables away from the wall and placing it in front of the couch, Victoria dropped heavily onto the soft cushions there.

Pallasophia returned a minute later, carrying a plain tray that held four drinks. Two were identical and held a vibrant pink liquid that tasted like the idea of fruit. It also contained a variety of nutrients, including electrolytes and amino acids, that came in handy after a workout. As strange as the pink drink tasted, Victoria admitted it was still more palatable than a nutrient tablet.

The second pair of glasses were different. Victoria's came in a delicately stemmed glass that refracted light through the ruby-red liquid it held. Tritogenes told her what the drink was called, but Victoria could not call it to mind at the moment. He promised her her love of mixed drinks was not something he included in the Project plans, but it still gave the two of them something to talk about.

Pallasophia's glass was simpler, a squat tumbler containing a measure of vanilla-scented amber liquid. Brandy, she had explained one day, from First Lord Eurybia's vineyards on Kokkinos, although Pallasophia's preferred vintage actually came from vineyards overseen by First Lord Stephania some seventy years ago.

"I like to remind Tritogenes that I'm drinking something older than he is," she said over after-dinner drinks the day he made Victoria his Spatharios.

Pallasophia laughed and shook her head as she came into the room. "I should have known you wouldn't get dressed."

"It's more comfortable than my robe."

"Your robe won't soften up unless you wear it more often," Pallasophia said, setting the tray on the low table.

Victoria shrugged, taking the vibrantly-colored post-workout drink first. "It's fine for when I leave the suite, but otherwise..." She shrugged again and drained half the glass in a single go.

Pallasophia sat beside her and for several minutes, neither of them said anything as they drank. Finally, Pallasophia set the now-empty tall glass down and picked up her brandy. She swirled it around in the glass, taking several long moments to breathe deep of the sharp, vanilla scents. Victoria was not sure exactly how much of that actually improved the drink and how much was simply for show because it was simply "what you did" with a drink like that.

"You seem calmer," she observed.

"Than what?"

Pallasophia took a sip of her brandy before continuing. "I've caught you smiling during the last few matches."

"I've almost beaten you twice now under these new rules," Victoria said. She pointed at Pallasophia with the hand not holding her drink. "You, who, I might add, were Limani's champion wrestler."

"That was once," she countered, "and it was nearly fifteen years ago. There's more to it than that, though. Isn't there?"

"Is there?"

"Doctor Iro would say you're being unnecessarily defensive about it."

"I enjoy our time sparring," Victoria said. She frowned, took a sip of her drink, and said, "that's all."

Another few minutes of silence fell. "What I mean," Pallasophia ventured again, "is that you don't seem as angry."

Victoria bit back the start of a heated retort. That was exactly that sort of thing Pallasophia was talking about, and also the exact thing she had been trying to control. She might take her time in a combat situation, but interpersonal relations seemed to be a very different sort of encounter.

Here, her temper was much shorter, especially with certain subjects.

"Especially," Pallasophia continued, "about Tritogenes."

Certain subjects, Victoria reflected, like that.

She spoke carefully, easing the words out of her mouth so that they did not come with a growl or snap. "Tell me something, then."

Pallasophia's face darkened with apprehension for just a moment, but it passed. She smiled, bright and disarming. "Yes?"

"Why can't I stay mad at Tritogenes? I wanted to strangle him the entire way here, but once we met, he seemed so damned reasonable."

"I want to tell you it's because he's charismatic," she said, "but..."

Victoria's heart suddenly hammered in her chest. She was not sure exactly what emotion it was that gripped her right then. Some mixture of fear, anger, surprise, and feelings she had no name for swept over her, choking off the words in her throat before they could even form.

Pallasophia sat watching her, allowed her face an open show of concern. She said nothing, however, and instead slowly sat her glass back on the low table.

"God's between," she swore, having picked up the expression from Pallasophia. "You did."

She nodded. The movement was glacially slow and through it she never took her eyes away from Victoria's face. "It was Tritogenes's idea."

She growled. "I suspected as much. So I'm *programmed*," she practically spit the word, "to be nice to him?"

"No," Pallasophia replied. She spoke slowly, and Victoria knew her careful choice in words was to avoid hurting her feelings. "He. We. I. I made you to always see the best in people and their intentions."

The expression on her own face changed as Pallasophia cycled through pronouns. Anger slowly gave way to contemplation as the Second Lord spoke. She knew it was plain to see and made no attempt to conceal her feelings. In that moment, Victoria knew her own reactions proved how true Pallasophia's confession was.

Victoria sighed. "Tritogenes wanted more, didn't he?"

"He was afraid of you and he wanted you..." She stopped. "I don't want to say 'obedient,' because that's not quite right, but..."

"Tractable," Victoria supplied.

"Yes."

Victoria laughed, letting some venom into it. "The thing is, my immediate reaction to that is, 'oh, that makes sense.' I *want* to be angry about it, but it's too damn logical."

Silence hovered over them as Pallasophia reached for her glass, took a slow drink, and set it back down. "I doubt he would ever tell you this, but last year I stumbled across Tritogenes in his quarters, face in his hands, empty glass on his table. It was shortly after the death of... of the one we called Ninety-Four. You can imagine the state he was in."

"Doctor Iro told me the Project, quote, 'weighed heavily on his soul.'"

Pallasophia nodded. "I was about to leave him alone when he looked at me. Even as close as we'd worked, I'd never seen his face like it was in that moment. You know what he said to me?"

"What?"

"He asked me, 'is it worth it?'"

Victoria sat back against the couch cushion, sinking into the soft material. She rested the base of her stemmed glass on her thigh. "I'm here, talking to you now, so I can assume what your answer was."

Pallasophia nodded, visibly fighting the urge to look away.

Victoria had no desire to meet Pallasophia's eyes just then, but did so anyway. The surface was calm, collected, but deep beneath that, Victoria could see pain. She wondered if Pallasophia herself even knew it was visible.

Finally, she continued her story. "He stared at the carpet for a long time, silent. I was about to leave him alone, when he looked at me again. 'I pray that one day whoever walks out of that pit can forgive me.'"

She growled again, this time with what sounded like defeat. "It seems I don't have a choice."

"You've always got a choice."

"And if I walked away from it right now?" she demanded.

"A lot of people are counting on you, Victoria."

"I repeat. It seems I don't have a choice," she said. She let her voice reveal a little of her resignation. Inwardly, however, she knew the truth. If she walked away, a lot of people *would* likely die. The mastigas battleship was on its way, pointed at Dasos, and she had mere months to figure out how best to stand in its path.

Before Pallasophia could say anything, Victoria continued speaking. "None of us do, not now, not morally. You're as trapped in this as I am. If we just sit here, the mastigas will burn Dasos like they burned Kipos."

"'She has a destiny,' Tritogenes told me the other day. The others, as far as I know, were volunteers. Are you sure you want this?"

"No," Victoria admitted, finally pulling her eyes away from Pallasophia. She frowned, angry and the sentiment but *still* unable to be angry at the Hexarch who voiced it. "I want this, but I'm not sure if I *want* to want this. I want to fight, to protect people, but I don't know how much of that is me and how much is..."

"Me," Pallasophia supplied. She placed one hand gently on Victoria's shoulder, but said nothing else.

"I'll do it, you know."

Pallasophia took her hand back. "I never had any doubts."

"No," Victoria mused, "I suppose you wouldn't."

"I'm sorry."

"Don't be."

Confusion crossed her face, then Pallasophia asked simply, "why?"

"Tritogenes made me, programmed me to be who I am, perhaps, but the person I see in the mirror is me. Without everything you put in my head, I would not be the same person, and I can't feel any regret over a life I might have had. I can't fault your goals. The logic is sound—one life, ninety-nine deaths, to save millions. My life isn't yours or his to offer in trade, but you allowed me to see what the trade would be, and make that decision. I'll pay that price myself."

Pallasophia pulled away slightly. On anyone else, Victoria might have explained the expression on her face as fear, but on Pallasophia's face all she saw was a hardening around her eyes. "The others," she again spoke slowly and carefully. Her voice was quiet, almost reverent. "What do you remember?"

Assembling her reply took several tries. During that time, Pallasophia sat quietly, watching and waiting. Victoria was thankful for that. Images flashed across her mind as she spoke: blood, broken bones and torn flesh, the sound of poisoned bile on the floor, the panicked feeling of a dying body trying to put its intestines back into a torso that could no longer contain them.

"I remember them all dying, Pallasophia. That's not something anyone else can understand."

Pallasophia reached out a hand, hesitated, pulled back slightly, then touched Victoria's shoulder again. "I'm so sorry, Victoria. None of us knew how your mind would process the information."

"It's all very vivid still."

Victoria reached up to her shoulder and covered Pallasophia's hand with hers. For the moment, she still refused to actually look up and meet the Second Lord's eyes, but the physical contact was enough in that moment. The memories calmed, still there but no longer tinged with blood and death and pain so personal she could still feel it. She smiled. "Thank you."

"For?"

Victoria finally looked up. "You're the only person so far who doesn't treat me like I'm sort of of savior or warrior goddess. When I'm here, I'm just..." She sighed, letting out tension she had not even been aware she was carrying. She met Pallasophia's eyes and smiled. "Me. And..."

Pallasophia waited a moment, then gently said, "yes?"

"The memories aren't as bad when I'm here. Out there," she said, then gestured vaguely at the entire world. "Anything could remind me of a moment from Aphelion: a shadow, a noise. Here, it's quiet. I can relax. I suppose what I'm trying to say is that I appreciate your companionship."

A smile tugged at the corners of Pallasophia's mouth, then her face brightened into a true smile. Over the last few days, Victoria had grown to appreciate that expression. "I could say the same thing. To you, I'm not 'Project Director Pallasophia,' or 'Lochagos Pallasophia.' Like you said, I can just be myself for a little while."

Victoria, suddenly aware of Pallasophia's hand on her should, sank back into the couch. "Yeah."

"Come on, we..."

Pallasophia never completed that sentence, stopping as the floor beneath them shuddered. A heartbeat later, the sound reached them through the air, a great tearing and crashing noise.

Victoria sprang from the couch, somehow still holding her drink and not spilling it in the process, and jumped over the low table. Their suite had a balcony and she ran for it, looking outside and past the curve of Odyssey itself.

Nothing.

Victoria cursed and dashed back inside to find that Pallasophia already had the big holo on the wall active. It showed a stadium, or what was left of it, billowing black smoke.

She paused just long enough to read the caption at the bottom of the screen. "Molyvos," it said. By the time she processed that piece of information, Victoria was already in her bedroom and half into her black combat suit.

"I'm going out there."

"Not alone, you're not."

"What?"

***

They were halfway to the shuttle pad, and Victoria still had not accepted Pallasophia's assistance. She led the way, using her authority as Tritogenes's Spatharios to pass through the vast majority of the security doors. She avoided the public access areas, which sped the process considerably. The Hexarch's areas were nearly devoid of foot traffic, which made their running argument easier to maintain.

Now, only a few doors stood between the two of them and the open air of the shuttle pad. Despite the private corridors they took to get there, the landing pad was technically public, even though in practice only the Hexarchs and their staff used it. In a few minutes, their argument would be moot, at least because neither of them could hear well enough to continue it over the roar of emergency traffic they would doubtless encounter.

"Why do you need to do this alone?" It was not the first time she had asked that particular question.

Without missing a beat, Victoria swiped her palm across an access door's lock and passed through it. Pallasophia followed closed behind, slipping in before the door shut. She supposed that would give someone in the shuttle pad's security office a fit. By rights, she should at least have tapped the reader so that the system knew two of them were coming through, but that was last on her mind.

The hallway beyond branched off to either direction, but it was the door opposite them that was their goal. Now, Victoria had to stop, because the door to leave the Hexarch's area required a retinal scanner

161

just like the ones to enter the area. Allegedly, it was a security measure in the event something happened so that the perpetrator could more easily be caught. At the moment, Pallasophia was happy because it gave the two of them another moment to talk.

Victoria finally answered, but with a question of her own. "Why do you think I can't do it alone?"

"Because it doesn't matter if you can do it alone or not, Victoria. What matters is getting the job done, and if we both go the odds of that go up."

"We don't know what happened to that stadium. It's going to be dangerous out there."

Pallasophia bristled. She failed to see why Victoria was so insistent on this point. "That's why we need as many people on the scene as possible."

Victoria turned fully to face Pallasophia, folding her hands behind her back. She stood with her feet wide, imposing and dominating the space around her. Her visor was locked in place as it had been since she put the helmet on, but the subtle tilt to her head told Pallasophia something was on her mind. She imagined her jaw clenching and loosening, working its way around whatever words and ideas were there.

"Look," Victoria began. "It's dangerous out there. I'm Limani's Titan. It's my job to deal with it."

Pallasophia felt a spark of anger flare inside her. Victoria could not open the door outside until she raised her visor and she was not going to raise that visor until they finished their conversation. Her body language said as much.

Still, Pallasophia held her tongue. She still carried her helmet under her arm, and so her face was bare of everything except the day's makeup. Taking momentary advantage of that fact, she allowed her feelings to show on her face, relaxing the muscles there so that her anger and frustration showed through.

"You're a Spatharios," she said, leaving it at that.

162

Victoria's head tilted to the other side, more confusion. Her shoulders relaxed slightly, but her hands remained behind her back. Unlike before, whatever emotions sat behind that mask were effectively inscrutable now.

"What's your point?"

Pallasophia frowned. "If you want to lay things at the feet of a 'job,' then your job as Titan is to fight the mastigas. Your 'job' as Spatharios is to protect Tritogenes."

"You're seriously suggesting I *don't* go out there?"

"I'm not suggesting anything, Victoria. Damn it, I'm *saying* you're not going out there by yourself. Gods between, Victoria, I'm a Lochagos!"

A hand came forward, threatening, accusing. Victoria pointed a black-clad finger at Pallasophia, spearing the air with the gesture. "I don't want *you* putting yourself into that kind of danger."

Pallasophia stopped. That had not been what she was expecting to hear. Her expectation was that Victoria was being so stubborn because of her own sense of pride.

Thinking back on the things she said and did during the fighting in the labyrinth, Pallasophia supposed it made sense, but she had not expected that sense of protection to extend to her.

"I'm flattered," she said at last, "but as I said, I am a military officer. I'll be fine. Besides, do you know how to fly a shuttle?"

Victoria seemed to deflate. "No," she admitted. "I don't."

Pallasophia took that moment to shoulder past Victoria, saying, "good. We agree."

"Grudgingly."

Pallasophia leaned into the retinal scanner. Fortunately, the uncomfortable process only took a second and the door whisked into the wall. Pallasophia squinted against the sudden influx of light and dropped the helmet over her face. To her side, Victoria's visor darkened automatically, a feature they added after she realized exactly how bright the suns were from Prosgeiosi's surface.

When she stepped onto the shuttle pad, Pallasophia's ears were assaulted by absolutely nothing. The silence was disturbing as she and Victoria strode out under the cloudy sky. Off to the left, toward Molyvos, the only break in the sky was the pillar of black smoke she saw on the holo.

Pallasophia looked up. Not only was the landing pad completely still and quiet, nothing flew in the air above them. She keyed in a series of commands on her wrist holo, accessing the landing pad's control channels.

"We're in lockdown," she said, making the announcement as she read it.

Victoria scanned the shuttles assembled around them. Pallasophia wondered how much she taught herself about Technocrat ships in her downtime. Naval technology certainly had not been high on the list of knowledges she and Tritogenes provided.

The liner that brought them from Aphelion stood off to one side, hardly the largest of the ships available. Many around the same side congregated on that end of the pad, a natural evolution of their ship sitting there as long as it had. Beside them, several even larger ships sat. Some of them bore the scars and damage of work vehicles, but others seemed to be personal vehicles.

"That one," Victoria said, pointing. She indicated a sleek, silver craft with a flared engine at one end.

Pallasophia shook her head. "Even leaving aside that it's not our ship, that's a personal car. It's not designed for rapid deployment. We'd have to park and get out. No, what we need is something like..." She trailed off, examining the ships for the best options.

"That," Pallasophia said, finally pointing toward a small workhorse flier. She was three steps toward it before Victoria followed. A small business logo covered one side, claiming it as some sort of delivery vehicle. She hoped whatever it was there to deliver had already been unloaded.

"This?" Victoria asked.

"It will have an autopilot," Pallasophia said, "and that loading door in the side will let us, will let *you* jump out quickly."

Victoria nodded. "Lead the way," she said, then added, "Lochagos."

Pallasophia tapped on the side of the delivery vehicle, opening a dark blue holo. She first accessed the vehicle's owner record, leaving a quick note explaining who she was and why she was taking—commandeering, specifically—the vehicle. Second, she transferred a substantial sum of money just in case the Third Lord who owned the vehicle found it unrecoverable once they were finished.

Last, she threw Tritogenes's Hexarch authorization at the vehicle, unlocking it. Pallasophia gestured for Victoria to get in the back, adding a simple command. "If there's anything back there, try not to damage it."

Victoria nodded. Now that their argument had ended and things clarified, she seemed to have settled into a more martial mindset, ready to either follow or give orders. For the time being, she was following orders, but Pallasophia knew as soon as they hit the crisis area, Victoria would start giving orders and expecting them to be obeyed.

She was a fantastic commander, Pallasophia thought, and in a few minutes she would have a chance to truly prove that. She knew Victoria had not looked at the holo for more than a second to determine where the disaster happened. It was likely she missed seeing the other Titans already at work.

No matter, she thought. She would learn soon enough.

Victoria climbed into the back of the delivery flier. "It's empty!"

"Good. Find something to hold on to."

A moment passed, then another reply from the cargo ahead. "I'm good."

Pallasophia took the vehicle into the air, eliciting a shrieking alarm from the console. "Odyssey Control to permit holder B113. Air traffic is suspended. Land immediately."

Pallasophia considered ignoring the message, but it was likely that Odyssey control would remotely shut down their engine if she did so.

"Repeat," the control office's voice said, annoyance clear.

She tapped a holographic key. "This is Second Lord Lochagos Pallasophia of Limani, Underdirector of Project Titan. I'm taking this vehicle to the disaster site with Titan Victoria of Limani."

"On whose authorization?"

She frowned, cursing silently. If they bothered to check their system, the access authorization was already there, passed along to them automatically when she took control of the flier.

"First Lord Tritogenes, Hexarch Limani," she replied, patience already running thin. She had people to save, blue screen it. "If you shut down the engine on this flier, three things will happen.

"First," she said, "this vehicle will crash, and I'll make sure the owner knows why.

"Second, you'll delay us from getting to Molyvos, potentially putting more people in danger. Again, they'll know why.

"And third, you'll earn the personal enmity of First Lord Tritogenes."

A long moment of silence passed while she continued to push the flier into the air. Finally, the comm channel came to life again. "You have authorization to proceed."

A smile crept across her face and Pallasophia replied, "thank you, Odyssey control."

The channel cut off without a parting message, and Pallasophia chose to ignore the unstated insult.

Victoria poked her head into the driver's cabin. "Trouble?"

Pallasophia shrugged. "Nothing worth worrying about."

She nodded. "Good."

With no other air traffic to contend with, the flight to Molyvos took ten minutes. She deliberately padded the trip by a few minutes taking a slightly circular route. A straight shot would have only taken seven or eight minutes, maximum, but Pallasophia kept the burning stadium in her periphery instead of straight ahead.

It was easier that way.

With one hand, she scribbled a simple message to anyone on the ground explaining their identity and imploring the personnel on the ground not to accidentally shoot them down. She added a request for an open space for them to get out, then programmed the vehicle's autopilot to return to Odyssey.

A minute passed and the workers on the ground cleared an area a few meters on a side. Rubble littered the area around it, but since she did not have to actually land, that was of little concern. Pallasophia sighted the other Titans already on the ground and did her best to angle the ship toward them.

"Height?" Victoria called from the cargo area.

Pallasophia almost told her it should be obvious, but then remembered the back of the delivery vehicle had no windows. Victoria would have to come back into the cabin to see the outside, and she was not about to step away from the hatch until the moment came to step through it.

"Ten meters."

"Can you get us down to two?"

Pallasophia looked down at the rubble beneath them. "I can manage three and a half."

"It'll have to do."

"Air drop is not my specialty, Victoria."

Her laughter echoed in the metal cargo hold. "You're a Lochagos. You'll be fine."

"That's fair. I can roll."

Another laugh rolled out from the back of the vehicle. "Just tell me when to open the door."

"You can open the door now if you really want."

"Good. That will..."

Pallasophia turned around in her seat. Victoria stood facing the side door, helmet pressed against the metal. "It's alright, Victoria. If you need a moment..."

Victoria seized the door handles and flung it aside. "I'm fine," she snapped, then the tension left her shoulders. "Thank you."

"We're at three-point-three-nine meters. This is as good as it gets."

Victoria nodded. Pallasophia watched her breathing for a moment. Her ribs expanded once, twice, then a final time before her knees flexed and she jumped forward into the air.

Pallasophia chuckled to herself, setting the autopilot. Under her breath, she muttered, "face your fears indeed."

She programmed in forty-five seconds before the autopilot started rising again, which gave her about ten to stand in the doorway and take stock of things. She did, catching sight of Victoria on the ground coming out of a crouch. Several people faced her, some with raised weapons and some without.

She recognized some of the people below them by silhouette. Rivka, Helena, and Lelantos still wore their robes, making their identification easy. Aegesander was nowhere to be seen, or had faded into the crowd.

That was just as well, she thought. He was old and had no business being anywhere near this level of destruction.

The flier shifted around her, turning first. With no more time, Pallasophia stepped forward and pushed away from the doorframe. The descent through the air was an exhilarating few seconds, then she hit the dirt hard, tucking and rolling into a tight tumble.

As it happened, she came to her feet in front of First Lord Rivka. Lelantos, to her side, held his rifle at low ready, not quite pointed at Victoria.

She announced herself with a little bow. "Second Lord Pallasophia."

"First Lord Rivka," the Hexarch replied automatically, then added a nervous laugh. "But of course you already knew that."

"Orders, First Lord?"

"Get the civilians out first," she said. "Helena has been monitoring traffic. Follow her lead."

"And the snipers?"

Rivka blinked. "Snipers? That didn't make the public feed."

Pallasophia laughed. "Not the public feed, no. I checked some back channels on the way here."

Rivka nodded as a ghost of a smile flickered across her face. "Of course." A moment passed, and Rivka grinned. The expression was entrancing despite, or perhaps because of, the dirt and blood smeared across her face. "Resolutely go, Second Lord."

Pallasophia smiled. She knew who Rivka was, of course. Everyone in the binary knew the Hexarchs. Fewer people met with Lady Whipcord in that private garden on Kipos. Until that moment, she was not sure Rivka remembered, but "resolutely go" was a dead giveaway. No one but Lady Whipcord said that, just like no one outside of that garden gave the proper reply. "Stand Strong, First Lord."

Rivka smiled and turned away, back to work.

Pallasophia, too, snapped to attention. "Victoria!"

In an instant, she stood at Pallasophia's side. "Yes?"

"Take Lelantos, head into the stadium. Find every piece of information you can."

"With respect, Second Lord," Lelantos protested, "my weaponry is better suited out here."

She nodded. "Your weaponry, yes, but your talents at observation will be needed in there. Doubtless, whoever bombed the stadium and the snipers that attacked you were working together."

"Ouroboros," Lelantos growled.

"Do you have proof of that?"

169

"Helena does," he said. "Nothing physical we've yet uncovered points to a connection there. The snipers' bodies are gone."

"I didn't know, but I assumed that was the case."

Helena joined the conversation at that moment, gliding forward with eerie grace. "No one has been in or out of the damaged area of the stadium since the explosion."

Lelantos nodded, about to say something when Helena continued. "I have no other data on that location, Lelantos. Pallasophia is correct, your talents will be of more use in there than mine."

Pallasophia's eyed her as a cold feeling settled into her stomach. Tritogenes was right. She was unnerving. The world around them was noisy, smoke and fire, screams and yells, and Helena still managed to overhear a quiet conversation from six meters away.

She knew very little about Helena's skillset. Aegesander's security had been as good as, if not better than, Tritogenes's own security at Aphelion. Regardless, that could be addressed later. Right now, there was work to be done.

To one side, Rivka was speaking into a one-sided holo. Her face looked like she was shouting, but the ambient noise ate anything she was saying.

Pallasophia turned back to the Titans. The three of them, two Second Lords and an unranked Spatharios with no one in the senior position to start the greetings. After a moment, Victoria sketched a quick bow.

Of course Victoria took the social senior position, she thought, unsurprised.

"Spatharios Victoria."

"I know," Kipos's Titan replied with a smile, then, "Second Lord Lelantos."

Helena bowed first, then said, "Helena, Second Lord. If you will excuse me, Spatharios, there is still work to do."

Victoria nodded to her, then turned to Lelantos. "Are you ready?"

A muscle in Lelantos's neck twitched and his movements sharpened, becoming more precise. His eyes dilated, letting in more light. Even his voice quickened, syllables shortened to their absolute minimum.

"Yes, let's go," he said. "Into the smoke. If there's anything there, Spatharios, we will find it."

Chapter 10

Tritogenes watched the scene unfolding on his holos with distant horror. The media coverage was about five minutes slower than the direct message from First Lord Aegesander had been, but since the latter's exit from the scene, Tritogenes found the media feed to be the most reliable way of getting new information.

If it had not been his company providing the feed, he might have been angry about that particular issue, but as it was, he was not going to complain very loudly. With Rivka, the Titans, and Pallasophia all focusing on the crisis, he had few assets he could rely on. An actual damage control and information coordination team was on its way, but even using his authority as a Hexarch to bypass the grounding of all aircraft—for a second time, apparently—it was going to be the better part of thirty more minutes before they could get to the site.

So, instead, he fed the news crews valuable information on foot traffic patterns, safe areas, and anything else he could manage. He only began that process a few minutes ago, but already he was seeing some improvement.

In the chaos, each crew had only been able to report whatever was in front of them, but Tritogenes knew the area. True, it was not "his" area, but he spent enough time there and with Aegesander having been evacuated for his own safety, Tritogenes was the best chance they had for objective coordination.

Or so he hoped, mind racing with data from a dozen different feeds. How Rivka managed this much data at one time was beyond him, but with her on the scene in person, the job fell to him.

On one of the holos, the second row and third from the left to be exact, a news crew had either ventured dangerously close to the site or had a telephoto fixed on Rivka herself. Her face was hard, set into a mask of determination anger.

He stopped and zoomed in on Rivka's face. The sound on that feed, like the others, was muted, but the scrolling text at the bottom explained what was going on well enough. Rivka was directing the evacuation, shouting orders and directions at the steadily shrinking mass of survivors. He watched her for a moment, fascinated by the intensity of her movements, caught up in her swell of undisguised emotion in exactly the same way he would a character on stage.

No, he realized. Rivka was not "angry" and "determined," she was furious and resolute. He knew she had trouble with sudden danger and it seemed her rage gave her the energy to keep going, to give orders. The news about the snipers that went after her came in after the explosion and had been buried in that disaster, probably already forgotten by the majority of people.

He hoped it would stay that way. A terror attack like this was manageable. It had no target beyond "fear" and "destruction." No one felt like they might be next, provided they got out of the area. An assassination was different, and if people dwelled too long on the bullets that almost took a Hexarch from her people, they might start thinking they themselves would be next.

That—and Tritogenes frowned with annoyance and no small amount of fear—would spell chaos.

He returned the feed to its previous zoom level in time to see Rivka seize a Second Lord by the shoulders and roughly shove him in a direction perpendicular to the one he had been going. He wheeled on her, apparently registering the grab-and-shove but not her Hexarch's purple, and raised a hand to strike.

Rivka barked an order and two people melted out of the crowd. They bound the man's arms with expert skill before disappearing back into the press of people, carting her would-be assailant away.

She did not even stop to adjust her robe or dust it off, but went right back to giving orders.

Enyalios was wrong, Tritogenes realized. Rivka was not soft. Sure, she was kind and gentle on the surface, but this was not the demure Lord of Kipos the Council had grown accustomed to over the last five years.

His mind went to an old cliché: iron wrapped in velvet. It seemed appropriate here.

Then the last piece he needed clicked into place. Helena approached Rivka and leaned in close, whispering something directly into the First Lord's ear. Rivka straightened, then started gesturing in entirely different directions. Slowly, the crowd shifted, moving the way she indicated.

He realized ten minutes had passed. His relief forces were only twenty minutes away now, but that was immaterial if he did not act on this new piece of information.

Tritogenes pushed the panoply of news to the background, calling up a new window. He entered a transmission code, then a security code, and waited for it to connect. When he did, he wasted no time with introductions or niceties. He was the only person with access to this channel other than the one at the other end.

"Second Lord Nyx," he said, just to be sure.

"My Hexarch."

"Immediately when you arrive, coordinate with Second Lord Helena."

"Dasos's Titan, sir?"

"The same. Her implants are allowing her to interface with local surveillance systems, and she can see the area from above."

"She's probably patched into a mapping satellite, too."

Tritogenes nodded. That reaction was why he gave this relief mission to Nyx. Other people might have asked about Helena or her implants or how a human could directly access a high-security satellite using nothing but her machine-augmented brain, but not him. Nyx simply accepted things as Tritogenes presented them.

"Logical," the Hexarch agreed.

"Any other orders, sir?"

"First Lord Rivka is in charge of all ground-level operations. In absence of orders to the contrary, you will defer to her in all matters."

"Yes, sir."

"Go with the suns, Lochagos."

"Ten Thousand guide you through this, sir."

Tritogenes, to his credit he thought, waited until the transmission ended to scoff. He was going to need a lot more than the Ten Thousand if he was going to pull something good out of this disaster.

He tried to think laterally about the problem, which caused all sorts of new problems of its own. Objectively, he wanted Philip's help, but he stayed on Limani, and even though the two planets were fairly close at the moment, that was too much time lag between messages for even Philip's intellect to be of use.

That did not stop Tritogenes from keeping a file of notes and questions to send him later, but as far as live assistance went, Philip could offer none. Helena, on the other hand...

His mind raced only slightly faster than his hands as Tritogenes indexed Prosgeiosi's mapping satellites. Calling them up on a holographic globe, he immediately eliminated every single one on the wrong side of the planet. In the following moments, he worked his way inward, checking the focus area of each one until he found what he needed.

Had it been anyone else, he would have simply looked for a new location command in the satellite's recent history. Something told him Helena had not left something so mundane behind to mark her passage. Banishing the news feeds to the side in two columns of six, he expanded the satellite feed, zooming in on the chaos of Wisteria Road. Already, the area was largely evacuated. Helena, Rivka, and Pallasophia had been joined by a number of others, none of whom Tritogenes could recognize from the satellite feed. They might have been Rivka's people, or they might simply have been civilians Rivka felt she could entrust a measure of authority to.

"Hello."

The message flashed across the image itself. For a moment, Tritogenes thought Helena had somehow positioned giant letters in front of the satellite, but then he realized she was manipulating the camera feed. A quick glance at the news cameras told him her movement had slowed, becoming almost mechanical waves of her arms to direct people to safety.

"I know you're there."

Tritogenes had no way to reply, and so simply sat, waiting to see what Helena had to say.

"Remain connected."

The satellite feed vanished, and the globe along with it. A moment later, the holos from the news cameras flickered, but remained online. A moment later, the lights in his suite flickered as well.

A silhouette appeared on his desk, humanoid and about ten centimeters tall. In moments, it resolved itself from a shadow the color of midday sky to the exact person he expected to see.

"Tritogenes," the holo of Helena said. "Accessing the satellite was unnecessary if you simply wanted to speak."

He laughed. "You would think, but other than the news crews, who are using hardened cables to connect their equipment, I haven't been able to contact anyone down there."

Helena frowned. "We have had no trouble that I am aware of. In fact," she trailed off as the holo opened her own holo, tapped on the projection, and frowned deeper. "It would seem you are correct. Now that they are out of direct sight, I am unable to contact Victoria or Lelantos."

"That's concerning."

She shrugged. "I should have expected an EMP component to the bomb. I thought my difficulties in connecting to the satellite via nearby antennae were because the explosion damaged them, not because a magnetic pulse destroyed them outright."

"Were your implants damaged?"

She shook her head. "I have a headache, but my implants are shielded. I am fine."

"You seem distracted."

"This conversation makes a fourth thing currently occupying my attention. How may I help you?"

"Can you provide access to the satellite to one of the news crews?"

"It is technically illegal for me to access it."

Tritogenes shrugged, then laughed. "I'm a Hexarch. It's only illegal if I want it to be."

The holo nodded. "As you say. It will require a lot of bandwidth. Currently, I have access to seven different uplinks in order to maintain the connection."

"Give me a minute to figure out which crew has the best setup, and..."

Helena interrupted. "I have determined that already. If I combine the two largest cables, I can route the connection through them."

"Why didn't you do that already?"

"They were using them. It would have been rude. At present, I have access to the connections from three cafes, two bars, a jewelry shop, and..."

Now, it was his turn to interrupt. Tritogenes held up a hand. "I understand. I think."

Helena nodded.

"Instruct the news crews to assist in the evacuation. I've got a ship inbound in about ten minutes with equipment that should help clear the rubble."

"Excellent. It is most frustrating having to maneuver around the fallen stone."

A message alert appeared on the periphery of Tritogenes's holo display, pushing the news feed further to the side, but leaving Helena's projection alone.

"I have to go," he said. "Once you're connected to the hard line, you can contact me if you need anything."

"Of course," Helena replied. "Until later, First Lord."

Her holo vanished and the other windows automatically resized and repositioned themselves. Foremost were the globe with the satellite network, which Tritogenes no longer needed and immediately dismissed, and the high priority alert.

He tapped the alert, which revealed itself to be an audio-only message using Enyalios's encoding.

"First Lord," the message began. Tritogenes did not immediately recognize the voice, and it was only as he continued speaking that the First Lord realized it was Daniel. "I'm at the edge of the EMP zone. The field is *still* active. I saw your fliers on the way in. Instruct them to break off immediately." There was a pause, and then, "sir."

Tritogenes opened a communication channel, then froze for a moment. It was too convenient, he thought. For Daniel to arrive right before his forces only to find the EM field still active was a massive coincidence. In fact, his thoughts continued, for the field to still be active would require a constant source of power, which someone like Helena could triangulate with ease.

178

He wracked his brain to remember what, exactly the report said. The early details were sketchy, but it seemed clear enough that someone or thing called away Rivka's security with a false signal.

This had to be more of the same, he reasoned, but he still could not ignore the warning purporting to be from Enyalios's Titan.

He paged through video feeds from the area, trying to locate Daniel's armor. A minute into the process and he found it, exactly where the message indicated. It was unmoving, one arm and leg outstretched as though frozen mid-stride.

He frowned, pulse racing, and hit the key to open the communication channel.

"Nyx," he said as soon as the indicator turned blue. "I just got a report of a persistent EM field in the area. Slow your approach and investigate before landing."

"Understood, First Lord."

"Report back when you have something, but otherwise use your best judgment."

"As you say."

He cut the transmission as yet another priority message bearing Enyalios's encoding appeared in his queue. This one indicated an communication request, not a recorded message.

"First Lord," Daniel began. "The *Aegis II* just suffered a mechanical malfunction. I think airborne debris from the explosion got into the air vents and overheated parts of the mechanism. It will be upwards of an hour before I can scrub it all out. Orders, sir?"

Tritogenes frowned. "Is the EM field gone?"

"What EM field, sir?"

"I'll call you back."

He ended the call and punched in the code for Nyx's shuttle again. It sat unanswered for several heart-stopping seconds before the indicator changed color.

"Yes, First Lord?"

179

"Have you detected an EM field?"

"No, First Lord."

His frown turned into a scowl. "Proceed carefully."

"I always do," Nyx replied. "I... *Shit*."

"Nyx?"

"We're being targeted. I apologize, sir. Goodbye."

The conversation ended abruptly and as Tritogenes reached for the holo controls to contact Daniel again, yet another alert appeared.

Tritogenes cursed. Today was *not* going according to plan. All he wanted was to watch Helena and Lelantos compete, then possibly have dinner with Victoria and Pallasophia. Instead, he had to deal with a terrorist attack.

It took a moment, but he *did* castigate himself for that moment of selfishness, admitting in his own self-apology that the sudden stress of the last hour was quickly fraying his nerves.

This newest alert represented another recorded message, this time video. He hit the play key as soon as the hologram rendered itself, pushing the other windows aside.

A man who once had long hair and a full beard, but who now sported an uneven cut to both along with a severe burn to that side of his face, appeared on Tritogenes's screen. He wore a gray navy uniform with green stripes indicating his rank as a Third Lord. His face was bare of any makeup, though the smears of soot and grease could easily have been confused for some new fashion.

"First Lord Tritogenes," he began. "I hope this message reaches you. Ground control promised me they would pass it along."

From behind him, another voice growled, "get on with it!"

Tritogenes looked past the man, seeing the background for the first time. Unless he was mistaken, his messenger sat in the cramped confines of an escape pod.

"My name is Third Lord Mihalis," he continued, ignoring the complaints behind him. "I'm from Kipos, but my father was from Limani and died aboard the *Asphodel*."

"Hurry up, gods damn it!" another voice snapped.

Mihalis ignored it as well. "I enlisted after the mastigas attacked Kipos."

"The First Lord doesn't give a shit about that, Mihalis!"

"Would you three shut *up*?"

Tritogenes frowned. Those escape pods were only designed for two people, not four. No wonder everyone was grumpy.

Mihalis continued. "I was able to save the navigation data from the *Phlegethon*'s computer. First Lord, I think we can use it to plot their course even without..." He paused and swallowed hard. A deep breath, and he said, "without the *Tartarus*."

"So what do you need from me?" Tritogenes asked the recording.

As expected, that was the next piece of information the apparently tangent-prone Third Lord supplied. "The drive is badly damaged, and I'm no good with computers. First Lord, if you would meet with me, I can give it to you directly. I'm sure you've got people smarter than I am who can make use of it."

The message ended so abruptly that Tritogenes was afraid for a moment that something happened to the escape pod. Pulling up the orbital traffic told him that was not the case. A number of escape pods, each tagged with the ship they came from, huddled in a cluster outside the normal lanes. As he watched, orbital traffic was hurriedly rerouted to allow the pods passage through.

Tritogenes checked the ETA. Mihalis's pod was about an hour out, which gave him plenty of time to gather people who could make use of his data. He considered sending another wave of orders to his people at the stadium disaster site, but he left standing instructions that Rivka was in charge.

He made a face of distaste. Tritogenes hated micromanagement, and in a tragedy like this, all it would do is confuse and distract people. They had their orders.

***

Third Lord Mihalis had only ever seen Odyssey once before, and that was as a very young child traveling with his parents. That was nearly twenty years ago, and his memories of the place were fuzzy at best. For that, he was glad to be led around by an escort.

Of course he knew what Odyssey looked like, everyone did. Pictures were everywhere, and he could pull of a guided tour of nearly anywhere in the city on his holo. Unfortunately for Third Lord Mihalis, his holo, along with most of his personal possessions, had been destroyed when the *Phlegethon* went down. It would take him weeks at best to set up a new device—not a process he was necessarily looking forward to.

Tritogenes agreed to meet him in a public place. It was easier, he explained, to position his security teams for their protection than it would have been to add Mihalis to his access list for the Hexarch's areas.

Privately, Mihalis was glad of that. The escape pod had not exactly been the most pleasant or comfortable experience. Too many people occupied that little pod for too long, overloading the air recyclers and waste disposal system, to say nothing of the complete lack of bathing facilities. The overcrowded space quickly turned rank with so many people in it, and there was only so much a fresh change of clothes could do.

He frowned at that. Mihalis himself was not exactly what anyone would call fashionable, himself included in that list. He did as was expected of him, chronicling his achievements in stylized embroidery like everyone else, but most of those achievements were military in nature. Having forged his birth certificate to join the navy at a too-young age, he had little else to celebrate. Still, *some* things had gone well over the years and gotten put on display here and there.

Most of those things went onto his dress uniform, which was somewhere amid the wreckage of the *Phlegethon*, assuming it had not been reduced to atomic particles when the mastigas destroyed the ship. All he had now was a hastily bought Third Lord's robe from the customs shop right outside the Odyssey landing pad.

And now, he thought, he was going to meet First Lord Tritogenes, his Hexarch by choice. That he was going to do so in an unadorned robe still creased by the folds from the store shelves and stiff as paper was such an affront that even Mihalis in his current mental condition was bothered.

Still, he thought, at least it no longer smelled like the escape pod.

He did not ask for it, but Mihalis was more than relieved when Tritogenes proposed meeting in an open plaza outside a shopping center. The roof was high, especially for Odyssey's standards. Plants hung from the ceiling three meters above them, vines trailing pinkish-red tufts of blooms.

Mihalis shuddered. Those blooms were not the color of blood, not quite, but the sight of so much free-floating red made him uneasy. He considered asking his guards-slash-guides to take him elsewhere and if they would explain it to Tritogenes somehow, but decided against that. Lots of things in the binary were red, and if he was going to run from everything that shared a color with human blood, he would not get very far in life.

Still, he wove a meandering path through the flowers, not moving within arm's reach of any of them if he could avoid it.

Flowers are nice, he told himself.

Tritogenes sat alone at a table outside a sandwich shop. Filters hidden around the area pulled most scents from the air after a meter or so, and Mihalis could smell nothing. If it smelled anything like the slowly rotating skewer of meat in the window looked, it was going to smell very nice when he got closer.

Tritogenes was still young, very young by the standards of his fellow Hexarchs, but that was something Mihalis liked about him. He might have been forty years older than Mihalis himself, but he was twenty years younger than Rivka, the next youngest Hexarch. They shared that, he supposed.

He also looked distracted, monitoring something with quick jerks of his head on a single-sided holo. The back was a dark orange, featureless except for a subtle star pattern. He looked tired, Mihalis realized as they got closer, and tense. Like all the Hexarchs, Tritogenes usually excelled at hiding his emotions in public and putting on the impassive mask that was Technocrat custom for their leaders. At the moment, however, he looked as tired as Mihalis felt.

To Mihalis's right, one of the guards unobtrusively tapped his holo and a moment later Tritogenes looked up. He seemed confused, then that vanished as he stood and smiled.

Mihalis supposed the Hexarch's confusion was because he washed his face and quick heal was already mending the burned areas. He had to look different than he did on the message recorded yesterday.

Tritogenes waited for him to approach, then for his guards to step away and take their seats at nearby tables, before crossing the rest of the way and extending his hand.

Mihalis froze. This was *Tritogenes*, after all. He grew up hearing his father's stories about working for the man and for the better part of two decades that goal had been in the back of his own mind. Of course, Mihalis wanted to meet Tritogenes as part of an Elevation ceremony or because he did something great for the Technocracy, not like this.

Tritogenes raised his eyebrows a millimeter, breaking Mihalis out of his thoughts. He seemed to be asking if Mihalis was alright, a question which the Third Lord answered simply by moving again.

He took his Hexarch's hand, grasping him by the wrist as was customary. Another wave of shock passed over him when Tritogenes placed his other hand on Mihalis's. Shaking hands was normal enough,

184

but for someone like Tritogenes to greet him with both hands was an honor he never thought he would receive.

Mihalis was not so taken by surprise this time that he forgot to return the greeting.

Tritogenes smiled again, and the spell was broken. In that instant they were old friends greeting one another after a long absence. "I see you've availed yourself of Odyssey's finest fashions."

"I, ah, apologize, sir. It was all I could get on a short notice."

Tritogenes's smile turned mischievous. "Better than a shipboard uniform, though. Yes?"

"Yes, sir."

He waved to his table. "Come, sit."

"Yes, sir."

Tritogenes took his seat first, leaving Mihalis standing there in a tense moment of indecision. He finally moved when Tritogenes gestured to the seat a second time, now with an impatient raise of his eyebrows.

"Sir..." Mihalis began.

Tritogenes raised a hand, interrupting him with a gesture. He smiled again. "Call me Tritogenes. If that doesn't suit you, then First Lord is fine. I've had enough people calling me 'sir' today to last all week."

"The stadium explosion?"

He nodded. "So you do get some signal inside those pods."

"Some, si—First Lord, yes. Mostly we played a lot of holocards. Petroula tried to get people to play polychess with her, but after she beat everyone..." Mihalis laughed.

"It must have been tense."

Mihalis felt his face flush. "Yes. It was. We were all bridge crew, so being together was not bad. I heard..." He trailed off, unable to finish around the sudden tight lump in his throat.

"I heard about what happened in pod two-seventeen."

185

Mihalis wiped his face, not sure if the moisture there was from his eyes or not. "So few of us made it out that even one pod was..." Another pause, then, "terrible. It was terrible."

"You don't have to talk about it if you don't want to."

Mihalis nodded. "Thank you, si—First Lord. I'd really rather not." Tritogenes stayed silent, presumably waiting to see what Mihalis would say or do.

Contrary to what he just said, Mihalis felt his mouth open and the story start to pour out. He began with the alarm and ended when the mastigas ship targeted the *Phelgethon* directly.

"But your friend, Third Lord Aella. She survived as well?"

Mihalis nodded, feeling himself smile. He did not have a Hexarch's control over his expressions on the best of days, and right then he felt himself making those expressions and having those feelings without actually feeling any of them himself. "Yes. The mastigas breached the magazine, but it was one of the most well protected parts of the ship and held together long enough to get to the escape pod."

"The log says she was on pod four-nine, correct?"

Mihalis shook his head. "I don't know. I don't... She told me. We spoke for a few minutes once we were all away from the ship. None of us wanted to open a comm channel while the mastigas were still shooting."

Tritogenes nodded. "Smart. Give them nothing to lock onto."

He shook his head again. Despite the artificial sun overhead, Mihalis felt cold. "It wasn't that. None of us wanted to be the one talking to a friend when the other end of the conversation..."

"I understand."

"I just need some time, I think."

Tritogenes nodded, face impassive. "Take whatever time you need. For right now..."

Without thinking about who exactly he was talking to, Mihalis interrupted. "The nav data, yes."

If the interruption bothered the First Lord, he did not allow it to show on his face.

Mihalis reached into the pocket of his new robe, retrieving one of the only things there. The data disk was about the size of his palm, though most of that was the armored shell around it. When the *Phlegethon* started taking fire, he downloaded every piece of data he could to one of the ship's armored courier packages. Most of the gold and paint had been rubbed off during the trip from the binary's outer rim to Prosgeiosi, but some remained.

Tenderly, and very slowly, he extended it across the table.

Tritogenes took it with both hands and immediately placed it in an inner pocket of his own purple robe. He wasted no time examining the decorations on the outside or even any of the mundane aspects of the drive, such as the state of its connectors. Mihalis knew the First Lord had people who could recover the data even if the drive itself was damaged, so he had no reason to leave it out in the open for more than a moment.

"Does this have weapon data as well?"

"As much as we could get. There was a moment when the mastigas..." Again he stopped, taking a moment to work past the cold knot in his throat. "When they destroyed the *Tartarus*. Our sensors went dead and we have no data whatsoever."

Tritogenes's face fell for a moment, then brightened and opened again. "But you do have targeting data, weapon yield, that sort of thing?"

"I believe so. I really can't say. That wasn't my post, si—First. Lord."

"Of course."

"What I can tell you is that the last course that ship put itself on was aimed at Dasos."

Tritogenes nodded. "I'll make sure Aegesander gets a copy of the data."

"Thank you, First Lord."

"Now," Tritogenes said, rising to his feet. Mihalis did likewise automatically. Tritogenes continued, "I suppose you're ready to bathe and sleep, yes?"

Mihalis laughed, tension bursting out in that moment. "That would be nice, yes."

Tritogenes rounded the small table and clapped him on the shoulder. "Good, good. Go now, I'll contact you if I need anything further."

Mihalis's guards rose from their posts at the nearby tables, again taking up their posts beside him.

"Let's go, Third Lord. If you please."

He nodded, started to follow, then stopped and addressed the Hexarch again. "Thank you, Tritogenes. This, ah, this isn't how I wanted to meet you, but thank you."

"Go with the suns, Mihalis."

He felt his face flush and his throat tighten. *That*, coming from Tritogenes himself, almost made the last few days worthwhile. "Thank you. Gods bless you, Tritogenes."

"This way," one of the guards said, gesturing.

Mihalis nodded, following. They left the plaza behind, twisting and winding through Odyssey's hallways. For nearly thirty minutes they walked in silence while Mihalis took in his surroundings. The corridors and ceilings were narrow by the standards of most cities, but after years aboard the *Phlegethon*, even Odyssey felt spacious.

He was especially fascinated watching the mishmash of historic and modern elements as they moved through the halls. Some things were clearly one or the other, while some were clearly modern installations or additions designed to mimic the look of the older parts of the ship. Mihalis was not sure what to think of the decorating style inside the dome of Odyssey. He appreciated the emphasis on the preservation of history, but his textbooks said Odyssey used to be a ship, and Mihalis hardly thought the Navy was a good judge of what was and was not fashionable.

Another ten minutes passed, and his rather limited knowledge of Odyssey finally caught up with their current location. He assumed his guards were taking him to the residential section or, barring that, taking him out of the city to stay in a hostel nearby. He had been hoping Eantio, but would not be picky so long as the ceiling was higher than he could reach with his hands.

Where ever they were now, it was neither of those places. His guards had led him deeper into the city, far away from any sort of exit.

"Where are we?" he finally asked.

"Somewhere safe," was the only reply for a moment.

At his inquisitive stare, his second guard said, "we just have some questions for you, but wanted to let you meet with Tritogenes first."

Mihalis nodded, still feeling awash in events rather than in charge of anything. That particular feeling only abated in the few minutes he had to copy the ship's nav data. Otherwise, Mihalis had not felt any real sense of agency in days. Questions and protection were logical, he thought, and then thought no more about it.

They stopped before an unmarked door. One of his guards entered a code on the panel next to it and it hissed into the wall. They gestured him inside.

Finally, something in his brain registered a problem. "This isn't a military facility?"

"It's a secure facility, Third Lord. That's the important part," the first guard said.

Rather than reply, his second guard simply placed a hand on his shoulder and shoved. Mihalis tried to resist, but he was too tired. Days cramped in the escape pod with little sleep or food sapped his strength, and he stumbled into the room.

Behind him, the door hissed shut with his guards outside.

He turned around, examining the room in which he now found himself. Contrary to what he might have expected, it actually had decorations. The walls were painted a pleasant shade of brown that mimicked wood and several pieces of furniture and artificial plants decorated the space. Two doors sat in the back wall, and between them a desk.

Mihalis did not recognize the woman sitting there, smiling a welcoming and quite disarming smile at him. She wore the robe of a Second Lord decorated in a lifetime of glittering designs.

She rose, gestured to the seat in font of her desk, then sat again.

Mihalis did as instructed. He assumed that, whatever was happening, making a fuss would only cause more problems that it would fix. Besides, his guards might have been rough with him for a moment, but he *had* hesitated. No one had actively—or passively—threatened him.

He did, however, have questions. First among them, he asked, "who are you?" followed by, "where am I?"

"I'll answer the second first, because it's easier. The short version is that you're somewhere safe. News of what happened to your ship caused quite a stir and, well, we don't want it causing a panic."

"I wouldn't do that."

"Oh, I'm sure of that. But you can't be sure of what will happen when the news really gets out, can you?"

"I... suppose not."

"As for your other question, you can call me Tethys."

"Tethys?" he asked. Something in her tone told him that was not her real name. "Not Second Lord Tethys?"

She shrugged. "Titles mean less here than they do," she gestured upward, "up there."

"And where is here?"

Again, Tethys smiled. "Safe."

She rose and extended a hand. Mihalis took it automatically, letting her pull him to his feet. As they shook hands, his eye fell upon an intricate and quite beautiful design embroidered on her wrist.

In silver and gold, a serpent wrapped around her wrist, devouring its own tail.

190

Chapter 11

The hulking Aegis armor moved with surprising grace. Pallasophia had to admit to herself that Enyalios's creation performed better than she expected. Power armor was nothing new for the Technocrat military, but most existing suits were bulky and ponderous, little more than glorified tanks with too many weak points. The machi-machi, as Daniel referred to it, was an entirely different machine altogether.

As she watched, he stacked yet another multi-ton piece of rubble on one of the many growing piles around the area. There was little he could do to actually dispose of the debris, but having it all in a predetermined series of spots would make eventual cleanup that much easier. It also, and this was the part that kept Pallasophia's throat tied in knots, made it easier to uncover the bodies of those unfortunate enough to be near the stadium when the bomb went off.

Panatakis and Korakti arrived a few minutes after Daniel got his suit working again, kitted out and ready for combat, just like she and Victoria were. Pallasophia and Rivka quickly put them to work sifting through debris and helping the injured that remained unable to move on their own. That, at least, had gone well. Panatakis's implant-induced synesthesia helped locate a great many survivors, and Korakti's charisma kept them in surprisingly good spirits during the whole thing.

Thus far, the body count had been low. Perhaps a dozen dead and forty or fifty wounded. Those numbers were not exactly good, but they could have been much worse if the bomb makers planted their explosives anywhere else. They also used very high-power explosives, and the blast scattered many small pieces of rock around a wide area, rather than a few large pieces. Most of the injuries were no worse than they would have been if someone simply threw those stones at people.

The real danger came from the crowd itself in the first few minutes. Even with Rivka and Helena already on the scene, over a dozen people had been trampled to death with some hundred more injured in some form or fashion.

It made Pallasophia sick to her stomach, even going to far as to unnerve Helena. Rivka, on the other hand, was angry. Her every movement carried fire and strength. On any other day, or in any other situation, Pallasophia would have found that inner strength beautiful, but seeing it so close was something different. The Hexarchs at times talked about Rivka as though she were naive, but that was not true. This close, Pallasophia was almost frightened by her unwavering intensity.

Despite that power, Pallasophia needed to get Rivka somewhere safe. There had already been one attempt on her life that day, and she was not about to let a Hexarch get killed on her watch. More to the point, the crowds were all but gone, with nothing left but volunteer first responders, and even they were being replaced by actual relief troops.

For the moment, Rivka stood off to one side, splitting her attention between a mass of one-sided holos and the work going on.

"First Lord?"

"Yes, Second Lord? Sophia, was it?"

She nodded. "Pallasophia, First Lord."

"I apologize. There was little time for proper introductions earlier."

Pallasophia laughed as the lack of expression in Rivka's tone snapped a cord of tension that had wrapped itself around her thoughts. Yes, she thought, things had been somewhat hectic over the last hour. At least Tritogenes had the quickness of mind to adapt the local news crews to help coordinate things—they worked for him anyway, after all.

Rivka raised an eyebrow, but nothing else passed across her face. If she was tempted to refer to any previous meetings with Pallasophia—with Rosethorn, that was—Rivka's face betrayed nothing.

"Sorry, First Lord. It's just that this isn't how I expected the Titans' first public mission to go."

Rivka chuckled. "Yes. Lelantos and Helena were going to have an exposition match in the stadium, and..."

"I apologize, First Lord, but that was scheduled for today?"

She nodded, not bothered by the interruption. "Yes. What about it?"

"Who else knew?"

Rivka laughed. "Everyone, Second Lord. It was a public..."

"No, no. I'm sorry again, but that's not what I meant. Who else knew your itinerary? No one just *decides* to take shots at a Hexarch right when a bomb *just happens* to go off a few blocks away. Someone knew where you were going to be and when."

Rivka nodded. "My security teams are tracking down any possible leak now."

"Can you trust them?"

"Can I..." she trailed off for a moment. "I'll forgive the presumption, Second Lord, because you don't know my people, but yes. I trust them all with my life. In fact..."

Helena, who had been working on what she believed to be scraps from the bomb casing nearby, suddenly stood straight up. She took two steps then vaulted over the railing of the empty cafe's patio that separated her from Rivka and Pallasophia.

"Forgive the dramatic entrance," she said, "but I just finished analyzing recent communication traffic and I believe you should see this."

Rivka nodded. "Go ahead."

Helena initially opened a one-sided holo, showing the results only to the Hexarch, but a gesture from Rivka and Helena mirrored the information for Pallasophia to see as well. A series of spectrographs in the same four colors dominated the display. Numbers and labels accompanied them, noting frequency and a host of other information. Each graph showed a representation of a different chunk of comm traffic and various encoding signatures and transmitter markings.

Pallasophia was impatient, ready to ask her what the point of it was, but Rivka waited while Helena walked through not only the data, but her process of analysis as well. Data security and architecture was one of Pallasophia's strong suits, but her patience had been worn thin by the tense atmosphere at the feet of the still-smoking stadium.

Still, she listened. Helena had sifted through hours of messages, examining the metadata to determine where and how they had all been sent. At the end of it, she came up with three that did not match what they were supposed to be.

Helena overlaid two of the of the graphs, then eliminated the most obvious of the spectral lines.

"What are these," Rivka asked, "specifically. I see my own access code in there."

Helena separated the graphs again, and the primary lines reappeared. She indicated the first one with a gesture. "This one is a message sent to First Lord Tritogenes while his relief ship was on the way, it claimed to originate from Second Lord Daniel's suit. The second is the message you received shortly before the first sniper shot Second Lord Josephine."

Rivka's face darkened, but she nodded appreciation.

Helena took that as her cue to continue, and said, "they shared a carrier wave modulation pattern."

"Which means?"

Pallasophia spoke up now. If she was going to stand there, she reasoned she had to contribute to the conversation somehow. "It means they came from the same place, using the same equipment."

"Yes," Helena said. "But when they were broadcast, the origin signal was hidden."

Pallasophia leaned closer to the holo. "Not just masked, but changed. These transmissions weren't just bounced from place to place, they were actually downloaded and rebroadcast."

"Yes."

"Can you trace them?" Rivka asked. No, Pallasophia realized, she *demanded*. The fire was still there, but it had cooled somewhat, and Pallasophia realized that her impression earlier had been wrong. Rivka was not frightening solely because her spirit was capable of such ferocity, rather because she could summon and direct it at will.

"I have already begun the process, but there are two complications. First, it has proven difficult to follow the signal exactly, as there appears to be a feedback mechanism in place. I regret that several network hubs have been destroyed already."

"That explains why half of the news crews stopped relaying information," Rivka mused.

"And the other thing?" Pallasophia asked.

"There was a third signal, one I was only able to detect for a fraction of a second. The carrier wave data is incomplete, but the signal itself was simple and easy to decode."

"How simple?"

"It was a single packet of data, an activation signal."

Rivka paled. "For the bomb."

"I detected it mere seconds before detonation."

Now, finally, Rivka cracked a smile. "Aegesander said you tackled him and threw him under a table."

Helena's face did not register surprise or anything else. "The tables at that cafe were topped with particularly strong stone. Braced as we were, it would have taken a significant..."

Pallasophia held up a hand. Helena, according to her file, had been a computer technician before the Project, and Pallasophia knew enough of those sort of people to know she would continue talking for as long as she could once she started down a technical path. "But can you trace it?"

"As I said, I have already begun the process. The feedback prevents a direct contact, but in what First Lord Aegesander would call an ironic twist of fate, their own security protocols have provided the means to track them. Put simply, they bounced the signal too many times, creating a dead zone that will narrow the search immensely."

Rivka nodded. "Good, good. Second Lord Helena, call the other Titans. I want the six of you to find the origin of that signal as quickly as possible and eliminate it."

Helena nodded. "Understood." She stepped away, placing a hand on her ear to signify to the other two that she was using her comm. The gesture did nothing for her; Helena's comms were all internal, part of her implants, and fed directly into her aural nerve.

It was more comforting to see, Pallasophia thought, than watching her stare into space or be doing something else entirely while having a complete conversation in silence.

She turned to Rivka. "First Lord, you need to get to safety."

"What I need, Second Lord, is to find out who did this."

Pallasophia nodded. "You've set the Titans on the task. Gods between, you kept six strong personalities from bickering and jockeying for position. Everyone here is safe, and Tritogenes's people will help the last of the injured. Please, let me take you back to Odyssey."

Rivka's eyes flicked to the side, a gesture that almost looked like reflex. The only reason Pallasophia knew it was not reflex was that she followed it to the bombed-out section of the stadium where Victoria and Lelantos were still working. Now, they headed up an entire crew of

196

people, all sifting through the wreckage for bodies or clues about the bombmakers.

"They'll be alright," Pallasophia heard herself say. "You can trust Victoria."

Rivka inhaled sharply. "Lelantos," she began, then stopped. "He's a good man. I've known him for years now, and the Project has changed him. Oh, he's still the same person inside, but so much is different now. I wonder if he even realizes it some days.

"What was Victoria like before the Project?"

Pallasophia hesitated. Despite the declassification of a lot of Project Titan's assets and processes, no one knew exactly where Victoria came from. In a way, though, that made it easier because she did not have to lie to Rivka. Pallasophia shook her head. "I don't know. I didn't know her then."

Rivka put a hand on Pallasophia's shoulder. "Lelantos will take care of her. Come on, let's get you to safety. I know a nice garden not far from here."

Pallasophia smiled, wondering when the conversation became about getting *her* to safety and not Rivka. Despite that, she said, "I think I've been there."

***

The Titans were able to officially hand off responsibility for the disaster area to the regular forces once relief elements from Aegesander and Enyalios arrived to supplement Tritogenes's troops. Rivka's own people were out in the area around Molyvos, tending directly to the evacuees, searching for any other threats, and staying out of sight as much as they possibly could.

A coordinated effort from Helena, Panatakis, and Daniel's Aegis suit set up an aerial search grid for Hyperion's ships. Fortunately, the quick decision to ground all air traffic seemed to have paid off. If the terrorists left the area, they had to do so on foot, and Eurybia's troops partnered with Rivka's agents to patrol the pedestrian access areas.

Now, it seemed like Helena herself finally found the location of their base.

A holographic representation of Odyssey, cut-away to show the internal structure of the ship-turned-city, hovered a few centimeters above the ground. The image was being fed by all six of the Titan's holos, allowing any one of them to manipulate it.

The Titans, with the exception of Daniel, were seated on the ground around the meter-tall hologram. He lounged slightly higher, resting in a chair made from the Aegis's crossed arms, taking advantage of the suit's inflatable crash cushion. As usual, Panatakis and Helena sat together, with Victoria and then Lelantos seated next in the circle. Korakti stretched out along the ground on her stomach, chin propped in her hands.

"Regrettably," Helena said, "the satellite I was using to triangulate the last transmission proxy was destroyed by Ouroboros countermeasures."

"So it's definitely Ouroboros?" Korakti asked.

Panatakis nodded. "Yes. They accosted First Lord Eurybia already."

"And Rivka received a warning about their potential danger moments before the shooting began," Lelantos added.

"Now, when you say 'destroyed...'" Korakti began.

Helena interrupted, momentarily replacing the holo of Odyssey with that of a what appeared to be a standard communication satellite. Victoria squinted, trying to see what was out of the ordinary about it, but she knew nothing about the design or function of satellites like that. A moment passed and electricity arced from some component near what Victoria assumed must be an antenna. Another few seconds passed before a series of rippling explosions tore the satellite apart, raining flaming holographic debris on the ground in the center of their circle.

"That was not an accident," Daniel said, shifting position in the couch he made from the Aegis's arms.

198

"No," Helena agreed. "None of the other satellites reacted that way either. Fortunately, the debris will rain harmlessly down somewhere in the Mesithalassic Ocean."

"So it's a dead-end, then?" Korakti asked.

Helena shook her head and gestured, and the freeze-frame of debris vanished, replaced by the same projection of Odyssey from before. She gestured again and an antenna on the roof of the massive dome started glowing yellow.

"The detonation signal came from there."

"Wait a minute," Daniel said, urgency in his voice. He sat up, summoning a miniature version of the same projection on the ground. As he manipulated his, the larger one turned and adjusted to match. Pieces of the city's outer layers fell away as Daniel literally picked the diagram apart.

After removing much of the visual obstruction, he traced out the conduits from the antenna as they ran through the city. The one Helena highlighted passed through the residential area, the Hexarch's quarter specifically, intersecting a series of corridors that Victoria did not recognize.

Several conduits ran to the antenna, and Daniel highlighted them in different colors. Red for power, blue for incoming signals, and the same yellow Helena used for outgoing signals. Power was straightforward enough, and the blue line ran to the city's central data hub, neither of which were useful pieces of information.

Victoria hoped the yellow lines would give them a better place to look, but Daniel seemed to have no such luck. The network branched out like roots, connecting potentially hundreds of different places through the Hexarch's quarter.

"What are you looking for?" Helena asked. "Perhaps I or another have already searched for something similar."

"I don't know yet."

Korakti grunted in annoyance. "I can help you look if you tell us what you're looking for, Daniel."

He sighed. "This is Enyalios's area. If the signal came from here, it means one of my compatriots is working for this Ouroboros group."

Victoria frowned at the diagram. Something there was wrong, but she could not place her finger on what it might be. Odyssey had a chaotic history, she knew that, but the current core systems were nearly identical to the ones that operated when the city had been a ship, and *those* had been designed and built with very specific things in mind.

One of those things, she knew, was redundancy.

"If I may," she said, not waiting on Daniel's say-so before taking control of the holo with her own miniature interface.

"Go ahead," he replied, "apparently."

Korakti laughed.

A variety of antennae fed signals into and out of Odyssey. Most were located on the upper surfaces of the dome, but not all. For a moment, Victoria highlighted all of them, which turned out to be seventy-two. She was very glad the computer could automate that particular task.

"Now," she said. She addressed Helena by tone and eye contact, but the comments were meant for everyone else. "Helena established a time window for us, so let's start by eliminating every array that did not send out a signal inside of that timeframe.

Helena nodded, and sixty-three of lines vanished in an instant. The remaining nine still produced a tangled network that would take hours or days to parse without further information to narrow the search.

"Hey," Korakti said. She pushed herself up off the ground and swung her feet around, narrowly missing Lelantos in the process. The end result was surprisingly graceful if Victoria ignored the near-miss between her boots and Lelantos's head. Sitting up now, she finally activated her own holo.

"Yes?" Helena asked.

Korakti ignored her question, navigating the menus herself. Despite that, she narrated her thought process, muttering under her breath the entire time. "Detonation signal's not complicated, can't rely on that." Pause, another command entered into her holo. "Spoofing a distress sig—no, still small. Probably used text. Hey, Limani!"

It took Victoria several seconds to realize Helena was addressing her, and confusion gave way to a flash of anger as she wondered if Korakti actually knew her name, or was just calling her by her alleged planet of origin to needle her.

Either answer produced the same reaction: annoyance.

Still, she had work to do. Victoria asked herself what Pallasophia would do in the situation, quickly coming to the conclusion that the Second Lord would shrug it off unless it impacted mission performance, and then have a long conversation with Korakti in private later on. Hiding her annoyance would have been much easier if she never took her helmet off.

So, Victoria did her best to smile. "Yes?"

"You said the message your Hexarch got was a complete fake, right?"

"The one that was supposed to be from me?" Daniel asked.

Korakti nodded. "Yeah."

"I only heard about it second hand from Pallasophia, but yes. Apparently everything was faked from Daniel's access codes to his voice."

"Worse," Daniel said, "they relied on the fact that the machi-machi *was* stopped right at that moment. Someone was watching me, probably watching all of us. And," he continued, "it continues to get worse. I thought the suit shut down because it overheated because debris got into the air intake."

"A directed EMP took his systems offline even as the warning about an area-wide EMP was sent to First Lord Tritogenes," Helena supplied.

Daniel grimaced. "Fortunately, the Aegis II's systems are hardened *and* redundant. I was only down for about two minutes."

Victoria frowned. "Sounds like Ouroboros didn't count on the upgrades."

"Which means their intel is accurate," Daniel said, "but potentially old."

Korakti's face brightened. "We can use that. We cycle codes and things *now* and we lock out everything that doesn't match."

"Agreed," Helena said. "Give me some time, and I will handle it."

"Good call, Dasos," Korakti said. She shifted again, turning her attention back to the holo. She frowned. "They fabricated a whole-ass message, voice and security and everything. Packet like that's going to be big. It'll leave a trace. Where..."

"Here," Panatakis said. A section of the city illuminated, and the rest fell away, fading at the edges as the holo zoomed closer. Two major branches of the communication system converged momentarily. "These trunks converge in the same spot, and..."

"Both were active at the exact same time," Korakti added.

"Do we inform city security?" Panatakis asked.

"Better," Lelantos said, "do we go ourselves?"

"I will contact Odyssey security and inform them of our discovery," Helena announced. "It should take no more than twenty-one-point-oh-three seconds."

"No," Daniel replied.

"What?" Korakti demanded. "Look, I know just because it's your Hexarch's area that you feel like you've got a personal stake in things, but we need to start somewhere."

"Explain, please," Helena ordered. Victoria found her voice sounded much more like that of a commander than Korakti's did. She was firm, but curious. Daniel's wide-eyed expression of alarm would have given Victoria pause as well.

"That's not a random point inside Enyalios's residential area," he explained, "that *is* Enyalios's quarters."

"Bull*shit*," Korakti cursed. "There's no way a Hexarch is behind this."

"The timing and location of the sniper attacks would point to someone with significant inside information," Lelantos said. His face was set into a hard mask, difficult to read as anything other than simmering anger.

"We can't search Enyalios's quarters," Daniel protested.

"We *can*," Lelantos said. His voice sounded just short of an outright growl. "And we *will*."

"But..."

"But, nothing, Daniel. We are *Titans*. And if that's not enough for you, these *people* tried to kill Rivka."

"They tried to kill you, too," Victoria added.

His glare softened for perhaps half a second. "They tried to kill my friend, Victoria. How would you feel if they shot at Pallasophia?"

Despite her attempts to control it, Victoria felt rage boil up inside her. A surge of anger washed over her unlike anything she felt since watching Pallasophia's squad being killed by mastigas deep in Aphelion's belly. Her nerves blazed and her blood froze in the same instant.

Victoria had no idea what her face looked like at the moment, but her voice was expressionless. "I would kill them all."

"Calm down," Korakti said, addressing both of them.

"I agree," Helena said. "It may well be that Enyalios or someone working for him is behind this, but we will not move against a Hexarch without undeniable evidence of his crimes. We cannot."

"So what else do we have?"

"At this moment?" Helena asked. "We have nothing else."

Lelantos growled. "Then we search everything near that juncture."

"Wait!" Daniel snapped, harsh enough that the other five of them took notice immediately and looked his way. "Just give me a second. There's something else here. Two size three trunks merge, making them effectively a size two, right?"

Helena raised a hand. "It's more complicated than that and the ability of the cables to carry data is not quite a geometric scale. In fact..."

"But it's close enough, right?"

Helena stopped herself, then nodded. "Yes."

"Let the man speak," Korakti added.

"Then why," Daniel continued once the others quieted down again, "are the only things that emerge from that spot a single size three and one size four?"

Korakti laughed, slapping one knee. "Are you telling us there's a secret cable in there?"

Lelantos stood. His fingers twitched. His voice sounded strange, clipped in the same short way it had been when he and Victoria went into the ruined part of the stadium. "He's grasping at hairs trying throw us off the trail."

Daniel blanched. "Are you seriously trying to say that I..."

Helena rose to her feet as well, cleared her throat. "Both of you, stand down."

"Yeah," Korakti said, "cut the shit."

Victoria came to her feet as well. She still felt the fury Lelantos's suggestion elicited in her, but now that anger had a focus. Daniel was right, she reasoned, and at the very least they needed as much information as they could get before they made any decision.

"Helena," she said, "is there a way to check for comm lines that don't show up on the main diagrams?"

She closed her eyelids, but Victoria could see her eyes frantically tracking something nonetheless. "Give me a m—yes. Two years ago, a communication line was decommissioned from that very junction box by First Lord Enyalios."

"I knew it," Lelantos said, balling his hands into fists. Victoria wondered how much that gesture was for show and how much was to prevent him from reaching for the pistol hung from his belt.

Helena's eyes were still closed as she spoke, eyes still frantically moving. "According to this, the First Lord's reason for disabling the comm line was that it did not work, and when it did, it, quote, 'had poor signal, prone to distortion and data loss.'"

As suddenly as his anger came before, Lelantos's fury dissipated. "Helena, show us a map from before that date, please."

She opened her eyes, blue crystal momentarily awash in strange emotions. The holo in the center of the group shifted. A few lines appeared or disappeared, most of them small. The change they were all now looking for was there, however. The missing communication line from Enyalios's junction box appeared, branching and twisting all the way to the depths of the city.

Helena highlighted an area. Most of the branches had been small, leaving the final cable still easily within what Victoria assumed would be a size five.

"And that's big enough to transmit enough data to fool Tritogenes's system?" she asked.

Helena nodded. "It's easily twice the size required. None of the other branches retain the bandwidth at their termination points, however."

"Got ya!" Korakti said, already celebrating.

"We go here first," Victoria said.

Helena nodded. "Agreed."

Panatakis and Korakti rose, the last to do so. Daniel stepped down from the impromptu cushion he created with the Aegis's arms, remaining near the suit as the crash bags deflated so that he could re-enter its armored confines.

Lelantos approached the Aegis, moving at the edge of Victoria's vision. She turned just far enough to keep both of them in sight, but made a show of looking over the damage to the stadium instead.

"Daniel."

"What?"

"For what it's worth, I'm sorry I accused First Lord Enyalios of being complicit in this. I am..." he sighed. "It has been a long day."

Victoria could not quite make out his expression, but Daniel's voice had an edge to it. "Don't mention it," he said. "Ever again."

***

Victoria had no idea what the door was when the city had been a starship, but the current generation of Technocrats used it as a loading dock. The lowest levels of the dome, buried deep within its still-armored shell, still played host to the massive former ship's internal machinery. Reactors, factories, and other assorted industrial facilities filled the lowest levels.

That close to the base, the dome might as well have been a wall. The curve was so subtle there that Victoria had to crane her neck upward at a sharp angle to even get a hint of the shape of the city. Even next to the dome's vast bulk and with layers of bridges and tall towers all around them, that was not an experience she wanted to have twice.

Victoria kept her gaze carefully at the horizon level, only going higher if she had to. The great expanse of open sky overhead glimmered though the mass of air traffic. She could look at other things, instead.

Specifically, the important "other thing" was the heavy door in front of them. Helena's best guess as to the false signal's origin point was a level above them, but that entrance required the six of them to pass a visual inspection.

Korakti had laughed at that as they made their way downward. She argued that the best way was to go in guns blazing. Lelantos, back to his usual reserved self, agreed with her, but Victoria was certain he would not have agreed if someone had not shot at Rivka earlier.

Between Helena and Victoria, they talked Korakti and Lelantos down, putting the need for stealth first.

Now Helena returned from inspecting the door, a disappointed frown on her face. "It's locked."

"So hack it!" Korakti said. "Gods between, everyone talked up your ability to compromise computer systems, and a door is what stops you?"

Victoria assumed "everyone" meant "Hyperion," but was not about to engage on that particular tangent. Let her vent, she told herself. It was what Pallasophia would do.

Helena's frown darkened for a moment, but she too did not address Korakti's statement directly. Instead, she gestured back toward the door. "It is *locked*," she repeated with more emphasis. "There is a mechanical lock keeping those doors shut and the only place for a key is on the inside."

"I suppose security won out over not being suspicious," Daniel rumbled. The Aegis's external speakers added more bass to his voice, probably to reflect the size of the armor, Victoria assumed.

"So it would seem," Helena said.

"Looks like we're going to be breaking in anyway," Korakti said. She did not address Helena directly, but the subtle sidelong look was enough. Victoria grit her teeth—Korakti was exactly as good as she thought she was, and therein lay the problem.

Her ego also did not mean she was wrong, though Victoria did cut off her next boast with a gesture when she agreed.

"They may escape," Helena warned.

"They may," Victoria agreed, "but they will be more likely to escape if we have have to pass a checkpoint first."

Helena turned on her heels just fast enough for her tattered robe to flare slightly. Like the others, she had not had the luxury of changing clothes. Worse than most, she had been caught in the initial blast. "Daniel, how quietly can you force that lock open?"

The suit was silent for a moment before a couple of surprisingly light footfalls turned it to face the four-meter door. Another minute passed before he said, "the machi-machi isn't detecting any structural weaknesses, and the doors close flush."

"Impressive," Korakti said.

"And frustrating," Victoria added.

"That too. Can we blow it up?"

"I doubt it," Daniel replied. "Well, I could blow it up with a bit of work, but collateral damage would be a problem."

"And Odyssey's exterior, or the majority of it anyway, is considered a cultural landmark," Panatakis supplied. "It wouldn't do to defeat Ouroboros, defeat the mastigas, and have everyone hate us because we damaged the dome."

Victoria laughed. That idea was so absolutely ludicrous that she knew it had to be true. In her brief time on Prosgeiosi, she acquired an unshakable belief that the citizens here, especially those who considered themselves lucky enough to live inside Odyssey's walls, would most certainly vilify anyone who deliberately damaged the structure of the city.

"We wouldn't have to open it much," Daniel said. The Aegis's hand was pressed against the spot where a chin would have been on a human being. For the armor's part, it simply lay flat against the lower half of its impassive faceplate.

Daniel, via the Aegis, gestured with his other hand. "The doors are pretty wide. If I can get them open even a little, I can probably pry them apart enough to let you through."

"What about the Aegis?" Helena asked. "Our odds without it drop by nearly forty percent."

"We're spending too much crashed time talking!" Korakti snapped. "Daniel, break us in with as little noise as possible, please."

The armored head of the Aegis could nod a little bit, and it did so before Daniel lumbered toward the locked door. Korakti started to offer advice, but Victoria quieted her again. "You've got to learn patience."

Korakti growled. "I didn't train sunrise to sunsdown just to stand around and wait. I want to *do* something."

"We're a team. Talk to Helena, let her know what your strengths are and she'll find a place for you."

"I'll make my own plans, thank you."

"First Lord Rivka made it clear that Helena was in charge of this mission."

"First Lord Rivka ain't here," Korakti retorted. Her expression relaxed a moment later, and she put a friendly smile on her face, or at least an approximation of one. "But you're right, Limani. I'll talk to her."

Victoria watched her go for a moment, just long enough to make sure she *was* going to speak with Helena, before turning her attention to Daniel. A blade extended from the left forearm of the Aegis, and he was using it to pry the doors far enough apart that he could cram the suit's armored right hand into the gap.

After several minutes he was successful, and discarded the bent and damage blade to use both hands to pull the door open. Thankfully, it appeared to be well maintained and the only thing making noise was the angry grinding of the door's locking bolts as Daniel bent them out of shape.

"Thirty seconds," Daniel's voice announced. He had switched to communicating through the team's comms rather than "speaking" aloud from the suit's speakers.

"Korakti, you will go in first," Helena's voice instructed in her ears.

"First good order you've given me all day," she muttered, cursed, and in a louder voice that indicated she now remembered her mic was active, said, "good idea, Second Lord."

"With respect to Second Lord Korakti's skills, perhaps I should go first. My implants will give me a greater acuity of information." Panatakis said. His voice was formal, but something in his tone betrayed a hint of indignity to Victoria's ears.

"Second Lord Korakti is best suited to handle any immediate threat. You will enter soon after," Helena replied.

"Understood."

"Victoria, you're with Korakti," Helena continued. "Then Panatakis, myself, and Lelantos last. Daniel will then allow the doors to shut if they are able and take point.

"On my signal."

Victoria and Korakti approached the door, careful to stay out of immediate line-of-sight. Before drawing her weapons, Korakti extended a hand to Victoria. "You ready to do this, Limani?"

Inside her helmet, Victoria allowed herself to frown, then glare. After a moment, she took Korakti's hand and shook it. "Only if you stop calling me that."

Korakti cracked a smile. "Of course. Sorry if it bothered you."

Victoria originally did not have time to visit an armory and gather weapons before she and Pallasophia deployed to help at the stadium. She made a mental note to acquire a permit to keep at least one set of guns in their suite at all times. That would prevent this sort of thing from happening again.

When Tritogenes's lightly armed troops arrived, they brought a standard array of weapons and gave Victoria a shotgun they had no use for. It was not the carbine she preferred but, in the close confined she suspected they were about to enter, it would do well enough.

Korakti on the other hand drew two weapons. In one hand she held an oversize pistol. It looked vaguely like some sort of competition pistol, but the rig was different from anything Victoria had ever seen in recordings. It was also much larger, with a barrel that seemed purpose built to fire high-caliber rounds.

In her other hand, Korakti held a heavy saber. That sword, Victoria recognized. It was nearly identical, except for the edge, to the one she used in her exposition match on Pteryga before she and Hyperion left to come to Prosgeiosi.

"Remember, these people aren't going to be wearing uniforms. Probably. Don't shoot unless they shoot first."

Victoria laughed. "I assumed I would have to tell you that."

"You've only just met me, so you don't know me that well yet. When it's time to get serious, it's time to get serious."

Victoria nodded. "Hyperion chose you for a reason."

Korakti laughed now, loud and boisterous. "He chose me because I'm the best."

"We go on Helena's signal."

"Of course."

That signal came moments later, and Korakti burst through the door, pistol and sword held high. Victoria followed quickly after, sweeping the corridor with the shotgun, ready to fire at anything that looked dangerous.

She found nothing.

"It's empty."

"Blue screen it!" Lelantos cursed. "What..."

Helena's comm overrode anything else he was going to say. "Are there obvious signs of equipment or vehicles recently being there?"

"Not that I see," Victoria reported.

"Let me take a look," Panatakis said. He appeared behind Victoria a few seconds later, weapons at his side. His eyes and facial muscles twitched, seemingly at random, as his head swiveled back and forth. "This is the place the bomb was made, but I can tell little else."

Helena entered then, followed by Lelantos. Daniel released the door, which creaked and slammed about halfway back to where it was supposed to be.

Korakti slapped the Aegis's thigh and tapped Lelantos's shoulder. She gestured for them to follow. "Come on, let's find out where that bomb came from. The machi-machi can scan for that sort of thing, right?"

Daniel laughed. "Of course it can."

"Good, let's go."

The two humans flanking the Aegis looked like children in tow behind a massive athlete as they walked away.

"Should we go with them?" Victoria asked.

Helena shook her head. "No. They will be fine on their own. It will be easier not having my instructions questioned."

"I suspect they packed up and left after the bomb went off. That would be the smart thing," Victoria said.

Panatakis agreed. "Of course. They had to know we were coming. There's something here waiting for us; I can smell it."

"No," Helena argued, "I circumvented a great many security protocols and destroyed a lot of hardware to trace this signal. While it's logical that they evacuated some time ago, a trap would be unlikely."

"Still, everyone be careful," Victoria cautioned.

"The computer terminal is in that room," Helena said, gesturing.

"There is nothing on the other side," Panatakis added. Victoria knew they were speaking aloud for her benefit, and wondered how many steps ahead in the conversation they were in the mental space Tritogenes talked about them sharing.

"Then it should be safe."

"You misunderstand me," he said, pushing the door open. True to his words, the room was empty, the only marks from where a desk sat against the wall and where a hardline had once been attached and since cut.

"Crash!" Korakti swore over the comm. "We found the room, but everything's gone."

"At least we now know one location they are not," Lelantos supplied. Despite her building frustration at the situation, Victoria laughed.

Chapter 12

"You don't have to follow so close, you know," Daniel said. He tried to speak quietly, but the machi-machi was not exactly built for stealth, and even a "quiet whisper" from the suit's external speakers came out somewhat louder than conversational volume. If he really needed to speak so that he could not be overheard, the suit could use a radio communicator identical to the models in the other Titan's helmets.

In front of him, Korakti laughed, but the comment had not been directed at her.

"Your suit takes two minutes to take a single step," Lelantos said. "I will have plenty of advance warning should you move unexpectedly."

"Two minutes? No it doesn't, it..." Daniel stopped, then laughed at himself. "Oh, you're under right now, aren't you?"

"I have been steadily administering the chronodrug since we arrived, yes."

"What's it like?"

"Hmm?"

"The drug."

"Ah," Lelantos said, then let out a long sigh. "Your religion recommends meditation as a way to commune with your gods, correct?"

Daniel was not about to get into a theological discussion or debate with Lelantos in the middle of what should, by rights, be a combat zone. Practically speaking, his error was minor. His religion, unlike the majority of those practiced across the Technocracy, only recognized a single god. Others, such as Selene or the Ten Thousand, were manifestations of that single god, not separate entities, so his religion had no quarrel with any other.

Prayer, also, was not quite meditation, but that too was a hair too fine to split right at that moment.

So, Daniel nodded, a motion which was picked up by the suit and translated as well as it could be given the Aegis's reinforced neck.

"Imagine, then, reaching a state of meditation where you should go about your everyday life with the same feeling."

"Don't you get bored?"

"Do you get bored meditating?"

Praying, Daniel thought, but again resisted the urge to be pedantic. "Sometimes," he admitted.

Lelantos nodded, visible at the fringes of Daniel's vision where the Aegis compressed the view behind him into his periphery. "I used to."

"But not anymore?"

A shrug. "No. Too much happens that one's eyes can miss when one lives at a normal speed. The wings of birds, the flow of hair in the breeze, the ripple of muscle. There's beauty all around us, Daniel."

"That's a good way to look at it."

Lelantos's thin face split into a grin and he laughed. "It was that or drive myself insane waiting for things to happen. Surely, you had a similar experience when you first donned the machi-machi?"

Daniel felt his face frown. He could not see himself inside the armor, which he supposed was for the best. "I shouldn't have put on the armor when I did. I was," he paused, "angry. The previous Titan candidate was

214

a good friend of mine and when his suit failed in a combat test, I stormed into First Lord Enyalios's office and would not leave until he allowed me to take his place."

"I'm sorry."

"His name was Nikos."

Lelantos tilted his head to the side, throwing a questioning glance at the Aegis's back. Daniel was surprised Lelantos knew the Aegis had circular vision, but very little actually astonished him about his fellow Titans.

"If you pray," Daniel said, "his name was Nikos."

Lelantos nodded. "I understand."

Korakti slowed her pace, coming even with the Aegis. "I hate to be the one to tell you guys to hush, but hush. There'll be time for that kind of talk once we're done here."

Daniel nodded, feeling the armored head of the Aegis move with him. "Of course."

"Orders, then?" Lelantos asked.

"If Helena's done her job right, we should be getting close."

Daniel did not ask what they would do if Helena had make a mistake in her calculations, because he was not entirely convinced Helena *could* make a mistake in her calculations. Instead, he called up a holomap and projected it into one corner of the heads-up-display inside the Aegis's helmet. He should have had it there the entire time, but until that moment he had been relying on Korakti's map instead.

"Do you think they know we're coming?" he asked.

Korakti shrugged. "I'd be surprised if they don't with the racket we're all making. Either way, it's about time to make sure they know we're here."

He nodded, pleased. That part of the plan, at least, was working. Helena's group, consisting of herself, Victoria, and the other cyborg, Panatakis, was elsewhere. Hopefully, they were on the far side of what Helena's data indicated was the Ouroboros base. Panatakis and Helena were supposed to be locking doors, preventing the terrorists from fleeing again, while Victoria, as Korakti put it, got ready to crack some heads.

Head-cracking was certainly *their* task, he thought, keying up the volume on the Aegis's external speakers.

"Cover your ears," he said, speaking for the moment through their private comm channel. A moment passed as he waited to make sure both of his teammates had their ears covered, then Daniel activated the suit's external speakers.

"THIS IS TITAN DANIEL OF KATARRAKTES, ACTING WITH THE AUTHORITY OF THE COUNCIL OF HEXARCHS IN GENERAL AND FIRST LORD ENYALIOS IN PARTICULAR. THROW DOWN YOUR WEAPONS AND SURRENDER, AND YOU WILL BE TREATED MERCIFULLY."

Ten seconds passed and nothing happened, then from somewhere at the far end of the corridor came a dull thump. Warning lights inside the Aegis's head came on, bathing everything in a red glow. Before he could consciously react, the suit painted the source of the sound on his HUD, tagging it helpfully as "rocket powered grenade."

Daniel raised one armor-clad arm. The machi-machi reacted to a combination of his movements, the focal location of his eyes, and the data it generated about the targets around itself to determine how best to aim the machine gun attached there.

Before the heavy, triple-reinforced servos in the suit's shoulder brought the arm level, Lelantos fired twice. According to the data presented by Daniel's suit, the first shot impacted the RPG, detonating it. Thermal overload from the explosion kept his sensors from seeing what, if anything the second shot hit.

***

On the opposite side of Daniel's hulking armor, Korakti cursed. Lelantos did not spare the attention to listen to the entire thing, drawn out as it was from his perspective over several minutes, but he could make a reasonable guess about why she was was upset. They expected forward defenses. In fact they counted on it, which was why the three of them spent most of the walk chatting loudly. However, what they hoped for was that their frontal attack would interrupt a retreat attempt, allowing an easy push into the Ouroboros base.

As it was they were still half a kilometer from where Helena's refined data said their center of operations was. Finding active defenses this far out was one of the worse-case scenarios, but he was not about to suggest a retreat. Regular troops, diverted from disaster relief at the stadium, were on their way. The Titans' job was to prevent the terrorists from fleeing until the entire area could be contained.

That, of course, had been the plan before he realized Ouroboros had rockets at their disposal.

Lelantos cursed silently. To curse out loud, considering his distorted view of time, would take too long. Especially, he realized, because his second shot either missed the wielder of the RPG or because they had more than one at their disposal.

He squinted, trying to make out the source of the noise and fervently wishing he had Panatakis's abilities in addition to his own. If he could "see" through the smoke from the first rocket, things would be much easier.

Instead, Lelantos had only a few seconds even from his perspective between the moment the second grenade came through the smoke and when it would impact its target.

He fired again, working the action on his rifle as fast as he could. Thanks to the chronodrug, his movements were faster and more precise than any one else's would have been. The ability to perceive time as intensely dilated as he did allowed Lelantos to shave considerable fractions off a second any action he took.

Most people would not even be able to determine whether or not their first shot hit or missed. Lelantos saw the trail of burning gas behind the bullet, saw that it would not intersect with this second grenade, and had another round ready before it impacted its target.

217

Unfortunately, while he still technically had time to line up a shot and fire, it would do no good. When the chamber of his rifle slammed closed, the grenade was a mere meter away from the Aegis's chestplate.

Lelantos had thirty seconds to make a decision. His physical body could not do much in that time, scarcely half a second of real time, but smaller time margins had saved or killed soldiers in combat before.

He threw himself backward and to his left, aiming for the spot behind the Aegis.

For twenty-seven seconds—Lelantos counted them all—he sailed through the air, moving perhaps a meter in that time. The RPG struck the Aegis before Lelantos hit the floor and heat and pressure washed over him faster than even his drug-slowed brain could follow.

Fortunately, "heat and pressure" was all that hit him. The armored bulk of the Aegis shielded him from the worst of the explosion, especially the fire and shrapnel. Smoke already billowed around the armored Titan, shrouding the area.

The blast did have another effect. Lelantos realized that in the same instant as he realized he was still in the air, only now twisting and turning in an unexpected direction.

He cursed again. The floor looked uncomfortable.

Lelantos hit the floor hard, sending a shock through his nervous system. This was one of the major downsides to the chronodrug. Pain was a response from the body, not the mind, and that meant the impact between his shoulder and the floor lasted sixty times longer than it would have normally, sending shocks of agony through his arm and neck the entire time.

Gunfire thundered overhead as the Aegis finally opened fire with the machine gun on its right arm. Every second and a half, from his perspective, Daniel's gun fired once.

Korakti yelled something too distorted by the chronodrug, the explosions, and gunfire for Lelantos to understand.

The Aegis lifted its foot, pushing forward as Daniel tracked gunfire down the hallway.

He rose, aimed. The Ourobors soldiers were still shrouded in smoke. Daniel seemed to be firing for their most likely positions without any more data than Lelantos had.

He Aegis took a step.

Lelantos lowered his rifle. Moving as quickly as he could, he accessed the holographic controls on the side of the weapon's scope. Their visual intensity, flicker rate, and everything had been carefully adjusted through trial and error for his use while under the effects of the chronodrug.

Hoping these terrorists were not as smart as he feared they were, Lelantos adjusted the scope so that it produced an image from infrared data. With the smoke, and no other tools at his disposal, it was as good as he was going to get.

Raising the rifle again, he focused through the scope, trying to peer through the haze. Waste heat from the Aegis distorted his immediate short-range vision, and he moved away from the hulking suit of powered armor for better view. It helped some, but the problem continued to aggravate him.

The next problem was the smoke. Cooler still than human skin, it was nevertheless warmer than the surrounding air, which further reduced infrared contrast.

Added to that was the distance itself. Infrared was only really accurate over short distances, and the scope registered the enemy combatants at the end of the hallway as little more than vague blobs a few fractions warmer than their surroundings.

One of the blobs moved, rising. Its weapon gave off no heat until it fired, a stuttering burst of six rapid fire bullets separated by two seconds of dilated time.

Lelantos zeroed the scope on what should have been the blob's head. He aimed at the top of the warm area, just above the gunfire. Two more bullets raced his direction—rather, they raced toward the Aegis. He was a minor target next to that giant war machine—and the warm blob descended again.

The air remained warm in its wake, further compounding the problem of aim. Worse, the target cooled dramatically when it dropped, indicating some sort of cover or barricade.

The next blob moved, separating itself from the first slightly. By his count, Lelantos had line of sight on potentially six or eight people. He was sure there were more, but he could not discern them through the miasma of heat and smoke.

He glanced upward. The Aegis continued to fire the machine gun on its right arm. The heavy autocannon on the left was, for the moment, silent. Lelantos was glad of that. While the autocannon might punch through that barricade, they had no idea where Helena's half of the team was and, worse, the overpressure from the cannon would make his job even harder than it already was.

The Aegis took another step, and Lelantos shuffled to keep up without losing his sight picture. He knew Korakti was somewhere off to his left, on the other side of the Aegis, but that was all.

One of the blobs rose, and Lelantos automatically centered his sights on it. A single bright flash of heat erupted from its location, momentarily masking everything around it for a meter or more.

"Rocket," he said, enunciating carefully into the comms. "About thirty degrees left of center."

He shifted his aim. Despite the rocket's speed, it was hot and bright in infrared. Thanks to the chronodrug, Lelantos had plenty of time to track its path. He centered the scope and several things happened in such quick succession that even he could not tell the order.

First, he squeezed the trigger. The heavy rifle bucked in his hands, but the heat from the rocket made it hard for him to miss.

Second, the Aegis took a step and the floor creaked and shifted under its heavy weight. The stone under the armor cracked and the damage

220

propagated like lightning. The end under the Aegis sank and the end under Lelantos's feet rose.

He stumbled.

A hot knife of blazing agony ripped through his thigh in that moment, turning a loss of balance into a catastrophic fall that lasted three hellish minutes.

His leg burned and spasmed. Even through the haze of smoke, he could see the blood pouring from the wound. It looked shallow, easy to treat, but that was as far as his brain got before the neverending torment warped his perception beyond the point of usefulness. He knew he was screaming, but that was about it.

He lay there for an hour, unable to administer the chemical that would counteract the chronodrug, as blood poured from his leg and agony wracked every moment.

Sometime in the second hour, he felt himself moving. Hands took his shoulders and the floor passed by underneath. A staccato rhythm punched the air every second and a half, accented every three minutes by a deeper thud. Every so often discordant sounds, scatter and scrabble from an unknown source, interrupted the louder noises.

The sounds quieted slightly as the pain finally started to recede. The sweetest feeling of elation and mercy filled his mind where the pain had been, and Lelantos opened his eyes finally. Korakti's worried face hovered a few hands-breadths away, then she reached forward and wiped a soft cloth across his lips.

"You alright, Slim?" she asked.

Weakly, though with growing strength every moment, he nodded. His tongue and lips did not want to cooperate, and his response came out slurred. "M'ok. Thid dyu gib me kik theal?"

"Quick heal?" she asked. "No, I dosed you with painkiller first. Was about to do that, though."

He shook his head, pushing backward against what he assumed to be a wall. With his eyes open all the way, he looked around. Korakti seemed to have dragged him into a side corridor, away from the main fight. Daniel's Aegis traded fire with enemies out of sight as a rocket streaked in and impacted against the suit's chest armor.

"Bet he's glad he's in that can, hm?"

Lelantos nodded, then turned his attention to his leg. It was still pouring blood. Rational thought and calculation told him it had only been a few minutes since he was shot, and that the chronodrug only made it feel like hours.

He extended a hand. "I'll do it. You get back out there and support Daniel."

Korakti nodded and pressed a full vial of quick heal into his hand, then stood up. "It's pretty smoky out there and we're going to hit some bad close-quarters shit in a few minutes."

Lelantos nodded. "My rifle works close up. Just need to change out a few pieces."

Korakti nodded. "Good. Get back out here as soon as you can."

Once Korakti was out of sight, Lelantos set the quick heal on the floor beside his leg. Slowly, he withdrew a small knife from the front of his uniform and used it to cut the hole in his pants leg open wider. The wound turned out to be fairly superficial, which made things easier. He had no real desire to try and dig out a bullet or to apply quick heal to a deep wound cavity.

He inhaled deeply of the smoky, acrid air.

When he picked up the quick heal and dialed it to a topical application, a little holographic instruction box appeared. Its flicker rate had not been set for his drug-slowed eyes, and he could only barely make out the dosing instructions. Rather than risk using too little, he set it to dispense what he knew was "too much." In fact, another box appeared to warn him that using the entire contents at once was not recommended, but he dismissed it.

Lelantos had become a patient man, but it appeared that getting shot had somewhat of a negative effect on that part of his personality. He wanted to get on his feet *immediately*.

For topical use, the quick heal came out in a thick gel to better stick to—and fill, when needed—wounds. Lelantos dumped the entire ampule on the wound on his thigh, watching in slow motion as the gel first mixed with the blood pouring from the wound and then as it staunched the bleeding.

Getting the gel to set properly was a lengthy process even without the chronodrug altering his perception of time. Lelantos relied on it too much to give him an edge in combat, and did not want to completely counteract its effects, however the idea of sitting there for what would feel like hours was not appealing. Fortunately, adjusting the dose was easy, an in moments time sped up to the point where things were only one third their normal speed.

At that rate, he still had to wait almost ten subjective minutes, but he could accept that much delay. After the gel set, he wrapped his wounded leg with a bandage.

For the moment, he left the dosage of chronodrug where it was. He could always slow things down again once he caught up to Korakti and Daniel.

Lelantos came to his feet, picked up his rifle, and began the modifications as he regained his balance. His right leg was still weak, but it would get better as the quick heal took effect. While he shuffled toward the firefight, he removed the scope and barrel from his rifle, replacing them with a low-power sight and a shorter barrel respectively. A holographic control on the side of the weapon adjusted the firing rate to something better suited to close range.

He stepped out into the hall, following the obvious sounds of gunfire and explosions. Twenty meters away, Daniel and Korakti were still trudging onward. A number of bodies lay on the floor between them and where Lelantos stood, and Korakti seemed to be watching behind them as much as she was watching ahead.

Daniel's voice crackled over his comm as Lelantos reconnected. "How much further?"

"According to Helena, not far."

Daniel grunted in frustration. "Machi-machi's chest armor is down to forty percent and both legs are showing severe wear. The right arm's out of ammo and the left is running on half right now."

"Crash," Korakti muttered, then. "Slim! You're ba—"

She never finished that sentence where Lelantos could hear it because a roaring, thunderous explosion overrode both the comm channels and any chance of actually hearing her actual voice.

The wall to his left, about three-quarters of the distance to the Aegis, exploded inward, showering the area with debris. Lelantos hit the stud on his collar that would administer an emergency full dose of chronodrug and everything slowed to a crawl in moments.

From overhead, a piece of the ceiling shifted and a blast door slammed shut, pulverizing the stony debris like so much stale bread. Even to Lelantos, that door closed *fast*.

From the opening, he saw shadows moving. Thanks to the chronodrug, he had several extra seconds to react and threw himself backward, returning to the hall where they treated his wound.

"Blue screen it," he muttered under his breath.

***

Second Lord Korina led the assault through the breached wall, weapon braced against her shoulder. The charge was supposed to detonate after Enyalios's Titan passed, locking that crashed machine inside. Thus far, it had followed the bait perfectly and if Korina had objections to their methods, she could not fault the results.

A quick glance to the right told her how expensive it had been to trap Enyalios's metal beast. Six people lay dead—four from gunfire, one who had been ripped in half by the power armor's cannon, and one who had been killed with a sword.

Korina frowned. They were supposed to have killed her first. Like the rest of Ouroboros's operatives, Korina was no stranger to Korakti's skill. Indeed, Hyperion saw to it that her exploits be broadcast to the entire binary. If she was in there with—she wracked her brain. What was his name? Nikos?—then it would be much harder to take that suit out of the picture.

Castor, Metis, and Timon followed her through the destroyed section of wall. The rest of their forces would still be inside, split between the monumental task of destroying Enyalios's Titan and dealing with the sweeping tide of death coming at them from the back end of the facility.

She suppressed first a shudder and then a curse. *No one* told them about Tritogenes's Titan until it was too late. When she showed up in Molyvos, that was the first time they got any real data on her, and then she and those damned cyborgs found their staging ground.

Korina straightened, glad her helmet covered her face. It would not do to have her subordinates see the concerned thoughts bubbling just beneath the surface.

"Metis, Timon," she ordered, addressing the two on the right of the trio following her. She had no idea if those were their real names and even less of an idea of what their faces looked like. In fact, those names had been chosen by a random generator and, except for a handful of high-level operatives, they all wore masks around one another. It was safer that way.

"Yes, Lochias?" they replied in unison.

She nodded, pleased. At least they retained their military discipline when the base was under assault by the Titans.

She gestured to the rubble-dusted security door. "Keep an eye on that door in case Enyalios's Titan tries to turn around."

"As you say, Lochias," Timon replied, crisp and proper.

"If the Titans attempt to breach the door, send out a universal alert."

"Understood."

Korina waited just long enough to double check their positioning before turning away. Not knowing their real names or faces also made it easier to order them to their deaths like that. If the Aegis did in fact turn around, "Metis" and "Timon" would die very quickly.

"Castor, you're with me." Korina gestured down the hallway, toward the door the Titans used to enter the facility. "We're going to secure the main entrance. According to our best estimates, we've got no less than fifteen more minutes before reinforcements arrive. We need to make sure everythis is ready for them."

Castor nodded, falling in beside her. "Does command know whose forces will be coming first?"

Inside her helmet, Korina eyed the man beside her for a moment. Careful not to betray anything in her tone, she said, "unknown, but given the rapidity of deployments so far, I would expect Tritogenes or Enyalios."

Castor nodded, then rolled his shoulders as though a weight had just been lifted from them. Not for the first time, Korina found herself wondering which Hexarch it was that Castor served publicly.

Korina frowned. She hoped he had not pledged himself to Hyperion or Aegesander. Neither option would be good once Ouroboros eliminated the Titans and the social and political fallout hit.

"You have a question?"

He hesitated. "Can we expect reinforcements?"

"Unknown," she replied. "Our job is to secure the entrance and sound an alert when troops arrive."

"Understood."

"Problems?"

Castor shook his head. "No, Lochias."

"Good. Now..."

Off to the left, a shadow shifted against the light in a side corridor. Korina instinctively froze in place and raised her weapon again.

She opened her mouth to shout an order. She was going to tell Castor to "get down!" or perhaps alert him to the potential presence of one of the Titans, but she did not have the time. She barely had time to turn, to raise her own weapon to her shoulder, when a sharp crack filled the air.

Castor's head snapped back. His feet, suddenly bereft of instruction, stumbled and tripped. He collapsed to the floor like a marionette with its strings cut.

Korina could not see the Titan. He stood at the far end of the side passage. Castor had been a step ahead of her and the walls of the corridor itself shielded the Titan from her line of sight.

She cursed. It had to be Rivka's Titan, the sniper of Kipos. Unless Tritogenes's Titan had still more abilities they had not seen, he was the only one capable of making a shot like that without giving himself away in the process.

Korina threw herself backward and to the ground as another shot rang out. It cracked the wall opposite where she would have been standing had she taken another step forward. He knew exactly where she would be when she stepped into view, exactly where she would have to pause to aim her own weapon, and the shot was already lined up and timed.

Metis and Timon rushed forward. She and Castor had only gone a few dozen meters, and her other two soldiers covered that distance in seconds.

Metis knelt beside her. "Lochias!"

She shook her off, tried to warn Timon.

Timon turned before he cleared the edge of the hallway. Smart, she thought, but probably not smart enough. He had no idea who or what was down the hall, but his weapon was already up, braced against his shoulder. Human flesh could withstand a hail of bullets, and they *knew* the Aegis was elsewhere.

He fired his rifle on automatic, spraying several rounds into the wall on the near side of the corridor before sending the next few down the long hallway as he continued to strafe sideways.

The first shot hit his shoulder, throwing his aim off and sending the hail of gunfire uselessly into the ceiling. The second shot turned Timon's thigh into a mass of red pulp, and the third and fourth punched fist-sized holes in his ribcage.

Timon staggered back, masked face looking downward as he dropped his rifle and groped at the missing parts of his rib cage. His hands came away bloody and empty and he looked at them with horror as his wounded leg buckled and he dropped to his knees.

His masked face turned towards Korina, bloody hands reached out for her. In his horror, he grasped again at the empty air, then stopped. His masked face tilted to the side as if to ask a single question.

Why?

Korina could not answer. Instead, she grabbed Metis violently by the shoulder and hauled her to her feet. Together, they crossed to the edge of the corridor entrance where Rivka's sniper waited for them.

She withdrew a flashbang grenade, gesturing for Metis to do the same. She did, and Korina counted down from five on her fingers. On zero, they activated the grenades and hurled them down the hallway.

Korina again counted to five, then she pivoted around the corner. A sidestep, a step forward, and Metis did as well.

For a moment, the corridor was empty. No one waited on them. Then *he* came around the corner. He moved with a languid grace that Korina found disturbing somewhere deep in her gut. Nevertheless, she and Metis both raised their rifles to fire. The least they could do was manage to kill *one* of the Titans.

Metis was faster. Her weapon was at her shoulder, ready to fire, when the Titan's own rifle spat fire. The first shot struck Metis in the right hand. She screamed and dropped the rifle. The second would have hit her in the left hand, but she recoiled when the first shot hit her right hand, and the second grazed her elbow.

Korina fired, tracking shots across the back wall. One, two, then the sniper of Kipos fired again.

Metis's head snapped back and she crumpled to the ground, dead in an instant.

Korina's attention broke for just a moment as Metis fell, and when she looked up again, the sniper was gone. She cursed and broke into a run even as her instincts told her that was the worst thing she could do.

Her instincts were right.

She rounded the corner, expecting to see the sniper several meters back, ready to shoot again. She would have been ready for that. Her rifle was at her shoulder, finger on the trigger. Instead, he struck out from just past the corner.

His first blow knocked her rifle sideways, and her reflexive burst of fire missed completely. The second strike was to her solar plexus, right under her chest armor.

Korina staggered back, dropping her rifle, as her diaphragm spasmed and left her unable to move or breathe. A dim part of her brain was thankful for her mask, because this blue screened devil would not see the sudden look of wide-eyed terror on her face.

Her state of shock did not last long. She had been well trained before Ouroboros, and her time since then had only improved upon those skills. Korina moved on instinct, ready to fight with or without air.

Korina threw a punch with her right hand, lightning fast. The sniper's facemask turned towards it by millimeters and his left hand shot up, brushing her fist aside like a fly. She did not let up, aiming a vicious uppercut at his stomach. He pivoted, moving with alarming speed, and placed his hand against hers as it rose. His movement adjusted her strike just enough so that it missed, disrupting her balance and rhythm.

No one should have been able to take advantage of that mistake, she thought. The break in her movements was too small, too quick.

Yet, he did. The sniper of Kipos flowed toward her, moving like a snake cornering its prey. One hand, open palm, struck her in the center of the chest, further ruining her balance. The second strike buried the knuckles of the other hand in her throat.

Korina tried to continue the fight, but every time she make an attack, he was already there.

Now, the sniper of Kipos had a knife. She was not sure if it had been there before. No matter, she thought, it would not be important for long.

His final strike was to ram the knife upward, under her chin and into her brain. As she fell, Second Lord Korina had one final thought: what *is* he?

Chapter 13

The air flared bright red as Daniel's announcement echoed through the Ouroboros base's halls. The reflections from the walls were dimmer, cooler in color, but only served to make a confusing mess of everything Panatakis could see. When the grenade detonated a few seconds later, the sound washed away the red glare of his announcement with a dull thump the color of old blood.

Gunfire joined in a moment after, flashes in several different colors that muddied together into a useless brown. At this distance, and though as many twists and turns as the sound traveled, he could get no useful information from any of it.

Panatakis turned down the volume on those specific frequencies, and the world around him cleaned itself up considerably. The sudden gunfire concealed everything, disorienting him for a moment and preventing him from hearing anything but Helena's running commentary in their shared mindspace.

<Devil take that woman,> she said. Even through her presence in his mind was not a physical or even a visual one, Panatakis could practically see the frown on her face as her voice spoke.

<Problems with the lock?>

Next to him, Victoria tightened her grip on her rifle. Her gloves creaked as they tightened, a cluster of blue-green ripples that painted her rifle with a swirl of color, gone as soon as it appeared.

"She's early," Victoria said. She was watching the hallway, not listening in on their conversation—because how could she, he asked—but the remark seemed timely nonetheless.

Aloud, Helena replied to both of them. "She was supposed to wait another twenty minutes to allow enough time to finish this task. Until then, she was supposed to distract them, not engage them."

<Perhaps she thinks she *is* being a distraction?> Panatakis asked. When Victoria did not reply, he repeated the question, this time with his voice.

"I knew we should not have separated into two teams."

"Korakti had a plan in her mind," Victoria said. Her tone was calm, not argumentative, but Helena bristled nonetheless.

When she spoke, Helena's voice had turned a cooler blue, almost the same icy shade as her eyes. "I *know* she had a plan. Her plan was also risky and overly direct, allowing the terrorists time to escape. Preventing that escape is the exact reason we are here," she pointed at the exposed control panel on the wall that was currently flashing a series of warnings. "Instead of there."

Victoria called up her copy of the facility's map. The area they deemed the "base" had been highlighted in red. Their position showed as three blue dots and the location of Korakti's team as three green dots. Thanks to a quick field modification, her holo emitted a soft and quite low-pitched tone that Panatakis's implants could focus on, allowing them to render anything she displayed as visual data.

So far, Victoria's was the only one with that modification, as Helena could simply show him anything he needed to see by projecting the image into their mindspace.

She highlighted the doors Helena locked with yellow markers. "We've got four more to go," she said, "five if you count this one."

"Too many. There's a high probability that Ouroboros agents will escape through one of the doors we have yet to seal."

"How soon until we can move again?"

"It will be another one-hundred-and-forty-five-point-one-one-seven-four seconds for this one. Each of these doors has been sealed with a code of at least thirty characters. We will advance as soon as possible, I assure you."

Footsteps, soft and brown and suppressed by soft-soled shoes, echoed around a corner three meters away from where they stood.

"They are coming," Panatakis said aloud, speaking more for Victoria's benefit than Helena's. She could multitask easily enough, but the more additional tasks she had, the longer it would take to bypass the door's security and lock it.

Victoria nodded, her helmet a sonic dead zone. Watching her made Panatakis's rather jaded skin crawl. Whoever made her uniform did the job exceptionally well, and he could only see parts of her uniform by the lack of noise they made against the regular background hum of her body.

"Where?" she asked.

Panatakis pointed. "It's hard to tell how far they are."

She nodded again, moving closer to the end of the hallway with her borrowed shotgun at her shoulder.

"Come back," Helena ordered over the comms in their helmets. "We do not have enough data on their numbers or movements."

Victoria froze in place, caught in a moment of indecision. Her body language, even as still and hard to hear as it was, clearly said she did not approve of Helena's order. Victoria wanted to be at the front of whatever battle was to come, not standing in the back.

Finally, she turned and started back towards Panatakis. She moved quickly, without any reluctance now that the order had been given and her mind made up.

<If only Korakti followed orders like that,> Panatakis quipped.

<Second Lord Korakti does as she sees fit,> Helena replied, almost instantly. <Her plan was not a bad one; my wish was only for better coordination.>

Panatakis frowned. <Her plan didn't involve any coordination at all.>

<Her plan involved all of us at the front. She didn't take into account the necessity of locking the exit routes.>

<You're entirely too understanding, Helena.>

<I cannot change her mind without understanding her reasoning first.>

<Still,> he thought at her, <you need to have a talk with Korakti after this is over.>

<Such a conversation will happen, I assure you.>

<Good.>

He knelt, waiting on her, rifle raised to his shoulder. He would have preferred something a little more specialized, but he did not have enough time to visit Eurybia's armory and retrieve the platform her personnel crafted specifically for him. For the moment, a standard-issue battle rifle would have to do.

Panatakis squinted. His implants read the muscular signal and narrowed his aural focus, amplifying the volume on quieter sounds. Even with the distant gunfire nearly muted, he was having trouble picking things out of the cacophonous morass of noise filling his sight with sludge.

<I can no longer see their footsteps.>

<It would be highly unlikely to have overheard random footsteps and for them to then vanish. We will need...>

Helena continued speaking in his mind, but Panatakis ignored her as a few more footsteps reached him. It had only been a few seconds since Helena ordered Victoria away from the end of the hallway, so it made sense that the terrorists approaching their position had paused for a moment.

Either way, they were close. He whispered as much into the intercom half a second before a trio of Ouroboros soldiers came around the corner.

"Victoria!" he snapped.

She did not reply verbally, instead acknowledging his shout by pivoting on her heels and dropping into a crouch.

Nearby gunfire was a set of frequencies that his implants automatically corrected for. The alternative was to leave them at their real volume and let the noise flares drown out everything else.

Victoria opened fire as soon as enough of the first enemy soldier's body came around the corner. The shotgun coughed a single red-orange burst, huge and deadly. To Panatakis's ears, it looked almost like the visual flare of bullets in the darkness. Most of the pellets pocked the walls in a scatter of crystalline blues, but enough hit to matter.

The Ouroboros soldier staggered and collapsed amid shouts from around the corner that came as yellow-green flashes and sparks.

Panatakis shifted his aim and his own rifle kicked against his shoulder as a burst of gunfire raced down the hall faster than even his eyes could make out. The soldier fell the rest of the way, clutching at the bleeding wounds from his rifle.

"Time?" Victoria shouted, loud over the comm.

"Ninety seconds," Helena replied. "Get closer!"

Victoria nodded. "As you say!" she replied, sprinting down the short hall.

<Changed your mind?>

<Recalculated.>

Panatakis chuckled. <Of course.>

Noises came from around the corner, mingled with Victoria's heavy footsteps, then a small object sailed through the air. It hit the wall to his left with a light thunk, metallic and green and small.

"Grenade!" he shouted, not sure if he yelled aloud, into Helena's mind directly, or both.

The grenade hit the floor between himself and Victoria. Her head snapped to the right, toward the Ouroboros soldiers. She raised her shotgun, fired, stepped forward, and...

Anything else Victoria did was smothered under a blanket of disorientation and pain. Panatakis had jumped backward, away from the grenade, then to the side in order to shield Helena from the blast should the little metallic object turn out to be a high-explosive.

It was not. Instead of fire and destruction, when the grenade broke open, it did so with a soft puff of air. Looking at that puff had been his mistake, because that first sound turned out to be a small charge propelling a number of microgrenades into the air.

Almost as one, the grenades detonated. Magnesium flash-ignited, filling the hallway with enough light to blind someone with normal senses or knock out cameras. The sound that accompanied them was a high-pitched whine, shrill and painful. It was loud enough to damage or destroy microphones and potentially rupture the eardrums of unaugmented humans nearby.

Panatakis was *not* an unaugmented human. The cluster of lights and sounds ripped into his cybernetic senses, overloading and shutting them down completely. Fortunately, from his perspective, that meant the white fire that burned through his nerves only lasted a few seconds before everything shut down.

Terror set in quickly, however, because the modified flashbang did not knock him unconscious. He could still move and potentially still speak, but without ears, eyes, or a sense of touch, nothing he did had any real effect on the world around him. He might have been screaming, but he could not tell. Even smell and proprioception were gone, locking him into a state of pure sensory deprivation.

For a moment, Panatakis thought he was moving based on nothing more than resistance and difficulty in certain actions, but then even that stopped.

The first sense to return was smell. Four things hit all at once. Blood, gunpowder, and sweat assailed his nostrils. Strongest of all, however, was a scent much more pleasant and familiar—Helena. Whatever was happening, she was still there with him, alive and breathing and very close.

Second, sound returned. Distant gunfire and explosions continued to fill the air, the sounds of Korakti's team still fighting. Nothing came from their immediate area, however, and he hoped that was because Victoria defeated the soldiers attacking them, not because she had been killed and Helena dragged him to safety.

Nearby, footsteps reached his ears. He tried to pinpoint the location, but realized that he was actually *hearing* the sound, not visualizing it. The noises reaching his brain were exactly that: noises.

His eyes burned and ached as something dripped down his face. It might have been blood or tears, or even a mixture of both. His implants were offline thanks to the flashbang, reverting his senses back to the state they were in before the Project. It was his misfortune that, in that state, he was blind.

The burning in his eyes stopped as the footsteps came closer. He tried to tense, but none of his muscles responded yet.

"How is he?" Relief flooded his system at the sound of Victoria's voice.

"His implants will take several minutes to recover. This is a contingency we did not plan for, and countermeasures will have to be devised before our next sortie."

He felt the corners of his mouth move, raising into a smile. The expression was automatic, a reflex brought on by his emotions acting on their own. The pathways between his conscious brain and muscles, nearly all of which ran through his implants, were still offline, it appeared.

"Thank you for doing this."

"I could not leave a fellow Titan undefended."

"You didn't have to..."

"No," Helena interrupted. "I did not. But I chose to. He is a friend, someone else like me. I could not allow harm to come to him."

"I know the feeling."

"Are you...?"

"I don't know. It's possible." After a moment, Victoria asked, "how long until he can move again?"

"Another minute, perhaps."

Above him, a shotgun cocked. Victoria's footsteps receded.

Helena leaned close. Panatakis only knew that because he could suddenly smell her perfume and sweat much more clearly. Her robes rustled in his ear, real sound making real noises.

"Your implants are damaged, my friend. I am doing all I can, but it may be some time before full functionality is restored."

Panatakis fought against the numb feeling in his face and tongue, forcing them to cooperate, at least a little bit. "Thh...aaa...*k*. Ye."

"Of course."

Panatakis had no way of telling how much time passed while he lay there, but eventually the rest of his senses started to come back. Small muscles started working first, followed slowly by larger ones until he could sit up at last. With them came speech and his general sense of proprioception.

Despite all that, he was still blind, but at least now everything else worked right. That was nothing new. He had been blind before.

"How do you feel?" Helena asked.

Panatakis turned his face toward her, wondering how he looked to her. Perhaps his implants had scorch marks and his eyes were unfocused, or perhaps he looked normal except his eyes did not know where to point. "They knew exactly what to do in order to shut down my implants."

"It would seem that way. Victoria found something that would seem to support that hypothesis."

"Look at this," she said.

Panatakis turned his face to her, unfocused eyes seeing nothing but blackness. He waved a hand in front of his face to drive the point home.

"You're," she paused, "blind?"

He nodded. "Did Helena not tell you?"

"I thought your sight would return as your implants recovered."

"It should, but it hasn't."

"I'm sorry," Victoria said.

"Don't be. You didn't know."

"Hold out your hand."

He did so, and she placed what felt like a boot into his hands. The material was soft all around. The upper layers were made of a double layer of strong, woven fabric that was probably cut resistant.

Panatakis flexed the shoe. The top moved like fabric, and inside was a stiffer insole, but even that was no more rigid than a piece of gel armor. By feel, he suspected it had just enough protection to keep the soldiers' feet safe from minor hazards like rocks. The outer sole was made of the same material as the upper, soft and pliable fabric, with a sticky coating laid out in chevrons on the bottom.

He tapped the shoe against the floor at his side. It barely made noise, and he slapped it against the ground harder. Even then it was only slightly louder than someone in their stocking feet would have been.

Dropping it, he frowned. "Yes. They knew exactly how to counteract our skills."

"Hexarch Tritogenes managed to keep the events at Aphelion secret," Helena said. "That included your training and skills, Victoria."

She must have nodded, Panatakis thought, because Helena paused for a moment before speaking again.

"Proceed to the rendezvous at center of this facility. It is statistically probable that Ouroboros has little or no data on you, Spatharios. I will care for Panatakis and rejoin you when I am able."

"As you say." Victoria's footsteps vanished into the distance.

***

239

Panatakis was blind and Helena remained pinned down, held in place by stronger security protocols than they expected. She wanted to curse Korakti for jumping the proverbial gun, but could not muster the anger to direct that way. Not, she realized, for the same reason Tritogenes remained so frustratingly personable, but rather because the problems that suddenly plagued them were not actually Korakti's fault.

Her mind raced, trying to fit the actions of the Ouroboros soldiers into some sort of rational framework. The bomb in the stadium had been only superficially devastating. An hour later and it could have killed thousands. Instead, it caused property damage and a few unlucky fatalities.

And now...

Now, she came to a dead stop in the middle of the corridor, fading into the shadows thrown by a deep set door. Another trio of soft-soled killers passed, oblivious to her presence for a few precious seconds.

The trio marched past, looking for all the world like normal military—or, at worst, militia. Only the serpent-like coil wrapped around the wrists of their uniforms gave them away as being part of the organization she and the other Titans came to destroy. Masks obscured their heads, but even those looked like standard-issue equipment, designed to protect the delicate parts of the face and not for purposes of intimidation.

Her attention fixed on their shoes, however. *That* was the problem. Normal soldiers were not issued soft-sole boots. Those shoes would offer no protection to the top of the foot and very little to the bottom. The only purpose they served was making as little noise as possible.

Inside her own helmet, she scowled. It was the exact sort of thing *she* would have worn in order to defy someone who relied on sound to visualize the world around him.

At least they shared the same singular flaw that hunter-killer teams often had. She saw it in the mastigas, as well. These soldiers were so fixed on fighting Panatakis and letting the computer occupy Helena, that they failed to account for her presence.

Perhaps, she thought, Helena was right. Ouroboros did not know much about her.

Victoria grinned. It was time to change that.

She leveled her borrowed shotgun without moving from her hiding place. The soldiers were perhaps three meters away when she squeezed the trigger the first time. The nearest of the trio doubled forward, heavy clothing preventing the splatter of blood she expected. There was no mistaking the result of that shot, however. Knees did not simply stop working unless the spinal cord had been severed.

The two remaining soldiers turned back in time to see their comrade hit the floor with a wet thump. One had the presence of mind to pivot toward Victoria, unleashing a hail of bullets on the spot where she had been standing.

Unfortunately for the soldiers, Victoria was already moving long before either had a chance to aim. They were fast, that much was true, and certainly well-equipped, but Pallasophia's soldiers back at Aphelion had been better than these second-rate terrorists.

And still, a dim part of Victoria's mind thought, none of them would survive against even one mastigas loose in these hallways.

She darted toward the slower of the two soldiers, throwing her weight to the side in order to completely clear the arc of their muzzles. Her shotgun did not have much of a stock, but it served its purpose well enough when she slammed the back end of the weapon into the nearer soldier's skull.

He grunted and cursed, spitting something that might have been, "bitch!"

Her strike did what she needed it to, though, and he doubled over forward. She jammed an elbow into his exposed spine, forcing him even lower and turning him into an ersatz firing stand just long enough to center the bore of her shotgun on the last soldier's face and pull the trigger.

That one did not scream.

The last soldier alive, however, was still very much in the fight. He lashed out with a vicious kick that struck Victoria in the shin. Armor or not, he hit with enough force to leave a painful throb in the bone.

His next strike was aimed not for her, but for her shotgun. He swept upward with the butt of his own rifle, hitting Victoria's gun between her hands and sending it flying through the air. It hit the floor somewhere off to her right, but that was low priority for the moment.

Much more important was the location of her enemy's rifle as it lowered toward her face.

She ducked, swiping upward with her left hand and driving the right into the man's solar plexus. He grunted and tried to bring the butt of his rifle down on her head in an instinctive counterattack but was slowed slightly by the muscles of his stomach refusing to cooperate.

Victoria rose, wrapping her arms around his in a sudden, violent spiral and tearing the rifle out of his grip. It clattered to the floor but, like her shotgun, was quickly forgotten in the face of something much more important to worry about.

He staggered back, raised the bottom of his mask a few centimeters and spat blood into the floor. "You're all going to fucking *die*, Titans."

"Why?" she demanded. "Gods between, we're here to fight the mastigas. What could you possibly have against that?"

"Don't play games with me," he shot back. "We all know the real reason behind Project Titan. Ophion laid the groundwork thirty years ago."

Victoria was aghast. "You think *Ophion* was responsible for the mastigas?"

The Ouroboros soldier laughed. "The mastigas? No. They're just blue screened bad luck. He and the other Hexarchs just used them as their excuse to set Project Titan in motion."

"Project Titan started five years ago. Ophion has been dead for..." She paused, searched her memory. How long had Tritogenes been a Hexarch? "Twenty years!"

The soldier scoffed. "Is that what they told you? This has been going on a lot longer than that!"

"To what end?" Victoria demanded. "Why?"

"It's simple. Haven't you seen the military buildup over the last three decades? The increased police and security presence everywhere? You six are just the final nail and you don't even know it."

"You're lying."

"Prove it."

She almost said, "I know Tritogenes," but decided against it. Should this man get away from her, he did not need to tell his compatriots that she was Tritogenes's Titan. Instead, Victoria replied, "I know the Hexarchs. They wouldn't..."

He interrupted. "They did! The fact that you're here, now, proves it. They sent you, their pet jackbooted thugs, to silence us!"

Victoria felt her face heating up. Her muscles tingled, skin going numb as adrenaline flooded through her. Her fingered itched and twitched. "We're here because you're a bunch of crashed terrorists who blew up a stadium."

He laughed. "No, you're here because we needed you to be. Kokkinos and Dasos are down, and if the others are doing their jobs right, Katarraktes and Pteryga should be dead soon."

"You forgot one."

"The sniper?" The man laughed again, and Victoria wondered if he had been dosed with some sort of chemical to suppress fear, or if he really was this twisted. "He's alone, last I heard. A man who can barely carry his own weight isn't going to be a problem for long."

Victoria gestured to the two dead Ouroboros soldiers on the ground. "And them?"

He shrugged. "They don't matter in the grand scheme of things."

243

"They were your friends!"

His laugh turned deep and bitter. "Friends? I didn't even know their names. Now, Titan of Limani, if your curiosity is satisfied, are you ready to die?"

"No."

Victoria shot forward, knees bent deep and arms forward. He reacted, coming to guard then trying to throw a punch at her head. She brushed it aside, sinking onto one leg for balance, and then springing up with the next step.

As she straightened, the back of Victoria's hand shot out like an uncoiling rope, striking his chest directly over the heart. The gel armor there made the back of her hand sting, but that was irrelevant. She barely even felt the pain.

He was not so lucky. The skin of his neck where his mask had not properly settled back into place went pale as his heart stuttered under the shock of her hit.

Victoria struck again, this time with the heel of her hand at the underside of his chin. Any armor there was meaningless, as the force of the impact was directed at his neck. His head snapped back and Victoria's arms snaked around as she finished circling with her feet.

There, one hand was in the right place. A breath, a thought: these people are no different from mastigas. Her other hand was in position. She exhaled, twisted. His neck cracked like a wet twig and he fell to the ground, limp.

Her borrowed shotgun had slid down the hall and sat some distance away. Victoria briefly considered going to get it, but the weapon only had one shell left inside. She had no spare ammunition for it, meaning after one more shot it would be nothing more than a glorified club. The troop carrier she borrowed it from would surely want it back, but they could collect it when the regular forces swept through this facility.

A quick look at the Ouroboros soldiers told her they all carried some variant of the same weapon. They looked superficially like military

244

rifles, sporting the same basic features, but each one had been customized in a different way. Some of the modifications looked useful, but many looked like worthless add-ons that did nothing.

One of the first to die carried the shortest of the three, which suited her fine. The trigger and safety were all in the right place, so she adjusted the bloody strap and slung it over her shoulder. Picking over the bodies gave her several large magazines which fit well enough in the pockets of her black uniform.

She checked the magazine of the weapon, finding it to be missing a no more than one or two rounds. It had been the other soldier who shot at her, then.

Stepping away from the bodies, Victoria called up the facility's map, projecting the holo image in front of her visor so that she could follow herself through the corridors in real time. Her goal was marked with a green dot, but she could only see it if she zoomed out or panned her way around the map.

She adjusted the map to where she could see herself and the goal both, then moved it to the periphery of her vision where she could consult it if needed.

"They're no different from mastigas," she whispered. That made things easier. She could worry herself about taking human life afterward, but for the moment there was only herself, her goal, and her enemy.

Weighing her options, she settled on stealth. The angry, violent urge in her blood wanted her to abandon stealth, but even there in the depths of Odyssey, the same voices that guided her through Aphelion resurfaced. Haste, they told her, would kill her. Be quiet, they urged, be careful.

Ninety-nine dead souls all urging her toward the same end made a very persuasive argument, and Victoria crept her way down the hallway.

She made her way deeper into the facility, up a set of stairs and then down a smaller one. According to the map, she was getting close now. Unfortunately, the team agreed upon comm silence to prevent Ouroboros from overhearing, and she had no idea where Korakti's team was. Random gunfire erupted, echoing off the walls, but with no way to pinpoint its source, Victoria went on.

Trust the team, she repeated to herself. Korakti was early and Helena would likely be late, but she needed to trust the team. Everyone had their role to play, and this was hers.

Ahead, around a corner, she heard voices. They spoke in low, hushed tones, trying to be quiet but making just enough noise to be overheard. Victoria flattened herself against the wall next to the corner, listening, trying to determine the number of voices. She heard at least two distinct tones, but nothing more than that.

She checked map again. According to Helena's data, she was close to her destination now. That meant this was likely a trap. She replayed the conversation with the Ouroboros soldier, adding it to the soft-soled boots they all wore. They knew the Titans were coming, they planned for nearly every ability and skill the six of them possessed.

Of course this was a trap, she reasoned. If the outer forces failed, the ones tailored to everyone's skills, then this inner guard would have to hold out long enough to kill them. She took a deep breath, thinking through how she would do such a thing if their positions were switched.

The best conclusion Victoria could come to was guns, lots of guns. If "special" tactics failed, then she would simply bait her enemy into an open area and fill that area with bullets. According to the map, their goal was on the far side of just such an open area, which itself waited on the other side of a small room that could easily be turned into a close-combat nightmare.

Fortunately, and she smiled a thin and sour smile at that thought, Victoria *was* a close-combat nightmare. She just had to get there.

She rounded the corner, bringing her rifle to her shoulder as she did so. One Ouroboros soldier had the misfortune of being in the exact wrong place—or, from Victoria's perspective, the exact right place—and fell immediately under her sights.

She fired and the gun kicked gently into her shoulder. Whatever else these Ouroboros soldiers were, they at least had nice weaponry, she thought. Her enemy staggered, flailed, and then dropped to the floor under a second barrage of bullets.

Others came into sight as she closed toward the doorway. One threw a grenade at her, while another took aim with a rifle similar to hers. Victoria aimed for the rifleman and sprayed the area with bullets in the same motion as she threw herself backward and retreated around the corner.

The grenade detonated, a high explosive this time, filling the corridor with fire and pressure.

Voices reached her ears, followed by footsteps. They were coming closer. They would try to prevent her from escaping, from warning the others about the trap waiting for them.

Unfortunately for her enemies, Victoria had no intention of escaping.

She dropped the magazine from her rifle, letting it clatter to the ground, forgotten. It might have been empty or half full, but she was not about to go up against these people with anything less than a full magazine. For a moment, she was thankful Tritogenes's machines taught her how to do that, because the movements came automatically and without hesitation.

She pushed the replacement magazine home a moment before the first soldier rounded the corner.

His rifle was ready, level at his shoulder, and hers was not. Rather than fight to aim or shoot from the hip, Victoria lashed out with the weapon's stock. Her attack hit her enemy's chin and he staggered back into the soldier behind him. That gave her a moment, which she used to shoot the soldier next to them, then drove forward with her shoulder into the pile of staggering limbs.

They fell to the floor, shouting and cursing. Gunfire erupted from the pile of tangled limbs, but Victoria was fairly certain that none of it actually hit her.

She wondered if she would notice if it did.

She whirled in a circle, counting. One down, out of the fight but still moving, two more down and quickly getting their bearings. Three more closing on her, about to fire.

Victoria dropped as quickly as she could, landing heavily on top of the two soldiers on the ground. A thought flashed through her head, riding on the voice of one of her dead memory-lives. It asked her what Pallasophia would do in that situation.

The soldiers under her reacted quickly, despite their predicament. They tried to grab and hold her, but got in one another's way. She seized on a pair of hands, not caring which enemy they belonged to, and heaved, bucking with her hips.

They flipped over, sandwiching Victoria between the two Ouroboros soldiers. With one arm, she drove her elbow into the woman below her. With the other, she grabbed a weapon. In that moment, Victoria had no idea if it was hers or belonged to one of the Ouroboros soldiers on the floor with her.

Right then, the owner of the weapon did not matter. Right then, *she* owned that weapon. She wrapped her hand around the grip, found the trigger, and emptied the magazine in the direction of the rest of the Ouroboros team.

Sudden screams told her that her plan was at least marginally effective. She drove her elbow into the woman below her again, then again, unsure if the cracking feeling was her enemy's sternum or armor. Regardless, it gave her a moment to deal with the person on top of her who now had his bearings again and was trying to wrench Victoria's arms in painful directions.

She wrapped her legs around his middle, heedless of a sudden flare of pain in one calf, and threw him to one side. He landed a meter a way with a grunt, but was quickly back on his feet.

Including the man she threw, who was now throwing his own rifle aside after a frustrated growl when the weapon clicked empty, three

Ouroboros soldiers now faced her. One held a rifle in one hand and a bloody knife in the other, and the furthest away still had a rifle.

Unfortunately, that last soldier's rifle was also pointed directly at Victoria's chest. She dove to the side, knowing it would not be fast enough, as his shot tore into her side.

"Gods between," she muttered, trying to catch her breath. "This is not going according to plan."

A bullet spalled the floor beside her head as the last gunman fired again, missing by a scant few centimeters. Before he could fire again, his head snapped sideways. Before his body hit the floor, two more shots struck him in the right shoulder and left elbow.

Victoria scrambled to her feet, sparing just a moment to look for her assistant. Precise shooting like that would only come from one place, but she could not see Lelantos. Wherever he was, he remained far enough away to keep himself safe from these soldiers.

The woman she elbowed on the ground was now coming to her feet as well and Victoria reached for her rifle. Her hands closed on nothing, then she spotted the short-barreled weapon on the ground, near where she went down the first time. The shoulder sling was only attached from one spot now.

She cursed, sparing a second to look for another replacement. When nothing presented itself, Victoria dropped to one knee in long-practiced reflex. One hand drew the dagger, one of the same ones she took from the fonias in Aphelion's depths, and her other plucked her gigas baton from where it hung from her belt.

A smile spread across her face as the familiar weapons settled into her hands. This, she thought, was how things should be.

She charged the nearest of the three soldiers, the one with the bloody knife. He dropped the blade, took his rifle in both hands, but it was to late. Victoria jerked to the side and slammed the rifle with her baton. It fell from his hands, expensive add-ons destroyed. Before he could react, the mastigas dagger in her other hand slashed diagonally downward across his throat and chest, then horizontally back across his torso, and finally she thrust upward into his skull.

Victoria kicked the Ouroboros soldier aside in time to see the woman she grappled with drop her rifle and clutch at a pair of bloody spots on her chest. She toppled, and Victoria raced past her to meet the last enemy soldier in the middle of the room.

To his credit, her enemy struck out with more skill than the others. His fist glanced off what would have been her cheekbone without her helmet on, and she stumbled. That stumble turned into a fall as her wounded leg chose that moment to sent a stab of pain through her nervous system.

She hit the ground hard, the impact on her knees tearing at the wound on her side.

This, she thought, was familiar, and not in a good way.

Victoria lunged forward, wrapping her arms around her enemy's thighs as he rained blows down on her head and shoulders. They both hit the ground hard and she scrambled on top of him. He tried to fight her off, but she snaked her way past his hands exactly as Pallasophia had done to her countless times, and drove her dagger into his eye socket.

He screamed.

She withdrew the weapon, then plunged it in again and again *and again*. Breathing heavily, Victoria only stopped when a calm, slow voice came over her helmet comm. "He's dead, Spatharios. You can relax."

She nodded, rolling to the side and catching her breath as the rush of combat started to fade and her oxygen starved body screamed for fuel.

By the time Lelantos joined her in person, Victoria mostly had her breathing under control. "Where are," she panted, "the others?"

"I could ask the same question," he replied, "but won't. We got separated."

Victoria nodded. Her lungs burned, but her side and leg burned worse.

"You're injured," Lelantos said.

She looked down. Blood indeed soaked her side and lower leg. Adrenaline and endorphins still coursed through her body and she laughed. "I've had worse."

"Of course," he replied. "Still, you should take a moment and apply a dose of quick heal. I suspect this was light resistance compared to what awaits us."

Victoria nodded and sank to the floor. She wiped the blood away from her leg and side. The leg was a stab wound, but it did not hurt. The knife must have been razor sharp, which made healing easier. She emptied most of a vial of quick heal into the wound, then switched the device to general application and drank the rest.

The wound in her side was deep enough to no longer qualify as a "graze," but not so deep that her memory-lives were sending her warnings about life-threatening injuries. At a guess, it passed through soft tissue and missed her organs. Still, she emptied an entire vial into the exit wound, then applied most of a vial to the entry wound. Once again, she drank whatever remained, letting it to go work on her general bruises.

While she attended to her injuries, Lelantos kept watch.

"Are you ready?" she asked. The quick heal was already surging through her bloodstream, invigorating her tired muscles. Her body tingled with warmth.

He nodded. "I have been ready for hours."

She laughed, unsure whether to take that at face value or as a comment about his time-dilating drug. "Let's go, then."

Another nod, fast and jerky. "I will look ahead."

"Good plan. You can get a lot of information in just a second, right?"

"Yes."

With Lelantos in front, the two of them made their way into the room that had previously housed the six Ouroboros soldiers they just fought. It was of medium size, but relatively nondescript. Two tables had been turned into makeshift barricades, but otherwise, nothing in the room looked useful.

A whir from the large room on the other side, however, told a very different story. The whir sounded mechanical, but the bullets that shattered the tile in front of them explained exactly what made the noise.

Victoria dove behind one table and Lelantos took shelter behind the other. "How much did you see?" she shouted.

"Not much." It sounded like a confession, not a report. "But I did see that the source of that gunfire was a heavy automated turret, and it was not the only one with a fix on this location."

"Gods between," she muttered. "And today was going so well."

Chapter 14

Security camera footage in the area where the Titans were fighting Ouroboros was surprisingly good. According to record, some years back, the area had been a bustling factory owned by First Lord Diomedes. Until that very afternoon, Aegesander thought it had been abandoned by anything of note. Of course, space was at such a premium inside Odyssey that nowhere was ever "abandoned," but no news or products of note had come out of the area in at least seven or eight years.

He frowned at the wall-sized holo. Now he knew why that was. Of all the places where a group like Ouroboros could set up, he asked himself why they chose the very heart of Odyssey itself. His frown deepened into a scowl as he continued that line of thought: of course they put their base in Odyssey's core. No one on the Council of Hexarchs would think to look inside their own dome for a rogue element like this.

Aegesander picked up his drink and brought it to his lips just in time for his door chime to break his reverie. He sighed—at least nothing of interest was going on right at that moment. Daniel's Aegis and Hyperion's Titan moved carefully through the halls. Lelantos had been injured and separated some time ago, and he had not seen Helena or her half of the team since the mission began.

His door chimed again. He knew it had to be another Hexarch. No one else would even *be* in the hallway outside, and the list of his fellow Councilmembers who would come to bother him was very short indeed.

"You know you're allowed to simply enter," he said, pitching his voice so that the microphone by the door would pick it up.

It slid silently into the wall. With his back to the doorway, itself a sign of trust that was only slightly subverted by the hidden gun and computer-controlled targeting system aimed at the door, the only way he knew the door was open was the sudden influx of warm air from the hallway outside.

"Hello, Eurybia," he said. Still without turning, he quirked an eyebrow. "Have I missed a meeting?"

She laughed the barb aside. "None yet, but if you brood in here much longer, you'll run the risk of being absent from your own Council session."

"Yes," he said. Aegesander waited a moment, then gestured to the holo projected in front of the wall. Not much had changed in the environment other than the width of the halls. Daniel and Korakti seemed to have stopped, and she was adjusting something on the far side of the hulking armor. "I would like to see the resolution of this before we begin the meeting."

"Even if it means postponing the meeting that you yourself scheduled?"

He nodded. "Even so. I would know this Ouroboros is dealt with before we address the issue at all."

Eurybia appeared at his side, glass in hand. Aegesander was sure he had not opened a bottle of red wine in some time, nor had he dusted off his personal wine glasses, but she still managed to find both in a short time. "Why? When you contacted the others earlier, you stressed the need for haste to deal with the stadium attack."

"I did," he admitted, "but that was before we made the connection between it and the vandalism to your suite. And," he gestured to the holo against the wall, "it *is* being handled with all haste."

"Tritogenes was first on the scene, not counting yourself or Rivka," she said, needling.

"I have no quarrel with Tritogenes."

Eurybia laughed, allowing a mocking tone to come through. "You? No quarrel with Tritogenes?"

"I did not stutter, Eurybia."

She eyed him for a moment, then shrugged. "This is news to me."

"I may not like him very much. He, like Rivka is young and inexperienced in the ways of politics. He believes charisma and a smile is all he needs to dictate order and safety to his people. Despite that, I have no professional quarrel with him, and I will not slight any achievement of his." Aegesander paused just long enough for it to feel deliberate. "They are, after all, so few."

Daniel and Korakti were on the move again. Despite some difficulties moving brought about by the heavy work the suit had been part of that day, the Aegis moved quite well. With it, Daniel took the lead. Korakti followed, keeping watching on their sides and rear.

Aegesander nodded with approval. After the first ambush, neither of them had been taken by surprise by anything from a side passage. Since being separated from Lelantos, Korakti would ghost ahead, inspecting anything the Aegis was too large or cumbersome to deal with. It was an admirable adaptation, he thought, and once that reduced the damage they both received significantly.

Eurybia sipped her wine, made an approving nod.

"It's from Kokkinos," Aegesander supplied.

"I know. I can tell one of Stephania's vintages even if you've not kept this bottle in the dark as you should."

"How can you..."

Eurybia laughed. "My dear Aegesander. I've been Hexarch over the planet with the binary's best vineyards for nearly six decades. You just learn these things after enough time has passed. I could not, for instance, differentiate between tea from Dasos or Kipos."

A smile spread across his thin face. "I see your point."

"Enough of trivial matters," she said, gesturing with her free hand at the holo on the wall. "How did you access the feed?"

"As it turns out, our esteemed Katarraktean colleague took my advice last spring and installed a complex ECM suite in his Titan's armor."

"Electronic countermeasures," Eurybia supplied, "that apparently include the ability to suborn local security cameras?"

Aegesander nodded. "That little adaptation came from Daniel's predecessor in the Project. He argued that the ability would prove useful, perhaps improving his ability to lay down indirect fire."

"Has it?"

"In tests, it seems to have performed adequately."

She gestured to the holo on the wall where the Aegis was prying open a door to allow Korakti passage. Gunfire flashed on the far side of the door, followed by a rocking shudder in the Aegis's arm. Even without sound, a burst of automatic gunfire from the powered armor was easy enough to identify.

"And in the field?"

"Ouroboros seems to have put better security in place than we would have expected. The Aegis has two ways of connecting to computer systems. First is traditional wireless, and it seems like the Ouroboros systems are completely isolated from that avenue. The Aegis also has laser communicators, but those require line of sight, so his ability to use them to 'look ahead,' as it were, is limited."

"But you can watch over his shoulder well enough."

"Enyalios graciously allowed me to access the feed from the Aegis."

"What of the others? Are they all in pairs like this?" Eurybia frowned, clearly unhappy with that idea.

256

"No, in fact," he said, then proceeded to explain what had happened to Lelantos since the fighting started, then explained what he knew of Helena's plan. "Since they separated after leaving the staging area, I have had no contact with Helena."

"Pity. I wanted to see her in action."

"That time should come soon enough. I believe Daniel and Korakti are approaching the rendezvous point."

"Then I came at the right time."

"Indeed. Now, enough talk. Let us see how our Titans handle themselves, yes?"

The Aegis made short work of obstacles that would have stopped an older generation of armor in its tracks. The first time Aegesander watched the massive suit effortlessly vault over a barrier, even he had been impressed.

In fact, the First Lord continued to be surprised with the advances Enyalios made in agility for his armor. Prior to the start of the Project, powered armor like the Aegis was much larger and bulkier while being less effective and able to operate on its own. Its only real use had been in places where traditional vehicle support was impossible.

The Aegis, by contrast, moved almost as effortlessly as a real person.

"Take a seat," Eurybia offered from across the room. "How long have you been standing there, anyway?"

Aegesander laughed. "Only for a few minutes before your arrival. This feed has been active all afternoon and I've devoted more and less attention to it as things happen. You caught me at a time when I was considering the future applications of Enyalios's technology."

She scoffed. "A stronger military?"

"That will always happen with new technology," he replied. "No, I was thinking of how it could be applied to other areas. It was quite adept at search-and-rescue earlier."

"So I saw."

As he crossed the room to where Eurybia sat, a notification appeared on his personal holo. Floating above his forearm was a simple message indicating that the current feed would be out of range in a few moments. Aegesander selected a new one, which moved the camera a few dozen meters down the hall.

The process repeated itself twice more over the next twenty minutes, providing the only change in the events unfolding before them. Whatever was happening deep beneath the Hexarch's feet, Korakti and Daniel had slowed down considerably.

The pair rounded a corner, speeding up slightly, and quickly stepped out of view. Unlike previous changes, the camera was not out of range of the Aegis, but now a wall sat between it and the armor, cutting off the line of sight required to maintain contact. It happened so suddenly that his system did not have time to produce a warning, and instead simply switched to another feed at random.

This one was on the far side of the hallway Korakti and Daniel just turned down. Barricaded in front of a door were two human figures. Or they were, at least, humanoid. Aegesander shuddered when he got a clear look at the pair of them. Despite knowing exactly who she was, Tritogenes's Titan's mastigas-inspired uniform still unnerved him. Something about it looked wrong; she looked like *them*.

The black-clad Titan gestured to Lelantos, who crouched next to her, peering over their makeshift barricade. His slight frame and thin face made the other Titan look even larger than she already was. It did not help matters that Lelantos was dressed in what remained of the once-fancy robe he wore for his intended lunchtime plan of visiting Molyvos with First Lord Rivka.

He gestured back, then to the Aegis and the corridor beyond. His shoulders fell and he shook his head.

"I would like to know what's stalled their progress," Aegesander muttered.

Daniel raised the Aegis's arms, gesturing with them as he would his own. After a few moments, he made a pair of gestures, palms down, that clearly indicated levels. One arm was much lower than the other, nearly at the floor as the suit's knees flexed.

Aegesander had no idea what they were discussing. The camera still had no sound, but the image was entertaining enough to bring a smile to his face. The Aegis was humanoid and, perhaps because of its size, for a few moments it looked like an adult explaining something to a group of children.

Tritogenes's Titan crept away from the barricade, only standing upright when she was completely out of line of sight from the door on the far side. She came close to the Aegis, talking and gesturing as though in whispered confidences.

Eurybia hummed. "Spatharios Victoria is taller than I would have expected. Nearly two meters, it seems. I can see why Tritogenes chose her for the Project."

Victoria, he thought, remembering the name at last. Tritogenes's security had been so complete that the name was all Aegesander had been able to glean during the Project. Her presence and identity were no secret anymore, but unlike the other five, Victoria had not made a public face of herself since her arrival on Prosgeiosi.

"What are they hiding from?" Aegesander asked.

"What are they hiding *behind*?" Eurybia added.

He squinted, enlarging the holo. This camera's feed was not as good as the others and the details were scant. A number of bodies lay in the doorway, but otherwise, the camera offered no more information about the area beyond.

"Tables," he said. "Hmm."

"Ouroboros may have fixed weapons on the far side."

He scoffed. "Fixed weapons? This is a terrorist cell we're dealing with, not a militia. They're probably just waiting on the entire team before they push through. Helena and Panatakis are supposed to be securing the exit routes, so I expect they'll be along shortly."

As it happened, "shortly" turned out to be another ten minutes. Eurybia had left the room to refill their drinks and came back in time to see Pantakis and Helena approach the makeshift barricade.

At Victoria's insistence—whatever explanation she gave was punctuated by enough gesturing that the gist was obvious even to Aegesander who still did not have the benefit of sound—Helena and Panatakis crouched low to pass the doorway.

Panatakis remained at the barricade, resting his back against it. Victoria seemed to fuss over him, prompting Eurybia to ask what happened.

Aegesander shrugged. "I don't know. This is the first time I've seen them as well."

Helena stood facing Korakti now. Her face was turned slightly away from the camera, far enough that Aegesander only knew she was talking by the subtle bob of her chin. Korakti retorted hotly, waving her arms and gesturing widely.

Aegesander laughed to himself. "How like Hyperion."

"Why do I suspect they are all a little like us?"

"You would be wrong. Helena and I have very little in common. I wish that were not the case, but it is."

"Are you so sure about that? I rather suspect she is taking Korakti to task for not following some minor element of her carefully laid plan."

Aegesander smiled, sipped his drink. "I will not rise to your bait, my friend. You must try harder than that."

Korakti gestured to the doorway, then patted the nearby Aegis on the side. She laughed, gestured something accusatory at Helena. Helena, for her part, remained largely unmoving.

Aegesander admitted silently that he admired her composure and ability to remain impassive in the face of all manner of things. He was not going to admit that aloud, however, lest he deal with another round of Eurybia attempting to compare the two of them.

After a moment, Helena said something, gestured to Lelantos, then returned to the barricade, crouching behind it next to Victoria.

Even on the grainy feed, Korakti looked abashed. She too approached the barricade and sank down next to Lelantos. Even trying to parse their hand gestures led Aegesander nowhere, and so he turned his attention back to the Aegis.

Unable to hide behind the barricade, the Aegis simply waited off to the side, standing watch like a statue.

"What could they be hiding from that's dangerous enough to warrant that much caution, but weak enough to be stopped by a table?" Eurybia asked. "Unless...."

Aegesander raised an eyebrow. "Unless what?"

"What if it's not weapons they're hiding from, but surveillance? They're all coming very close to talk, closer than people generally do."

Aegesander hummed for a moment, then nodded. "It would made sense. I'm sure there are still weapons, otherwise the six of them would simply storm the room, but you may be correct. If their position keeps them out of the line of fire, whatever weapons await them are likely raised and firing downward at an angle."

She nodded. "Creating a crossfire just inside the door rather than using it as a firing lane. Smart."

Aegesander frowned. "I'd rather not consider the people who bombed my stadium as 'smart,' if it's all the same."

Eurybia shrugged. "They can be smart and evil at the same time. Haven't you picked anything up from Enyalios's military lectures? Respect your enemies' capabilities and all."

He nodded now, though it was not without a considerable feeling of reluctance. "Again, you have a point. I'm letting my frustration with the situation cloud my judgment, another reason to postpone the Council meeting until this is all done with."

Eurybia frowned. "As you say."

"Something's troubling you."

"You are going to tell the other Hexarchs about this, yes?"

He scoffed. "Of course, don't be absurd. They'll hear about it from their Titans if nothing else."

She nodded, and a cloud passed over Eurybia's face. "Good."

Her tone bothered him. Eurybia had a habit of distancing herself, turning cold and aloof like this whenever something was eating at her. "What else is bothering you?"

"Nothing relevant to the Titans' current engagement."

"Eurybia."

She was silent for a long moment, likely gathering her thoughts. Very few people held on to their secrets around him for very long, which was the way First Lord Aegesander preferred things.

"The mastigas. On the way here, I got an update on the ship."

"An update?" he demanded, suddenly energized with a frantic tension. His fingers flew across his personal holo's interface, dismissing menus and messages without even noting what they were. Dimly, Aegesander was aware of his heart hammering in his chest. "I had been so focused on this mission that I had not..." He stopped, read the message in front of him, and cursed.

The mastigas ship had changed course and applied a solid four hours of acceleration. That enormous warship, the one that lurked at the edges of their binary for thirty years now, was no longer nine months away. At its current speed, even factoring deceleration time, it would reach Dasos in less than four months.

In one-hundred and seventeen days, the mastigas would do to *his* planet what they did to Kipos five years before.

"We have to pull the Titans out," he said.

"Now?"

"They need to be in top shape, training every day until the mastigas arrive. We can't risk their lives for," he gestured to the holo on the wall, "this."

"Don't be absurd. This kind of task is what they trained for."

"No," he retorted, letting his temper get the better of him. "What they *trained* for is to fight mastigas."

Eurybia narrowed her eyes. "They trained to be our protectors. Pulling them out now would be a mistake."

Aegesander sighed deeply, not wanting to admit she was right. The Hexarchs had been reckless before, acted on emotion rather than logic. He would not let this be another of those times. Yet, a thought remained, "the mistake would be letting them get killed down there. We need to approach this more carefully."

"Aegesander," Eurybia began softly. "The reason the Titans exist at all is to fix our mistakes, to expunge our sins. The Council made mistakes dealing with the mastigas before. Interrupting the Titans would be *another* one."

Aegesander felt a flare of anger deep in his heart, but snuffed it out. Still, his voice was cold when he spoke again. "You've been talking to Hyperion."

"We're not getting into that right now, Aegesander. I don't want to rehash an argument we've had a thousand times."

He sighed, searching her face. For the first time in a great many years, Aegesander found her face hard to read. Her emotions and thoughts hung behind a deep, dark curtain. Despite that, it was Hyperion who most often referred to "their sins" in relation to the poor handling of the mastigas, and Eurybia knew more about the decisions of thirty years ago than anyone who was not there in person.

Aegesander also knew she resented him for it. Not, as he might have expected, for "bringing her in," as it were, but specifically for the things he and the others chose to do and not do when the mastigas were first an issue.

Now, with that ship—that scourge—on the move again, every one of them was experiencing the same anxiety and terror that he and the others felt thirty years ago.

Eurybia pointed to the screen, drawing his attention out of the sins of the past and back to the present. "They're moving!"

Indeed, the holo showed a sudden flurry of movement. Lelantos kept watch at the barricade while Victoria stood between Helena and Korakti, gesturing at both of them. Her apparent explanation also included—perhaps centered upon, if her body language could be read as easily as Aegesander read most people's—Daniel.

Victoria turned a placating hand to Korakti, then gestured at Helena, making some grand expression with both hands.

Helena nodded, making a single curt gesture with one hand that seemed to drive the point home to Korakti, who nodded in what Aegesander read as approval. Not happy approval, he realized she she crossed her arms firmly over her chest, but approval nonetheless.

At Victoria's signal, everyone but Daniel and Helena pulled the tables making up their makeshift barricade away, opening the passage once more. Daniel's Aegis stood well back, away from the opening, and Helena seemed to be taking shelter behind his armored bulk.

Tritogenes's Titan gestured to everyone in turn, and they all responded with affirmative nods and some sort of ready gesture or indication toward their weapon. After checking with everyone, Victoria nodded in approval and gestured to the Aegis.

The armored head nodded once, and Victoria took position beside Panatakis. The two of them stood to the left of the door, backs pressed against the wall, out of sight of anyone or anything on the far side. Korakti and Lelantos stood on the opposite side, weapons raised.

Before the Aegis could move, Aegesander entered a quick command to disregard his previous instruction regarding the video feeds from the Aegis. Rather than the strongest, he wanted to make absolutely sure that whatever feed his holo shifted to next was inside the room they were about to turn into a battleground.

The Aegis took off at a sudden sprint, using the wall opposite the door to kick start its momentum. It hurtled into the room and the feed went dead for less than a second before switching to an overhead shot.

The Hexarch scanned the area. It looked like this had once been the primary assembly area for this factory before it had been abandoned and re-purposed. Ouroboros were clearly not using the open space for assembly, but rather to create an otherwise impossible gauntlet of automatic and computerized weapons.

He could not see the entire room, but at a glance it appeared that no less than six automated guns tracked the Aegis into the room. A further four or five manned squad weapons added to that total, making the dozen or so individuals with personal weapons seem almost superfluous.

"Selene's Grace," Eurybia muttered. "Even the Aegis can't stand up to that kind of firepower. Can it?"

"I honestly don't know. It's held up against everything else so far, but I fear Second Lord Daniel is out or nearly out of ammunition. Whatever Victoria's plan is, let us hope it works, yes?"

Eurybia nodded, opened her mouth to speak, but the Aegis came under fire in the same moment. The machine guns opened fire first, but repeated losses apparently taught them that small arms like that could not penetrate the Aegis's armor. Instead, they saturated the area directly beside the armor, preventing the other Titans from coming forward.

Aegesander sat forward in his seat, drink forgotten on the side table. He was aware that the posture, especially with his elbows on his knees and his chin resting on his knuckles, was not exactly dignified. In that moment, he did not particularly care.

Bullets hit the Aegis uselessly, but Daniel did not fire back. He ran forward three more steps, forcing the autocannon to track him before they could fire, then dropped to the ground. He pulled the suit's knees up, then wrapped his arms around them, tucking everything behind that multi-layer of armor.

The computer-controlled autocannon tore into his armor, leaving great divots in the metal. Still, none of the other Titans entered the room for a full two seconds.

The rumble reached Aegesander's suite, a constant thump-thump-thump as the report from the autocannon vibrated the very bones of the Technocrats' greatest city. He felt his face go pale as the realization of how much firepower was at Ouroboros's disposal sank in. He, like everyone else involved in the day's missions, thought Ouroboros to be nothing more that a terrorist cell. At most, he reasoned, they might have a few machine guns and explosives, but this was *military* hardware aimed at the Titans.

The first through the door, ducking low so that the machine guns ricocheted off the Aegis rather than hitting her, Helena ran with more urgency than Aegesander had ever seen her exhibit.

Like the Aegis, she did not engage the guns or Ouroboros personnel in the room. Rather, she too dropped to the ground and sat with her back pressed tightly against the Aegis's metal spine.

"What is she doing, Aegesander?"

He narrowed his eyes, trying to bring her gestures into focus, and failed. The information displayed on his personal holo indicated the image was at maximum magnification unless he wanted to artificially magnify it, but that would just make things grainy and indistinct.

He frowned, unwilling to admit a failing, even in front of a trusted colleague like Eurybia, but found no other way to answer her question. "I don't know."

Whatever she was doing, Helena held her hands in front of her chest, directly in front of the tattered remnants of the planetary seal of Dasos that had been embroidered there.

Cannonfire continued to tear into the Aegis. Its arms were all but gone now, and the heavy bullets were making short work of the internals there and of the armor of the suit's legs.

Aegesander wondered how much time he had before those shots would breach the suit's chest armor, then decided he did not want to contemplate that.

Then, as one, the cannonfire stopped. The people operating the machine guns around the room, as well as those carrying smaller rifles all stared at their equipment in confusion as it stopped working. Aegesander could not read the error messages, but the angry red was unmistakable.

The calm underfoot was eerie. Even though the weapons had only been firing for a few tens of seconds, the sudden absence of vibration left things feeling flat and incomplete.

Helena stood up, stumbled as though dizzy, and placed both hands on her head. She bent forward, retching, but Aegesander could not see if she actually vomited or if it was merely a muscle spasm.

Then the autocannon exploded. First one, then two more, then three, then the final sixth and seventh in a stuttering series of blasts that shuddered up through Odyssey's structure like an earthquake.

"Did," Eurybia stopped, awe in her voice. "Did *Helena* do that?"

Aegesander went pale. His blood froze as a great abyss opened in his gut.

No. The thought repeated itself over and over in his head. No, no, no, no.

On the holo, the other Titans poured into the room, but he was only dimly aware of them. Korakti seemed gleeful, ready to fight. Panatakis and Lelantos were more reserved, staying close to the ruined bulk of the Aegis. Victoria raced forward like Korakti lagging behind only because one leg moved slower than the other. Still, she climbed the stairs and rails to engage the Ouroboros militia directly.

267

He barely noticed. The cold sweat on his brow was more interesting in that single, terrifying moment. He raised a hand a wiped his forehead clear.

"Aegesander?"

He asked himself a single question: what have I created?

"What's wrong?"

His thoughts raced, and he repeated his silent question aloud without realizing it. "What have I created?"

"You've done what we all did."

"No."

"You created a supersoldier."

"No! Afraid of the monsters nipping at our door, I created a monster of our own."

"Helena would not turn against us."

"Have you looked into her eyes, Eurybia?"

"Have I...? Aegesander, you're not making sense."

He dropped his head into his hands. "There's nothing human there. Ten Thousand, what did I put that poor girl through?"

Eurybia said something, some platitude that failed to make it from his ears to his brain. Aegesander's attention was fixed on his personal holo, where he navigated a series of menus, passwords, and biometric security measures.

Finally, he found what he was looking for, one single command represented by a single key press. Despite all the security, this system would still only accept input from his hand. He raised one finger.

"Terminal Security Protocol?" Eurybia said, reading the text over his shoulder.

Aegesander cursed silently. "Yes."

"Why?"

"I told you!" he snapped as his temper momentarily broke free of his control. "Did you see what she did? In a matter of seconds, she shut down and destroyed an entire roomful of equipment."

"Isn't that what you wanted?"

He took a deep breath. "I never knew what she would become, and as the Project accelerated, it was like Helena was dictating the pace of changes. Eurybia, she *isn't human anymore*."

Before she could argue, before her raised hand could reach far enough to stop him, Aegesander hit the key. His holo blinked red once, then the key vanished. The failsafe he never wanted to use, and would never need again, was active.

On the large holo by the wall, Helena dropped to one knee. Victoria and Korakti were too far forward to see, but Panatakis rushed to her side while Lelantos sped up the pace of his sharpshooting.

Aegesander let out the breath he had been holding and sagged back into the couch.

Eurybia's face reddened. "You killed her!"

"I did what I had to," he replied. He knew his voice was weak. A tired old man spoke to her rather than the statesman with a spine of steel he was when dealing with the outside world.

Aegesander raised a hand to his personal holo to deactivate the main viewer. He had seen enough of the Titans and their endeavors for the day.

His hand froze halfway to the control. On the holo, Helena rose to her feet, swaying with obvious vertigo. He frantically re-accessed the termination protocol. "Silence," he called it. It was inactive, having already been used.

Helena raised her head. Even in the relatively low quality image, Aegesander *knew* she was making eye contact with him through the camera. He could feel it deep in his soul.

His hands shook, unable to turn off the video feed.

Helena raised her pistol and fired, destroying the camera. Aegesander recoiled as though the shot had been aimed at him, which, he supposed, it was.

"I was right," he breathed.

"You tried to kill your Titan!" Eurybia shot up from the couch, making her way to the door. Her voice was thin, hurried, and full of seething rage. "The others will hear of this, Aegesander! The others wi—"

"The others will hear nothing!" he barked. It was not his usual strength, but he found some fire nonetheless. He rose to his feet. "This does not leave this room."

"The Council," she said, then stopped herself. "No, *Hyperion* will know."

"Hyperion is a snake! You will tell him nothing!" Aegesander roared. "Do not forget, Eurybia, that you are party to our secrets now. If any of this comes to light, any fate that comes to me will come to you as well."

She scowled. "I'm only party to *your* sins, Aegesander, because you chose to tell me. Now, *I* am choosing to leave this room."

"And?"

"And nothing!" she snapped.

Aegesander returned her scowl, meeting her acidic glare with fire. No one spoke to First Lord Aegesander like that. "Does your Panatakis have such a protocol, I wonder?"

Eurybia's face darkened in apoplectic rage. She opened her mouth, but no sound came out. Instead, she took several deep breaths. The anger never left her face, but her voice calmed. "I will keep your secret, Aegesander."

Chapter 15

Victoria did not return to her suite until an hour after midnight, nearly eleven hours after and she Pallasophia arrived on the scene of the stadium explosion. Quick heal staved off the worse effects from her injuries, but as her adrenaline ebbed on the return trip, fatigue and pain slowly crept in.

After returning from the Ouroboros facility, Victoria handed the rifle she had been using over to Odyssey security. She had no reason to keep it—the weapon was simply an unusually expensive piece of battlefield salvage as far as she was concerned—and was happy enough to get rid of it. At the same time, she filled out a request for a permit to be allowed to keep her personal carbine in her suite.

"Better response time," was her reasoning. She was not sure if that was sufficient, but the Third Lord working as a clerk in the armory seemed disinclined to argue with the blood-and-grime smeared Titan.

The six of them parted ways after that, each ostensibly to their own Hexarch's area. Korakti tried to get Daniel to go drinking with her, but he refused with as much politeness as any of them could muster at that point. Lelantos immediately called Rivka, and was deep in conversation with her even before Victoria left. Helena and Panatakis went somewhere on their own; she was not sure where.

Walking hurt. The knife that stabbed her leg might not have torn her flesh very badly. In fact, it was probably the least painful wound she had experienced in her life, or any previous life's memory. The problem was that it went deep, and as her adrenaline faded, she became acutely aware of exactly how deep.

Now, she carried her helmet in one hand, cracked and damaged from the fight. Her helmet prevented any cuts, but simply being knocked around left bruises on her cheekbones. Her eyes felt swollen and heavy. Her uniform covered the worst injuries, but even it had been badly torn. Blood, hers and that of numerous Ouroboros terrorists, soaked fabric and left stains darker than black.

Even this late at night, Odyssey was not quiet, and people gave her space as she walked. She was sure she looked terrible, perhaps even dangerous or monstrous despite their best efforts to clean their hands and faces in the armory. Bruises could not be washed away, nor could the cuts and stains on her clothing.

She let people see her face as she passed. Some shied away, but others watched her go with respect. At worst, they were leery, but the many people she passed seemed to be regarding her with, of all things, *awe*. Noises from the gunfire and explosions reached far and wide, and they all knew where she had been.

Image, she thought; let them see for themselves exactly how hard she fought to keep them safe. She was tired, she hurt—yet she kept her head high and returned every greeting, every smile. She was bloody, dirty, but the people she passed needed to see that she won, that all six Titans won. Odyssey was safe, and all she had to do to enforce that idea was keep her head up just a little longer.

People she did not recognize thanked her, congratulated her. They addressed her by name, by rank, or even just as "Titan of Limani." Her feelings came and went. Some she simply nodded acknowledgment, and

272

others she spoke to. She gave them few words, but those words seemed to carry a great importance, no matter what she said.

Victoria was not sure she knew what she said.

She stopped in the corridor outside her suite, catching her breath and leaning against the wall with one hand. This was the time when she should have been curled up, sleeping under an air duct or behind a nest of pipes to steal some rest before the next mastigas attack.

Instead, she had a bed to go back to. Real, hot food and cold drinks awaited her just a few more meters away. With a deep breath, she pushed away from the wall, catching a concerned glance from a passing Second Lord.

Before he could ask, Victoria wordlessly waved him on. He nodded and continued down the hall. "Thank you, Titan," he might have said.

She paused again in front of the door to her suite. Several deep breaths later—it would not do for Pallasophia to see how tired she was—Victoria reached for the door lock. At least, she thought, she was no longer *actively* bleeding.

The door slid into the wall on silent tracks, unleashing a wave of pleasant scents. In the moment, Victoria could not discern which of them she was happiest to smell, the sharp scents of cooking meat or the soft smell of tea.

The door slid closed, locking automatically, and Victoria looked around the room. Pallasophia had reset the furniture, something which they had no had time to do before leaving for Molyvos. The Ouroboros facility felt so similar to Aphelion's depths that Victoria again felt the shock of stepping into some place that was both *clean* and *safe*.

If that shock put her on edge, those feelings vanished as Pallasophia stepped out of their shared bathroom, drying her hands. She wore a loose shirt held up by a pair of thin shoulder straps and shorts that barely reached the top of her thighs. Both articles of clothing were made of some soft, pale blue material.

Unlike many Second Lords who felt their rank's color was only for their robes, Pallasophia actually liked the color.

She smiled, opened her mouth to speak, and then closed it again. Instead, Pallasophia crossed the room and threw her arms around Victoria's neck.

The sudden jolt sent a spasm of pain through her side and calf, but it was nothing truly unpleasant. If anything, their relative height differences would have made the sudden embrace amusing if it had not been such a pleasant surprise.

After a long moment, Pallasophia stepped back. Some, but very little, of the dried blood and grease from Victoria's uniform transferred, but she seemed not to care. "I was just going to point out that if you were trying to surprise me, I knew you were coming as soon as you came through the door to this area, but..."

"This was a better greeting," Victoria supplied. She smiled, or thought she did. Her face moved, but she was too tired to tell exactly how it did that.

"Yes."

"And there's food."

"Food?" Pallasophia smiled, then laughed. "I ate hours ago."

"Oh. I could still smell it, and..."

She laughed again. "Of course I'm heating it back up for you, Victoria."

Now, Victoria laughed as well. The sound was not quite as vibrant as Pallasophia's had been. She laughed with a harsh undercurrent of fatigue, energy drained by hours of stress and fighting. "Sorry. It's been a long day."

"I imagine so," Pallasophia said. She made a show of summoning a clock on her personal holo, checking the time, then waving it away. "Take some time to clean up while the food finishes heating. I'll bring you some tea in the meantime."

"How long?"

"Hmm?"

Victoria stopped, already halfway to her bedroom. "How long until it's time to eat?" Pallasophia laughed once more, then shrugged her shoulders. She smiled, and the fog in Victoria's brain parted. "Whenever you want. Why?"

She stepped into the bedroom, leaving the door open. "I'm going to draw a bath and try not to bleed in it."

"You know," Pallasophia called from the main room, "coming from anyone else, that statement would alarm me."

Victoria laughed, but said nothing. Instead, she opened the suite's controls on her holo and opened the faucet in the bath. She then set the temperature and waited until the system heated and the sounds of water came from the bathroom before doing anything else.

While the bath filled, she turned her attention to getting out of her combat uniform. Ostensibly, it was an easy task, but two things complicated matters. First, her wounds still made certain movements difficult. Quick heal closed them up, mostly, and sped the healing process along, but it was no magic cure. Second, one of the buckles securing her gel-reinforced jacket had been crushed during the fight.

Victoria cursed quietly, trying to make the twisted buckle detach. After a minute of fruitless straining, she took a knife and cut the strap instead. The piece fell to the floor with a soft thump, weighed down by the dense gel plates.

She tapped a quick note into her holo about the problem and sent it to Tritogenes's armorers. She also included the location of her gunshot wound and a not-too-subtle note that perhaps they could improve the protection on her side.

Piece by piece, she dropped her armor pieces into a grimy pile on the floor, telling herself she could pick them up later. She was *safe* here, and not everything had to be done immediately. Even the voices of her past deaths had no argument against that.

Underneath the armor, her suit showed less damage than she expected. Except for a few instances, both of which entered her mind again as stabs of pain shot through her body, the high-strength fabric seemed to have done its job. Moreso than even the mastigas fabric she scavenged from her would-be killers, this suit, made specially for her, did its job and kept minor cuts away from her skin.

Minor cuts, Victoria reminded herself as she undid the closures holding the top together. It dropped to the floor, starting a pile next to her armor, fluttering with a few more openings than it had when she put it on that afternoon.

Even without removing her undershirt, the worst of her injuries still stood out against her skin. The scar from the mastigas elite was a clean white line across her side. Above it, the mark left by the second sophont's handmade gun was still a red-tinted patch of twisted tissue. Thankfully, it no longer hurt, but from the look of the damage there, it was not quite healed yet, either.

That, or, Victoria thought with something between a grin and a grimace, she re-opened something internal in her shoulder. The multiple doses of full-body quick heal she administered should, theoretically, fix any potential problems there, but if it started bruising, at least she would know why.

By far, the worse injury was on her flank opposite the elite's sword-scar, although she could not see the very worst of it. The entry wound stopped bleeding shortly after the first direct application of quick heal, and looked like it would leave a much smaller scar than the sophont's low-velocity bullet.

A "through and through," one of the voices from a past life called it. The feeling that came with it implied she should feel lucky, because if the bullet had tumbled, the damage would have been much worse.

She could not twist around enough to see the exit wound without pain, but Lelantos had showed an image to her while they waited for the other Titans. That wound was much larger, which was perhaps a small mercy because it made it easier to apply quick heal directly to the damaged tissue.

Victoria reached behind her and felt of the area gently. The skin was sensitive there, and the solidified quick heal bandage remained mostly in place. It had cracked and torn during the final fight, however, and she amended her earlier thought.

At least she was not bleeding *much.*

Her shoes went onto the pile with armor, then pants onto the clothes pile. Other than the wound on her calf, her legs were fairly free of damage. Victoria supposed she had that much to be thankful for. Memories of an older self crippled by a torn thigh muscle, one of the few things she did not vicariously experience during her time in Aphelion, surfaced amid a wave of panic and nauseating pain.

Victoria pushed those images aside as her real, undamaged muscles twitched in response. Her legs were tired and sore as it was, and she had no need to add imagined pain and damage to that.

She then knelt to examine her calf. The wound there had originally been clean, done by the cold edge of a very sharp knife. Yet, it was in the meat of her calf, and since being stabbed, Victoria had done a lot of running, walking, and climbing. The once-clean edges of the wound had torn, ripping through multiple liquid bandages and smearing a mixture of quick heal and blood across her lower leg and into her shoe.

Probing the area, the wound was warm to the touch, which set off no end of mental alerts among her past selves. A hot wound, they all told her, meant infection. Infection, they continued, meant death.

Death.

Death.

Victoria grit her teeth, then took several deep breaths. She tried to remember Helena's meditating hand gestures, failed, and contented herself with simply interlacing her fingers as she fought to control her suddenly racing pulse.

If her past lives were real, she would have scolded them, told them to leave her alone. She was safe and an infected wound just meant that it hurt more and would require more care.

But they were not real, and continued to scream death into her mind for another minute before she organized her thoughts.

Those memories might have saved her life in Aphelion, but anymore they were becoming less useful and more intrusive. She supposed a meditation routine might help and made a note on her holo to talk to Helena once the cyborg woman was healthy again.

She placed her underclothes on top of the pile made by her black suit. Leaving aside the blood and grime, she suddenly felt much more comfortable. The black combat uniform was exactly that, a uniform. Now, without it, she felt like she could relax.

In the next room, the faucet shut off automatically. Victoria rose and went into the bathroom, pleased that, unlike her room at Aphelion, the floor here was not cold on her bare feet. Absently, she marveled at how something so unimportant like that could make such a big difference in comfort, but it did.

This bathroom was larger than the one at Aphelion, too, meant to be used by both of the suite's occupants. A large counter with a pair sinks dominated the wall to Victoria's right, with a toilet nearby. A pair of small shower stalls filled the wall to her left. In the center of the room, taking up much of the available area, a spacious bathtub sat, already filled with gently steaming water thanks to the automated system's control.

Victoria both longed for and dreaded the next few moments, but took a deep breath and stepped with her un-wounded leg into the hot water. The temperature was exactly where she wanted it and already was starting to soothe the tension in that foot.

It was the other leg—and by extension her side—that was going to be the problem. She gently lowered that leg into the hot water, taking deep, quick breaths to dispel the pain as the water touched the stab wound.

By comparison, the shock when the water hit the gunshot wound in her side was rather minor.

After a minute, however, temperatures started to equalize and the throb from deep inside those two newest wounds slowly faded into the background.

Pallasophia knocked on the only closed door in the room, the one leading to her bedroom, then entered with a mug in each hand. She handed one to Victoria, then went to the showers where a towel-draped wooden chair waited. She pushed the towels onto the floor, looked at them, shrugged, and carried the chair to the side of the bath.

"You look like hell," she observed.

Victoria laughed. "You should see the other guys."

Pallasophia smiled. "I have, actually. Rivka provided a copy of her after-action report."

Raised a questioning eyebrow, Victoria asked, "I thought it was classified."

"The official report is, yes. To be honest, I'll be surprised if even the official report explains exactly why you six went down there. First Lord Aegesander is already calling the stadium explosion a 'pyrotechnics accident' to assuage the populace's concerns."

"Those explosions reached people all the way up here," Victoria said. "They told me."

Pallasophia nodded. "I know. And I'm sure they suspect what happened, but Aegesander is pushing the Council to keep things quiet to avoid inciting a panic across the binary."

Victoria scoffed and sank deeper into water that was already turning a dull shade of red. "What did Rivka's report say? And, more importantly, why is hers different from the official report?"

"Let's just say that First Lord Rivka and I are old business associates."

Victoria snorted a moment of laughter, then turned a sarcastic grin toward Pallasophia. "As you say, Second Lord."

"It was different working with her in person, though."

Victoria nodded. "First Lord Rivka is an impressive woman."

"She is."

Victoria finally took a moment to take a deep, deliberate inhalation of her tea. Simply holding it, she noticed some floral aromas and some kind of spice or fruit, but her mind had been otherwise occupied at that point. Now, she took a deep breath, savoring the smell of rose, chamomile, and a handful of other scents that traveled deep into her mind, relaxing her.

She sipped the tea, hotter even than her bath water, and that feeling of relaxation intensified, radiating outward just as the heat from the water seeped in.

Victoria laughed. "If you've got Rivka's copy of what really happened, I suppose I don't need to explain what took so long."

"You don't have to," Pallasophia replied, "but I would appreciate hearing it."

Victoria took another sip of her tea, then began her explanation with the empty bomb-making facility. Pallasophia seemed especially interested in Victoria's attempts to coordinate Helena and Korakti's conflicting personalities, though even that took a proverbial back seat to the spectacle that was Helena's show of power.

"And she did that with her mind?" Pallasophia asked.

Victoria went to take another sip from her tea, found it empty, and frowned. Pallasophia took the mug and placed it on the floor beside her chair with a gentle clack.

"Her implants, which I suppose at this point is the same thing," Victoria replied after a moment's thought. She let her hands sink under the water now that she no longer had a mug to keep out of the bath. Her blood made little swirls as she swished her fingers through the warm water. The filters took care of most of it, but the worst of her wounds were still open—not that she cared as long as the tub's heater continued working. "It still took almost forty minutes to finish that fight, then over an hour to break into the Ouroboros computer system."

"Rivka said as much. Between us, I suspect there will be very little 'official' that happens from those records."

Victoria frowned. "I don't want to agree, but I do."

"What's wrong?"

Victoria explained what the Ouroboros soldier told her about their beliefs, that Project Titan was part of some sort of multi-step plan to consolidate power in the hands of the Hexarchs.

Pallasophia's eyes went wide with surprise, then she laughed. "That's stupid. They *already* have all the power in the binary."

"I know that, but these people were willing to die over it."

"Stupid," Pallasophia said, "and troubling. Still, I'm glad you're alright."

Victoria laughed and lifted her injured leg out of the water. A trickle of blood ran down her calf. The filters, the only thing preventing the water from becoming a disgusting soup of bloody sweat, would take care of it soon enough.

"Yes," Pallasophia said as Victoria returned her leg to the water, "but you're alive. I was... worried."

"We had this discussion," she replied. "I'm a Titan."

Pallasophia reached out and put a hand on Victoria's shoulder. Her palm was cold, at least compared to Victoria's bath-warmed skin. "Doesn't mean I can't worry about you."

Victoria put a hand over Pallasophia's, leaning her head against their hands in automatic reflex. "Thank you. I..." For a moment, she was not sure eaxctly what words she wanted to say. "I appreciate it."

They sat like that for longer than Victoria would have expected. It could not have been comfortable for Pallasophia to lean forward like that, but she did not seem bothered. For her part, Victoria was rather unwilling to let go of the other woman's hand.

Finally, Pallasophia took her hand off Victoria's shoulder and sat back in her chair. "So."

"What?"

She frowned, deep and dramatic. "You got shot again."

Victoria laughed, relaxed and almost as bright and carefree as Pallasophia sounded that morning, before things started exploding. "It wasn't my first choice."

"I imagine not."

The companionable—comforting, even—silence lasted for a while longer before Victoria felt the tug of fatigue finally pushing through as her muscles continued to loosen. "I need to actually wash all this dirt and blood off before I get in bed."

"No food?"

She laughed. "Ok, yes. Soap, food, bed, in that order."

"Let me help," Pallasophia said. Her tone indicated that, while Victoria was free to refuse, it was not exactly a request. When she did not reply for a moment, Pallasophia pushed a little harder. "You're injured. I watched how you moved when you came in. At least let me get your back."

"I can reach."

"You can," she said, "but that doesn't mean you should, or that you can without it hurting."

Victoria knew she was right, and no argument her fatigued and heat-fogged brain could conjure was strong enough to counter it. Twisting to reach her back would be painful, she knew that much from trying to apply quick heal to the wounds there. More important, Pallasophia was offering to help her because she cared and wanted to make the healing process easier.

Victoria's thoughts continued racing. More important than convenience, she actually *liked* the suggestion.

"Alright," she said after a moment more of thought. Victoria sat up in the bath, conscious of the changes in Pallasophia's eyes as they traveled down her torso to the gunshot wound in her side.

Pallasophia got out of the chair and moved around behind her, making her the first person to be that close to Victoria's back without eliciting a fight-or-flight reaction. "Gods between," she muttered. Victoria assumed she was reacting to the bullet's exit wound.

Pallasophia ran water and a soft washcloth over the wound, but otherwise stayed away from it as much as possible. The whole process only took a few minutes, but during those fleeting moments Victoria realized something that she had not quite processed before.

She rather enjoyed the touch of Pallasophia's hands on her skin.

***

The rest of the bath did not last much longer. The cleaner she became, the more Victoria's stomach growled. With her skin free of dirt and grime, and mostly free of blood, she tried off and let the bathtub drain. Pallasophia excused herself at that point, and when Victoria came into the main room, she found food and drink waiting for her.

They did not speak very much while she ate, instead sharing a comfortable silence broken only by occasional curses as Victoria moved in unexpected directions. She took her own plate and glasses to the kitchen, they said their goodnights, and Victoria finally made her way to the bed.

She had yet to turn off her room's lights when Pallasophia returned, knocking on the perpetually open doorway with her knuckles.

"Helena's on her way here," she said.

Victoria's head shot up. It had to be nearly two hours after midnight, perhaps even later than that, and Helena should have been asleep already. Of course, *Victoria* should have been asleep already, so she could hardly hold a bout of insomnia against her.

Yet, an unexpected visit was rather different.

Her pulse spiked suddenly, surprise and concern flashing across her face quicker than her still-developing control could stop. One deep breath, then two, and her pulse began to slow. "Has she contacted us?"

Pallasophia stepped fully into the room, shaking her head. "No. Truthfully, I only know that it's Helena because my system just got a ping that Tritogenes was headed this way, and I know for a fact that he's visiting First Lord Enyalios right now."

Victoria nodded, though that revelation did little to calm her down. If anything, it made things worse as she began to put the pieces together. Impersonating a Hexarch was a serious crime, and the ability to convincingly do so was limited to a small number of people. So, her thoughts continued, either Helena *was* on her way, or Ouroboros had more in common with the multi-headed hydra than a self-renewing serpent.

She explained her thought process aloud, then added, "so get a weapon, just in case."

Pallasophia nodded. Her facial expression said she agreed, but she was not about to waste a moment doing so verbally. At that point, even Victoria's system, which did not have the same high-profile access her Second Lord suitemate enjoyed, pinged an alert that "Tritogenes" was on "his" way.

Victoria threw on a simple black robe, a gift from a wealthy Second Lord, that served as a housecoat when she did not want to get dressed, but could not in good manners sit around completely unclothed. Intricate, embroidered flowers covered it from top to bottom, picked out in vibrant shades of purple. The note that came with it had been anonymous, but entreated her not to take rank too seriously.

She secreted a small knife in a band just under her left breast, the handle angled so that she could withdraw it through the overlapping front of the robe without having to move too much fabric out of the way.

Emerging from her bedroom, Pallasophia had a similar thought, only her plan was a pistol strapped to her otherwise bare thigh. She had not changed out of the tank top and shorts she wore when Victoria returned home, and the weapon was plainly visible.

The door chimed and Victoria moved to it. Pallasophia tried to interpose herself between Victoria and the door, prompting a brief—if wordless—argument between the two of them.

Victoria indicated her stature. If it was not Helena, she was better suited to am immediate fight. She tried to explain that with a series of gestures, most of them relating of her height and shoulder breadth.

Pallasophia frowned and pointed at her pistol.

Victoria shook her head, placed a hand on Pallasophia's shoulder and stepped toward the door.

Pallasophia pointed at Victoria's side, to the gunshot wound.

Victoria waved that away, patted her knife. She was fine, she tried to show. She smiled. A little combat right then would be a good way to unwind, she thought, a fitting epilogue to the problem that had been Ouroboros.

Finally, Pallasophia indicated the door, her pistol, and Victoria, in that order.

Victoria nodded, assuming she was trying to say she would cover her if anything bad happened. She went for the door, stopped, and whispered, "these rooms are soundproof, aren't they?"

Pallasophia shrugged. "You started it."

Victoria laughed, then tapped the control next to the door. A key helpfully labeled "audio," stood out next to a grayed-out toggle for "video." She tried the video key unsuccessfully, but the audio button depressed easily enough.

"Tritogenes is..." She started to explain that they knew Tritogenes was not the one in the hallway, but Helena's voice cut her off.

"I know that. I apologize for stealing his access codes and will pay whatever fine he feels necessary. This is urgent."

Helena's tone rose the hair on the back of Victoria's neck. She sounded panicked, and even the flashbang temporarily shutting down Panatakis's implants had not filled her voice with that much obvious fear.

Victoria did not waste another moment, reached out for the holo control next to the door and opened it. It slid into the wall, as always, with silent motion, but the sight on the other side was anything but normal.

Helena had changed clothes and taken a bath since the mission ended. That much was obvious. Her robe was as immaculate as ever, if it seemed a little bit older and more frayed at the edges than something she would have normally worn.

What was unusual was her face. Unlike Victoria, Helena fully indulged in the Technocrat custom of extravagant makeup, but at that particular moment, her face was bare. That in and of itself would have been strange, but Victoria looked beyond that to her skin. The flesh around Helena's implants was reddened, swollen.

She pushed past Victoria, into the suite. If she noticed Victoria's knife or cared about Pallasophia's pistol, she did not make a show of it.

"Victoria," she began, then paused. She eyed Pallasophia.

"I trust her," Victoria said, reading the obvious question in the cyborg Titan's expression. She added, "completely," a moment later.

Still, Pallasophia stepped out of the room.

"Coffee, please."

Victoria watched Helena as she spoke even that simple request. Despite the politeness, the movements of her jaw were forced and painful-looking. Every time she went to open her mouth or close it, some force seemed to be fighting her.

Rather, Victoria realized as she watched Helena *stumble* her way to the couch, nothing was actively fighting Helena's movements. Instead, she moved like Panatakis did when the flashbang damaged his implants and he was just regaining consciousness.

More to the point, Helena moved like she had been moving since destroying the Ouroboros turrets. She had not taken part in much of the firefight afterward and had been tense and angry during the aftermath.

Victoria frowned as Helena sank into the couch like an old woman. Korakti blamed it on her injured pride, that Victoria's plan had been the successful one, and Helena herself claimed she simply had been struck by debris that left her with a sense of vertigo.

No, Victoria realized, crossing the small room in Helena's wake. Something had gone wrong with her implants. If she was there, rather than somewhere in Aegesander's or even Eurybia's sections, then that something had to be catastrophic indeed.

Victoria eased herself into a chair opposite the couch. She might not have felt the fatigue and pain that was obvious on Helena's face, but her wounds would continue to ache until she had a decent night's sleep. At that point, that was looking to be a very unlikely scenario indeed.

"Did you see me collapse?" Helena asked.

Victoria raised her eyebrows, both of them, opening her face in interest and confusion. "Collapse?"

"During the fighting, after the turrets exploded."

She shook her head. "Lelantos said something, but I assumed you overloaded your implants accessing so many devices at the same time."

Helena's eyes fell. The sudden absence of their usual blue brightness made her face seem hollow. "There was a problem with my implants, yes. In fact, you are correct that they overloaded. They experienced an energy surge four-thousand percent in excess of their usual maximum."

Victoria sat back, folding her hands in her lap. "But."

"The energy surge was not a by-product of my exertions. Two-point-oh-oh-three milliseconds before the surge, I became aware of a subroutine within my implants. Until that moment, I was unaware of its existence, though now that I have become aware, I have discovered several other links and concerning data clusters within the system architecture."

287

She continued to explain the problem for several more minutes. Pallasophia returned with a cup of coffee and two mugs of watered honey wine in Hyperion's signature style for herself and Victoria.

Ordinarily, Victoria might have interrupted her, urging Helena to get to whatever point it was she was trying to make. She long since lost Victoria amid the technical terminology and esoteric phrases—though Victoria suspected Pallasophia was able to follow along much better. Helena continued to be agitated, however, and so Victoria allowed her to talk until she seemed to come to a natural stopping point.

"So someone tried to have you killed."

Pallasophia set her now-empty mug on the table. "It sounds like someone managed to slip a corrupted data packet into your system. Possibly a failsafe from the Ouroboros base?"

Helena shook her head. "If that was the case, I would not be here."

Rather than reply directly, Victoria waited, watching over the top of her half-full mug.

Finally, Helena's mouth opened. No sound came out for a moment, and she shut it again. Taking a deep breath, she started to speak again, grating the words through clenched teeth. "Aegesander. Did. This."

"Selene's Grace," Pallasophia swore. "Can you prove it?"

Again, Helena's eyes fell. "No. No traces of the program remain. They erase themselves even as I find them."

Victoria rose. Without realizing it, she tightened one fist and the other slipped into her robe, touching the rough plastic hilt of the knife secreted there. "What can we do?"

"To him?" Helena asked. "Nothing. None of us, not even myself, could get close enough to him."

"Better question," Pallasophia said. "What can we do for you?"

"I came here to request a place to stay until we leave for the mastigas ship."

"All we have is the couch," Victoria said. "It's comfortable enough."

"It will do. Even in their current, suboptimal state, my implants will manage enough autonomous functions so that I will be able to sleep comfortably on any surface you make available to me."

Victoria turned an inquisitive glance toward Pallasophia, who nodded. "Do you have any possessions you need to bring?"

"Others will bring them," she said. "People who can move through my quarters without attracting too much attention. They are all small items, easily hidden."

Pallasophia nodded again. "In the morning, I'll program the door for you."

Helena smiled. Victoria suspected the other Titan could have re-programmed the door herself if she so chose, but it was the gesture that was important. "Thank you."

Victoria rose. "If you need anything, wake me."

"Of course," Helena replied. "Thank you again. I will repay you this kindness."

Victoria smiled. "We're a team. This is what we do."

"Of course," Helena replied. "Good night, Spatharios."

Chapter 16

A Second Lord—or at least that was what the blue robe usually meant, except this robe was completely *blank* of any designs—wearing a mask stepped into the room Third Lord Mihalis was rapidly starting to think of as "his." The mask sported a stylized serpent eating its own tail painted in black on an otherwise featureless gray expanse. Even the holes for the eyes, nose, and mouth were covered by a fine mesh indistinguishable from the rest of the mask in the dim light of his room.

The Second Lord waved a hand and the room brightened. Mihalis sat up on the bed, eyeing his visitor. They eyed him with a curious tilt of the head that Mihalis might have called interest or disdain if he could have seen their eyes.

The first few times this happened, the visitor actually woke him up, but recently, Mihalis's sleep had been rougher and less deep. This morning—at least he thought it was morning because now was the time they chose for him to wake up—he had been awake and waiting for his visitor for some time.

"Good morning, Mihalis," she said. With the robe and mask, the sound of her voice was the only clue he might have had to her identity.

Even then, it was muffled and distorted by some kind of modulator inside the mask itself.

He did not answer.

"Your breakfast will be brought soon."

Still, he did not answer.

"Is something troubling you today, Mihalis?"

He considered maintaining his silence, but the urge to simply *speak* to someone screamed at the back of his mind. After a moment, he said, "Third Lord."

His visitor tilted her head in question.

"I'm a Third Lord. I'd like to be addressed as such."

She nodded. "Very well. Let us start over, then. Good morning, Third Lord Mihalis."

Grudgingly, or perhaps spurred by the fact that this person actually was doing what he asked, he replied, "good morning, Second Lord."

"You may call me Larisa," she said.

Silence.

"If you wish."

He frowned. "'Second Lord' is fine."

"Of course. As I said, your breakfast will be around shortly, Third Lord."

"Thank you. What am I being fed today, Second Lord?"

"A hand pie with meat and cheese, fruit, and sweet cream. Your ration of coffee has been replaced with hot chocolate, I believe."

He wanted to frown or scowl, he really did, but *gods between*. These people fed him well. Mihalis supposed that was all part of their plan, and he had to admit that it was working.

So, Mihalis said nothing, but simply nodded in acknowledgment.

"Are you ready to talk about what you saw?" she asked.

"I saw the mastigas ship destroy our squadron one by one, including the *Tartarus*. I watched..." He choked up. The attack had not been long ago and the images, even the sanitized images from the ship's sensor

291

display, still clawed at the back of his eyelids every time he closed his eyes. "I saw twenty-two *thousand* people die."

"It must have been terrible, Third Lord."

"The mastigas are en route to Dasos even now."

"Are you sure it was the mastigas you saw?"

He scowled. It was the same question every day. "It was the mastigas."

"And where did the mastigas get their ship?"

He refused to answer.

The Second Lord knelt down, bringing her masked face to a level lower than his. She looked like she was pleading now, but her voice lost none of his power or authority. "Why do you think they attacked, Third Lord?"

Mihalis maintained his silence.

"Are you sure their attack was unprovoked?"

He scowled. "It was unprovoked, just like the attack on Kipos five years ago."

The Second Lord rose to her feet again. "When the mastigas attacked Kipos, the Hexarchs created Project Titan. Now that it is complete, the mastigas attack again. Ask yourself if that could be coincidence."

"I've seen mastigas with my own eyes, Second Lord. They're real."

"Of course they're real, Third Lord. No one denies that. But we both know these attacks are not unprovoked."

Mihalis grit his teeth, reminding himself to keep his temper. These people, they called themselves Ouroboros, held his life and comfort in their hands. Until he could figure out a way out of wherever this prison was, he had a part to play.

"Are you sure, Third Lord, that the *Tartarus* did not bait the mastigas into attacking? Ask yourself why the lives of your crewmates were thrown away like they were."

his inner thoughts urged him to say something, to fight back, even verbally, but he did not. Mihalis kept his lips very tightly shut. He kept his hands in his lap, right on top of the left, tightening the fingers of his left hand into a fist. He wanted to yell, but he did not.

"Ask yourself, dear Third Lord Mihalis, if you do not want justice for what was done to you."

Finally, he raised his eyes. His resolve shook, cracked. "I want justice," he said. "Against the mastigas."

The masked face turned toward the ground. He imagined her eyes, closed in regret. Slowly, she turned to leave. "Perhaps tomorrow, Third Lord, you will be ready to tell the *right* story."

***

Third Lord Mihalis woke up in the darkness of his room—his cell— and kept himself perfectly still. Despite being kidnapped by what he could only assume was some sort of terrorist organization or, at best, a paramilitary militia, he was still being treated rather well. They had not beaten or otherwise physically mistreated him beyond simple imprisonment.

They even seemed quite reasonable, telling him that they were hiding him away "for his own protection" in case the general population got word of his news that the mastigas were on their way.

Apparently, they tried to intercept him on the way to his meeting with Tritogenes, but were unsuccessful. He learned that when one of the guards let slip that he was on "prisoner detail" because his squad failed to get to Mihalis before he got to Tritogenes.

When the guards said that, they thought, as they did at the moment, that Mihalis was asleep. In truth, he had not been sleeping well for several days, which allowed him to gather a great deal of information about his surroundings.

Unfortunately, none of that information was useful. All he knew for certain is that he had been moved multiple times, including at least one orbital flight. It was not long enough to leave Prosgeiosi, so until proven otherwise, he was prepared to simply assume it was a flight around the capital planet that his captors stretched out to deliberately confuse him. They knew he was a navigator; such tactics were logical.

Even blindfolded and locked in a passenger compartment, he could at least tell basic things about the flight. Angle of ascent and descent, for instance, were easy enough. Past that, he knew nothing.

Really, he thought, if it were not for the blindfolds and complete lack of freedom, he might have supposed he really was in protective custody. The constant leading questions, however, blew that theory apart. True protective custody would not involve trying to get him to change his story.

None of the soldiers bore the emblems of Hexarchs, which was the biggest clue of all. Instead, everyone he had seen wore a blank robe or uniform suit with the same serpent mask.

The only clue to their affiliation was the name "Ouroboros," but that meant nothing to him. Mihalis spent years in the outer system, watching over the mastigas battleship. For all he knew, this Ouroboros was a well-known group, but they took his holo away and he had not been able to access any news or other data for days now.

Two nights ago, at least as far as he could calculate "night" based on when he got tired, he overheard the guards talking about Project Titan and the mastigas. They seemed to distrust Project Titan, claiming it was a military takeover by the Hexarchs. That made no sense, no matter how he tried to look at it. The Hexarchs already controlled the binary, and they did so generally quite well, and he failed to understand the motivation they might have to force a military coup of any sort.

That, he thought, was bad enough. It explained why they tried to prevent him from talking to Tritogenes, anyway. It was the rest of the conversation that prompted him to escape or die trying—a decision that, made by anyone else, anywhere else, he would have called overly dramatic.

The mastigas, they said, were not a real threat. No one could deny that the mastigas existed; those terrifying soldiers attacked the outer rim before he was born. They attacked Kipos five years ago, and the footage was real enough. Instead, they said the Hexarchs were simply using the mastigas as a smokescreen and justification for Project Titan. As an organization, Ouroboros believed the Hexarchs were baiting the mastigas into attacking and that, if left alone, the mastigas would simply leave the Technocrats alone.

That, they said, was why they kidnapped Mihalis—and, apparently, many of the other survivors of the battle. His story of unprovoked aggression from the mastigas could not be allowed to get out. It would, they said, galvanize popular support behind Project Titan.

Mihalis wanted to strangle the man who said that, who reduced the deaths of tens of thousands of people, many of whom Mihalis knew personally, to a piece of their political agenda. At that moment, he was supposed to be asleep, which he supposed was the only reason the guards were being so loose with their conversation.

Second Lord Anaxagoras, Mihalis's now-deceased CO from the *Phlegethon*, would have had more than a few words to say about the lack of discipline among his anonymous, masked guards.

So he continued to feign sleep, listening, waiting.

He wished Aella was with him. She could have rigged something out of the simple electronics around them, but he had no such skill with anything other than navigation plots. On the other hand, that lack of skill would, he hoped, come in handy in just a moment. He could not build anything complex, but he was rather good at taking things apart.

The guards outside his door shifted around, bored. That was another part of his "not a prisoner" prison. The door was open at all times, ostensibly allowing him the freedom to leave whenever he wanted. In reality, two guards waited just past the door frame. More stood in the hall at regular intervals, but he had only seen them on the way in.

Mihalis was trapped in a room with smart technology and without weapons. Even his food was brought to him by uniformed and masked Ouroboros members. Early on, he refused to eat, but finally someone in a half-mask sat down with him and silently ate half of his meal. When his apparent food taster did not die or suffer any ill effect, Mihalis accepted it and ate.

That, at least, he was glad for. He was not looking forward to being a prisoner *and* starving.

Finally, the guards outside his room changed shift. He could not recognize anyone by their voice, but most of the guards who came in after midnight displayed much less discipline than their day-shift comrades. Mihalis had been instructed to go to sleep some hours before, meaning there was a good chance this was the midnight shift.

He rolled over in bed, turning his face away from the door. In his hands rested the light diode from his bedside lamp. What good that lamp was supposed to do was a mystery, as he was not permitted any reading material, but that also meant he never turned it on. Also scavenged from the lamp was a simple manual control stud.

Mihalis draped a piece of the gray bedsheet over the light and switched it on. He wished the light would get hot enough to set the bed on fire, but that was not an option without more technical engineering skill than he possessed.

Instead, it bathed his face in a dim, gray glow. He waved his hands in front of the light, pantomiming the sorts of movements he would make to navigate a holographic interface. Some of the movements were so ingrained in his muscle memory that pretending was almost as easy as actually doing them. A wave here and a key press and he would have been checking shipboard messages, then another flick of a finger would scroll the readout past the high-priority messages from the *Phlegethon*'s captain and take him to the ship's social boards.

Mihalis's throat tightened as he mimicked the actions he made every day for years. His brain went to the people who would never contact him again, and to whom he could never reach out.

So many lives lost in the blink of an eye. It ate at his soul, weighing it down like an anchor.

"We are the gods' justice made flesh," one of his interrogators said the other day. He talked about how the Hexarchs arranged everything from provocations against the mastigas to the groundswell of popular support behind the Titans.

When Mihalis refused to agree with him, the man left him alone in his cell. "You'll understand in time," he said. "Goodnight, Third Lord Mihalis. We will speak again in the morning. In the meantime, ask yourself: do you not want justice?"

Mihalis scowled. If these Ouroboros terrorists wanted justice, he would give it to them. At that thought, he laughed—gods, he was getting dramatic as his imprisonment wore on. That laugh choked in moments, turning to a hastily swallowed sob.

He had work to do. His hand trembled, but he continued the act. He was doing this for *them*, he told himself. Mihalis ground his teeth together and continued paging through imaginary menus. His actions cast tall shadows on the walls, impossible to miss if the guards would only look through the door and check on him.

The guards outside his door made a noise, shifting around. Neither of them talked yet. That was good, he reasoned.

Mihalis laughed. Rather, he made a noise that might have been laughter if it was prompted by anything other than a need to draw attention to himself so that he could put the next part of his plan in motion.

"The fuck?"

"Hey!"

A cold pit opened his his stomach and a chill went down his spine as Mihalis fervently hoped keeping their prisoner *alive* was part of his guards' orders. They could just as easily shoot him and be done with the whole affair, but since they went to the trouble of not beating him routinely, he put the better odds on not getting immediately executed.

That did not stop those thoughts from raging through his brain as the two guards approached his bed.

He hit the power switch for the light and covered it with a quick motion of the sheet, exactly as someone trying to hide a real holo would do. For a moment, neither guard spoke or did anything, probably trying to decide if they actually saw anything or if they just imagined it. After all, Mihalis had been thoroughly searched and every personal item confiscated.

One guard kicked the bed and Mihalis sprang into motion. He squeezed the activation stud for his makeshift light and threw it at where he assumed the guard had to be standing in order to kick his bed. The man cried out in surprise as Mihalis surged up from the bed, tackling the other guard and taking him to the ground in a tangle of limbs.

Mihalis was not a strong man, but he was large. He passed the navy's combat tests by quite literally throwing his weight around. That tactic worked then just as well as it was working against the Ouroboros guards.

He and the guard hit the deck, and Mihalis's weight drove the air from the man's lungs. The other guard, temporarily half-blinded, took a step in the wrong direction and tumbled to the floor on top of Mihalis. The fall drove the air from his lungs as well, but the man on the bottom of the pile had it the worst. He let out a cry of surprise and pain, which turned into a gurgle as Mihalis elbowed him in the side of the head.

Mihalis thrashed around, rolling himself onto the bottom guard's head and pressing his back into the man's face. He had no real idea what to do from that point, but his attention was on the guard on the top of their pile.

That guard was almost as large as Mihalis and ostensibly better trained. He reached for Mihalis's arms to pin them or lock up his wrists and shoulders. Mihalis resisted, but his legs were free. He wrapped them around the guard's waist, and tried to twist back and forth. The other guard's skull and teeth ground against his spine, crushed against the floor, but the top guard would not go down.

So Mihalis squeezed. He was, after all, a big man and his legs could put out a significant amount of power. The guard's face turned red with effort as he struggled, then purple as Mihalis's legs forced the air from his lungs and literally crushed the life out of him.

It took several minutes, and he sustained a rather nasty punch to the left eye socket, but finally the guard stopped fighting and went limp. Mihalis maintained his hold for another minute before he realized the fight was over and released.

He stood up. His legs wobbled. The man at the bottom of the pile was dead, suffocated either by Mihalis himself or by the blood dripping from his nose and mouth. The other guard was also dead, ribs cracked. Bloody pink foam dripped from his lips.

Mihalis wobbled on shaky legs, stepped away from the dead guards, and vomited the remnants of yesterday's dinner onto the floor. He looked back at the dead men and vomited again, this time little more than acid and bile.

The dead men watched him with eyes that no longer saw, but somehow still judged him. Gods Between, he silently swore. No one warned him how it would *feel*.

It took a minute, but Mihalis swallowed the rest of the vomit in his throat and searched the bodies. Neither had a gun, probably for this exact reason, but they did have a pair of military-issue holocomputers. Their holos did little other than communication within the facility, providing no information about their location or anything else.

He assumed the holos could be tracked and left them there. Instead of guns, the guards carried batons, weapons that would certainly have turned their scuffle against him had they deployed them. He took one of the batons, tucking it under his right arm as he finished his search.

They took his shoes, but Mihalis was not about to steal either of the dead men's boots. If nothing else, they looked like the wrong size.

He stopped, thought about it for a moment, and took the other guard's baton.

Carefully, Mihalis made his way into the hall outside his room. The lights were dim. Whatever time it actually was, the facility's clock obviously said it was night. He wished he had a window. At worst, he would continue upward until he found the roof and go from there.

No one waited outside his room and he picked a direction at random: left. A few meters that way, the hall took a turn to the right and he peeked around it. Another guard waited about four meters away, and this one had a gun.

The words of Second Lord Tryphosa, Aella's CO in the *Phelegethon*'s magazine, came to him in that moment. In matters of ship combat, it was best to think and aim, but in personal combat, thinking got people killed. Do not think, she would say, only do.

Mihalis did. He had two batons. He stepped around the corner and threw one as hard as he could at the guard. He knew it would not kill and probably not even injure, but it did its job. She let out a grunt of surprise and pain when it impacted her shoulder. That slowed the rest of her reactions as Mihalis ran forward.

He slammed into this newest Ouroboros guard with his shoulder, then lashed out with his baton at the side of her head. Her skull snapped sideways and she fell to the ground. Mihalis did not stop to see whether she was alive or not. Instead, he simply took her rifle and ran.

Around another corner, two guards. No thinking, he reminded himself, only action. Mihalis raised the rifle and squeezed the trigger. The weapon kicked three rounds down the hall, then another three, burst after burst until enough bullets found their mark and the two guards fell to the ground in a rapidly spreading pool of blood. The spray on the wall behind them left little chance that they survived.

Mihalis had no idea how many bullets he fired, only that it was a lot. He was a bridge officer, not a Marine or ground soldier, and counting bullets was not a skill he practiced. Rather than run the risk of emptying the magazine, he dropped the weapon altogether and picked up one of the fallen guards' rifles.

Another corner, another guard, another burst of gunfire. This one was ready and shot back, but Mihalis was fairly certain he was not hit. Again, he dropped his rifle and took the dead soldier's weapon as a replacement.

Next to where the soldier had been standing was a plaque that gave general directions. Arrows indicated things like "lobby" and "holding area." Another arrow gave him what he needed, pointing out "stairs."

An alarm blared overhead and Mihalis took off at a sprint in the direction the plaque indicated. Despite the alarm, no one intercepted him between that spot and the stairs, and be shouldered the door open.

Mihalis panted, short of breath and already sweating. This time, he avoided reminding himself that he was a bridge officer and instead focused on the fact that he was part of the Technocrat military and if he needed to sprint up every stair between himself and the roof, he would do so.

That turned out to be true only because Mihalis convinced himself that it was either die of a heart attack in the stairwell or get shot when the Ouroboros soldiers found him. Six floors up, the stairs ended and he leveled his rifle with one hand, reaching for the door with the other.

His weapon shook with fatigue, but if someone waited on the other side of the door, a shaky aim would not make much difference at a meter's distance.

He threw open the door, revealing an immediately empty hallway. A shout to his left told him that would not last long, just long enough to read the sign directly in front of the stair door. According to the helpful arrows, somewhere to the right was an observation deck.

He ran that way, panting. His lungs burned, filling his mouth with the metallic taste of blood. By contrast, his legs had long since stopped hurting. Now, they simply moved as he willed. Somewhere deep in the muscle, energy remained, pulled from a place of numb strength deep within.

If he stopped moving, even for a moment, Mihalis knew he would never start moving again.

So he ran.

Around another corner, two soldiers and a man in a Second Lord's robe waited. They looked surprised, but that did not last long. Mihalis opened fire, spraying bullets across the trio. They returned fire as he ran and something stung his left arm. He nearly dropped the rifle as that arm went limp, but fired another burst down the hallway. Running, and with one hand, his accuracy was terrible, but the gun held enough bullets to make that less of a problem than it might have been.

He danced around the still-falling bodies, distantly surprised at how much agility his aching feet and numb legs had.

Things blurred together. Run. Shoot. Run. Drop weapon. Steal weapon. Run.

Up ahead, he saw a door. Beside the door was a sign. The sign told him this was the observation deck. If Mihalis could lock or barricade the door, he could take the time to rest, catch his breath, and figure out where he was.

He hit the door with his shoulder, but it did not open. He tried to lift his left hand to the holo lock next to the door, but that arm did not want to function. His rifle chose that moment to fall from his shaking right hand, and rather than retrieve it, he pressed his palm against the lock, hoping that the door would open for him.

It did, and he stepped through, turning now to pick up his rifle. The door slid shut and Mihalis first shot the lock, then the opening mechanism itself.

Finally, he turned, sagged against the door, and looked up. Overhead, stars speckled the sky, but they were strangely clear. No light pollution distorted their gleam, and he saw more overhead than he had anywhere other than...

"Space," he whispered, voice horse from running. Then, "shit."

Wearily, he forced himself to his feet. Stars had patterns, so matter where they were being seen from, and reading those patterns was something Third Lord Mihalis was very good at. He craned his neck upward, trying to piece together the constellations and use those to triangulate his location.

When he looked to the left, however, he found a shortcut that eliminated a great many options. There, just above the horizon, hung the edge of a brilliant blue orb. Prosgeiosi sat there, a beacon that, when combined with the stars overhead, told Mihalis exactly where he was.

"Faros," he said, turning to draw a line across the sky with a shaky finger. "That means Pyrsos is over there, probably just under the horizon." Mihalis laughed, hollow and tired, but somehow full of mirth. "Figures. I always liked the other moon better."

He racked his brain, trying to figure out why Ouroboros would take him to Faros, other than to take him away from Prosgeiosi. After a moment, he realized the more important question was, "how?"

He looked around. Everything was plain, utilitarian, like a military base, but it was also old. Some of the colors and minor design elements were dated, things his father's generation would have put in place.

"That's it," he muttered, still forcing his aching legs to move, pacing around the room. "I'm on Faros. This is a military base, an old one, probably decommissioned. That means it ought to have communication equipment, right? But if I use it, they'll shut it down if they haven't already. Have they? No, they need to be able to talk to the planet, which is why we're *here* and not on another world."

Someone beat against the room's door and Mihalis looked around. Tables and chairs littered the area. He pushed a table against the door, raised it onto its edge, and leaned it against the door. Another one he pushed straight in, bracing it. He then wedged several chairs around the tables and fervently hoped it held and Ouroboros did not simply blast their way in.

That thought brought a chilly glance at the dome overhead. If they really wanted to get to him, that was where they would come from, but there was nothing there he could reinforce. The best Mihalis could hope for is that Ouroboros saw blowing the dome as a last-ditch option.

With that thought looming overhead, he searched the room for a holo, finally finding one built into the back side of what appeared to be the serving bar.

"Alright, Mihalis," he said. "They're going to shut this down as soon as they realize you're in the system. What do you say? Who do you send it to?"

His hand hovered over the holo control for a minute as he thought. Until he had a plan, Mihalis was unwilling to even touch the holo for fear of tripping an alarm somewhere.

"Location data. That needs to go out and it's easy enough to include. Gods between, I'm no good at this, but I don't have a choice. They'll kill me otherwise. Ok, so. Location data? Yes. Then a simple S.O.S.. But to whom..."

A light overhead interrupted his thoughts and Mihalis ducked behind the bar, hoping the gunship outside was looking for him and not simply there to put a few holes in the dome and wait until he suffocated.

The ship moved on. Mihalis hoped it left because it had not seen him rather than because it was getting into a better position to open fire.

Another minute and he hit record on the holo. Location data would be added automatically. "This is Third Lord Mihalis. Ouroboros is holding me prisoner on Faros. They're going to kill me soon. Help me."

He did not take the time to review the message. In fact, he could not even be sure in his fatigued state if he even spoke the words he thought he spoke. The facility's location was tagged to the message however, and that was good enough. If the system was still operational, it should send out the message in every direction, coded to the only frequency he had memorized other than the now-useless code for the *Phlegethon*.

He sank to the ground as his muscles finally gave out. "Let's hope Tritogenes is willing to come get me twice," he said, or thought he said, before passing out.

The fight was no longer going well.

The woman who, when she put her mask on, called herself Second Lord Larisa cursed and balled one hand into a fist. She refrained from striking out with it, but that decision was primarily motivated by the simple fact that there was nothing for her to hit. The panic room in which she had locked herself contained only her holo and a hardline cable so that she could continue overseeing what had rapidly become an evacuation.

She knew Third Lord Mihalis, the man they code-named "The Spark" would try to escape. In fact, that had all been part of the plan. The guards on the lower levels had not gone to their posts that morning planning to die, but the expectation was always there. Ouroboros went on, regardless of whether any individual member did or not.

Larisa briefly wondered why the founders had not called it "Hydra." That seemed more accurate, a thousand heads of an unkillable beast. It was probably for the best, she reasoned. Hydras had such a negative, destructive image. The Ouroboros, symbol of rebirth, was a much better choice.

Rebirth, she thought, even if everyone had to die in the process.

Even letting Mihalis get to a computer to contact someone from the outside was part of the plan. The entire facility where they held him was an abandoned military testing ground. Each building, even the observation dome, had been constructed to withstand heavy bombardment from above.

Nothing was perfect, however, and when the attack started, Mihalis and the other survivors of the mastigas attack were to "accidentally" be killed by falling debris. Then Ouroboros would make its exit, after having quashed his story but not before broadcasting the footage of the Hexarchs' soldiers killing "defenseless" captives from the air.

When the attack ship did not open fire, but rather disgorged ground troops and vehicles just outside of their defensive envelope, Second Lord

Larisa knew she had to change the plan. Things could still work, but now they would actually have to break into the observation dome and execute Third Lord Mihalis the old fashioned way.

It would have made their job harder, but such was the way of life. Crushed by debris caused by Hexarch weapons was easy enough to spin, but dead from a bullet to the head during a rescue operation was much more difficult to explain in a way such that it benefited the narrative they needed.

For the first few hours, it seemed even that would not be needed. If the military force simply died outside the facility, they could spirit Mihalis away and deal with him at their leisure.

Of the two hundred and fifty troops, thirty died in the first six hours. They tried to split into two groups, trying to flank Larisa's base, but she had the advantage in firepower. As the actual fighting began, the Hexarchate's military reacted poorly, moving in different directions as though getting conflicting orders.

Typical, she had thought at the time. Six militaries trying to work together was going to produce no end of inefficiency. Ouroboros would win in the end because they only answered to a single voice. Growth, birth and death, these were the natural order of things, and order would always defeat chaos.

Then the fighting stopped for an hour, giving her plenty of time to devote a crew to laying a trap for Mihalis and flushing him out of the observation dome. That plan was almost ready when the attack force outside finally started moving again.

The second wave was different. Yes, soldiers fell to her guns, but fewer than before. They moved under a single command now. One of the Hexarchs must have over-ruled the others—probably Aegesander or Enyalios, she thought. Of the six, those two bloody-minded men would be the best suited to commanding an army.

At least the planetside force succeed in trapping and killing the Titans, she thought, watching yet another sector on her map turn hostile red. One hundred and seventy-five soldiers moved methodically through the facility—through *her* facility—eliminating or capturing anyone they came across.

She revisited her earlier thought. Such brutal efficiency could only come from Aegesander's mind. Enyalios would provide the guns, be Aegesander knew into whose hands to place them.

Second Lord Larisa hit a key that sent a cancellation order to the crew trying to get into the observation dome. She blanked that screen without waiting to see if they acknowledged or obeyed.

Sinking back into her chair, Larisa covered her masked face with her hands. She hung her head backward, staring up at the ceiling. Thirty Ouroboros personnel remained in the facility. The others were either dead already, possibly captured, or had fled into the underground tunnels of which she hoped the attacking army had no knowledge.

Another sector in the map turned red. That only left three still green. Fortunately, one of those was the access for the tunnels. She might not have known the names of the people under her command, nor had she ever seen their faces, but still Larisa felt the pain of defeat. They were all prepared to die for the cause, but that idea was predicated on dying for the cause actually doing something.

If she lived, her superiors were going to be *very* unhappy with her.

She sat up and swiped angrily at her holo, dismissing it. Dying here did nothing for Ouroboros, except perhaps if her own death provided a chance for the others to escape and continue the fight if they could.

Even if they succeeded today, it would be some time before Ouroboros was ready to move again. The Prosgeiosi bases were all written off the moment their bomb went off. Anyone left there would die when the Hexarchs' militaries stepped in. The great serpent would slumber once more.

Her holo reappeared automatically, showing the last sector of the map, the sector that contained her panic room, turn red. It was now only a matter of time before those soldiers would find her and try to take her prisoner.

"Try," she thought aloud, "because I'm not going with them."

With a stability in her movements that surprised her, Second Lord Larisa rose to her feet as something large and heavy slammed into the panic room's door. She exhaled and picked up her pistol from the table beside where her holo had been projected.

She considered taking the easiest option in front of her. It would allow her to die on her own terms, a martyr rather than a casualty of the fighting. Her own gun, her own bullet. There was a certain poetic symmetry to it, she thought.

Ouroboros, after all, was symbolized by a serpent eating its own tail. Rebirth through death was etched into the mask she put on every morning.

Still.

The door banged again, and the lock clicked.

Larisa had no time anymore. She raised the pistol, finger on the trigger, and aimed it at the door instead.

When the heavy door slid aside, it revealed five figures in non-regulation combat gear. Behind that group, she saw the bulky outline of heavy combat armor silhouetted against the dim glow of safety lights. The largest human, at the front of the group, regarded her from behind a glossy black mask.

Larisa squeezed the trigger on her pistol.

Click.

She stared at the useless gun in her hand in mute horror. It worked the last time it had been tested. It worked that morning. Her eyes snapped back to the tall, black suited figure as she strode into the tiny panic room.

In her pocket, her holo's processor buzzed violently and the image projected onto her desk crackled with static and then vanished.

Two of the soldiers in the back of the squad gestured to one another and stepped away. They were followed a moment later by a third who carried a heavily modified marksman rifle. They rejoined the armor, forming a protective cordon outside Second Lord Larisa's no-longer-safe safe room.

That left the largest and, behind her, second largest of the squad. The woman in front carried a bullpup carbine scarcely long enough to hold in two hands. Behind her, dressed in a movement-shrouding hybrid between a robe and a combat uniform, a woman with a sword in one hand and a pistol in the other stood in silent judgment. She slowly returned her pistol to its holster and sword to its scabbard.

Second Lord Larisa put it together a heartbeat before the woman spoke with a voice like warm iron.

"I am Spatharios Victoria, leader of the Titans. On the authority of the Council of Hexarchs and in the name of First Lord Tritogenes, you are under arrest."

The ground forces failed.

Larisa dropped the broken pistol—no doubt rendered non-functional by Second Lord Helena—to the floor and raised her hands. Despite everything in her brain screaming at her to fight, she knew she could not stop both of them, and Larisa did not resist as they bound her wrists roughly behind her back.

Chapter 17

Victoria awoke screaming. It was hardly the first time, but it was the first since before the mission to Faros to rescue Tritogenes's informant. She slept with a spare dagger under her pillow—not one of the mastigas daggers from her time in Aphelion, but a cheap knife bought at a shop in Odyssey—and her hand brandished it at the darkness, threatening and defending before her conscious brain even had a chance to catch up.

Other than her own pounding heart, the only noise for a moment was the low hum and gentle click-clack of the embroidery machine as it worked on her robe, finalizing some of the new designs before the farewell banquet the following evening.

Helena was first into the room, backlit by a soft glow from the suite's living room. Victoria supposed her implants were capable of dumping adrenaline into her system or somehow controlling her wake/sleep cycle precisely. She might have only been wearing a loose sleeping gown, but her face and posture said she was ready to fight or help.

A stray thought flitted through Victoria's brain. Helena really was beautiful, and the external components of her cybernetic implants gleamed in the darkness. Fierce protectiveness blazed in Helena's eyes. If any of them looked like a guardian spirit, it was her.

"Spatharios! I..."

Victoria waved Helena away with the hand still holding her pillow-knife. "I'm fine, Helena, but thank you."

"Should I get you anything?"

Victoria shook her head, dropping both hands to the sweaty, disheveled sheets. "No. Thank you."

She nodded and backed out of the doorway. "As you say."

From the living room came a rustle of fabric, the creak of a body settling onto the couch, and then the lights went out again.

Victoria waved her right hand over her left forearm, waking up her holo. It came on dimly, barely brighter than the light from the living room had been. She laughed, remembering the first time she tried to use the holo in the dark, before she knew about the adaptive brightness settings. Thankfully, it no longer blinded her.

The dim display indicated it was two hours past midnight. Victoria put her head in her hands, dismissing the holo, and sat there, breathing deep. She had been asleep less than an hour this time, though at least she woke up *in* the bed instead of under it or curled into the corner like she slept in Aphelion's depths.

From the door to the shared bathroom came a soft knocking. Victoria looked up to see Pallasophia standing there, holding a drinking glass.

"Are you alright?"

"I will be."

She stepped the rest of the way into the bedroom and offered the glass to Victoria, waiting until she accepted it before perching on the edge of the bed. "Water," she explained.

Victoria drank half the glass in a single drought, then wiped away the excess that spilled from the rim with her other hand. She passed the glass back to Pallasophia who finished it before placing it on the small table beside Victoria's bed.

"Want to talk about it?"

Victoria shook her head, then took a deep, shuddering breath. The images haunted her, and she knew once she started explaining the things she saw in the dark that she would never stop. She had a hundred lives, ninety-nine deaths, of nightmares to draw on.

And yet...

Another deep, ragged breath. "One of the older memories," she began. "At least I think it's a memory. It's hard to keep track. I'm dreaming about previous lives dreaming about their own previous lives. How can I be sure any of it was real?"

"Does it feel real?"

Victoria shuddered. "Yes."

Pallasophia put a hand on her shoulder, warm against Victoria's sweat-chilled skin. "Then they're real enough."

"This one, though. She had been wounded, a bite. It got infected. It slowed her down, fogged up her brain. She woke up to a pair of mikros, blood on their faces..."

Even in the dark, it was easy enough to see the sudden absence of color in Pallasophia's face. Rather than say anything, she reached out with her other hand, pulled Victoria to her, and wrapped her in an embrace.

The first deep breath started to calm her. Even in the middle of the night, Pallasophia smelled pleasant, comforting.

"I'm sorry."

Victoria pushed back far enough to look her in the face. In the dark, Pallasophia made no attempts at Technocrat propriety, and let Victoria see the full range of emotions she was feeling. Hurt, anger, regret all passed over her face, twisting and swirling into one another.

She laughed, once, quiet. "I would say that you didn't do anything, but we both know that's not completely true."

Pallasophia gave her a weak smile. "Yeah."

Victoria said nothing else, instead pulling Pallasophia, the only other human she could let be so close to her, back into a tight embrace.

Unbidden, Victoria felt a surge of emotions so varied and sudden that she did not have time to explain or even name any of them before they broke through and crashed against the real world. There, with her face resting in the crook between Pallasophia's neck and shoulder, Victoria finally allowed herself to experience the things she had been bottling up since the first mastigas dropped out of the shadows and tried to murder her.

Images of blood and death washed through her mind, carried on the sounds of the dead and dying. Mastigas, human, the screams of pain were not very different without a face to identify the source. Blood was still blood when it splattered on the ground, no matter what it was that bled.

Worse, her own wounds intermingled with those she had caused, feet and hands slipping on blood-slick tiles, grips faltering as the hands that held them paled slowly. Teeth and knives coming for her as her arms and legs failed.

Death, now, loomed over her, both her own and the deaths of the soldiers she fought beside. Their faces, so full of life and then suddenly blank and empty like failed sculpture, all clay and red water.

Again.

And again.

And again.

If Pallasophia cared about the tears soaking into the front of her shirt, she neither said nor did anything about it. Instead, the longer the well of emotions poured out from deep within Victoria's soul, the tighter she held.

Finally, some uncountable eternity later, the surge slowed and Victoria felt her thoughts becoming her own again.

"Can we stay like this?"

Somewhere above her, she felt Pallasophia's hands caressing her hair. "Of course. If it will help you, I'll stay."

Rather than reply verbally, Victoria disentangled herself from Pallasophia's arms and slid to the side. Pallasophia climbed into the vacant space and pulled up the sheets.

There, in the dark, just enough light bled from the holo displays around the room for Victoria's night-adjusted eyes to see clearly. She thought for a moment that Pallasophia looked sad, but the longer she looked, she realized that emotion was actually relief.

"Pallasophia, I..."

She shifted, withdrawing a hand from beneath the sheets, and pressed a finger to Victoria's lips to silence her. "It's alright."

Victoria shook her head. Before she could speak, a thought hit her: who else would she permit to touch her like that? After a moment, she persisted, saying, "No. I need to say this."

A deep breath in the darkness, pensive, then, "alright."

"I don't know how," she began, paused, then continued. "But you quiet my demons. Thank you."

Pallasophia smiled, touched Victoria's cheek, and said nothing.

They lay like that for a moment before Victoria shifted closer. She took a deep breath, tried her best to ignore the sudden spike in her pulse rate, and brought her face closer to Pallasophia's.

Their noses brushed against one another, then someone shifted. Victoria could not tell who moved first, but in a flash the distance between them vanished and their lips found one another.

***

Helena woke up long before Victoria or Pallasophia. By the time they finally got out of bed—a process that took much longer than it would have had both still been in their own beds—Helena had prepared coffee and a small breakfast for the three of them.

Pallasophia left a kiss on Victoria's forehead, then excused herself through their joint bathroom to her own room to change.

For her part, Victoria loosely draped her black and purple house coat around her shoulders and belted it.

"Good morning, Spatharios," Helena said, looking up as Victoria entered the room.

Victoria smiled, then let out a small laugh. "I've told you, you can call me Victoria. We're still equals."

Helena frowned, then smiled, or forced herself to put on a facial expression very like a smile. "But you are our leader now."

Victoria waved that thought away. "I'm the leader, because my job is to direct our team. That doesn't mean I'm your superior."

Helena nodded. "I understand. I will remember that," she said. "Victoria."

Victoria gestured to her, indicating her own house coat as well by the way she deliberately did not draw attention to it. "You've been busy since you got up."

Again, Helena nodded, once, precisely. "I woke up quite early and set to work. I believed it was for the best to allow you a few extra hours of sleep."

Her pulse hammered suddenly as she wondered how much Helena overheard. After a moment, thought it did nothing to calm her nerves in that moment, Victoria realized that did not matter. What mattered was her gesture of assistance. So, she smiled. "Thank you."

"How are you feeling?"

Thoughts not of horror and blood, but of Pallasophia's fingertips and lips filled her mind for a moment, though Victoria was fairly certain none of her sudden embarrassment showed on her face. Instead, she addressed the reason she woke up in the middle of the night in the first place. "I'm better, thank you. I," she paused. Fingertips on her spine. "We talked at length before going to sleep."

"Of course."

"Did you sleep well?"

"Yes. Once I left your room, I was able to use my implants to return my brain to a state of deep rest. Such is why I was also able to awaken early and prepare for the banquet."

Victoria nodded, finally taking a moment to process the intricate formal touches in the cyborg Titan's outfit.

Helena's black-dyed hair had been pulled back into the sort of twisted bun she would have expected to see on the back of a ballerina's head. Shot through those twists were silver wire, or possibly white fiber optic, that gleamed as she moved.

Her implants themselves, always a spot of color against her face, looked like they had been polished and painted with a fresh silvery-blue enamel. Following their metallic curve led Victoria directly to Helena's eyes—deep, blue, and the exact color she painted her implants. She even drew small spiderweb veins from the corner of her eyes to the nearby metal pieces.

Helena's lips were likewise painted in the full formal style. At first, Victoria thought they were simply a dark, matte purple, but instead they sported a carefully stenciled swirl of blue and red.

In keeping with the high formality of everything else, Helena's robe was a blue silk so dark it was almost black. The designs embroidered in it, in contrast to the usual style of metallic thread for major accomplishments, were picked out in a variety of blues and greens, and even reds and purples in places, just a few shades brighter than the fabric itself.

For contrast, she wore a white sash like a belt. It might have been, and probably was, embroidered as well, but Victoria's eye could not pick anything out.

"I suppose I'll have to get myself ready soon enough," Victoria mused.

"Yes. I must be on my way, however. I finished my own prep early because I am having lunch with Panatakis."

Victoria glanced at the time projected above the table, the room holo's default screen. "You've still got two hours."

"I know, but we are meeting in a cafe in Eantio, and I wish to walk. I have been ferried about by military transports too much lately."

Victoria smiled. "I can't blame you."

"Until tonight, then."

"Wait, one more thing."

Helena raised one eyebrow. The effect was exaggerated by the makeup lines drawn around the implant there. "Yes?"

"When we return from the mastigas ship, you can have my room. I..." This time, the thoughts that came were of lips and sweat, and she knew she could not hide the sudden flush on her cheeks. "I don't think I'll be needing it anymore."

"Of course," she replied. "Thank you."

Pallasophia came out of her room as the door shut behind Helena.

"Eavesdropping?" Victoria asked.

"I'm sure I wouldn't do such a thing."

Victoria smirked. "Of course not. Helena made breakfast."

"I heard," Pallasophia replied. "More importantly, I smelled."

Victoria placed both hands on her stomach in exaggerated pantomime of hunger pains. "I, for one, am not going to let food go to waste. Care to join me?"

Pallasophia smiled, and in that smile Victoria once again felt her demons shrink back. "Of course. Any idea how much more time is left on your robe?"

Victoria went to the machine in the corner, where a complex of arms, needles, and threads was still hard at work on the designs she chose, including the personally-chosen symbols of the other Titans. At the moment, it was hard-to-impossible to tell what part of the design the machine was actually working on.

The important thing was the holo display floating in front of it. "Three hours," she called over her shoulder.

From behind, Pallasophia wrapped her arms around Victoria's waist. "Then there's plenty of time to relax."

Victoria sank back against her for a moment before straightening. "Do you want to talk about last night?"

Pallasophia shook her head. "No. Perhaps later today, before the banquet, but not now. Now, I just want to enjoy your company."

"And Helena's breakfast."

Pallasophia laughed. "Yes, and that."

***

It was a rare day that they had nothing do to. With the launch coming up, the Titans and their respective Hexarchs had very little to do other than take a few precious hours for themselves. The banquet remained, but otherwise no major events, no speeches, nothing stood to disrupt their time.

The original plan, Victoria learned, had been an extensive training program, perhaps taking as long as six months. They were to work together, to learn how to coordinate with the Technocracy's military, and generally how best to utilize their skills and training.

The mastigas ship's destruction of the picket around it and the sudden rise of Ouroboros destroyed any chance they had of making those plans work. Instead, they had scarcely more than a month between their arrival on Prosgeiosi and Victoria's impending departure that evening.

For the moment, she and Pallasophia spent it in silence, reading and making a point to do as little as possible. They had yet to discuss last night, but as the day went on, Victoria started to feel like that was not as much of a problem as it could have been. The comfortable air between herself and Pallasophia said more than words could.

The other five Titans were busy doing *something* that day. Helena and Panatakis were touring the towns around Odyssey, "taking in the culture" he called it when extending the invitation shortly after lunch. She admitted that did sound like a pleasant way to pass the time, but Victoria very much did not want to deal with crowds at the moment.

Korakti and Daniel were likewise out and about. Korakti's note said little, but the subtext was clear enough, especially with Daniel in tow. Odds were good, she thought, that Korakti was taking him to whatever seedy bars she could find and talking some poor soul into any one of a hundred classic bar bets.

Lelantos sent a message to everyone just to keep in contact. He, like Victoria, was staying in for the day.

So, instead of going out, Victoria currently nursed what remained of a cup of once-steaming tea in one hand. The other hand held a book—a real, paper and ink book from Pallasophia's personal collection.

She would have to put her robe on soon enough, and her combat uniform after that. For the moment, her house coat, belt long since forgotten, was clothing enough. After dealing with Ouroboros and an endless string of shallow wounds, the feel of the soft fabric against her skin was luxury enough.

Pallasophia sat opposite her, cradling a now-cool mug of tea against her chest with one hand and scrolling through what appeared to be a lengthy article or story on her holo. She had privacy mode off, which meant the "back side" of the hologram was not blank but rather a reversed version of what was shown on the front. Even so, the text was small and backward, giving Victoria no idea what the other woman was reading.

Victoria turned a page in her book and, a moment later, the embroidery machine beeped. The constant hum that filled the lower registers of sound for the past two days fell silent, and suddenly the air felt strange and hollow.

Pallasophia looked to Victoria without moving her head, then back to her holo. When Victoria turned another page rather than get up and retrieve the garment, Pallasophia finally looked up. "You know it's finished, right?"

"I heard."

Pallasophia laughed. "Usually Technocrats are hovering beside the machine the last half hour, ready to snatch their robe out and examine the new design."

Victoria smiled, but turned her attention back to her book. "Yes, but were they in the middle of the last chapter of the last book in the *Blue Sun* trilogy?"

Pallasophia laughed again, dismissing her holo. "Not usually, no."

"I'd prefer to finish this before I head into certain death."

"You have been fairly dedicated to it."

"It's your doing, you know."

"I do not feel a need to apologize, Spatharios," she replied, affecting a stiff, and quite false, formality.

Victoria looked at her, raising her eyes without moving her head, shook her head with an amused laugh, and returned to her book.

An hour later, Victoria finally set the book down, proclaiming that the end to the series was a good one and thanking Pallasophia for giving her the time to finish it. She stretched in her seat, simultaneously aware of the tightness in her joints and muscles from sitting for the last several hours and of Pallasophia's eyes on her as she moved.

She stood slowly, making a show of pretending not to notice she was being watched, then dropped her housecoat onto the chair. It fluttered into a pile of soft black, dotted here and there with purple.

Victoria stretched again as memories from the night before flitted through her mind. Pallasophia's fingers and lips on her scars, tracing and memorizing every jagged piece of torn flesh. "Don't worry. I'll bring some new scars back from the mastigas ship."

Pallasophia flushed, but said nothing as Victoria withdrew her robe from the machine. She might not care for it from a comfort perspective, but at least putting the thing on had become easy.

Once on, she took a moment to admire the six symbols stitched around her wrist. Each emblem, designed by the Titans themselves, represented a different member of their team. Daniel chose a raised, mechanical fist. Korakti, whose flamboyant personality never flagged, drew a single spread wing. Lelantos initially drew crosshairs, but decided that was "done to death," and replaced his initial sketch with something that could be a twisted infinity loop or an hourglass.

She turned her wrist over. Panatakis's symbol was first, a stylized eye. Next to it, Helena's emblem glittered, simple and mysterious. A square sat inside a circle, connected to it at the corners.

Last and, in her case, largest, Victoria's own emblem was a single upward-turned arrow. The pride she felt was natural, she supposed, but some part of it felt a little silly taking as much pride as she did in the simple fact that the six of them had become a team.

Pallasophia sighed dramatically, an overacted gesture that, for reasons Victoria never could articulate, always amused her. She stood, went to the bedroom, and returned minutes later with her own robe, proving still to be much more adept at donning it than Victoria.

"I suppose we need to get ready, then," she said.

Victoria nodded. "You know I'm going to want help, right?"

Pallasophia laughed. "Yes, I remember what happened the last time you tried to do your own makeup for a formal event."

"Let's not talk about it, then."

"As you say, Spatharios," she replied formally. She maintained that stiff posture for several more seconds, then dissolved into a fit of giggles. "Come on, let's get yours done first."

***

Victoria continued to stare at herself in the mirror. The face that looked back at her was hers, clearly, but the vast swath of color that had been painted on her face hardly made her look human, let alone like she was used to seeing.

Starting at her hairline, Pallasophia painted what she could only describe as a melting starscape across the upper half of Victoria's face. Bright silver and white stars speckled a field of swirling reds and purples that would have not look out of place in the background of a piece of fantasy art. The colors were solid and heavy until the "mask" passed her cheekbones, after which it dripped down her cheeks and neck in long, trailing splatters that *still* looked like they were actively running. Liquid starlight dripped across her jaw and neck.

Lips colored the same shade of deep red as the mask across her forehead and cheekbones and lined in black completed the look.

Victoria reached up and touched one of the drips, again expecting it to smear, but it did not. The paint was well set and nothing short of a shower or liberal application of makeup remover would alter it.

"I may not have much use for these formal events," Pallasophia explained after the first hour of painting, "but when they happen, I make it my business to be the best-dressed person there."

Waiting by the door, Pallasophia herself looked equally different. She dyed the underlayers of her hair an iridescent purple that shimmered between reds and blues as the light caught it. The upper layers had been braided in spots, pulling her hair away and revealing the color underneath. Her makeup was no less bright than Victoria's; sapphire blue shone above her brown eyes, terminating in curls of blue-green flecked with gold that framed her cheekbones.

After finishing Victoria's space-themed makeup, Pallasophia explained that her own would be deliberately styled after the deep sea. Her blue-green lipstick seemed—at least to Victoria who had never actually seen the sea except in holos—to fulfill that aim rather well. The right side of her face had been painted in cooler colors and the left in warmer tones, sunset and sunrise.

Victoria stood, sparing another look in the mirror at the artwork that her face had become. Even excluding the time it took to finish the newest designs on her robe, preparing for this banquet had taken the better part of a day. She was glad, for whatever it was worth in her position as Tritogenes's Spatharios, that events with this level of formality were comparably rare in the grand scheme of things.

She adjusted the folds of her robe, pulling at the black fabric until the silver mastigas elite skull, impaled on his own sword, sat in the place of prominence she wanted. Some achievements called for subtle designs, especially if the person wanted to fill a single robe with as many as possible, but Victoria considered killing an elite to be something worth drawing a little overt attention.

Pallasophia's robe was perhaps even finer than Helena's had been that morning. Where the cyborg Titan's robe was all mathematical precision and drape, Pallasophia's "dress robe" was a multi-tone blue swirl of color whose pleats—an old style that these days was rather rare in modern Technocrat fashion, she explained—flared dramatically with every movement.

"Are you ready?" Pallasophia asked.

"To see the others again or for the banquet?"

"The banquet."

Victoria hesitated. While she was much less averse to crowds than she once was, such a public event was still not something she would willingly attend if she had a real choice in the matter.

Reading her hesitation as a no, Pallasophia smiled and said, "you can foist most of it off on Korakti."

She laughed. "She does enjoy the spotlight."

"At least one of you does."

Another laugh. "Fair. One of us must."

"You seem to enjoy it some days."

Victoria frowned. "I tolerate it. Are *you* ready?"

Pallasophia shrugged. "The banquet is fine, and the parade won't be anything new, really. I'm actually looking forward to the pre-banquet, though."

Victoria raised an eyebrow and absently wondered how visible that was given the mask of red and stars on her face. "Oh? What *are* you going to be doing while I'm being forced to entertain the Hexarchs?"

"Meeting with the other so-called 'seconds in command.' Eunike, Hyperion's daughter-slash-business manager; Ilias, Rivka's new head of security; and so on. You'll meet them at the launch, I suspect, but

Hyperion wanted us all to meet officially now that Project Titan is effectively over."

That phrasing stirred something disquiet in Victoria's stomach. She *was* Project Titan, after all.

She pushed that aside. "We should be off, then. The sooner we get all this fanfare out of the way, the sooner you can get back do doing your real job."

Pallasophia blinked and a smirk flashed across her face for half a heartbeat, the expression Victoria was used to seeing when she was being obvious about not rolling her eyes. "After you launch, I start the process to decommission Aphelion. I might be done when you get back," she said, laughed, and added, "with the paperwork, that is. Don't worry. You won't miss anything exciting."

She smiled. "Remind me why you wanted that job again?"

Pallasophia placed a hand on Victoria's shoulder and gave a slight squeeze. "It has its rewards."

"I'll take honest work over politics any day."

"Honest violence, you mean."

"That, yes."

"That's why you're going to that ship and I'm staying behind."

"I'll never understand your fascination with politics."

"It's fascinating," she said, and as she spoke, her face lit up. "Imagining the different ways people might react to or do something, plans and counterplans, layers of contingencies," and..."

Pallasophia stopped herself with visible effort, then laughed. "Listen to me. If you let me talk like that, we'll never get out of here."

Victoria smiled as something stirred in her stomach, migrating to her throat where it sat for a moment. "I'd be happy to listen," she finally said.

"I know. Now..." Pallasophia leaned in closer, saying, "in case I don't get a chance before you board the ship..."

Pallasophia might have initiated the kiss, but Victoria quickly took charge of it. She placed a hand on the back of Pallasophia's head, holding her close for a moment longer. Yes, a dim part of her brain thought, this was good.

Finally, Victoria pulled away. Flecks of red dotted Pallasophia's sea-green lipstick now, an artistic concession to that moment. Pallasophia held Victoria's eyes with her own and rested a hand on her cheek as though trying to memorize the contours of her face.

"Come on," she said at last. "We've taken up enough time as it is."

In the hallway, they both fell back into the sort of propriety that was required of two high-ranking Technocrats in public, but it was not lost on Victoria that the two of them walked just a little closer than they had before.

Chapter 18

The walk to the banquet hall was not a long one, but it did take the two women through the public corridors. Despite—or perhaps because of—their extravagant makeup, everyone recognized Victoria as they went, and stopping to exchange pleasantries with people slowed down their progress considerably.

Most of the conversations were short, just a few words here and there. Some congratulated her on her success dealing with Ouroboros, while others simply expressed admiration or gratitude for Project Titan itself. If anyone shared Ouroboros's anti-Titan viewpoints, they chose not to speak up.

Victoria gestured, and the two women ducked into a side passage. About five meters down, the crowds thinned out and no one payed enough attention to the two extravagantly-dressed Technocrat women to worry about. The banquet was today, after all, and *everyone* was dressed up.

"Everything alright?" Pallasophia asked. She allowed worry to be written across her beautifully-painted face.

Victoria let out a deep lungful of air and leaned against a wall. "Part of me still wishes the mission was a secret."

Pallasophia laughed. "It *was*," she said. "Right up until Ouroboros started shooting at you with artillery."

"A lot fewer people would want a holo with me if they still thought all we were doing out there was cleaning up after a 'failed pyrotechnics test.'"

Pallasophia shrugged. "They know the truth. They know you beat them," she said, then smiled. "Twice now."

Victoria snorted a single amused laugh. "There's not much subtle about dropping an army on the moon, is there?"

"No," she agreed. "No there is not."

"Until you six showed up covered in blood and grime, people were willing enough to believe what they heard was just more pyrotechnics tests. But when Enyalios and Tritogenes launched a very public assault on Faros, people started asking questions. Eurybia and Tritogenes..."

Victoria interrupted with a laugh. "That's a crashed unlikely pair."

Pallasophia grinned. "That was my thought. Anyway, they broke the news about the stadium, the mission to the lower levels, everything."

Victoria nodded. "Good on them. Any repercussions?"

She shook her head. "Minor ones, sure, but nothing major. Turns out Enyalios had been passing notes to the Seconds for some time and about a thousand people were ready to pull support from Aegesander if he didn't let Tritogenes speak."

"Messy."

Pallasophia shrugged. "That's politics."

Victoria frowned. "I don't have to like it, though."

"Just be glad you're not a Hexarch, then."

"There are worse things to be, I'm sure," she replied with a sly grin. "Not many, of course, but I'm sure there are a few."

Pallasophia grinned, nudging Victoria with her elbow in a moment where she was fairly certain no one was watching. "Just keep smiling and playing nice with people."

"Yes, yes. You've explained how important moral support is many times now." Despite her unease with the crowd, Victoria laughed.

Pallasophia eased her tension further when she smiled. "Doesn't it feel good to know how many people are behind you?"

Victoria shrugged one shoulder, eyeing the crowd pushed through the big arterial walkway nearby. "Perhaps. I would rather have more soldiers to fight the mastigas, but if kind words and thoughts are what we get, then we'll make do."

"It's not all empty words, you know. A lot of these people are going to be working in support roles for your mission."

"I know," she said, fighting a sigh. "It's just that I get tired of having the same conversation a thousand times."

"Why?"

She started to reply, then closed her mouth. That question was harder to process than she expected it to be. She gestured back in the direction they were supposed to be going, and Pallasophia followed as they pushed back into the dense flow of people.

They shouldered their way through more people, more ten-second conversations. When the air was clearer again, Victoria finally replied. "I wish I had something to actually give them."

"You're going to stop the mastigas," Pallasophia whispered. Victoria barely heard her. She spoke so quietly, especially the word 'mastigas,' that her sentiment was nearly lost amid the crowd noise.

"But I haven't yet."

"You stopped Ouroboros."

Her reply was delayed by a trio of passing Technocrats who wanted to take a holo with Victoria. When they were gone, she simply replied, "I'll give you that one."

"Then give *them* that as well."

She took a deep breath, held it, then exhaled. The momentary pause helped get her thoughts back in order. "Alright."

They walked along as the crowd grew thick again. Victoria's towering height made it easier for her to push through the press of people, but it also put her spectacularly painted face high above most everyone else.

As people parted to let them through, much of the time only doing so after exchanging a few words with Victoria or taking a quick holo-picture, more would fill the void. They approached a tram station, which explained the sudden increase in people, but it did mean their progress slowed dramatically.

The decorations around them changed as well, aging and becoming plainer. When she first arrived, Victoria thought it odd that such a well-traveled area would have such a bland exterior, but it was all part of the way Odyssey presented itself. Some things, especially old things, did not change inside the Technocrat's domed capital.

The trams, like much of the larger structures within the dome, dated back thousands of years or more. They had been the primary transport system for the massive structure since the days when Odyssey the city had been *Odyssey* the ship.

Victoria touched one of the exposed support beams as they—finally—approached the tram itself. It looked new, especially on the inside, and had been built with luxury in mind. Warm colors, soft carpets, and comfortable seats filled the cars ahead. The outside was painted in vibrant color as well, which sat in strange juxtaposition with the bare metal and thin carpet of the station.

"How much of this is actually original," she asked, "and how much is restoration?"

"I honestly don't know. All that information is publicly available, but..." Pallasophia shrugged. "It's never been an interest of mine."

"I might look it up when I get back, then. Learn something you don't know."

Ahead, the tram pulled out of the station. In its place, a holo screen appeared counting down the five minutes until the next one arrived.

Pallasophia pointed at it, and laughed. Victoria detected a hint of annoyance in it, but nothing major. If missing a single tram would upset their nonexistent schedule that much, she knew Pallasophia would have pulled rank and used Tritogenes's access codes for the Hexarchs' transport system instead.

But, Victoria reminded herself, meeting people and "being seen" was the important part of their walk. A few minutes more of that was more important than being at the pre-banquet that much sooner.

Most of those who stopped her to talk had been adults, though Victoria was at a loss to define any sort of average age range. The crowd started to blur together almost from the moment they left their suite. A few stood out here and there, couples and triads whose interactions with one another were more memorable than anything they said to Victoria directly, older men and women who talked about a time before the mastigas, and even a few bubbly and excited teenagers who were just thrilled to meet a personal hero.

As they waited for the tram, however, a girl in a silky red robe approached Victoria and quietly asked if she could speak to her.

Victoria looked down, conscious of how much taller she was, and smiled. Her first instinct was to kneel to be closer to the girl's level, but she felt like that might be misconstrued as being condescending rather than helpful. She was no expert at guessing age, but given her height, she had to be a young teen, at best, or perhaps twelve. Technocrat gene-therapy did not take effect until after puberty ended, and the girl was nearly half a meter smaller than Victoria.

So, instead, she replied with a simple, "hello. What's your name?"

"Sixth Lord Alexis, ma'am. I was supposed to leave for Limani today, but they let me push my flight back to tomorrow so I could watch your launch."

Victoria smiled. Children, she realized, did not bother her nearly as much as adults did. "I'm glad you're able to stay. Are you from Limani?"

Sixth Lord Alexis shook her head. "No, ma'am. I'm from Kipos. I came to Prosgeiosi to meet First Lord Rivka, but that was before Ouroboros blew up the stadium."

Victoria chuckled. Hearing those events, something that resulted in a rather harrowing and dangerous set of missions for her, talked about so casually was interesting. That was the best word for it, she thought. It was neither a good feeling nor a bad one, but it certainly was a curious one.

"I'm sorry your meeting got interrupted."

"It's alright. I got to meet her after everything was cleaned up. She's nice. Have you met her?"

Victoria smiled and nodded. "Yes. I agree. First Lord Rivka is," she searched for the best child-friendly way to describe her, "a good person."

Alexis stuck a hand into her pocket and withdrew a small length of thin rope. She reached out a hand to Victoria, who took it. In her hand, it was clearly not just a random piece of rope, but a braided necklace with a small red stone in the very center.

"I hope it's the right size," Alexis said, suddenly embarrassed. "I didn't realize you were so tall, ma'am."

Victoria smiled again as a curious weight suddenly appeared in her throat and she realized that her earlier statement about having nothing to give was wrong. She closed her hand around the necklace. "I'm sure it will fit."

Alexis brightened, nearly bouncing in place. "Yay! I mean, thank you, ma'am."

Victoria eyed the tram countdown. Two minutes left. "So, what's bringing you to Limani?"

Now, Alexis positively beamed, smiling broad and bright with childlike enthusiasm. "I'm going to be competing in a marksmanship contest next week!"

331

That, Victoria reflected, was not what she expected. "Really?"

Alexis nodded. "Yes!"

"I'll have to see if the other Titans and I can watch while we're on the ship."

"Would you? That would be amazing! Thank you so much!"

"It's the least I can do."

Some sort of alarm dinged on Alexis's holo, and she started to turn away, "Thank you again!"

The crowd surged forward toward the incoming tram, and the girl melted into the mass of people. Pallasophia nudged Victoria with an elbow. "Still think it's not worth it to be out here?"

She laughed. "I've changed my mind, if that's what you're asking."

"Good. Now, let me help you put that on."

Victoria nodded, passed the necklace to Pallasophia, who slid it under her black robe's folds and tied the ends together. Satisfied, she patted Victoria's robe back into place as they stepped onto the tram, and the rest of the short walk passed in a blur.

***

As Victoria feared, she was the last to arrive at the pre-banquet celebration. The only positive to that, she thought, was that the others already present had opened a great many of the bottles on the bar. Platters of appetizers and finger foods were scattered around as well, likely to placate them until the actual celebrations started. Even though she was "late," technically, people would not even begin to be seated in the banquet hall for another two hours.

There was a way things were done, she reflected. Although, because everyone knew that the timeline for the day had been—she searched her mind for the best term for several moments—extended, the support staff provided the twelve people in the room with a sufficient amount of foods and liquors to pass the time.

The door slid shut behind her and, despite her best intentions, everyone looked up. Korakti waved with her mug in big, boisterous movements, and Victoria returned gesture with a much more subdued wave.

Most of the other Titans sat together. The exception was Lelantos, who currently stood to one side of Rivka, participating tangentially in his Hexarch's conversation with Eurybia and Aegesander.

In fact, several small groups dotted the room. Even though these people were not the ones she needed to impress with public appearances and visibility, Victoria decided it would be rude to simply waltz through the center of the room, take her seat with the Titans, and not speak to anyone else.

Closest to the door, not that she was surprised, were Tritogenes, First Lord Enyalios, and First Lord Hyperion. This was her first time meeting the other two, but not only did they look exactly like their holos, makeup or not, there were few people who would dress *that* extravagantly.

In a robe of purple so dark it was almost black sat Tritogenes, holding the remnants of some dark liquor. His robe shimmered when he moved; the minute designs that covered every centimeter of fabric had been picked out in silver and gold. At first, she thought his makeup was simple, but the longer she looked, the more detail Victoria picked out. The colors he chose made a gradient that seemed to put the bottom half of his face perpetually in shadow, no matter which direction he looked.

By contrast, Enyalios went to the same sort of intricate detail Victoria sported as part of her own look. His face was divided by a crisp vertical line. One half was an artistic skull picked out in reds and oranges. The other side was a cluster of butterflies in blues and greens. The two sides seemed to have no interaction with one another, but the dichotomy when he looked directly at her was, if nothing else, dramatic.

True to form, at least from Tritogenes told her about him, Enyalios's outfit only grew more gaudy from there. Metallic thread had been braided into his hair and the embroidery on his robe had been accented with polished silver rondels that caught the light when he moved.

Victoria would have recognized the third man in their group under any level of glitter. First Lord Hyperion sat nearly a full head taller than Tritogenes, and his piercing blue eyes watched her from the middle of a wide swath of black like the shadow of a great bird across his face. That shadow abruptly ended at his snowy beard, where six glittering rubies had been braided like drops of blood.

To his side, Tritogenes leaned in and said something too quiet to carry. Hyperion's deep bass laugh, on the other hand, filled the room.

Victoria approached them first, watching as a silent struggle passed between Tritogenes and Hyperion. Technically, the senior of a pair was supposed to be the first one to offer greetings. That, like many other things about the day, was simply how things were done, an unspoken law of Technocrat propriety. Matters became more complicated when the people were of the same rank or when two people of similar rank were greeting a third.

After a moment, Hyperion closed his brilliant eyes and laughed again. "By the Ten Thousand, Tritogenes. She's *your* Titan."

Tritogenes smiled, teeth bright against the makeup-induced shadows on his lower face. He stood and extended a hand to Victoria. She took it first with one hand, then with two.

"I'm glad to see you got sufficient rest after your trip to Faros," he said, grinning.

Victoria laughed. "Yes, thank you, First Lord. Having a few days off allowed me to finish some personal projects."

Tritogenes sank into his seat and Hyperion rose. He offered first his hand, then a curiously raised eyebrow. "Personal projects, Spatharios?"

She took Hyperion's hand, finding his grip iron solid, warm, and dry. He stood as tall as Victoria, a fact alone which surprised her, and even broader through the shoulders. Korakti had not exaggerated when she described her Hexarch as a "big guy," but holos of Hyperion did not do him justice.

"Books, First Lord. Catching up on my reading."

Hyperion's eyes glittered mischievously. "Good, good. It's important to keep yourself well read."

"It's actually why I wasn't here earlier."

Hyperion laughed again, and Victoria could already see why his people loved him. If she had relatives, she supposed Hyperion might have been a favored uncle or grandfather. "What book, then? I may have to add to my own collection. Eh, Tritogenes?"

"If you did that, old friend, you'd have to buy another moon to hold them all."

"Precisely! No library can be large enough. So, Spatharios? What captured your attention so?"

"The *Blue Sun* trilogy. I was on the last book."

Hyperion nodded thoughtfully. "Not something to 'add' to my collection, since I've read those books many times. Tritogenes, my friend, you didn't give your Titan *my* copies, did you?"

Tritogenes laughed. "No, Hyperion. Those are safe back on Limani."

"Good," he said with a nod. "Give them to her when she gets back."

Tritogenes smiled. "As you say, First Lord."

The conversation quieted for a moment as Hyperion sat, which Enyalios took as his cue to stand and introduce himself. Rather than anything dramatic or flowery, he stuck out one hand, shaking Victoria's when she took it, and said, "You've been here too long without a drink, Spatharios. Let us fix that."

"Enyalios knows his liquors!" Tritogenes called as the heavily-decorated Hexarch led her to the bar.

Enyalios, for his part, laughed and waved Tritogenes's comment away. He smelled like alcohol, but Victoria could not notice any waiver or stumble in either his steps or his words. "What do you like to drink?"

Her mind raced. Pallasophia made her several drinks, but she had not exactly been given much down time to cultivate anything approaching the sophisticated tastes she felt she needed to fit in with the Hexarchs.

To cover that issue, she simply smiled and said, "I'm not picky. Make me something you like, First Lord."

Enyalios grinned, apparently pleased with that answer. While he mixed, she stepped away to the other end of the bar where the other three Hexarchs sat. Aegesander and Eurybia occupied stools on the front of the bar while Rivka sat in the one around the corner. Lelantos already departed their conversation and now sat with the other Titans.

"Victoria!" Rivka called, breaking off from the conversation for a moment. Her face was bright, decorated with purples and lavender hues, through the orange on her lips and eyes might easily have been fire. No pattern or design dominated her makeup, rather it was a full-face swirl of color, like she had been hewn from colorful stone.

Rivka extended a hand and, when Victoria took it, clapped her other hand on Victoria's shoulder. The gesture was much less formal, but the bright smile on her face made it all that much more important to Victoria. Unlike the others, even Tritogenes, she and Rivka had worked together side-by-side in the field. As far as she was concerned, that meant something.

"It's good to see you again."

"You as well, First Lord."

"Rivka, please. For the next hour or so, we're all equals."

Enyalios approached, silently pressed a thin-stemmed glass into Victoria's hand, and returned to his seat next to Tritogenes and Hyperion. She sniffed the ruby liquid, smelled cranberry and an abundance of alcohol.

Victoria took a sip. The drink was tart, cold, but very tasty. She could easily see herself having one too many of them because, despite the smell, the drink itself did not taste like alcohol at all.

She offered some to Rivka, but the Hexarch waved it away, saying she was, "not a fan of cranberry."

"I met a fan of yours," Victoria said. "Alexis, a Sixth. Says she's got a tournament next week on Limani?"

"Oh, yes!" Rivka brightened. "She's a bright girl, and quite good, too. That reminds me. If you'll excuse me, Victoria, I need to talk to Tritogenes."

"Of course."

Rivka nodded, then patted Victoria's shoulder as she passed.

When Victoria turned around, Aegesander was on his feet, watching her curiously. Like Tritogenes, his makeup had been applied more simply than the others, only his was in a radial, almost star-like pattern centered on his eyes. The effect drew Victoria's gaze to the center where his dark, intelligent eyes watched her.

He waited a moment, studying her, perhaps waiting to see what she would do. Aegesander had to know she knew what happened to Helena. It was no secret that the other Titan had been staying with Victoria since the initial Ouroboros mission.

After a moment, he nodded in recognition. He did not, she noticed, offer his hand for her to shake. Victoria tried to assure herself that he was simply keeping his distance because of her newfound friendship with Helena, but she could not shake the feeling that Aegesander was lumping her in with his feud with Hyperion and Tritogenes.

"You're a mystery," he said, then with extra emphasis on her nonstandard title, added, "Spatharios Victoria. I couldn't find any information on you in the records."

While they studied one another, Eurybia stood. She exchanged a nod with Victoria, then brushed past her on her way to speak with Tritogenes's group. Aegesander's eyes followed her for a moment, but he gave her no other attention.

Victoria smiled. This was the sort of exchange she had watched Tritogenes have many times. "Well, the official word is that I grew up in a religious sect and never formally gained a rank, but in truth..." She paused, grinned. If she told him a truth so outlandish that it could not be true, then he would assume it to be a lie. "I just sort of *appeared* one day out in the rim. Seems like there's a lot of that sort of thing going on, First Lord."

His eyes narrowed for less than a heartbeat, but Aegesander nodded. A mysterious, and hard to read, smirk crossed his features. "Of course. Shall I let you speak to the other Titans now?"

She, barely, resisted the automatic urge to frown at his sudden breach of propriety. Asking her like that, especially with that sort of phrasing, was rather more rude than simply telling her to exit the conversation or doing so himself.

She almost retorted in kind, but resisted that urge as well. The purpose of the pre-banquet was for them to unwind and relax in one another's company, and riling up Aegesander would not serve that end. More to the point, as Tritogenes told her in the past, the man simply liked to argue, and *not* giving him one would irk him more than if she gave in.

Instead, she gave a polite nod, and turned to leave.

The other five Titans were sprawled out in various positions on what seemed to be little more than a pile of cushions. At one point, it might have been a couch or even a set of chairs, but anymore it was little more than a backdrop for the least formal group in the entire room.

At the moment, Panatakis sat in the middle of the circle. If he and Helena had not coordinated their makeup, she would have been surprised. Every color and pattern on his face was opposite hers: dark where hers were light, red where she was blue. He laughed with genuine amusement, eyes unfocused and staring at nothing.

She could not hear what they were all saying over the general din, but the others were holding various objects near him. She suspected it was some sort of guessing game or it would have been with a normal person. With Panatakis's augmented senses, she suspected they were trying to see how easily they could trick him.

From the way the amused smile on his face persisted, Victoria assumed they were losing.

Daniel turned and waved to her, smiling and more relaxed than she had ever seen him. Unlike the others in the room, he had not gone to much of an effort with his appearance. From what little they had spoken, she knew he was a technician before becoming Enyalios's Titan, and his lack of attention to his appearance was likely part of that. He died stripes of red into his beard, but otherwise did little out of the ordinary.

Next to him, practically leaning against him, though not in anything resembling what Victoria would call a romantic way, was Korakti. Done in blacks and a red that was surprisingly similar in shade to what masked half of Victoria's face, Korakti wore a painted mask that looked similar to her existing features, but larger and more exaggerated. Her painted eyes extended past her real ones, creating an effect that was an unnerving mix of cartoon and devil.

She raised her glass high—though Panatakis said, "beer mug, three-quarters empty," before she could speak—and said, "here's to our glorious leader! Last to arrive!"

Victoria felt her face flush, but raised the ruby drink made by Enyalios as her reply. Already feeling an amused smile cross her face, she sank onto the pile of cushions opposite Helena. "What have I missed?"

"Panatakis was just telling us what made him volunteer for the Project," Korakti said. She reached for the spigot of a nearby keg and filled her mug.

"Yes, yes," he said. As always, he seemed to speak with his hands as much as his voice, though the effect was greater now that they were all relaxed. "What I didn't say before is that my vision wasn't "bad," it was nonexistent. I'd been blind since I, as a foolish Fourth Lord, had the misfortune of being a living example of laboratory safety." Panatakis grinned. "Do not add water to acid," he said, then laughed. "When I learned what First Lord Eurybia was developing for the Project, I volunteered immediately."

"Did it hurt?" Korakti asked.

339

"Early on, yes. Even once the implants themselves healed, to say nothing of upgrading them every so often, which worked about like you would imagine, there were some issues before I learned how to manage the neural pathways. Light or sound would get routed to my pain sensors. It was fine the other way around, but when the lamp next to you suddenly starts burning your skin," he shook his head, grinning. She knew that expression, either sink into the misery or learn to laugh at it. "Not something I want to do very often."

Korakti pantomimed a dramatic shudder. "Now I'm almost glad I got my skill the old fashioned way: getting my ass kicked in front of a million people!" She laughed, a boisterous sound which was quickly taken up by the rest of them.

"What about you, Victoria?" Panatakis asked. "We never spoke much before. Why did you join?"

Her mind raced. She, for whatever reason, had never expected this question. After a moment, one in which she was keenly aware they were all looking at her, she decided to tell a filtered version of the truth. Thinking and speaking slowly, she said, "I woke up one morning. I dreamed I had been attacked by mastigas. Me, personally."

"Damn," Korakti muttered. "Rough dream."

Victoria nodded and continued. "In that dream, I was naked, armed only with my fists. They almost killed me. When I woke up, there was something, I don't remember what now, about Project Titan in the news. I got in touch with First Lord Tritogenes, though it took a while, and volunteered. Once I really thought about it, I didn't see that I had any other option."

One by one the other Titans nodded.

"Sounds familiar," Panatakis said.

"What about you, Helena?" Korakti asked. "Surely, you've got an exciting story to tell."

Panatakis turned, almost looking at Helena, but stopped. His eyes aimed at nothing a meter or so to her right, but his posture clearly said his attention was focused on her. A quick flash of emotions passed across his face as they spoke to one another across their mental link.

"I was a programmer for First Lord Aegesander, working on security systems. I wrote much of the code that governed his systems as well as those used by many others in the binary. He requested me, personally, for the Project. I wrote the code that governed how I operate," she said, then quickly added, "the implants, I mean."

"You tested them on yourself?" Victoria asked.

Helena nodded. "It was only right that I undergo the procedure. It was only right that, if it failed, I would be the one who... died."

Daniel waved a hand at Panatakis. "First Lord Eurybia didn't seem that worried with yours."

"Hers are somewhat more advanced than mine are," he replied. "I couldn't begin to understand how hers work."

Victoria nodded, then raised her glass. "To us."

"To us!" The others answered.

"Titans!" Korakti bellowed.

Victoria took a long drink, finishing the cranberry cocktail Enyalios prepared. Korakti downed her drink in one go, as did Panatakis. Daniel and Helena seemed more reserved.

Korakti cheered, then stood up. From somewhere nearby, quick enough that Victoria did not see the tray before it was in her hand, Korakti produced a plain black platter. "Come, give me your glasses! I'll bring more."

Daniel dropped his glass onto the tray first. He laughed, and his blessing was an old and ironic one, but Victoria still felt a bit of a dark cloud settle over her mind because of it. "Drink and be merry, my friends, for tomorrow we may die."

Helena and Panatakis placed their glasses on the table, explaining what they had been drinking and asking for more the same. Lelantos, silent until then, asked for whatever beer she and Daniel were drinking.

341

Victoria's glass clinked onto the tray and, rather than more of the same, she gave Korakti the same instruction she gave to Enyalios. "Surprise me."

Chapter 19

The embarkation area had been cleared of all the guests and general population. They had been allowed near the ship, under observation more intense than they would have been before Ouroboros, up until an hour before, when the area closed to everyone except the Titans, guards, and "VIPs." In this case, "VIP" meant the Hexarchs and their seconds in command.

The banquet itself went on for several hours, though things were still surprisingly close to the proper schedule. The ship would be departing Prosgeiosi in just under two hours. The suns set some time ago, but Odyssey's launch pad was fully illuminated by a ring of floodlights. From the ground, it might as well have been noon.

For the moment, the three groups stood apart from one another. First Lord Hyperion, with more than a little bit of trepidation in his heart, watched the Titans as they interacted. As intended, they stood just far enough away that none of the Hexarchs, himself included, could overhear their conversation.

Hyperion smiled. The six of them looked *happy*. Perhaps Aegesander was right after all, and this was the final thing that would atone for their previous mistakes and sins when it came to the mastigas.

He stepped away from the other Hexarchs, leaving behind a muttered, and apparently heated, conversation between Aegesander and Eurybia. Hyperion cleared his throat and raised both hands. His voice naturally carried a ways, but the pad was loud, and he relied on a microphone in his collar to boost the volume.

"The carrier in orbit is ready to depart," he began. "I will be brief. When First Lord Tritogenes first proposed Project Titan five years ago, I was skeptical. His dreams were lofty: to save us all from the mastigas. But his dreams were necessary, because no one else was willing to step up and do something."

He continued. "We were paralyzed by fear. Fear of the mastigas. Fear of the unknown. Fear of making mistakes.

"You six represent the antithesis of our fear. I send you on this mission not because I want to, but because it must be done. You go now to fight a fight that should not need to be fought. You go now to cleanse our sins. Upon your shoulders rests the fate of all mankind.

"Go with the suns, Titans, and may Selene's grace be with you all."

Hyperion paused for a moment, then bowed deeply from the hips. It was not a gesture in common use anymore, but it had been the preferred greeting for the previous generation of Hexarchs, those who ruled the binary when Hyperion was a child.

His bow had the desired result, and one by one the Titans returned the gesture. Helena bowed first, followed by Daniel. Panatakis and Korakti, then Lelantos joined. Finally, Victoria did as well. She bent low, lower than First Lord Hyperion had gone, and held that ancient position of respect for several seconds before straightening.

"Now go," he continued, still using the microphone. "Speak to whomever you wish. Time may be short, but it is not yet gone."

Rather than approach anyone, Hyperion stood and watched the three crowds break apart. Many of the seconds in command fell back. If they had any sort of relationship with the Titans, it was little more than business. Only Rivka's security chief, Ilias, and Tritogenes's Project

Director, Pallasophia, stayed around. The others, including his daughter Eunike, had other work to worry about.

Korakti approached him directly. Somehow, her robe fluttered in what might have been a breeze if there was one. After a moment, Hyperion realized she was deliberately swishing her hips and arms to produce the effect she desired.

He chuckled. "Showoff."

She must have heard him, because Korakti laughed. "Crash my code, old man. You *did* keep it short after all."

Hyperion laughed. There would be time for propriety later. He clapped Korakti on the shoulder harder than he would have anyone else. "Make me proud."

Korakti smiled, swallowed hard, and said, "yeah. Yeah, I will."

***

Lelantos broke away from the other Titans almost immediately and headed in her direction. Rivka knew they were his friends now, and so she no longer worried about his general lack of sociability. Even before the chronodrug, Lelantos was not exactly a social butterfly.

When he smiled, the hollows he painted on his already-thin face shifted around. They turned his face from a glowering skull into something happier. The dark circles around his eyes thinned and pointed as he squinted against the lights overhead.

Today his face looked unusually animated, and not just because of the dramatic makeup.

Rivka's eyebrows rose. She meant to say something more profound, but at that moment, the only thing that came to mind was, "you're not slowed right now?"

Lelantos laughed, then shrugged his shoulders. Even through his robe, the increased metabolism from the chronodrug kept him stick-thin, obvious even through the heavy fabric he wore. Most people would not be able to tell—the extra layers to his robe masked the boniness of his silhouette well enough, but Rivka had worked with him for years now.

345

"No," he said. "I wanted to enjoy today's celebrations like a normal person."

"Is that it or did you just not want to sit through a two-day banquet?"

"That was part of it, I admit." Lelantos held out his hands, flexing his fingers into claws and then relaxing them several times. "It feels weird now, being like this. Everything is so fast, I almost forget what it's like."

Rivka felt a lump in her throat. Since meeting the others, she learned about some of the misfortune they suffered both during Project Titan and afterward. Rivka used to feel ashamed for what happened to Lelantos's predecessor, but after learning about Tritogenes's Aphelion Facility, she felt lucky that her tragedy was so small in comparison.

She smiled, letting her feelings through. Her smile was thin, lopsided, but genuine. "You've changed a lot for the Project, my friend."

"You say that every time."

"And every time it's still true."

"Look at this," he said. Lelantos withdrew a coin from his pocket and tossed it into the air. He tried once, twice to catch it. The third swipe was so late that the coin already hit the ground before his hand was even in motion. "With the drug, I could have plucked that out of the air before it even rotated once."

She nodded. "Your skill is..."

Lelantos shook his head, interrupting. "It's not the skill that's important, it's the experience. I had a long talk with Panatakis the other day. The world is different for us now, and I have you to thank for that."

"Just promise me..."

"Promise you what?"

She laughed, once, softly. "I was going to say, 'promise me you'll come back,' but that's cliché and silly."

Lelantos put a hand on her shoulder. "Of course I will. Ouroboros shot me in the leg and all it did was annoy me. There's nothing the mastigas can do to me. Don't worry, I'll keep Dasos from, well, you know."

She nodded. That annoying lump of emotion in her throat was back. "From becoming another Kipos, I know."

"Anyway," he continued, taking his hand back. "How's working with Ilias?"

She took a half step back. Ilais stood off to the side, doing his best to look like he was not eavesdropping on the conversation. Lelantos knew that, not only was Ilias doing exactly that, but it was likely that at least one other member of Rivka's new security staff was listening in to their conversation as well.

She beckoned him over and Ilias approached with a fluid grace that telegraphed "dangerous security agent" to everyone watching. It was not a persona he adopted often, in fact such an obviously threatening display would make his routine job harder, but for an event like this, Lelantos knew the man would let his more dramatic side take over.

"Yes, First Lord?" he asked. Ilias looked at Lelantos with his eyes, smiled, but kept his face locked on Rivka.

"You can relax," she instructed. "There's no one here to impress."

"On the contrary," Ilias said with stiff, almost comical, formality. "I believe if I can convince Second Lord Korakti that I've more martial skill than her, First Lord Hyperion will allow me to fight in his arena."

Lelantos laughed. "Ever the showboat, brother."

"One of us had to be."

"Is she keeping you busy?"

"Right now?" Ilias asked, then threw his head back and laughed. "You've no idea! I haven't slept more than two hours at a time since taking this job."

"I'm sorry to hear that."

"Don't be. I love it! First Lord Rivka has kept me busy, ah, let's call it 'cleaning house.' After the incident in Molyvos, there was a great deal of mess to attend to."

Rivka put one hand on each of their shoulders, but she addressed Lelantos first. "Thank you for introducing him to me."

"Yes," Ilias said. "Thank you, Lelantos."

"Lelantos," Rivka said. Again, that upwelling of emotion, but this time it hit her stomach and throat at the same time. Propriety be damned, she thought, and took Lelantos by both shoulders, pulling him closer for an embrace.

"First Lord?" he started to ask, then gave in and returned the hug.

"Come back to me, my friend."

***

Tritogenes fully expected her not to speak to him. Their meetings had been fairly pleasant when they happened, but Victoria never sought him out when she had time off like the other Titans did with their respective Hexarchs.

That was just as well, Tritogenes thought. They had very little in common.

He was going to leave the launch area without saying anything to her, but footsteps behind him stopped his attempt at a surreptitious retreat.

"You're not going to just leave, are you?"

He turned, smiled. Tritogenes was not the tallest of men, and Victoria towered over him. She held out a hand, stealing the role of social senior from him—typical. Tritogenes laughed when he saw that, but took her hand anyway.

"I didn't think you'd have anything to say to me, Spatharios."

Two simultaneous emotions passed over her face. Amusement flitted across her lips in a thin smile while her eyes darkened with anger. "There are many things I *want* to say to you, First Lord."

"I suppose that's not a surprise."

"Not all of them are bad."

He smiled, picking up some of her amusement. "That, however, is a surprise."

Victoria took her hand back and stood watching Tritogenes. After a moment, he realized where exactly he had seen that sort of thin-lipped, amused smile before.

"So," he began. "Pallasophia?"

Victoria flushed. He supposed it was fortunate she was facing him, and thus no one else, because Victoria did not seem pleased by her sudden blush of embarrassment. Still, she was not going to argue, it was not in her nature. "How did you know?"

Tritogenes smirked and tapped his forehead. "I used to be an actor, remember. Reading between the lines is one of the few things I'm good at."

"You're good at a great many things, First Lord," she responded. "Don't sell yourself short."

"I think that's the first truly nice thing you've said about me, Spatharios."

"Victoria," she corrected.

He nodded. "Victoria."

"Tritogenes, listen," she ordered.

That tone of effortless command was another thing he thought she picked up from Pallasophia, but Victoria took it to another level. She managed to unite Korakti and Helena during their mission to Faros, after all. Tritogenes felt himself ready to listen to anything she had to say.

She continued. "You are I are going to have a very long conversation when I return. I've tried not to think about it lately, but there are some things that need to be said."

He nodded agreement.

"By both of us."

"Oh?"

"Yes."

"So, that's it?"

"Yes."

Tritogenes sighed. "I suppose that's more than I expected, to be honest. I have a lot to apologize for, Spa—Victoria."

"Save it for when I return," she ordered.

He grinned. "And if I don't?"

Victoria shrugged. "I'm getting on that ship in just a few minutes, so you'll have to write it down, and if you do that, I still won't read it until we're on the way back."

"Fair. So why...?"

"Because if I didn't say *anything* to you, it would bother me. This way, there's something to talk about when I get back. Stay safe, Tritogenes."

He laughed. "Aren't I supposed to tell you that? You're the one going toward that battleship, after all."

Victoria grinned. "Exactly. I'm going to be fine. You have to go back and deal with *politicians*."

"I suppose you'd see it that way."

Victoria tapped her forehead in mimicry of the way Tritogenes had done moments before. "You gave me a love for fighting. I'm going to go do what you," she paused, smirked, "*trained* me to do."

"And I thank you for that," Tritogenes replied. "Truly. Now, I think you have someone else more important to speak to?"

***

"I'm surprised you came to speak to me."

Helena nodded once. She was all mathematical precision and subtle movements, the same way Aegesander remembered her from the start of Project Titan. He wondered if it was intentional or if she was simply holding everything back in order to prevent him, or anyone else present, from seeing how she actually felt.

"It would be unseemly if I did not. People would ask questions."

"People *already* ask questions, Helena."

"I cannot be held responsible for that, First Lord."

"You cannot be?" he asked, "or you will not be?"

"We both know the answer to that."

"Who have you told?"

"Victoria knows."

"And?"

"And I do not feel obligated to answer the rest of that question, First Lord. It is mathematically unwise."

"Helena," he said. "I am sorry for what I did."

To Aegesander's astonishment, Helena's reaction was strong enough for him to pick up on. For just a moment, she looked genuinely surprised—no, he realized, shocked. "Then why did you feel that course of action was appropriate in the first place?"

"Your abilities concerned me," he admitted. Aegesander stopped then, and looked around. Even Eurybia, busy talking to Panatakis, was out of earshot. No one would hear him admit such weaknesses except Helena.

"You were afraid."

"Yes."

"Because," she started to say, then closed her mouth. Helena frowned, but said nothing else."

"I'll not answer that."

"I would not expect you to."

"Thank you, Helena. I wish this mission to have the best outcome."

Her eyes narrowed at that, and for a moment Aegesander wondered if she would actually speak again, but she did not. That, at least, he was thankful for. With luck, she would eliminate the mastigas, protect Dasos, and Aegesander would never have to lay eyes on her terrifying visage again.

Instead, her face simply darkened. Aegesander could only imagine the furious anger lurking there and hope he would not have to face it again.

Helena turned away and walked straight for the shuttle.

***

351

"You're talking to her, aren't you?"

Panatakis nodded. His eyes were aimed at Eurybia directly, something for which she was rather grateful. Having a conversation with him while he stared off into space watching birds sing was unnerving at best.

"Is she alright?"

Panatakis nodded again. "She said what she needed to."

Eurybia sighed. "I tried to speak to Hyperion about the whole thing, but Aegesander," she paused, "convinced me that it would be better if I let the subject be."

"How?"

She shook her head. "It's not important now."

"Did he threaten her?"

"It's..."

Panatakis's jaw tightened and his unseeing eyes bored into her. "Did he threaten Helena?"

"I," she began, stopped, then, "no. He threatened you."

Panatakis flinched as though physically struck. "Me?"

"Yes."

"Helena said he targeted her implants and," Panatakis's eyes went wide. "No! He told you he would do the same to me?"

Eurybia nodded. "I had, *have*, no way to prove he doesn't have that kind of access. Even Helena didn't realize that failsafe was there, did she?"

"No. Aegesander did a number of things to her implants that she's only now figuring out."

Eurybia frowned, then shook her head. She felt her face relax. Both Helena and Panatakis would be on their way to the Mastigas ship soon enough. The two of them would them be far out of reach of any signal from any of the Technocrat planets, giving them the time and space to fix those issues.

"Panatakis," Eurybia began.

"Don't," he said.

"What?"

Eurybia expected him to be angry. Her reaction to his words came before her reaction to his tone. She expected him to be angry, but he was not. If anything, Panatakis's tone was sympathetic, perhaps even pitying.

"No," she continued, "I do have something I need to say, Panatakis."

He watched her for a moment, or it felt like he did anyway. When the implants first started working, he explained how they changed his worldview, allowing him sight and access to senses that the rest of the world could only dream about. Now, however, it felt like he was actually looking at her, boring holes through her with eyes Eurybia knew did not work.

After a moment, he nodded.

Eurybia raised a hand, intending to put it on his shoulder or touch him in some way. Anything she could do to create some kind of physical connected between the two of them would be fine, she thought, but it did not feel right. Too many failed opportunities already passed for that to matter, and Eurybia dropped her hand back to her side.

"I know you want to rejoin Helena and the rest of the Titans," she began, "so I'll be brief. If Hyperion can do it, so can I, right?"

Panatakis smiled, amused, but said nothing.

"I've not been the best friend to you, have I?"

"Not at all, First Lord. You have been an adequate employer, however."

"That's probably the best I could hope for."

He nodded. "I have not been displeased with our professional relationship, First Lord."

"You stressed professional."

"Did I?" He looked amused.

"We both know you don't say things you don't mean, Panatakis. Was our personal relationship, as people, not to your liking?"

"It could not be to my liking or disliking, First Lord, because such a relationship did not exist."

Her eyes fell to the ground for a moment. This was not how Eurybia planned for this conversation to end. "I see. I apologize. I found myself wrapped up in the Project and in my duties as a Hexarch and did not take the time to be your friend as the others have done. I thought providing you with luxury and freedom would suffice, but I fear it did not."

"I was never unhappy."

"That's good."

"But?" he asked, metal-clad eyebrows raised.

"Again," she continued, "I'm sorry. I should have been a better friend to you, Panatakis. Perhaps if I had done that, Helena, and by extension you, would be safer."

He smiled, then that smile finally broke into a laugh. "First Lord, we're headed to the mastigas battleship. 'Safe' is what awaits us here at home when we're done."

"Of course."

He turned and started to leave, then stopped. He no longer looked at her with his eyes, but after years of working with Panatakis, Eurybia knew his attention was still fixed on her. "First Lord?"

"Yes?"

"Thank you."

***

"Boss, listen," Daniel said, rubbing at a nonexistent itch on the back of his neck. "I'm sorry I never got to thank you for letting me pilot the machi-machi."

Enyalios laughed. "I don't recall you giving me very much choice."

"I suppose I didn't, did I?"

"Do you miss him?"

Daniel nodded. "Every day. Nikos was my dearest friend and not a day goes by when I don't blame myself or my crew for what happened to him."

"He..."

"Yes, I know. Nikos was a fool, but that's what would have made him such a good Titan. The others? They're all fools. They don't know what danger is, and I swear the sight of their own blood only makes them want to fight more."

"But not you?"

"I..." Daniel paused. "I suppose it's the same. Every time something hit the armor and bounced off, it made me that much more wiling to keep up the fight."

Enyalios laughed again. "Hell, it must have been a wild ride when you rode out those autocannon, yeah?"

Daniel laughed, this time with a little edge to it. "It was exhilarating, that's for sure. I'm just glad Victoria's plan worked."

"Helena definitely played her part."

"That she did. I felt bad when I saw how much it took out of her, though. I don't think I've ever pushed my body so hard that I puked."

Enyalios nodded, very careful not to let anything show of his face. If Daniel did not know what actually happened to Helena, he was not going to divulge the secret. That story was not his to tell.

Instead, he redirected the conversation. "How has the Aegis been performing since then?"

"About the same, truthfully. Most of the improvements to the suit were subtle. The biggest thing was the weapons. As much fun as it was having that autocannon, the ammo reserves were so low..."

Enyalios nodded. "That was a concern I had. The new model..."

"Two-point-one."

"Yes. It won't have as much firepower, but the ammunition capacity is nearly twenty times larger."

"And the mastigas don't have armored vehicles, so that won't be as much of an issue." He paused. "Do they?"

"No, but the gigas and elite are going to be harder to take out with those smaller-caliber guns."

Daniel grinned. "That's why I had the techs include that hammer."

"Did you name it, too?"

Daniel shrugged. "Not yet. I'll have to wait until I use it."

"Of course. And Daniel?"

"Yes, boss?"

Enyalios clapped Daniel on the shoulder and grinned. "Keep them safe out there."

"That's the plan."

"Anyway, it's about time to board the shuttle isn't it?"

Daniel nodded. "The machi-machi was loaded this morning and my bags went aboard this afternoon. All that's left is me."

Enyalios clapped him on the shoulder again, opened his mouth to say something, but kept silent.

"Boss?"

"It's nothing."

Daniel frowned. "Boss."

"Fine," he said, then laughed. "Look, goodbyes aren't my strong suit. Ask Tritogenes about that when you get back. Still..."

"Yeah, I get it. I'll buy you a drink when I get back, boss."

"That reminds me," Enyalios said. He reached into his robe pockets and withdrew a small steel flask. He shook it loudly, the liquid sloshing inside, then passed it over. "Bring this back empty, Daniel."

Daniel took it, opened the top, and took a swig without smelling to see what was in it. He coughed in surprise, then laughed. "Bourbon? I was expecting something sugary."

"It's not for me," Enyalios said. "It's a gift. Like I said, bring it back empty and I'll fill it up again. I owe you that much."

Daniel returned the cap to the flask, then dropped it into the front pocket of his robe. "Thanks, boss."

***

"You're going to come back safely. You understand that, right?"

Victoria smiled. "Of course. I'm going to have five of the most skilled people in the entire binary, not to mention a whole company of soldiers, behind me."

Pallasophia nodded, but her eyes were sad. Dark circles that could not be explained by her makeup sat there, pulling her entire expression down. "That's not what I'm worried about."

"What do you mean?"

"It's not *you* that I'm worried about, Victoria."

"It's the others."

"Yes."

Victoria reached out and took her by the shoulders, holding Pallasophia at something still approaching a respectable distance for public interaction, but very much closer than usual. "I'm going to protect them, all of them. The Titans are *all* coming home, Pallasophia. I promise you that."

She smiled. "Thank you, Victoria."

"Don't mention it," she replied. "Truthfully. Tritogenes..." She paused, then used the same word she used with the First Lord earlier, "*trained* me to fight, but protecting people is different. That instinct is mine alone. I think."

Pallasophia smiled, thin lipped. "Yes. That's something that's all yours."

Neither of them said anything for a minute. Around the launch area, the conversations between Titans and their Hexarchs were breaking apart. Tritogenes was long since gone, having left her to speak with Pallasophia in what amounted to privacy. Aegesander was likewise missing, making Helena the first to board the shuttle.

Pallasophia took a step back, ready to leave. Before she could, Victoria stepped closer and reached out a hand. She laid it on Pallasophia's elbow for a moment before shifting it to her shoulder again. "Hey, keep a piece of Aphelion for me."

She laughed. "Any preferences?"

Victoria shook her head, then thought about it. "Well, keep some sand from the arena and something from the pod room. And," she trailed off in thought for a moment. An idea sparked amusement and she laughed. "And something I can break."

She smiled and Victoria simultaneously felt her heart racing and her mind calming. "I can manage that."

"Thanks."

"And you'll come back, right?"

Victoria nodded. "Of course."

Pallasophia shook her head. "No, I mean, you'll come back *to me*, right?"

Her face heated, but she smiled. "Yes."

"I want to hear you say it," she said. "Please."

Victoria smiled, but instead of answering directly, pulled Pallasophia into a sudden embrace. After a moment, she stepped back and smiled. "Does that answer your question?"

"No," she replied, "but this will."

"What wi—"

Pallasophia lowered Victoria's chin with gentle pressure from one finger. Their relative height made that difficult while standing, but a moment's effort paid off. She might have had to rise onto her toes to further equalize heights, but that too was worth the effort.

There, propriety be damned, they shared one last kiss.

Epilogue

The command center was cold. It was also dark. A bare handful of lights illuminated the area, instrument lights and readiness indicators. They provided more than enough light, some of them even too bright. The others tolerated such things, perhaps even enjoyed them for whatever reason, but it did not.

118-Voice-of-Water was its name, a creature of the breed the humans referred to as a sophont. Its strong arms lifted it into the pod from where it would operate the great ship's weapon systems. That great mission had been directly ordered by the Speaker itself, and even if 118-Voice-of-Water disagreed, it could not have gone against that directive.

Its dexterous hands reached out and activated the controls. The great machine read the smallest of its movements, allowing 118-Voice-of-Water to control numbers eight-hundred through twelve-hundred.

The systems were operating at peak efficiency. The small ones deep within the system would ensure that nothing else could be possible. The wind from the Speaker reached even to them in the depths of the ship.

A new smell filtered through the room and 118-Voice-of-Water raised its head. All three eyes scanned the darkness. The smell was indistinct, either a door opened to a faraway hand or...

The dense muscles in its neck tightened and it used its strong hands to lift its body, rotating in place.

"Greet you, I, 7th-Grand-Fang. What purpose, you?"

7th-Grand-Fang, an elite, lumbered across the spacious area, shouldering past several smaller hands as it went. It came to a stop less than a thousand millimeters from 118-Voice-of-Water's station. The other sophonts pointedly did not pay attention to its hulking form.

118-Voice-of-Water inhaled deeply of the taller hand's scent, finally realizing why the others ignored it. It carried a smell that said it should be ignored. Only to 118-Voice-of-Water's nose, that smell was faint, almost impossible to notice.

118-Voice-of-Water squinted all three eyes in suspicion. That meant the great hand's scent had been deliberately tailored for this conversation.

"Spoke to the Voices, I," it said. It spoke quietly, voice pitched only for 118-Voice-of-Water to hear.

"Voices?" it asked, emphasizing the plural. "There is but one Voice and it speaks for all hands."

Slowly 7th-Grand-Fang's head rotated in negation. "Smelled 16-Green-Spectre lately, you?"

"No. 16-Green-Spectre has been assigned to the engines since five thousand seconds after beginning this mission."

7th-Grand-Fang placed two of its hands on the rail of 118-Voice-of-Water's control pod. Such proximity was uncomfortable. Their breeds were of equal smell—even the greatest of the single hands could not out-smell a double-handed breed like them—but 7th-Grand-Fang's smell was starting to influence 118-Voice-of-Water's own. Still, it leaned in closer, breathing its emotions directly into 118-Voice-of-Water's face.

It smelled like suspicion, or possibly something even more alien. It was possible, though unlikely in the extreme, that 7th-Grand-Fang smelled of *fear*.

"Speak to 16-Green-Spectre, you. Then together, you, find 4th-Skull-of-Emptiness and 33-Glittering-Tooth. Speak with them, you."

"Why?"

7th-Grand-Fang ground its mighty teeth together. "Cannot say, I. Smells are too strong here. Continue your work for now, but make time, you."

118-Voice-of-Water returned to its seat. 7th-Grand-Fang's smell receded after several moments, but its words never stopped echoing in 118-Voice-of-Water's mind.

Later, when it finished the fifty-thousandth second of its work, it considered returning to the mountain, but still the smell from earlier persisted. When it came to the Intersection, it turned right instead of left.

118-Voice-of-Water had questions.

When I took the original draft apart, I wanted to keep as much of it as possible. I still ended up cutting some tens of thousands of words between scenes and passages that were removed. I honestly lost track of how much got removed from what sections, but I feel like this part lost the most between versions. There was a lot of fluff that, when I took it apart, really was not needed. Once all of that was said and done, Book 2 ended up with 25% "original" material and 75% "new" material.

One of the hardest challenges for this rewrite was exactly how much I wanted to preserve from the original draft. The fact was, aside from the aforementioned fluff, it wasn't *bad* per se. Everyone who read it just wanted more of what was already there. So, when I took the original apart, I ended up writing a lot of scenes and chapters *in between* what I had already written. Sometimes, chapters or scenes would be moved around, but even so, the challenge remained. I had to write material that fit into a framework that was already there—points A and B became A and C and I had to write a new point B to fill it in.

Truthfully, that kind of thing is a *lot* harder than simply writing new material. The upside of it was that it forced me to really examine the world I created and make sure all the bits fit together.

Of course, this book wouldn't have been the same without two very specific people. First, Michael Huddleston, who supported me during the preorder campaign for *The Stars Have Eyes,* provided the framework for the character who would become Mihalis. We worked out the basics of the character, including some things that you won't see until book 3, and then I went and put him through his paces. Much of Mihalis's character development and decisions were my own, but all of his major decisions were filtered through Michael.

As one of my beta readers, he also got to see Mihalis's whole arc before anyone else, and was quite pleased. I hope are too, because it isn't over quite yet.

The other person who deserves special thanks for this book is Devon Wilson. I found myself stuck early in the rewrite. Book 2 needed an antagonist that was not the mastigas, someone "local" that could serve as the focus for bringing the Titans together as a team. The last thing I wanted to write was a run-of-the-mill, boring "team building arc."

So I texted her late one night and said I needed a name for a terrorist organization, something from Greek myth. She replied minutes later with a single word: *Ouroboros*. Rebirth, cyclic birth and death, and creation through destruction. Ouroboros's goals and methods spread out from there and I had the antagonist I needed.

The book also serves as what a friend refers to as the "romantic subplot" between Pallasophia and Victoria. That was not something I intended to happen (very few things in this trilogy were things I "intended to happen"), but as the story went on, I realized it was something important. Victoria needed something, some*one* who could, in her words, "quiet her demons." Romance isn't planned; it just happens.

Additional thanks to: Rick Lowden, Don Church, Jason McTeer, Ashley Ward, Steve and Diane Mitchell, Becky Spain-Kaiser, Jacob Forbes, Heather Green, Beth Davis, Kaycee Dortch, Will Nunn, Jan Parks, Sarah Philips, and Susan and John Farmer

https://www.facebook.com/tafarmerauthor/

https://www.amazon.com/Thomas-A-Farmer/e/B01A436HFO/

Born to geeky parents and raised on a diet of Star Trek and Babylon 5, Thomas started writing at an early age, working his way through fanfictions of all types. For good or ill, a lot of that early work has been lost.

Writing occupied much of his spare time throughout school and the years after, eventually culminating in an ostensible *magnum opus* he calls the "Chronicles of St. Michael." To this date, those stories still reek of many "early writer" problems, but he promises they will, one day, see the light of publication.

What can you expect next? Maybe he was wrong before, and he'll wrote some short stories next. We haven't seen Gideon in a bit, have we?

He also hosts a podcast (internet radio show, when he's feeling fancy) called "Authors in Abstract." As of this book, the show is well into its second season. You can listen to the podcast on a variety of platforms, or by going directly to www.authorsinabstract.com

When his hands aren't full with books, reading or writing, he fills them with swords. Four nights a week, as of this publication anyway, he teaches historic fencing, also called HEMA (Historic European Martial Arts) as one of the head coaches of the Knoxville Academy of the Blade (www.facebook.com/KABFencing)

He lives with his wife, Stephanie, their three cats, lizard, and snake.

www.ingramcontent.com/pod-product-compliance
Lightning Source LLC
Chambersburg PA
CBHW051323250626
47155CB00007B/2432